Several years ago **Jo**[...] during an operation [...] Afterwards, she disco[...] When her husband ca[...] Boons it took a solid m[...] reading the first one, but by the time she was fit to work again she had read them all and was hooked. Then her husband nudged her into action by daring her to write them, too! And the rest is history!

Laura Iding started writing at a very young age and loved to read, devouring everything in sight. As a teenager, she volunteered as a Candy Striper at a nursing home and fell in love with nursing. She worked several part-time jobs to put herself through nursing school, and one managing job and two degrees later, she found she could embark on an old dream: writing. Now Laura is thrilled to combine her favourite careers into one – writing medical romances for Mills & Boon.

USA TODAY bestselling author **Karen Rose Smith** has written over ninety novels. Her passion is caring for her four rescued cats, and her hobbies are gardening, cooking and photography. An only child, Karen delved into books at an early age. Even though she escaped into story worlds, she had many cousins around her on weekends. Families are a strong theme in her novels. Find out more about Karen at karenrosesmith.com

Their Twin Christmas Surprise

JOSIE METCALFE
LAURA IDING
KAREN ROSE SMITH

MILLS & BOON

First Published in Great Britain 2019
by Mills & Boon, an imprint of HarperCollins*Publishers*
1 London Bridge Street, London, SE1 9GF

THEIR TWIN CHRISTMAS SURPRISE © 2019 Harlequin Books S. A.

Twins for a Christmas Bride 2007 Josie Metcalfe
Expecting a Christmas Miracle © 2009 Laura Iding
Twins Under his Tree © 2010 Karen Rose Smith

ISBN: 978-0-263-27996-2

1219

MIX
Paper from
responsible sources
FSC™ C007454

This book is produced from independently certified FSC™
paper to ensure responsible forest management.

For more information visit: www.harpercollins.co.uk/green

Printed and bound in Spain
by CPI, Barcelona

TWINS FOR A CHRISTMAS BRIDE

JOSIE METCALFE

CHAPTER ONE

SHE was going to die!

Sara's eyes widened in disbelief as the car headed straight at her in the narrow side street. The headlights almost seemed to pin her in position and she knew in an instant that she would never be able to get out of its path in time.

Instinctively, she took a step back, her foot slipping as it tried to gain purchase on the uneven surface. Her hands flew protectively to her belly to cradle the new life nestling deep inside, a tiny corner of her brain acknowledging the fact that it was far too small to survive even if it were to be delivered by emergency Caesarean.

She heard the car's engine roar suddenly, almost as though its driver had floored the accelerator in direct response to the defensive gesture.

Then, in that final second before the powerful vehicle made contact, it was as if time ceased to exist. She could see everything around her with the pin-sharp clarity of a high-definition photograph—the gleam of the recent rain on the ancient cobbled street; the skinny cat that had been hunting in the gutter for scraps, quickly darting into the safety of the shadows; the harsh glitter of artificial light on expensive automotive paintwork and chrome, and the reflection of her own face in the windscreen where the driver's face should be…her reflection contorted in an expression of rage and… Even as she opened her mouth in a scream of denial the sound was cut off instantly as she was flung aside to land on the unforgiving granite.

She felt a sickening thud as her head struck the kerb with a glancing blow, then the world turned black and disappeared.

'I got the job I was after,' Sara volunteered diffidently into the lull when her vivacious sister finally stopped talking long enough to draw breath.

It was always this way when her shifts allowed her to join the family for a meal. Her mother listened avidly to every scrap of Zara's gossip—about the exotic places she'd been, the fabulous clothes she'd modelled, and the A-list celebrities she'd rubbed shoulders with—obviously believing every word.

Sara had her doubts.

She'd known for many years that every one of her sister's stories was carefully tailored to her audience, regardless of the truth. Even as she listened to yet another tale of her sister's glamorous life her fingertips were taking a well-worn path, absently tracing the line of scarring at her temple that had become the only way she and her twin could be distinguished from each other as children.

The rest of the world had believed Zara's tearful tale of

a childish prank gone wrong. Sara knew better; she had always known that her twin resented the fact that they'd been born identical and that Zara was the younger. The very idea that the injury might have been deliberate was unthinkable and had sickened her, but it had only taken one glimpse of the satisfied expression on her sister's perfect face, when she'd returned home from the accident department with a prominent row of stitches marching all the way from her shaven eyebrow into her uneven hairline, to know the truth.

From that day on, although she'd still loved her sister dearly, she'd never totally trusted her.

'I started the job a couple of months ago...in the accident and emergency department,' she added into the next pause, although no one had been interested enough by her announcement to ask her for further details. Even the father she adored was dazzled by the show his glamorous younger daughter put on for him.

Then a sudden imp of mischief tempted Sara into one of those rare attempts at competition with her sister. Would she never grow out of the childish urge?

'By the way, Zara, there are several rather gorgeous doctors in the department...one in particular is every bit as tall, dark and handsome as that actor who was chasing you a while back.'

The blank expression on her sister's face was enough to confirm Sara's suspicion that Zara couldn't even remember the story she'd told them after her last visit to the United States. In all probability, the rather famously married star hadn't done anything more than smile vaguely in her sister's direction at a crowded party. Then she saw her twin's expression change suddenly into a horribly familiar calculating look and instantly felt sick.

What on earth had made her draw Zara's attention to Daniel's existence? she berated herself the next day when her beautiful sister just happened to arrive at the end of her shift to be introduced to Sara's new colleagues. The last thing she needed was for Zara to turn up flaunting her perfection, especially when Sara was looking her exhausted worst at the end of a gruelling shift.

She and her handsome new colleague had quickly discovered that they worked well together, but as for their personal relationship, that was still in the fragile early stages, barely beyond the point where she and Dan had admitted that they enjoyed each other's company outside work, too, and wanted to see whether it could develop into something lasting.

Well, that had been as much as Dan had been willing to admit, so far. On her part, she'd known from their first meeting that he was special; that he could very well be the man she'd been waiting for her whole life. There had been something about the gentleness and compassion with which he treated his patients allied with the aura of strength and dependability that surrounded him...to say nothing of the fact that he was probably the sexiest man she'd ever met...

Those weeks of tentatively getting to know each other might just as well not have existed the day Zara walked into the department wafting her signature perfume and demanding to be introduced to all her sister's dedicated colleagues.

'Of course, the whole family is so proud of Sara for taking all those exams,' she gushed with a wide smile. 'I certainly couldn't do her job...all that blood and pus and...' She shook her head so that her artfully dishevelled locks tumbled over one shoulder and shuddered delicately.

Sara could have predicted exactly how the ensuing scene would play. From the day that puberty had given her sister that spectacular set of curves, she'd seen it so often before. She didn't need to watch to know that every male in the vicinity was about to make a complete fool of himself as they all vied for one of Zara's smiles, or, better yet, one of the sultry come-hither looks she sent them from under impossibly long dark lashes.

'You didn't tell me you were a twin,' Dan complained as he distractedly delivered the mug of coffee he'd been making for her before Zara's arrival. His eyes were flicking from one to the other and Sara suppressed a wince, knowing just how badly she would come out in the comparison. There was no way that she could compare with such a polished image of perfection while she stood there in crumpled scrubs without a scrap of make-up on her face, especially with her hair dragged back into an elastic band with only a few straggly tendrils to camouflage the worst of the puckered scar that drew her eyebrow into a permanently quizzical arch.

'Hard to believe, isn't it?' she said with a tired smile. 'Have you met her yet?'

She needn't have bothered offering, knowing deep inside that this introduction was the sole reason why her sister was here. In fact, Zara was already undulating her *way across the room towards them in her best catwalk strut, her slender legs seeming endless atop heels high enough to induce vertigo. Sara felt sick when she saw the intense way her sister's eyes focused on Dan as she drew nearer, almost devouring him piece by piece from his slightly tousled dark hair and broad shoulders to his lithe hips and long powerful legs.*

'So, this is the handsomest man in the department, is it?' she purred, all but rubbing herself against him and blinking coquettishly as she gazed up into his amazing green eyes. 'Sara was telling me I just had to come and meet you.'

It was far too late to wish that she'd kept her mouth shut.

What can't be cured must be endured, her grand-mother's voice said inside her head, and Sara felt an almost physical wrench as any lasting relationship she might have had with Dan was torn out of her reach for ever. She shut the pain away with all the rest she kept in the box in a dark corner of her soul, and summoned up the appro-priate words.

'Daniel, this is my sister, Zara,' she said formally, unable to conjure up even a pretence of a smile. 'Zara, this is Daniel Lomax. He's one of the senior...' She fell silent, realising that she may as well have saved her breath because neither of them was listening to her.

'Hi, Danny,' Zara breathed, and Sara winced, knowing that he hated that diminutive...only this time there was no automatic correction. Well, why would he object now that her sister had both hands wrapped around his arm, bla-tantly testing his muscles?

She knew how those muscles felt, the taut resilience overlaid with warm skin and silky dark hair. She'd been holding that arm on the way out of the hospital just last night at the end of their shift, delighting in the way his free hand had covered hers to reinforce the fact that he had been enjoying the contact, too.

'If you'll excuse me, I'll go and have a shower and change out of these scrubs,' Sara said, abandoning her untasted coffee as she made a strategic retreat, unable to bear the thought that he might give Zara's hands that same warm caress.

The last glance she threw over her shoulder as she reached the door left her certain that neither of them had even noticed that she'd gone.

Sara woke to a world of pain and noise and eye-searingly bright light. Slamming her lids shut against the unbearable glare, she groaned, unable to decide which part of her hurt the most.

Her hip was agony, but so was her shoulder…and as for her head…

What on earth had happened to her? Had she fallen out of bed in the night? With nothing more than polished floorboards around the new divan it would certainly account for the feeling that she was bruised from head to foot.

'Sara?' said an urgent female voice right beside her ear, but she tried hard to ignore it. It wasn't until she felt the familiar sensation of disposable gloves against her skin as a gentle hand awkwardly stroked the side of her face that she realised that she had an oxygen mask covering her mouth and nose. She tried to turn her head towards the voice but discovered that she was unable to move because of the padded blocks positioned on either side.

She had seen the situation far too many times not to recognise what those sensations meant. She was strapped to a backboard with her head and neck restrained because of the fear of exacerbating a spinal injury.

'Sara, can you hear me?' the voice said over the cacophony of bleeping monitors and voices snapping out orders. 'Sara, love, you've had a bit of an accident and you're in the hospital…' And with those few words terror gripped her. Suddenly she remembered everything that had happened to her in excruciating detail.

The car appearing in the narrow road just as she started to cross it on her way back to her flat…the brightness of the headlights as it came straight towards her…as it hit her and sent her tumbling to the ground…deliberately?

Then she remembered something even more important.

'My baby…!' she keened, her voice muffled behind the oxygen mask, panicking when she was unable to move her hand to her belly, so desperate to know by the familiar feel of the gentle swell that it was still safely inside her.

Then she heard the echo of what she'd said and guilt hit her hard. 'The baby,' she said, deliberately damping the forbidden emotions the way she'd been forced to right from the first day she'd had the pregnancy confirmed. 'Is it all right? Has anything happened to the baby?'

'Stay still, Sara,' ordered the familiar voice of the senior orthopaedic consultant. 'You know better than to move until we've taken spinal X-rays and checked them.'

'No! No X-rays!' she gasped, feeling almost as if she was trapped in a terrifying nightmare. 'I'm pregnant! No X-rays!'

'Hush, sweetheart,' said a softly accented voice, just another of those voices that she'd only recognised in the guise of colleagues before. Everything was so very different now that she was the helpless patient; they were her doctors and nurses and they would decide what treatment was best for her. 'You just lie there and trust Sean O'Malley to know how to take an X-ray without harming your child,' he said, coming to stand in exactly the right place so that she could see his familiar freckled face and carroty curls and the sincerity in his bright blue eyes. 'I promise you on my word as an Irishman that the wee angel won't come out glowing in the dark.'

Sara gave a hiccup that was part laughter, part sob and somehow found a smile. 'I trust you, Sean O'Malley,' she whispered, knowing absolutely that a man who delighted in every one of his four rambunctious red-headed sons would never do anything to risk anyone's child, let alone a colleague's.

The one voice she didn't hear, even though it seemed as if every last member of the A and E department was crammed into the resus room around her, was Daniel's.

What sort of irony was that? she mused silently, a tear tracking from the corner of her eye into her hair and stinging as it reached the place where her head had come into contact with the granite kerbstone. The one person she wanted beside her as she tried to cope with the terror, the one colleague who had the most to lose if anything happened to the child she was carrying—and he wasn't there for her.

'You're late, Sara,' her mother scolded, almost dragging her into the house as soon as she set foot on the doorstep. 'You could at least have tried to get here on time for your sister's big announcement.'

'Sorry, Mum,' she apologised automatically as she shrugged out of her voluminous jacket. 'Where's Zara going this time? Or is it a contract with one of the really big fashion shows?'

'Oh, Sara! You're not wearing that old thing again! You could at least have made an effort.' This time there was a sharper edge to her mother's voice as she saw what her daughter was wearing. 'I really don't understand why you always look such a dowdy mess. No one would ever believe that the two of you were identical twins.' She flung up her hands in despair as Sara glanced down at her favourite black trousers teamed with the soft ivory blouse that she usually wore with it. It had always been enough for a family supper before, so what was different tonight?

Then her mother opened the door into the lounge and she heard the buzz of conversation that could only be made by several dozen voices and froze.

'Mum? Is there a party or something?' she demanded, hanging back. She was suddenly horribly conscious that she hadn't bothered putting any make-up on after her shower and had done nothing other than run a brush through her hair either.

'Sara, you know very well that your sister and Danny

are making their big announcement this evening,' her
mother snapped as she beckoned her with an insistent
hand. *'She rang you up and told you all about it more than
a week ago and everyone else has been here for hours.
We've only been waiting for you to arrive.'*

'Dan...?' Sara felt her eyes widen as the implication hit
her with the force of a wrecking ball.

Zara and Dan?

A big announcement that her sister had told her about?

For just a moment she thought she was going to be sick,
but with her mother's hand now firmly clamped around her
elbow she had no choice but to enter the room beside her
as she pushed the door wide.

The room seemed to be crammed with people, every one
of them dressed to the nines in their most elegant finery,
but the glittering butterfly in their midst, effortlessly out-
shining them all, was Zara.

So why was it that the first pair of eyes she met were the
luminous green ones that belonged to Dan...eyes that only
had to glance in her direction to double her pulse rate and
send her blood pressure into orbit no matter how serious
the medical emergency they were working on.

Hastily, she dragged her gaze away, knowing that she
couldn't afford for anyone to guess just how much it was
costing her to keep herself together while her world fell
apart around her.

This was the first time that she'd seen her sister since
the day that she'd turned up in A and E to be introduced
to Dan, and when she'd heard nothing more, Sara had
dared to breathe a sigh of relief. Even if they had gone out

together, Zara's attention span was notoriously short and she was certain her fickle sister would soon tire of an escort who would never be at her beck and call.

She was so confident that the two of them hadn't hit it off together after all that she'd actually been contemplating screwing up her courage to ask Dan out for a drink later in the week, hoping that the two of them could continue the relationship they'd embarked on when she'd joined the department, longing to see where it would lead them.

The last thing she'd expected was that he and Zara had been carrying on a whirlwind courtship that would result in an engagement. Zara hadn't dropped a single hint...and she certainly hadn't phoned her a week ago to invite her to their engagement party.

It was a good job that she'd had years of practice at hiding her feelings from her manipulative sister. Even so, she needed a moment or two to compose herself, grateful for the time it took for her mother to walk across the room to join her father. Then he tapped the edge of his glass to attract everyone's attention. He beckoned Zara and Daniel to join the two of them in front of the fireplace before he cleared his throat portentously.

'Friends,' he began.

'Romans and countrymen,' added one of Zara's modelling friends with an inebriated giggle, only to be hushed by one of the older, more sober guests.

'Friends, as you all know, this is a very special occasion,' Frank Walker began again as Zara finally met Sara's gaze and she saw that, oh, so familiar smug expres-

sion followed by a cuttingly dismissive glance from head to toe that told Sara as clearly as anything that her sister had deliberately neglected to tell her about the purpose of this evening's gathering for exactly this reason.

If ever there had been a moment that demonstrated how different the two of them were it was this one, with Zara...flawless, beautiful Zara...the centre of everyone's admiring gaze while she was purposely relegated into the background, not even afforded the courtesy call that would have allowed her to look her best. No one would be left in any doubt why Dan would choose Zara over her dowdy, less-than-perfect twin.

'Audrey and I are delighted to welcome you all this evening to celebrate the engagement of our beautiful daughter Zara to this handsome chap here.' There was a muted cheer and happy laughter from a small group who could only be Dan's family—not that she'd ever had the chance of meeting them before. 'In case you haven't heard all about him yet, he's Dr Daniel Lomax, and I have no doubt at all that he'll soon be a consultant in emergency medicine at one of the top hospitals in the country. So, I'd like you all to raise your glasses to wish them both every happiness. To Zara and Danny!'

With all the glasses being raised and the voices echoing her father's words, the fact that she hadn't been given a glass shouldn't have been noticed, neither should the small detail that she was totally unable to utter a word, her eyes burning with the threat of tears. But Zara noticed, and once more smiled like the proverbial cat that had got the cream.

Then Daniel noticed too, his slightly dazzled expression replaced by a puzzled frown when he caught sight of her standing alone just inside the door with her hands hanging heavily by her sides.

Then Zara noticed the focus of her new fiancé's attention and put an immediate end to it, reaching up to cup his cheek with a hand that glittered with a million points of fire as the light caught her engagement ring, then she leaned possessively against him to give him a prolonged kiss that had the room hooting encouragement and left him branded with her scarlet lipstick.

This time when her gaze met Sara's from the circle of Daniel's arms her expression screamed just one word—mine.

'Relax. The baby's fine,' soothed the technician as she slid the probe through the gel on the pale curve of Sara's exposed belly. How few weeks ago it had been that she'd celebrated the fact that she was actually beginning to look pregnant. 'Look, Sara, you can see the heart beating for yourself and there is absolutely no sign of an abruption or any other sort of a bleed in there. Now, did you want me to print an extra copy for you? I might even be able to get a shot that tells you whether you're having a—' Her cheerful patter halted abruptly as she leant forward to take a closer look at the screen then moved the probe to change the angle of the view. 'What on earth...?' she muttered under her breath.

'What? Rosalie, what's wrong with the baby?' Sara demanded, the pain in her head intensifying with her fear for the life of the child. 'Is it something to do with the accident? Was the baby injured or…?'

'Not at all! There is absolutely nothing wrong with your baby,' the young woman announced as she turned with a wide grin on her face. 'In fact, there's nothing wrong with either of them. Look, Sara…it's twins! There are two heartbeats!'

Suddenly, Sara didn't know whether to laugh hysterically or cry. As if her life wasn't in enough of a tangle already. Now she was going to have to tell everyone that it wasn't just one baby she was carrying but two. Both sets of future grandparents would be ecstatic, without a doubt, but Dan would be the only other one in the family who would understand just how much more perilous this pregnancy had become.

As if thinking his name had finally conjured him up, there he was, standing in the doorway with an expression Sara had longed to see on his face for so long…concern for her welfare. Or was it, as ever, concern for the pregnancy?

'What on earth have you done?' he demanded as he strode in, grabbing her case notes as if he had every right to examine them, and she realised that nothing had changed. Any concern he felt was obviously for his precious offspring.

Disappointment made her headache even fiercer and lent an acid edge to her tongue.

'Don't worry, *Danny*, the baby's fine. In fact, you could even say you're getting a genuine bargain—buy one, get one free.'

'What on earth are you talking about?' he snapped, and turned towards the startled woman standing in front of the high-tech control panel. 'Has she been concussed?'

'No, I'm not concussed,' Sara insisted before Rosalie could even draw a breath to answer, completely ignoring the fact that she'd apparently been unconscious among a stack of soggy cardboard boxes for the better part of half an hour before anyone had found her after the accident. 'In fact, according to everybody, I've been extremely lucky. My foot slipped on the wet cobbles as I tried to turn away from the impact to protect the baby, so I only sustained a glancing blow from the car.' She ticked her injuries off on her fingers, a slightly difficult feat with one arm strapped across her body.

'I've had a couple of stitches and got a goose egg on my forehead and I'll probably end up with one or even two black eyes; I dislocated my shoulder, but that's been put back where it belongs—hence the strapping; my hip is black and blue where it hit the granite cobbles, but even without X-rays of the region the orthopaedic consultant's almost certain I didn't break anything there and he says the cracked fibula should heal without any complications. Oh, and apart from that, I feel as if I've lost several yards of skin from various portions of my anatomy.'

She'd been glaring at him throughout her recitation and couldn't help feeling a little remorse when she saw the colour swiftly drain from his face. Not that she intended letting him off the hook. After all, it wasn't Sara, the person, that he was worried about, it was Sara, the person who had been systematically browbeaten by her family into agreeing to carry a surrogate baby for Dan and her inexplicably infertile sister.

'So, let's get to the really good news,' she continued bitterly, with a gesture towards the image frozen on the screen between them. 'Exhibit A is the scan that not only confirms that there is no evidence of injury to the brood mare's procreative organs, but also the fact that she's carrying not one but two babies. Congratulations, Danny-boy! You hit the jackpot first time!'

And even though it brought tears of agony to her eyes to force herself to turn away from him, she made herself to do it, unable to bear looking at those heart-stopping green eyes any longer.

'Are you sure you don't want to change your mind about the pain relief?' Rosalie murmured, startling Sara into the realisation that the young woman was still standing there. She'd been so focused on her acrimonious conversation with Dan that for a moment she'd completely forgotten that there was anyone else in the room with them. Not only had the technician heard her swiftly muffled groan of pain when she'd turned away from the man but she'd had a ringside seat for every word that had gone before it. Now, the fact that she was pregnant by her sister's husband would be food for gossip right around the hospital.

'Hasn't anyone given her any analgesia yet?' Daniel exploded, confirming her suspicion that he was still standing behind her...still gloating over the image of his children, no doubt.

'I don't want any unnecessary drugs,' she snapped. 'I

used the Entonox while they put my shoulder back and stitched me, knowing that was safe for the baby…oh, excuse me, *babies*. I'm quite capable of deciding for myself if I want or need anything else. Now, please, go away and leave me alone. Shouldn't you be off duty by now? Zara will be waiting for you,' she added pointedly.

That thought caused a different pain altogether and was nearly enough to persuade her to accept the drugs on offer. The idea of wiping all the agony away with a swift injection was growing more attractive by the moment. After all, if she was unconscious, she wouldn't be able to think… wouldn't have to try to unscramble the images inside her head, the impossible images that were trying to tell her that it had been her own sister who had tried to run her down in that narrow side street.

CHAPTER TWO

'SARA! How could you be so clumsy? Your dress is ruined!' her mother exclaimed in horror as she followed her into her hotel bedroom.

Sara hid a grim smile of satisfaction as she unceremoniously stripped the torn dress off and kicked the revolting garment towards the bin in the corner of the room. Even in a crumpled heap in the shadows the colour was offensive and from the first horrified moment she'd seen it she'd realised exactly why her sister had chosen it, and had been determined to thwart her plan. Even if today was her sister's wedding, she had no intention of being made a laughing-stock in front of all their friends and family...and especially, she admitted guiltily, in front of Dan.

'I'll just have to step down from being a bridesmaid,' she said logically, putting Plan A into action even as her mother hurried across to retrieve the expensive dress to examine the extent of the damage. It wouldn't be nearly so hard to stand in the background while she tried to hide her emotions from everyone else; to hide the fact that she desperately longed to be the one standing beside Dan—the *man she loved—exchanging their vows. Zara was the twin accustomed to standing in the limelight and putting on the face that the rest of the world expected to see.* 'It won't take me long to put my smart suit on,' *she continued, refusing to think about anything beyond the immediate situation.* 'I'll catch up with the rest of you downstairs before the ceremony starts.'

'You can't!' *her mother wailed, wringing her hands.* 'You've got to be Zara's bridesmaid. You're her only sister...her twin! What would everybody think?'

'Does it really matter what they think?' *Sara asked with her head in the wardrobe, already reaching for the black silk suit she'd chosen as an elegant alternative to the burnt-orange meringue her sister would have had her wear.*

The thing that had amazed her was that her mother had apparently been oblivious to what had been going on right under her nose while the attendant's clothes had been chosen for the wedding party. She'd commented approvingly about the clever idea of a colour theme graduating from the creamy ivory of the bride's dress through various shades of gold and topaz for the dresses her wraith-thin modelling friends would wear, but how could she not have seen that both the colour and the style Zara had decreed for Sara's dress were an abomination that did absolutely nothing for her second daughter's colouring or more rounded shape?

And as for the hairstyle... Sara's eyes flicked towards the mirror, her glance taking in the simple severity of the swept-back style that would have complemented the fine lines of her face if it hadn't also revealed the imperfection of the scar her sister had inflicted on her so long ago.

The fact that her mother was oblivious to everything but that things should be exactly as her beautiful daughter wanted was an old hurt that was unlikely to go away any time soon.

There's none so blind as them that will not see, she could hear her grandmother say darkly, and Sara smiled, remembering that the indomitable old woman she'd adored had been one of the few who had seen straight through Zara. Granny Walker had been the person who had always known when her younger granddaughter had been practising her wiles and had taken no nonsense, especially when Sara had been the butt of Zara's machinations.

'You're not wearing black to your sister's wedding,' her mother pronounced as she whipped the hanger out of Sara's hand and angrily flung the contents onto the bed. 'There must be something we can do with your dress. It's a designer original. The man did it specially…as a favour to Zara because she's his favourite model.'

Sara knew without question that there was no way she was ever going to be able to wear that dreadful dress again. She'd made certain of that when she'd decided exactly what damage she was going to do to it. As far as she was concerned, everything about the dress was proof that the designer must have detested her sister…maybe even the whole female half of the world's population.

'How about this?' she suggested as she switched to Plan B and took out the dress that had been hanging in the wardrobe just waiting for the right moment. 'I was going to change into this after the photos. Do you remember it?

It was an evening dress of your mother's, from before Nana married Granddad. I thought that if I wore it for part of the day, it would be almost as if she were here, too.'

The dress was simplicity itself and while the fluid silk looked nothing special draped over a hanger, once she was wearing it, the rich honey-coloured fabric was so supple that it looked as if it had been poured over her curves with a delicate hand.

'Oh, darling...' As she'd hoped, her mother caught her breath at the sentimental idea and when she reached out a tentative hand to stroke the fabric, Sara knew that she had won the first skirmish.

'Shall we see if it fits me well enough?' she suggested, already knowing what the answer was going to be—the dress fitted her as if it had been made for her. This battle plan had been worked out in every detail, knowing that it was the only way she was going to outwit her spiteful sister. 'I remember you told me once that my hair is exactly the same colour as Nana's was.' Unlike Zara's, which had been lightened season by season until it was now at least half a dozen shades paler than Sara's dark blonde.

Her mother was quite misty-eyed as she helped Sara into the substitute dress, trying not to disturb either her hair or her make-up, and when she stood beside her in front of the mirror and had to resort to biting her lip so that she wouldn't cry and ruin her own mascara, Sara knew that the battle was won. There was just the matter of teasing out a few 'accidental' tendrils of hair to camouflage the twisted line of scarring that pulled her eyebrow up at an angle...

'Whatever you do, don't catch this one on the doorhandle,' her mother warned with a sniff into her lacy handkerchief as she bustled towards the door. 'I'll just go and make sure that everyone else is ready. Zara's hairdresser was just putting the finishing touches once her veil went on when you had your accident. We don't want to keep dear Danny waiting any longer.'

With those few words, the taste of victory over what she would wear was ashes in Sara's mouth. What did it matter how much better she looked in her grandmother's dress, or that her ugly scar was hidden? Dan probably wouldn't even notice she was there; he wouldn't have eyes for anyone other than his beautiful bride.

Zara looked like a flawless life-sized porcelain doll, Dan thought as he pushed open the bedroom door and found her lying on their bed.

It was hardly surprising that she'd fallen asleep. He was hours later than usual tonight, but he just hadn't been able to make himself leave any sooner. The thought that Sara might be stubborn enough to insist on going home, even after such a potentially fatal encounter, had found him hanging around until he'd made certain that she had agreed to spend the night in hospital and was settled into a side ward.

He smiled wryly when he saw how perfectly Zara was posed. It was as if she was expecting her favourite photographer to start clicking away, her hair spread artistically over the pillow and one hand draped elegantly over the edge of the bed. It would almost have been a relief to find her curled up in an untidy ball with creases on her face from the pillow. As it was, sometimes it felt as if he was married to a mannequin, with her face always perfectly made up and never a hair out of place, even on the increasingly rare occasions that they made love.

The heavy sigh took him by surprise and the weight of regret that accompanied it made him feel very guilty.

He'd realised almost as soon as he'd placed the ring on Zara's finger that he'd made a dreadful mistake, but by then there had been no way out.

Even if he *had* divorced his new wife, he'd known that there was no way that Sara would have stepped straight into her sister's shoes…what woman would, especially after the way he'd treated her?

He might only have met Sara a few months earlier, but they'd already admitted to a mutual attraction and had been exploring the possibility of a long-term relationship. For the first time in his life, he'd even found himself wondering about the possibility of marriage in the not-too-distant future.

Then he'd met Zara and discovered the meaning of the words 'whirlwind courtship', his feet hardly seeming to touch the ground before he'd found himself engaged and caught up in the planning of an uncomfortably high-profile wedding.

Up to that point, their relationship had been conducted largely in secret—at Zara's insistence that she didn't want to chance the media intruding—so he hadn't really noticed that she was such a favourite with her parents. It had only been after their marriage that he'd noticed just how little her family regarded Sara, in spite of the fact that she was now a qualified and highly proficient doctor in a busy A and E department. All their pride was definitely focused on their glamorous, vivacious, younger daughter.

In a strange way, he could even understand it, to a certain extent. He'd certainly been blinded by Zara's lively attractions when she'd set out to captivate him. What man wouldn't have been flattered to have such a stunning woman hanging on his every word in such an ego-stroking way?

How could he not have realised that she was all outward show with very little substance beneath it? Why had it taken him so long to recognise that Sara was worth a dozen of her self-centred twin?

Well, there was nothing he could do about it now. He was married, and even though he knew it had been one of the worst decisions of his life, he was not a man who broke a promise, so he certainly wouldn't go back on a solemn vow. He would just have to be content with the fact that Sara had agreed to carry a child for the two of them...two children, in fact, he recalled with a sudden surge of the same incredulous delight that had swamped him when he'd learned of it. Although how Zara would respond when he told her that she would shortly be learning to cope with being a mother to not one but two newborn babies...

'Zara?' he called softly, stifling a sigh of resignation. His wife was not going to be in a happy mood when she saw how late it was, even though it had been her sister's welfare and that of the babies she carried that had caused the delay. She was almost fanatical about preserving her looks with adequate sleep and certainly didn't like eating at this hour. 'I'm sorry I'm late, but it was unavoidable. Your sister had a rather...' He broke off with a puzzled frown.

She hadn't so much as stirred, even when he'd lowered himself wearily to the edge of the bed. Something rustled as it slid to the floor between the side of the bed and the cabinet—a letter she'd been reading before she'd fallen asleep? Perhaps it was a glamorous new contract she'd wanted to gloat over while she'd waited for him to come home?

He reached out and touched her hand...her curiously lifeless hand.

Suddenly, he switched into doctor mode as all the hairs went up on the back of his neck in a warning that something was seriously wrong.

'Zara!' he called sharply as he leant forward to take a closer look at the silent figure. He'd been standing in the doorway wool-gathering for several minutes and only now was he noticing that she was so completely still that she didn't even seem to be breathing.

'Zara, wake up!' he ordered harshly, his fingers automatically searching her wrist to find a pulse. 'Zara!' He heard the panic bouncing back at him from the expensively decorated bedroom walls when there was no sign of any rhythm under his fingertips. Was that because his ordinarily rock-steady hands hadn't stopped shaking from the moment he'd heard that Sara had been knocked down? Frantically, he probed her slender neck and breathed a sigh of relief when he felt the reassuring throb of the artery under his fingertips.

It was slower than it should be…much slower…and her skin felt cold and clammy. It was no wonder that he hadn't been able to see her breathing because her respiration was so shallow as to be almost imperceptible.

But at least she *was* breathing and her heart *was* beating, so that gave him precious time to try to make a diagnosis so that he could help her survive whatever had happened to her.

But first…

'Emergency. Which service do you require?' said a crisp voice in his ear as he continued to make his examination, trapping the phone in position with one shoulder.

'Ambulance,' he said tersely. 'My wife has had some sort of collapse. Her pulse and respiration are both depressed and her pupils are fixed and dilated.' He managed to give the operator his address even as he reeled with horror at the possibility that Zara was imminently going into cardiac arrest.

Without some secure means of administering oxygen and the supplies to set up an IV line he had no way of improving her tidal volume or boosting her systolic pressure above 80. At the moment it must hovering around 70 because her femoral pulse was barely perceptible. If it dropped below 60 the carotid pulse would disappear, too, and she would be just minutes away from irreversible brain damage and death…

'Come on! Come on!' he urged as he transferred her swiftly to the floor and began carefully controlled cardiac compressions to boost the volume of blood going to her brain, desperate to hear the sound of a siren drawing closer.

The weight of his guilt was almost crushing as he kept automatic count inside his head. If he'd come home when he'd said he would, rather than hovering over Sara and waiting till she was settled in her room, would he have arrived in time for Zara to tell him that she was feeling ill?

Would he have been able to prevent her collapsing in the first place?

A sudden hammering on the front door made him realise that he'd completely forgotten to release the catch for the ambulancemen to get into the flat.

'She's in here,' he directed as he quickly led the way back to the bedroom and dropped to his knees beside her again. 'Her systolic must have been close to 70 when I found her because her femoral pulse was barely palpable and her pupils were fixed and dilated.' He glanced across at the man who dropped to his knees on the other side of the body to begin his primary survey, and they came face to face for the first time.

'Dr Lomax!' the paramedic exclaimed, clearly shocked to see him, but he immediately became the consummate professional. 'Do you know what happened to her, sir?' the paramedic asked as he bent over the ominously still figure between them to check her pulse and respiration rates for himself.

As he did so, Dan heard the man's foot strike something to send it skittering under the bed but no one even bothered to glance at it. At the moment nothing mattered more than giving Zara a chance to continue her vibrant life.

Out of the corner of his eye Dan saw the man's colleague depositing an oxygen cylinder on the carpet and he

reached out for it, leaving him free to set up the defibrillator with the swift ease of much practice.

He was ashamed to see how badly his own hands were
trembling as he fumbled to tighten the mask against her
face, blocking out the heart-stopping thought that Zara
might already be in need of the defibrillator's violent
charge to reset her heart rhythm. It was several horrified
seconds before he remembered that it could also be used
as a valuable monitoring and diagnostic tool.

'I've no idea what happened to her,' he said, dragging
his thoughts back to the question he'd been asked, frustrated when he saw that the man was having trouble finding
a vein. But, then, with her blood pressure so low, it was
hardly surprising. Still, he had to fight the urge to take over
and do the job himself. They needed to get the IV started
and the lactated Ringer's running into her veins as soon as
possible to get her blood pressure up. If she'd had some
sort of spontaneous bleed that had caused a catastrophic
drop in her blood pressure…

'I came home from work to find her lying on the bed,'
he continued, forcing himself not to waste any time
second-guessing, even as the need to do *something* urged
him to continue CPR. 'At first, I thought she was sleeping,
but when I tried to wake her…' he shook his head in disbelief. 'That's when I realised how ill she was.'

'Do you know if she'd had any alcohol to drink before
you found her?' he asked, and Dan almost smiled.

'It's unlikely. She never drinks anything stronger than
a white wine spritzer…too many calories,' he added.

'Do you know if she's taken any drugs, sir?' the young

man asked as he peeled the gel pads from their protective backing and positioned them swiftly on Zara's chest, and even though Dan knew that the questions were necessary for him to do his job, the suggestion shocked him.

'No!' he exclaimed immediately, horrified at even the thought that this bright beautiful woman might have wanted to kill herself. Then he remembered a conversation he'd overheard at one of the parties she'd dragged him to earlier on in their marriage. He'd been shocked to learn just how many of her fellow models resorted to chemical assistance to maintain their almost skeletal slenderness.

'Oh, God,' he muttered, praying that Zara hadn't been tempted down that route. In a profession that valued the freshness of youth above almost everything else, her age was already counting against her. Had she been that desperate to extend her modelling career that she would use drugs to help her compete with all those younger wannabes?

'I don't know,' he admitted finally. 'I've never seen her taking anything, but…'

'Could you go and have a look in the bathroom, please, sir,' the paramedic asked firmly, as he gestured to his colleague to take his hands off their patient while he activated the machine to monitor the state of her heart. 'We'll take over here now.'

'Stand clear. Analysing now,' said the disembodied voice programmed into the machine as he strode into the *en suite* bathroom, almost grateful for an excuse not to watch if they were going to have to make her beautiful body convulse with the brutality of a shock.

It took precious seconds to search through a mirror-fronted cabinet crammed full of beauty products of every shape and size, but the only tablets he could find were those in a half-full plastic bottle of over-the-counter painkillers.

'No shock required,' the voice was advising as he came back into the room, and his heart lifted briefly at the thought that at least Zara hadn't gone into ventricular fibrillation or cardiac arrest.

'Did you find anything, sir?' prompted the paramedic as he rejoined them and he saw that in his absence they'd intubated Zara to secure her airway, rather than relying on the face mask, and had connected her to their portable oxygen cylinder. The monitor clipped to her finger was already starting to record an improvement in the saturation level in her blood.

'No drugs, other than some generic analgesics,' he said, disorientated by the fact that he was little more than a bystander in a situation where he was usually the one in charge. But this was completely different to working in A and E. There, he could work fast and effectively, treating any number of cardiac arrest patients in a single day with his brain working swiftly and clearly and every possible piece of equipment readily to hand.

Here, it felt as if his thoughts were travelling through treacle as he saw the paramedic's gloved fingers sort through the pre-loaded syringes in his kit. Somehow, he just couldn't get his brain to tell him what the man should be looking for, or why.

'They were paracetamol and the bottle was half-full,' he added, before the man could ask.

'What about the bedside cabinet?' prompted the other man, and Dan dragged his gaze away from what the two of them were doing to stride across and pull the drawer completely out. He upended it over the bed and several items fell off the edge of the mattress and hit his foot to land out of sight under the bed.

'Some herbal sleeping tablets and…a bubble pack of contraceptive pills,' he added in disbelief, suddenly wondering just how many kinds of a fool he'd been. So much for Zara's grief that she couldn't give him a child! If she'd been taking contraceptives to prevent herself getting pregnant, had anything about his marriage been real?

He reached under the bed to retrieve the items that had fallen, his first sweep revealing nothing more than a couple of pens and the locked diary that Zara had written in each night.

His second sweep shocked him to the core.

'*Barbiturates!*' he exclaimed when the empty bottle rolled into view and he caught sight of the name of the contents printed on the label. 'Where did she get barbiturates from?'

There was an awful silence in the room, with only the soft sibilance of the oxygen to break it, all three of them gazing at the slender beauty with varying degrees of disbelief, incomprehension and pity. They all knew that the incidence of barbiturate overdose had dropped considerably with the introduction of newer, safer sleeping tablets, but if the label on the bottle was genuine, the dangerously addictive drugs were clearly still readily available in other parts of the world to globe-trotters such as models.

Although why *Zara* would feel the need to take…

'We need to get her to hospital quickly, sir,' the paramedic said briskly, as he selected several syringes. 'Do you know your wife's approximate weight so I can give her the first dose of sodium bicarbonate?'

Thank goodness he'd found the prescription bottle, he thought, realising wryly that he was probably one of very few husbands who would know almost to the ounce what his wife weighed, the result of Zara's obsessive morning ritual had been a cause for alternating delight or despair for every single day of their marriage.

At least they now knew precisely which barbiturate she'd taken and that it was one that bicarbonate would promote more rapid urinary excretion—anything to get the drug out of her system before it could do any more damage. Zara was already deeply comatose and if he'd arrived home any later…

He shook his head, deliberately shutting that thought away as he followed every move that the two-man crew made with critical eyes. Not that he doubted their competence. From the moment they'd entered the flat they hadn't made a false move.

His colleague had already piled everything else back into their packs and as soon as it was closed he straightened up. 'I'll get the stretcher,' he announced and took off out of the flat.

'Do you want to travel with her, sir, or—?'

'I'll follow you,' Dan interrupted, and understood the look of relief that briefly crossed the man's face. He didn't know many paramedics who would be entirely comfort-

able about doing their job under the eagle eyes of an
A and E doctor, especially when the patient was a member
of that doctor's family.

Apart from anything else, he and his colleague were
probably wondering at the situation between Zara and
himself that could have led her to make such a desperate
gesture.

He sighed heavily with the realisation that there was no
way this would remain a secret, no matter how strict the
rules were over patient confidentiality.

'The last thing any of us needs is speculation and
gossip,' he groaned under his breath as he followed the
stretcher out of the flat and paused just long enough to
make sure the front door had locked behind him. It was
going to be hard enough to tell Zara's family that she had
made an attempt at taking her own life without the whole
hospital speculating what went on behind closed doors.

If that was what it had been, he continued agonising as
he followed the flashing lights through the busy traffic, the
urgent scream of the siren an audible reminder that the
outcome of the situation was far from certain.

Suicide? Zara? It still seemed impossible. Had she just
intended to give him a scare? Had it only been the fact that
he had been late that had made this such a serious situation, the extra hours giving the drugs so much more time
to do their damage.

And if she…*when* she survived? He hastily altered the
words inside his head, feeling a renewed stab of guilt that
he could even contemplate the alternative.

Anyway, he thought heavily, as far as her health was

concerned, no one could predict how well or how badly she would recover. Only time would tell how much permanent damage the drugs had done to her system.

The fact that she was his wife was another matter entirely. Zara wasn't anywhere near as important a model as she pretended to be, but any speculation that it might somehow be *his* fault that she'd come so close to death could start a media feeding frenzy that would ruin all their lives, to say nothing of his career. The lower end of the tabloid market would have the whole situation blown out of all proportion the minute they heard that she'd taken an overdose, especially if they unearthed the fact that the two of them had resorted to a surrogate pregnancy.

He followed the flashing lights all the way to the emergency entrance, his brain rerunning everything that had been done to try to stabilise Zara's condition. He was so preoccupied that he only just remembered in time to pull into the designated staff parking area rather than cluttering up the area around the emergency entrance.

As his feet pounded across the tarmac towards the emergency doors, the lights cast long shadows that made it seem as if the doors never got any closer, but finally they slid silently open in front of him.

'Dan? What on earth are you doing back here?' demanded his opposite number on the night shift, but he didn't even slow his pace, his long strides taking him unerringly through to the resuscitation rooms at the other end of the department.

'Dan! Come in,' called the consultant already standing the other side of Zara's ominously still body, his face creased in concern as he beckoned him into the room.

For a moment, as he shouldered his way through the doors, Dan was filled with dread. Had things got worse during the ambulance journey from his flat to the hospital? Zara's condition had been so serious that he was hardly likely to look across the clinically stark room and find her sitting up and preening herself in front of any males in her audience, but if the bottle of barbiturates she'd taken had been in her body too long, it was all too likely that she might never come out of the coma.

As he stared across at her, she looked even more like a porcelain doll under the unforgiving fluorescent lights, with an almost waxy sheen to her skin.

He slumped back against the wall and watched in awful fascination as his superior did everything *he* would have done if she were one of his patients, from aspirating her stomach contents to remove any tablets still undigested, to trying to neutralise any drug-laden fluids with activated charcoal before they could be absorbed by her body.

This just couldn't be happening, he thought, his helplessness making him feel sick to his stomach.

Zara had so much to live for, and before this he would have sworn that she was far too self-centred and conceited to ever think of suicide. Why on earth would she do something so…so…?

'I'm sorry, Dan,' the consultant apologised, and Dan knew that he was going to confirm his worst fears…*life extinct*.

Just the thought of those solemn words was enough to change the way he saw the woman who was his wife. Somehow her slenderness became mere gauntness without the aura of her vivacity, her expert make-up smudged into a caricature of its usual perfection and her shimmering blonde hair artificial and brassy.

He closed his eyes to try to block out the images, unable to look at her any more.

How *was* he going to break this latest news to her family? It had been bad enough when he'd been contemplating the best way to tell them that Sara had been knocked down, but *this*…

'We're going to have to put her on IPPV,' the consultant warned when a monitor suddenly shrilled a warning that her oxygen saturation was falling dangerously low in spite of the mask. Dan's eyes flew open and he blinked in disbelief. How had he managed to convince himself that Zara was dead when the room was filled with the sound of all those monitors?

'Her respiratory effort is so badly depressed by the drugs…' his superior continued, almost apologetically.

'It's OK,' Dan reassured the man, immeasurably relieved that all was not yet lost. 'Just do what you have to do. You don't have to talk me through every step. I trust you.'

More than he would trust himself at the moment, he admitted silently. The whole scene seemed totally unreal, especially coming so soon after Sara's narrow escape. How many disasters could one family cope with in a single evening?

At least he'd given in to Sara's request not to inform her parents what had happened to her. He'd been reluctant, knowing how excited they were about the pregnancy, but

Sara had promised that she would go straight to them when she was released in the morning, confident that hearing about the accident would be far less traumatic if they could see with their own eyes that she was perfectly all right.

Well, more or less, he temporised, imagining just how badly bruised she must be after such an event. Her pale skin would soon be all the colours of the rainbow, and as for the pain…that must be considerable, especially as she'd refused any further analgesia.

His respect for his sister-in-law couldn't have been any higher, as a colleague, as a person and as the temporary mother of his children. Sara might not always get along with her twin—an understandable case of sibling rivalry, perhaps?—but she'd certainly proved how much she loved her sister by putting herself through the traumas of a surrogate pregnancy.

Behind his closed lids he saw a flash of another image—that of two tiny hearts beating side by side. And he could picture equally clearly the fiercely protective emotions in Sara's eyes. It had been obvious just how much it had meant to her to see the babies for the first time and to know that her accident had apparently left them untouched.

A secret regret hit him afresh, one that he'd been living with for several years now.

He knew that he'd behaved stupidly when Zara had set out to entice him, had already realised, even then, that Sara had been more than halfway in love with him. He'd probably been heading in the same direction until her sister had started her determined pursuit.

And he'd been stupid enough to be flattered and intrigued by the prospect of being desired by a woman so confident in the power of her beauty. Had it been the fact that she was the twin of someone to whom he was already attracted that had made him believe he had been in love with her?

Enough!

Enough rationalisation! Enough excuses! Whatever the truth had been then, now was a different matter entirely.

He straightened his shoulders and deliberately opened his eyes to gaze directly at the woman he'd married, confronting his blame head on.

It had been his responsibility to protect her, and he'd obviously failed if she hadn't felt able to come to him with her problem—be it depression or a dependency on drugs. He had no idea when it had started or how long it had been going on...no idea whether her brush with death had been an accidental overdose or a deliberate one.

No doubt the police would have to be involved and would doubtless grill him at length about the state of his marriage.

How much worse would it have been if she'd died while he'd been hovering around Sara until she had been settled on the ward?

As it was, even if she did recover fully, it would be some time before Zara was in any fit state to answer questions. He certainly had no idea what had made her take this drastic action, so if the police needed to know why she'd done it, they would probably have to interview Zara's friends and colleagues as well.

'She's stable now, so we're transferring her up to ICU,' the consultant said, and Dan suddenly realised just how much time had elapsed while he'd been lost in his thoughts.

His superior patted his shoulder reassuringly, but there was something else entirely in the expression in his eyes, something that didn't need to be put into words. They both knew that there was no guarantee of a happy outcome.

'I've sent samples up to the lab, just to confirm what she'd taken to make sure we've done all the right things,' he said quietly, then added, 'Give them half an hour or so to get her settled up there,' exactly the way *he* would have done had she been one of *his* patients.

'How long before we know…? How badly is she…?' He couldn't finish a single question, knowing there were no real answers.

'I'd love to be able to tell you that she's going to be all right,' the consultant said, patting Dan's shoulder again. 'But you know as well as I do that only time will tell. Shall I leave it to you to contact the other members of her family, or would it be better coming from me?'

'I'll do that now,' Dan said, his voice sounding almost rusty as it emerged from a throat tight with too much emotion.

How *was* he going to break the news to Zara's doting parents?

CHAPTER THREE

SARA heard the all-too-familiar swoosh and creak of the door to her room as someone pushed it open, and barely managed to stifle a groan.

Not *another* member of staff preventing her from sleeping! There couldn't possibly be an inch of her body that hadn't been examined, poked and prodded...or had a needle stuck in it.

When nothing happened after several seconds of silence, she opened cautious eyes, wondering what was going on. Seeing Dan standing beside the bed, gazing down at her, immediately doubled her pulse rate, then she realised that the oversized gown she'd been given had slipped right off one shoulder. She had to stifle a groan of agony when she tried to hike it back into a more modest position with the wrong hand.

'Dan?' she croaked, trying for impatient but only managing to sound pathetic. 'I thought you were going home. You don't need to keep checking up on me, too. There's an army of nurses doing that every two minutes and...' She had to bite her tongue to stop herself delivering another tirade when she still owed him a massive apology for the first one. He'd come to see her just after she'd had her ultrasound scan to see if she and the babies were all right and she'd jumped right down his throat. It just wasn't fair that she was taking all her fear for the babies out on him.

'I didn't come to check up on you,' he said quietly, one hand going out to the chair beside her bed, then pausing.

It was almost as if he wasn't sure whether to stand or sit, and if it was sit, whether it should be on the chair or on the side of her bed. The whole incident took no more than a few seconds but it was totally uncharacteristic of a man who was usually decisiveness personified.

Finally, he perched uneasily on the edge of the bed, his lean hip nudging against her bruised thigh…not that she would say a word. Secretly, she still revelled in every occasion that he was close to her…close enough to smell the clean soapy scent of his skin and see the tracks where his fingers had raked through his hair. Close enough to see the lines of strain that had grown deeper still since she'd seen him just an hour or two ago.

'Dan? Is something wrong?' Panic struck her and her hand flew to cover the precious duo nestling deep inside her. 'Is it something to do with the babies? Has something shown up on one of the tests?'

'No!' he exclaimed, clearly startled. 'I'm sorry, Sara, I didn't mean to frighten you. As far as I know, everything's still fine.'

'So, what's wrong?' she demanded. 'I can tell you've got something serious on your mind and… Is it Mum and

Dad? I *told* you not to tell them about my accident. I was going to go and visit them as soon as I'm set free in the morning, so that they could *see* that I'm not—'

'It's not your parents,' he interrupted, then sighed heavily and shook his head. 'Sara, I'm sorry but there's only one way to tell you this. When I got home this evening, I found Zara unconscious. She'd taken an overdose of barbiturates.'

'*Barbiturates?*' she gasped, reeling. 'No! Not Zara. She wouldn't.' It was her turn to shake her head at the impossibility of what he was suggesting. Her sister might be selfish and egotistical but she wasn't anyone's fool. She'd seen far too many of her fellow models slide down the slippery slope of drug addiction, hooked when the desire for impossible slenderness came with an intoxicating high. With a few high-profile exceptions she'd seen it ultimately ruin their careers as model agencies and advertisers alike crossed them off their books.

Anyway, barbiturates were usually prescribed for people having difficulty sleeping, so they wouldn't be any use to someone wanting to get high. Deliberate overdoses were usually confined to people who were depressed and that definitely didn't sound like her vivacious sister.

'There was no name on the bottle and the drug name was generic…possibly bought abroad or over the internet…and the bottle was empty when I found it on the floor beside her,' he said quietly, and she could see from his expression that he was already blaming himself.

'How long ago…?' she began, only to halt in mid-sentence as a sudden thought struck her. If Zara had been at home, taking an overdose, then her crazy suspicion that it had been her own sister driving the car that had run her down this evening must have been just that…crazy. Unless she'd gone home after she'd done it and taken the drugs in her remorse…but, no, that didn't make sense either. Nothing made sense. Not the fact that she'd been absolutely certain that it had been Zara behind the wheel of the car that had deliberately aimed at her, or the fact that she would have access to barbiturates or would deliberately take an overdose.

'She was in a pretty bad way when I found her,' he said, answering the question she would have asked if her brain had been working well enough to formulate it. 'She was already comatose, her breathing and pulse rate both depressed, but when her stomach was pumped, there were a fair number of undigested tablets, so she must have taken them some time this evening.'

Sara's relief that her sister couldn't have been responsible for her accident faded with the realisation that there would still have been plenty of time for her to have returned home and swallowed the drugs before Dan had found her. But that begged the question: why would Zara do it, especially when Sara was expecting the child… *children*…that she'd begged Sara to carry for her?

'Have you told my parents?' Sara could only imagine the state her mother must be in, knowing that her beautiful perfect daughter had…

'Not yet. I had to come and tell you first,' he said simply.

Pleasure that he'd wanted to break the news to her *before* notifying his in-laws flowered inside her, only to wither to dust when he added, 'I didn't want you to get a garbled version if the news reached you through the hospital grapevine.'

That was more like the Dan she'd been working with for the last couple of years—logical and practical. Of course there hadn't been a personal reason why he would have wanted to give her the news in person. When was she going to stop searching for traces of the connection they'd made when they'd first met? When was she going to come to terms with the fact that any feelings he'd had towards her had vanished the instant he'd met Zara?

'Where is she? What treatment is she receiving? When can I visit her?' she demanded briskly, forcing herself to be equally logical and practical. She tried to push herself up in the bed and fell back with a groan when every muscle and joint complained.

'You're in no fit state to go anywhere yet,' he growled as he carefully slid one arm under her shoulders and effortlessly lifted her up, supporting her while he positioned the pillows behind her.

Sara shivered. Every tiny hair had suddenly stood up in reaction to the warmth of his arm surrounding her. Not that her hospital room was cold. If anything, it was far too hot. But somehow it was different when it was Dan's body heat in a wide swathe across her back where his strong arm held her, and as for the soft wash of his breath stirring her hair against her face and neck…

'But…' It was hard to get her thoughts in order when he was so close. Thank goodness they never did any more than brush against each other when they worked together, or she'd never be able to do her job properly. Still, she didn't dare to take a full breath until he laid her gently back against the pillows and released her to step back a little from the bed. The last thing she needed was another lungful of that familiar mixture of soap and musk to contend with.

'Sara, I'll let you know as soon as they say she's stable enough for visitors,' he promised, his green eyes darkly serious. 'At the moment she's so deeply unconscious that she wouldn't even know that you were there, and you wouldn't be doing yourself any good either. You need to give your body time to heal.'

'But you're going to have to tell Mum and Dad tonight, aren't you…about Zara, I mean?'

'And that means I'll have to tell them about what happened to you, too,' he pointed out.

'No! *I'll* tell them, when I—'

'Sara, think about it,' he interrupted. 'They're going to want to see you…they'll be *expecting* to see you when they arrive at the hospital, waiting outside ICU until Zara's consultant allows you in to see her.'

'But…' She closed her eyes in defeat. He was right, of course. And she wasn't in any fit state to be sitting around in the little relatives' room all night.

'Which would you rather—that they knew that you'd been involved in an accident or that they thought you couldn't be bothered to be with them when they need you?' he challenged, and she slumped back against the pillows, knowing that she couldn't argue against that sort of logic.

'You will tell them that the babies are OK, won't you…?

Oh!' she exclaimed with a shadow of her usual smile. 'They don't know that it's twins yet!' She groaned as she tried to reach into the bedside locker for the precious picture of the scan. 'Could you get the photo for me, so you can show it to them?'

'Actually…' He paused a second and she was startled to see a soft wash of colour sweep across the lean planes of his cheeks as he reached into his pocket to take his wallet out. 'I hope you don't mind, but I asked the technician to print an extra copy.'

For Zara. Of course.

'I should have thought of that…to get one for the two of you. After all, they're going to be *your* babies, so you actually have *more* right to a picture than I do.'

'Sara, don't,' he said swiftly, and startled her by trapping her hand in the warmth of his, the green of his eyes darkening as they gazed intently down into hers. 'I can't imagine how difficult the whole process is for you, but you have every right to a picture of the babies that are developing inside you. I'll never be able to thank you enough for what you're doing. An extra picture of an ultrasound scan is nothing in comparison.'

His sincerity was obvious and actually managed to soothe some of the ache that had been filling her heart ever since she'd been persuaded along this path. The last thing she'd wanted to do was carry the children of the man she loved, only to have to give them away. The fact that he genuinely seemed to appreciate the sacrifice she was making was like balm to her soul. All she had to do was make sure that he never had any idea of her true feelings towards him.

* * *

It had been every bit as dreadful as he'd thought it would be, Dan thought wearily as he propped himself against the wall of the ICU waiting room several hours later.

Unfortunately, it had been his mother-in-law who had answered the door of their smart suburban home, and when she'd realised that Zara hadn't been with him, something in his face must have told her that he was the bearer of bad news.

'She's had an accident, hasn't she?' she wailed. 'I *knew* something must have happened. I just knew it! I've been waiting all evening for Zara to call to let me know she'd returned home safely. I told her she should have asked you to drop her car off at the garage.'

As he ushered her through to her smartly decorated lounge, trying vainly to calm her down, a small corner of Dan's brain registered the odd snippet of information. What had been wrong with Zara's car that it had needed the attention of a mechanic? Both their vehicles had only recently been serviced.

'What's the matter? What's going on?' his father-in-law demanded gruffly from his favourite seat at one end of the settee. He fought to fold the newspaper that had spread itself across his lap and tried not to look as if he'd fallen asleep in front of the television.

'Our Zara's had an accident!' his wife keened. 'I told her she shouldn't be driving in London traffic. Danny should have looked after her. *He* should have taken her car to the garage if there was something wrong with it.'

'Is that true, lad? Is she hurt? How bad is it?' Frank might not be so openly emotional as his wife but it was plain that he was immediately worried about his precious daughter.

'Can we sit down?' Dan suggested, still uncertain just how much he should tell them. The results hadn't come back from the lab by the time he'd left the hospital, so he still wasn't certain what level of concentration the drugs had reached in Zara's body and what that would mean for her prognosis. If they had depressed her respiration and starved her brain of essential oxygen long enough to cause permanent…

'She's *dead*! My baby's *dead*!' Audrey cried hysterically, and for a moment he almost relished the idea that he might need to slap some sense into the woman.

'No! She's *not* dead!' he contradicted firmly, hoping that he sounded more confident than he felt. He took hold of both her shoulders and guided her until the backs of her knees met the edge of the settee and she collapsed next to her husband. 'Neither of your daughters is dead,' he said firmly, desperately praying that he was telling the truth.

'You mean, something's happened to *Sara*?' Frank demanded. 'But I thought… I'm confused. Did Zara ask you to come and tell us? Why didn't she come herself, or is she staying with Sara?'

'Is it something to do with the baby?' his wife demanded sharply. 'Zara will be *so* disappointed if anything's wrong with…'

Between the two of them he was having a hard time getting a word in edgeways. It looked as if he was going to have to abandon any idea of breaking things to them gently.

'Sara was knocked down by a car this evening as she

was walking home from work,' he announced bluntly. Too bluntly? he wondered when it looked as if the pair had stopped breathing.

'No!' He should have known that their mother would recover the power of speech first. 'Oh, Danny…how? Oh, tell me she hasn't lost Zara's precious baby.'

'She was knocked unconscious, her leg was broken and she's badly bruised, but she had a scan to see if she had any internal injuries—'

'She didn't have any X-rays, did she?' Audrey demanded sharply. 'I don't want my first grandchild being born deformed because it had X-rays.'

Not a word of concern about the injuries *Sara* had suffered, Dan noted, even as he had to stifle a smile when he remembered Sean O'Malley telling him just how fiercely Sara had objected to having X-rays. He could just imagine that she'd been the very picture of a lioness defending her cub.

'Actually,' he said, sidestepping the issue of X-rays entirely to focus on the news that still sent his spirits soaring, in spite of all the trauma of the last few hours, 'the scan showed us something we weren't expecting to see— that Sara's carrying twins.'

The momentary silence had a completely different feel this time, but even as they began exclaiming in delight he despised himself for his cowardice. He should be telling them about the much more urgent situation confronting their younger daughter.

His reprieve was all too brief.

'What did Zara say when you told her?' his father-in-law demanded with a beam. 'I bet she was delighted.'

'Well, I was very late getting home, after making sure that Sara and the babies were going to be all right,' he began, even as a voice inside his head jeered at him for trying to assuage his guilt for arriving home so much later than he'd intended. The outcome would have been very different. 'I thought she was asleep, but when I went to tell her the news, I couldn't wake her and had to call an ambulance to take her to hospital.'

'Hospital?' his mother-in law shrieked in disbelief. 'Zara's in hospital, too? Why? What's the matter with her?' She began to struggle to her feet, slapping viciously at her husband's hand when he tried to stop her. 'I've got to go to her straight away. *You'll* have to take me,' she declared with a glare at Dan.

'Why wouldn't she wake up? What's the matter with her? Do you know?' Frank demanded, clearly dumbfounded by the news.

'It looks as if she's taken an overdose of drugs…barbiturates,' he said, and was nearly deafened by the howl of denial.

'*Drugs!* That's a lie! My Zara wouldn't touch the filthy things.' Audrey was sobbing with rage now. 'Why would you say such a dreadful thing about your own wife? You should know she's the most beautiful, most perfect—'

He ignored the start of the familiar litany, interrupting bluntly. 'The bottle was found beside her, and some of the drugs were found still in her stomach when we got her to the hospital and pumped her out.'

'But—' Frank began, but as ever his wife's voice overrode his tentative attempt.

'Then you got them all out and she's going to be all right?' she demanded shrilly, in spite of the fact that her certainty about her daughter's convictions had been summarily destroyed. 'Did she tell you why she took them? It must have been a mistake…a…a…'

'They pumped out as many as they could, but she'd already absorbed enough to send her…' At the last moment he paused, wondering if the mention of the word 'coma' would be the final straw. Instantly, he knew that his mother-in-law would definitely have hysterics if he so much as mentioned the possibility, and sidestepped the prospect by choosing a less emotive word.

'Zara's deeply unconscious, so she's been taken into Intensive Care where she'll be monitored constantly until the drugs wear off and she wakes up.'

He hoped they were too shocked to notice the guilt he was trying to hide, but no way was he mentioning the very real chance that the drugs might have already caused significant damage. He knew that, as her parents, they had a right to information about their daughter, but he was hoping that he wouldn't have to be the one to tell them. It was bad enough that *he* knew that Zara might never wake up again, at least not in any meaningful way.

It might be cowardly, but he was intending to leave it to the consultant to tell them that, even when the effect of the drugs she'd taken did wear off, the daughter that the two of them idolised might already be lost to them for ever.

Sara was a different matter. There was no way he could

have left her to find out what her sister had done, not after the shock her system had already sustained this evening.

He stifled a weary sigh as he assisted his sobbing mother-in-law into his car, knowing that there would be very little chance that he would be seeing his bed tonight.

Hoping that his silence could be taken as the result of navigating the busy streets, he tried to get his thoughts in order.

He would definitely have to contact Human Resources as soon as possible to notify them that he wouldn't be in for his shift the next day…or for the foreseeable future, at least until the drugs had left Zara's system and he had some idea what sort of prognosis they were looking at.

He would also have to see if there was a relatives' room free for the Walkers to use. He couldn't imagine that anyone would be able to persuade Audrey and Frank to leave the hospital until their daughter was out of danger, but they might be persuaded to rest in between the short visits they would be permitted by her side.

Then there was Sara.

Bruised, bloodied and broken her body might be, but her spirit appeared even stronger than ever if the way she'd confronted him was any gauge.

He found himself stifling a grin when he remembered the way she'd turned on him like a spitting cat. It was the closest she'd ever come to telling him exactly what she thought of him, although he had a pretty good idea.

He'd barely admitted to himself how much of his time had been spent thinking about her, even in those first few weeks. Then he'd been stupid enough to allow himself to be snowballed into marriage with her sister, committing the oldest blunder in the book when he'd allowed his hormones to overrule his heart.

Then, when he and Zara had been unable to conceive, he'd been amazed and delighted when his in-laws had told him that Sara had volunteered to act as a surrogate mother for them.

How stupid could he have been? He should have known that her parents' desire to give Zara everything she ever wanted would have made them resort to any means to persuade her soft-hearted sister to agree.

No wonder she had so little time for him, even when he was concerned about her welfare. No wonder she'd been convinced that his only interest was that his child had been unharmed.

Children, he reminded himself with a surge of mingled joy and terror.

He'd been amazed and delighted to see not one but two hearts beating strongly on the ultrasound screen, evidence that they were both still snugly ensconced in their rightful environment and supremely unaware of their narrow escape. One side of him was ecstatic to see the evidence that his precious children weren't just a dream but a miraculous reality. It was the other side—the doctor side of him—that knew enough to be afraid; the doctor half of his brain that knew just how much more dangerous the existence of that second baby was, both to the pregnancy and to Sara herself.

Bearing a child was already one of the most dangerous things a woman could put herself through, and to carry twins...

He shook his head when he realised that he was already planning a session on the computer to access all the relevant statistics, irrespective of the fact that knowing the figures would worry him even more.

'What's the matter?' Audrey demanded in a panicky voice as she entered the relatives' room at exactly the wrong moment. 'Why did you shake your head? Did the doctor say something to you while we were in with Zara? She's not going to…? Oh, no! Please! She can't die. Not my beautiful girl!'

Dan swore silently as her voice rose shrilly with every word, his head thumping unmercifully.

'No one's told me anything,' he said firmly as he took her by the shoulders and leant down to force her to meet his gaze. 'Audrey, the only time I've spoken to Zara's consultant was when you were with me. The situation hasn't changed. We've just got to wait and see how her body copes with whatever it is she's taken. We've just got to be patient.'

'How *can* I be patient?' she demanded angrily, shrugging his hands off and whirling away. 'I'm her *mother*! You have no idea how dreadful it is not being able to do anything. Just waiting…'

'You could visit Sara,' he suggested. 'She must be wondering what's happening down here, worrying about—'

'If she were that worried she'd be here with us,' Audrey interrupted sharply. 'I can't believe how selfish that girl is, to be lying in bed when she should be down here with her sister…with us…'

'Sara's in no fit state to go anywhere,' Dan snapped,

rapidly reaching the end of his tether. It was unbelievable that parents could be so concerned about one of their daughters and so dismissive of the other. They seemed to care so little for Sara and were so unappreciative of her and everything she'd achieved that it bordered on emotional abuse.

It certainly wasn't something that he would ever do to *his* children. His heart missed a beat when he visualised the flickering evidence of those two tiny beings that would one day look up to him and call him Daddy. It was an awesome responsibility and he would make certain that they both knew that their father loved each of them as much as the other.

'Mum? Dad?' said a hesitant voice from the doorway, and Dan spun on his heel, his eyes widening with disbelief when he saw the shaky figure sitting in the wheelchair.

The bruises on her face looked livid and angry already, especially against the stark white of the dressing covering her stitches. He could only guess how many other injuries were hidden under the back-to-front gown she wore as a wrap, but nothing could hide the ungainly cast stabilising her broken leg.

'Sara!' He strode towards her when he saw her struggling one-handed to propel herself further into the room, her face so pale it seemed almost bloodless. He didn't know whether to be angry with her for being crazy enough to make the journey when every inch of the distance between her room and ICU must have been agony for her, or proud that her determination was enough to bring her here in case her parents needed her support.

All he knew was that he was suddenly filled with an overwhelming need to protect this valiant woman from anything that might cause her any more pain.

CHAPTER FOUR

DAN was still seething when he finally took half an hour to race home for a shower and a change of clothes.

'Those parents of hers are unbelievable!' he growled as he leaned wearily against his front door, almost too tired to make his way to the bathroom.

He was sure his mouth must have gaped when there hadn't been any evidence of sympathy at the shocking extent of Sara's injuries, not a single word of concern that she must have escaped death by the merest whisker, to say nothing of the possible loss of their grandchild…grand-*children*, he corrected himself and felt that crazy grin creep over his face again, banishing his bad mood at a stroke.

He reached for his wallet and extracted the precious image printed from Sara's first scan and awe joined his feeling of delight. Not one but two tiny beings were still growing safely inside her womb, in spite of their close brush with death. He could still feel that first surge of emotion when he'd seen the image of their minuscule hearts, the beats so rapid that they'd almost seemed to flicker on the screen.

'My babies,' he whispered as he outlined their precious images with a visibly trembling fingertip and was shocked to feel the hot press of tears behind his eyes.

This...*these*...were the one good thing that had happened in such a very long time. These two tiny beings made everything worthwhile.

Even the knowledge that your wife is lying dangerously ill in ICU? asked a disapproving voice inside his head. That brought him up short for a moment and guilt struck him hard that he was feeling such delight while Zara's health—her very life—hung in the balance.

His shoulders slumped still further when he realised that even though her situation was serious, with no guarantee for a happy outcome, he found it strangely hard to care any more than he would if Zara were just another patient brought into A and E in the course of his working day.

'That certainly took the smile off your face,' he muttered as he strode across the lounge towards the bathroom with the weight of a very long day pressing down on his shoulders again. At the last moment he veered towards the mantelpiece to prop the precious image in full view, torn between the desire to replace it in his wallet to keep it close to him and the equally strong need to keep it safe.

His first step inside the bedroom was like a punch to the gut. He and Zara were both reasonably tidy people so it was a real shock to be confronted with the shambles that remained from his efforts to keep her body functioning until the paramedics arrived.

The bedclothes straggling onto the floor were mute testimony to the way he'd hastily pulled her down onto the firmer surface, and there certainly hadn't been time to straighten anything up before he'd leapt in his car to follow the ambulance to the hospital.

He stepped forward and reached out to gather up the bedding then let it fall again, unable to find the energy to care that the bed needed making or, more to the point, the inclination to sleep in it at all when he thought about what had so nearly happened there.

He needed sleep. In fact, if he was honest with himself, he was nearly out on his feet with exhaustion, both with the stresses of a long hard shift and then the double shocks of first Sara's and then Zara's admission to hospital. Even so, he couldn't face the thought of climbing into that bed, not when he didn't know whether its last occupant was going to survive.

He nearly fell asleep standing under the shower, the fierce pummelling of the water jets on the back of his neck and across his shoulders almost as blissful as a massage.

Not that he'd had the time or inclination for massages recently. In fact, not since the last time Sara had taken pity on him in the very early days of their fledgling relationship.

'Don't go there!' he groaned aloud, but that did nothing to stop the images playing through his head.

It had been a rough shift, not unlike the last twelve hours, and he'd made the mistake of sitting down at the table in the staffroom rather than going straight home. The next thing he'd known had been Sara's voice in his ear, calling his name and waking him to the realisation that he could barely move his neck for the crick in it.

'Can I see if I can get rid of that stiffness for you?' she'd offered, and for a moment he hadn't been certain which stiffness she'd been talking about. Waking up with her soft voice and the warmth of her breath in his ear had matched perfectly with the dream he'd been having, and both had had a predictable effect on his body.

Her fingers on his neck and shoulders, alternately stroking then firmly kneading only helped his neck and shoulders. His other reaction he'd had to keep to himself until he'd returned to his bachelor digs with images of persuading Sara to join him there as soon as possible playing in his head.

Had there been a hormonal overload in his system at the time, because it had been just days later that he'd met Zara and been completely bowled over by her blatant interest in him…so different to Sara's more reserved manner and so flattering to the male ego.

The steam followed him out of the shower as he padded through to the wardrobe with nothing more than a towel wrapped around the back of his neck.

He was operating on auto pilot now, knowing that he needed clean clothes and to put something in his stomach and knowing that his duty was to support his in-laws while they waited impatiently for the scant five minutes in each hour that they were allowed to spend at their daughter's bedside. It was so wearing to sit with them knowing that they were pinning their hopes on finding a dramatic improvement each time they went in.

He was already running on his reserves and knew he needed to sleep, and sleep soon, but somehow…somehow he couldn't think about sleeping while Zara's condition was unresolved and especially while Sara was valiantly sitting with her parents, waiting for better news. She had worked just the same killer hours as he had and had then suffered the trauma of being run over.

The clean shirt made him feel a bit less ragged and he was just reaching for some bread to toast to fill the gaping hole where his stomach should be when his pager shrilled.

'Daniel Lomax,' he said, his heart in his mouth by the time the phone was answered in ICU and he was switched through to the consultant's office. He wasn't on duty but had told the ICU staff he was taking his pager home with him if they needed to contact him.

'Daniel, I thought you'd like to know that we've had another set of results back from the lab and—'

'I'm on my way, sir,' Dan interrupted, when he heard the strange note in the consultant's voice. Suddenly he knew that something was wrong, and a surge of adrenaline instantly banished his exhaustion. 'I'll be there in about eight minutes,' he promised, already halfway out of the door as he ended the conversation.

By the time he reached the street he'd fought his way into his jacket and had his keys and phone safely in his pocket. The rain was still lashing down and for a moment he considered going round the back of the flats for his car, then shook his head. The flat had been chosen because of its proximity to the hospital but the security system protecting the cars from opportunist thieves would take longer to get through than if he ran. Nothing was going to interfere with getting to ICU as quickly as possible.

He was soaked to the skin and so wound up that he was shaking by the time he made it up the last flight of stairs.

'What's happened?' he gasped as he reached the interview room, one of the nurses having pointed the way as soon as she'd seen him.

'It's good news!' Audrey exclaimed with tears in her eyes. 'They've found out that Zara *hadn't* taken an overdose of barbiturates after all. I *told* you she wouldn't. She's not into all that drugs nonsense.'

'Not barbiturates?' Dan said with a frown, turning towards Mr Shah. 'But the bottle was on the bed beside her when I found her. I don't understand.'

'It's possible that it was some sort of…' he hesitated a second and threw a glance in Audrey and Frank's direction. 'A decoy of some sort, to make you think she'd taken something else.'

'Well, it worked,' Dan said flatly, hating the thought that even in something as serious as an overdose of drugs Zara was playing stupid games. 'So what *had* she taken?'

'The lab results say that the majority of the tablets were paracetamol but there was definitely some phenobarbitone, too.'

'See!' Audrey exulted, obviously completely oblivious to the serious expression on the man's face. 'It was nothing more than some over-the-counter tablets. We'll soon have her home again, good as new.'

'We knew in A and E that there was something wrong when her stomach was pumped,' Dan said, remembering his shock when he'd seen just how many tablets there'd been. It had looked like handfuls of them still largely undissolved, to say nothing of the ones that must have already dissolved and entered her system. 'The label on the bottle meant it should have been capsules but they were bringing up plain white tablets.'

'Well, it looks as if she thought she was taking just enough phenobarbitone to send her to sleep, and miscalculated. She's still comatose.'

And that wasn't the worst of it, Dan knew with a sinking feeling, already working out for himself what Mr Shah was going to tell them next.

'She was given activated charcoal when she was brought into A and E after her stomach was pumped,' he recalled with a feeling of dread.

'Unfortunately, not long after the IV was set up, she had an adverse reaction to the antidote we were giving her,' the consultant said, obviously trying to keep things simple for Frank and Audrey. 'We've given her antihistamine to dampen the reaction but, because she's had the charcoal, methionine won't be an effective alternative.'

To say nothing of the fact that she was still unconscious and would be unable to swallow the methionine tablets, Dan added silently. He'd been horribly right in what he'd feared. 'That means you're going to have to start the same IV again at the lowest possible infusion rate so you don't trigger the reaction for a second time.' And *that* meant it would take that much longer before the drug in her body was rendered harmless—time in which it could be doing untold damage to her liver and kidneys, especially to someone who was borderline for malnourishment, the way so many fashion models were.

'So, how long will it be before she wakes up?' prompted Audrey eagerly. 'How long before we can bring our little girl home?'

The consultant sent Dan a wry look, sharing the knowledge that here was yet another set of parents who were only hearing what they wanted to hear.

'We're giving her medication to mop up the drugs still in her system, but everything else is largely up to her own body. She won't wake up until the sleeping pills she took have worn off, and we have no idea how long that will take. It's just a case of waiting,' he explained kindly, and Dan knew that the man had recognised that neither of his in-laws was capable of taking in the possibility of any other outcome. As far as they were concerned, Zara would wake up as quickly and easily as though she'd fallen asleep in front of the television the way she sometimes did after a long flight.

'Excuse us,' Frank said suddenly, getting out of his seat after a quick glance at his watch. 'It's our time to go and sit with Zara. We wouldn't want to miss it.'

'By all means,' the consultant said, getting up courteously to open the door for them. He glanced back at Dan as though asking whether he wanted to leave, too, but he didn't move. There were so many more questions he needed to ask, particularly about the lab results and the level of concentration of the paracetamol that had been found in Zara's blood.

At the last moment, just as the door swung closed, he caught sight of a slight cotton-clad figure in a wheelchair out in the corridor.

'Just a moment, sir,' he requested, and hurried across to open the door again, to find Sara making her laborious way towards her sister. Her parents must have passed her just seconds ago but had clearly left her struggling on her own.

'Sara,' he called gently to attract her attention, and stifled a wince when he saw how gingerly she turned her head towards him. She shouldn't be wheeling herself about when she was so badly bruised. She should be lying in bed, giving her body time to heal.

'Did you want to have a word about Zara?' he invited. 'The latest lab results are in.' He glanced over his shoulder to find that the consultant hadn't been quite so quick to mask his reaction to Sara's injuries. 'Do you have any objection if she joins us, sir? Zara is her twin, but Sara is a doctor on the staff here, down in A and E.'

'I've no objections at all. Come in, my dear. Let me hold the door for you.' He hurried to hold the door wide while Dan strode out to take hold of the handles and provide the propulsion she needed. 'My word, your family *is* in the wars. What on earth happened to you?' he asked as he gently shook her hand as though afraid she would shatter.

'A hit-and-run accident on my way home from work,' she said, as she used her hand to shift her cast to a more comfortable position, the wry smile that she sent him doing nothing to lift the evidence of pain from her face.

Dan ached for her, wishing there was something he could do, but there was no one on earth who would be able to persuade her to take painkillers if she'd decided against them.

'How bad were the results?' Sara asked quietly, as ever

going straight to the point. 'How much damage has she done to herself? I suppose she got the barbiturates on one of her foreign trips.'

'Actually, my dear, it's not the barbiturates that are causing the biggest problem,' Mr Shah explained. 'The majority of the drugs your sister took were paracetamol.'

Dan wouldn't have believed that Sara could have gone any paler until he saw it happen. Her lips were almost colourless and she had to lick them with a flick of her tongue before she could speak.

'So, she's on IV N-acetylcysteine? What concentration has the paracetamol reached? Is it still rising or is it on the way down now?'

'It's not rising any more, but it hasn't started dropping yet,' the consultant said apologetically. 'As you say, we put her on IV NAC, but she quickly developed side effects. We've had to administer antihistamine and drop the dosage of the drip right down.'

The small frown pleating her forehead told Dan that she had worked out for herself the reasons why they couldn't use the alternative antidote, and admired the fact that her brain was still working just as fast as usual in spite of everything that had happened over the last day.

'Also,' Mr Shah continued inexorably, 'we have no way of knowing how long the drugs have been in her system. If it is only a short time—less than eight hours—then it will not be such a big problem, but we cannot assume anything.'

Dan was watching Sara's face as the consultant was speaking, so he saw the sudden widening of her eyes and the deepening of her frown. The expression must have pulled her stitches if the wince and the protective hand that came up to cover the dressing was any indication.

For a moment it was obvious that she was conducting some sort of internal debate and the way her hazel eyes darkened told him it wasn't a pleasant one. Then her hand dropped to the curve of her belly in a protective gesture as old as time and panic roared through him. Was she in pain? Was she suffering a delayed reaction to her accident? Was she miscarrying?

'Sara,' he began, fighting for self-control when all he could think of was the precious picture propped on his mantelpiece, 'is everything all right? Are you feeling—?'

The sudden sound of a hasty knock at the door cut him off as the consultant excused himself before calling, 'Enter.'

'Mr Shah, Zara Walker seems to be waking up. Did you want to—?'

'Thank you. We will come now,' he said swiftly, already pushing back his chair. 'Do you want to follow me?' he threw over his shoulder, but didn't wait for a reply as he hurried out into the corridor.

'Here, let me. It'll be quicker,' Dan said as he took over the propulsion of her wheelchair, leaving Sara to slump back into the seat.

She must be really close to the end of her tether, he realised when he saw the slump of her shoulders. Zara might be the professional model but Sara had an innate elegance and style of her own and poor posture wasn't a part of it.

'Are you sure you're all right?' he asked, taking advantage of the fact that there simply wasn't enough space for the wheelchair in Zara's room—there were just too many people in there at the moment. 'For a moment, back in the interview room, you looked…worried. Is it the baby? You're not having contractions, are you?'

'*Babies,*' she corrected softly. 'And, no, I'm not having contractions, thank goodness. I was just…' She paused for a moment, then shook her head. 'No. It's nothing.'

'Are you sure?' Some sixth sense was telling him to press her. 'If it was something that could possibly help Zara…'

There it was again, a look of indecision, as though she couldn't bring herself to say something…detrimental about her twin. He had no right to insist that she speak to him and was still trying to find a way to persuade her to trust him with…well, with whatever it was putting that frown on her face when an all-too-familiar voice called his name.

'Danny?' it quavered, but whether the weakness was real or feigned he wouldn't like to hazard a guess. It could just as easily be either, knowing Zara. 'Is Danny there?' There was a plaintive note this time and he had to stifle a wry smile. Now certainly wasn't the right time to question Sara, but he was definitely going to make a point of it before he left the hospital this time.

'I'm here, Zara,' he confirmed lightly, straightening up so that she could see him above the general mêlée of medical staff and her parents. Her vital signs had already been checked and if he wasn't mistaken, there was more

blood being drawn for another lot of tests to track the
progress of the antidote.

'Come closer, Danny,' invited Audrey, beaming widely
and beckoning with the arm not wrapped around her
precious daughter's shoulders. 'Look! Isn't it wonderful?
Our Zara's back with us as good as new. Isn't she beautiful?'

Zara had been born beautiful, Dan thought dismissively.
It was all on the surface, not something she'd had to work
for…unlike Sara's medical qualifications.

Zara's initial expression when her mother drew her attention to him was one of open delight, then her wide
hazel eyes drifted to one side as though she was trying to
see what had attracted his attention away from her at such
an important moment.

He took a step aside so that she could see her sister
sitting in the wheelchair beside him. He was totally
shocked when, instead of an expression of concern or, at
the very least, an equally welcoming smile for her sister,
her look was one of…what? It was definitely more than
horror at the fact that she'd suffered such injuries, it was
almost revulsion, or even…hatred?

Impossible. He must be more exhausted than he'd
thought if he could imagine such a thing. Twins were
closer than almost any other people, and in their case, with
Sara putting herself through pregnancy on her sister's
behalf, they were bound to be closer than most.

Then, without a single question about how Sara came
to be so injured, Zara held out a hand towards him in a bla-
tantly theatrical plea.

'Oh, Danny, I'm so sorry for putting you through this but…' She bit her lip and peered up at him. 'I just couldn't cope with it any more. It was all just too much.'

'Couldn't bear what?' he asked, not buying her pantomime for a minute, although there must be something serious behind her actions. Someone as self-centred as Zara didn't do anything without planning it down to the last step, like her plan to seduce him.

'Well, didn't you read my note?' she demanded crossly. She was clearly wrong-footed by the fact that he didn't know what she was talking about, but he had no doubt he would be hearing all about it in exhaustive detail.

'I didn't see any note. When did you write it? Where did you put it?' he demanded. It certainly hadn't been on the mantelpiece when he'd put the picture of the scan there, although he hadn't really been looking at anything other than those two indeterminate dark blobs with the bright flashes where their hearts were beating.

'Oh, Danny,' she cried, and accepted the pretty handkerchief her mother offered, actually managing to squeeze out a tear or two. 'I poured my heart out to you…told you how insecure I was feeling…how afraid that… Oh, what's the use?' she said petulantly, and turned her back on him.

'She's overwrought,' Audrey said in a stage whisper. 'She'll feel better when she's had a good night's sleep in her own bed.' She turned her attention to Mr Shah. 'When can we take her home? Do we have to fill in any papers?'

'Oh, my dear Mrs…Mrs Walker,' he said after a quick glance at Zara's notes to refresh his memory. 'Your daughter is perfectly within her rights to sign her self out of hospital, but I certainly wouldn't advise it.'

'Why on earth not?' challenged Frank. 'We've all been waiting for her to wake up and now she has. Surely that's an end to the whole miserable episode.'

'I wish it were, sir, believe me,' the consultant said with a shake of his head. 'Unfortunately, the fact that your daughter has woken doesn't mean that all the drugs have left her body, and until the drip has neutralised the paracetamol, the drug could still be doing damage to her liver.'

'But…' Audrey looked almost comically disappointed.

'It really would be better if she stayed until we can give her a clean bill of health. She probably still feels rather shaky and tired and would rather not make a journey before she's absolutely ready.'

Dan smothered a grin when he recognised the way the ICU consultant had got the measure of the Walker family. To suggest, obliquely, that Zara needed specialist attention for a little longer was the one strategy that her parents wouldn't want to argue with.

After that, it wasn't very long before the senior sister had used a similar technique for persuading Audrey and Frank that it would be in everybody's best interests if they went home and had a good night's sleep.

Sleep! It had been so long since he'd done it that he felt quite punch-drunk, but something still wouldn't let him leave until he'd gone to check that Sara was finally getting some rest. After Zara's little pout he'd turned to say something to her, but neither the wheelchair nor its occupant had been anywhere in sight.

'What do you think you're doing?' he growled when he found her clothed in a set of baggy blue scrubs and trying to work out how she could use a pair of crutches with one shoulder taped up after a dislocation. 'Are you completely crazy? You should be in bed, allowing your injuries to start healing.'

'And that's exactly where I'll be as soon as I get home,' she countered with a stubborn lift of her chin.

'And exactly how were you intending getting there?' he asked, wondering what it would do to his credibility as a doctor if he stood in the middle of the corridor and screamed out his frustration. Why wouldn't the wretched woman see that he was trying to take care of her?

'Well, as walking is plainly out of the question until I'm a little more proficient, I would have thought that the obvious alternative is a taxi,' she snapped in frustration, standing on one leg and clearly in danger of losing her balance and falling over as she tried to put her coat on.

'And when you get home?' he persisted. 'How were you going to get up all those stairs to your little eyrie?'

He almost felt sorry when he saw her shoulders slump in defeat.

'I can't stay in here, Dan,' she said turning those golden hazel eyes on him in mute appeal. 'Won't you help me?'

'If you're really adamant about leaving, you've got two choices. Either I can drop you off at you parents' house—'

'No way!' she exclaimed with a shudder. 'I haven't spent a night there since I left for medical school and I don't intend changing that. What's the other alternative?'

'That I take you home to my flat.'

'*Your* flat?'

Her expression was so shocked that he hurried to continue. 'I—*we*—do have a spare room, Sara, and I'm sure that your sister would be delighted to know you're somewhere safe.'

Under her breath she muttered something that sounded very much like, 'I doubt it.' He almost asked her to explain but as she was conceding defeat over donning her coat it looked as if he'd at least won that round, even if was only to get her to stay here for the few hours left till morning.

'I'll give you a lift after morning rounds if the orthopod gives you the all-clear, and see what we can do to make you comfortable and safe...all three of you,' he added quickly when she bristled again at the suggestion that she couldn't take care of herself. He wasn't above using her pregnancy as a weapon if it got her to take care of herself. 'The last thing you need is to have a fall down the stairs. You might not be so lucky a second time.'

CHAPTER FIVE

Sara felt as if she'd been tricked into staying in hospital for the last few hours.

It had taken her some time to recognise the way Dan had played on her concern for the two tiny beings residing inside her to persuade her to agree, and she'd even had to smile at his astuteness, but she had no intention of staying any longer. Now was the perfect time to make good her escape, while the staff were all too busy elsewhere to notice her going. What did it matter that she would now be leaving in daylight in a pair of oversized scrubs that looked like a clown's baggy pyjamas and a coat that looked as if someone had rolled in the gutter in it—which she had.

'Maybe the dry-cleaners will be able to do something with it,' she muttered as she awkwardly balanced her borrowed crutches across the arms of the wheelchair to reach for the button to call for the lift. If the coat wasn't salvageable…well, it was easy come, easy go. It had been one of the items Zara had been throwing out because she'd needed to make room for more up-to-the-minute items, ir-respective of the fact that it was made of some horrendously expensive fabric like cashmere or vicuna. All Sara knew was that it was the most deliciously warm coat she'd ever worn and she'd be loath to lose it. She certainly wouldn't be able to replace it with anything as good.

'Making your escape?' said a deep voice behind her, and she jumped so high she had to scrabble to hold onto the crutches.

'Dan! Don't do that!' she snapped as her heart gave its familiar leap in response to his closeness.

'I had a feeling you wouldn't be waiting about this morning,' he said wryly. 'It's nice to be proved right.'

'Actually, I was just going to call in to ICU to see what Zara's latest results are. Have you already been? Do you know?'

The lift gave a quiet ding and the doors slid open to disgorge half a dozen assorted staff and visitors. 'Let's find out together,' he suggested as he took charge and wheeled her into the lift. Then the doors slid closed and the two of them were trapped in the enclosed space, isolated and alone in a way she'd been careful to avoid ever since the day Zara had turned up to be introduced to her tall, dark and handsome doctor friend.

'Sara, are you really well enough to be leaving so soon?' he asked quietly, and her heart gave a stupid extra beat when she saw the caring expression in his eyes.

He's a doctor. Caring's what he does, she reminded herself firmly, just in case she got the idea that it was her as a person that he cared about.

'I'll cope,' she said firmly. 'I'm a fit, healthy person, so I'll soon be on the mend. You don't have to worry about me.'

Her timing was perfect as the doors slid open just as she finished speaking, and the people waiting to board the lift prevented Dan from saying anything more.

'Ah, Daniel. Good. I'm glad you're here,' Mr Shah said, almost as soon as they'd set foot in the unit.

'Problems?' Sara heard the edge in his voice that told her he'd been expecting this conversation.

'More problems than I'd like,' the consultant admitted as he showed them into his office. 'Your wife's liver enzymes are raised and rising but time is critical. If only we knew exactly how long it was since she took the overdose. We'd have some idea how much further they might go.'

Sara felt sick as she took in the information. She knew that the raised enzyme levels were evidence of liver damage but she also knew that the number of hours between overdose and the start of treatment was very important. If a patient received the antidote within eight hours there was a far better chance of saving the liver from permanent, if not fatal, damage.

In her mind's eye she replayed the split second before she'd been struck by that car, the instant when she'd been looking straight towards whoever was driving it and had seen her own face looking back at her.

Had it been her own face, reflected back at her from the windscreen, or had the person behind the wheel been the only other person in the world with a face exactly like hers?

She didn't want to know, couldn't bear to know if it had been Zara, because whoever it had been, there was absolutely no doubt in her mind that they had aimed the car at her deliberately, that they had intended to kill her and the babies inside her.

But…logic told her that knowing might be essential for Zara's health. If she *had* been the driver, that would mean that she probably hadn't taken the paracetamol until she'd returned home. That would give Mr Shah the timeline he needed to gauge how much more aggressive his treatment needed to be if he was to be able to rescue Zara's liver.

She was still conducting her silent debate when one of the nurses ushered her parents into the office to join them.

'I'm afraid Zara won't be going home today,' the consultant stated firmly as soon as the pleasantries were over.

'But I've got everything ready for—' Audrey protested.

'She's not well enough to leave today,' he said. 'Her latest results are showing us a problem with her liver and she needs to stay here until we know she's stable.'

'Her liver? What's wrong with her liver?' Frank demanded with a look of disbelief. 'She's never been a big drinker, not like some of these girls who go out and get drunk all the time.'

'Partly she's having the problem because she's underweight,' Mr Shah explained patiently. 'Her liver didn't have enough reserves, so when her body started to break down the paracetamol, it began damaging the tissues of the liver.'

'So, how bad is it?' Frank was suddenly very subdued, as though the severity of the situation was only now coming home to him. 'And is it going to get any worse?'

'The damage means that her liver will develop areas of

necrosis—that means the tissue dies,' he explained hastily when he saw their puzzled expressions. 'We don't know yet whether it's going to get any worse. It's just a case of wait and see.'

'How long will we have to wait? Weeks? Months?' Audrey asked tearfully, clutching her husband's hand like a lifeline.

'Not as long as that. Usually, it's no more than a few days before we can tell whether the liver is damaged beyond repair.'

'What happens then?' Audrey was pale and shaky but clearly intent on fighting for her precious daughter. 'What are you going to do to make her well again? Will she need medication or dialysis or what?'

'Dialysis isn't an option—it can only be used for kidney failure—but some patients with quite severe liver damage can recover with the right diet and support. For the rest, there are surgical options, but we won't go into that unless it becomes necessary.'

The meeting broke up then, with her parents hurrying off to spend time with Zara while Sara was left trying to manoeuvre wheelchair and crutches out of the office without taking a chunk out of the door.

'Let me,' Dan said, and took over the propulsion again. And even though being this close to him caused every nerve in her body to tense up, she wasn't about to refuse the loan of some muscle power to get her to the lift.

'Thank you,' she murmured, careful not to look in his direction while they waited for the lift to arrive. She was grateful they weren't the only ones in it this time—the more people sharing the space the better if she wasn't to risk making a complete fool of herself. How long would it take before he realised that she'd never got over him, even though he'd abandoned her in favour of marrying her sister?

She could have groaned when he insisted on pushing her across the expanse of the main reception hall and out of the electronically controlled doors.

'Where do you want to go?' he asked, absent-mindedly flicking the keys in his hand against his leg.

'I can get a taxi,' she pointed out with a glance towards the couple already waiting outside the front of the hospital, their drivers chatting to each other with the ease of long acquaintance.

'Ah, but will it be driven by someone willing to stay long enough to make sure you get up your stairs safely? Are you willing to risk falling down and breaking something else—or injuring the babies?'

He didn't play fair, Sara grumbled silently as she tried to make herself comfortable on the plush grey upholstery. If he hadn't mentioned the babies, she would have stuck to her guns, she told herself as she tried to get her cast into the footwell, grateful that he'd thought to slide the passenger seat back as far as possible to accommodate her lack of mobility.

She breathed a sigh of relief when she was finally able to click the seat belt into position then regretted it when she drew in that tantalising mixture of soap and man that would forever signify Dan.

Think of something to talk about, she told herself sternly as he pulled out of the car park, but the only topic that came to mind was Zara. Still, it did prompt an idea.

'Nice car,' she commented blandly. 'What sort is Zara driving these days?'

'I didn't think you were into cars.' There was a hint of laughter in his voice, the laughter that she'd loved to share with him when she'd believed they'd had a future together. 'You don't even own one, do you?'

'I didn't see the point of buying one for the sake of it,' she said stiffly, fighting off the memories. 'I live within walking distance of the hospital and the shops, and if I need to go further afield, there's always a taxi or the train.'

'So, why the interest in Zara's vehicle?'

'Just wondering if you ever let her drive yours.' That was bound to get her the information she wanted. She knew how much he loved his bad-boy black BMW with its pale grey interior, had been with him the day he'd taken delivery of it, the first new car he'd ever owned.

'No way!' he exclaimed fervently. 'But she insisted that she needed to be able to get about and wanted something equally sporty, so…'

'His and hers? Matching cars?' she teased and held her breath.

'Well, yes,' he admitted uncomfortably, then added, 'Except hers is metallic silver with black upholstery.'

'Big difference!' she teased again, although how she found the words she didn't know. A silver car with dark upholstery. That was an image that would be imprinted in her memory for the rest of her life.

But there must be thousands of silver BMWs. It could

have been any one of them, said the corner of her brain that didn't want to believe that her sister could have done that to her. Except, she argued with herself as her fingers crept up to trace the scar on her forehead, you know what she was capable of when she was just a little girl. She's grown up now, but has she grown out of such tendencies or has the scale of them grown with her?

'I hope you won't mind if I stop off at my flat first,' he said, and she was so relieved that he was interrupting the darkening spiral of her thoughts that she would have agreed to almost anything. 'It shouldn't take me long, but you can come up and wait for me if you like.'

'And have to go through all that effort of posting myself back into the car? No, thank you,' she said. 'If you park in the underground car park, I'll be quite safe while I wait for you.'

He tried to change her mind but she was adamant, a new plan already fully formed in her head.

As soon as he disappeared from view she opened the passenger door and began the time-consuming struggle to extricate herself from the car. All the while her pulse was racing, afraid that she wouldn't have time to achieve what she wanted to before he came back.

'A silver BMW with a black interior,' she muttered aloud, having had to admit defeat with the crutches when her recently dislocated shoulder refused to take the pressure. Anyway the pain was too great and she didn't dare to do it any more damage or it could be a problem for the rest of her life.

So it was her eyes rather than her feet that set off along

the row of cars while she leant against Dan's, her eyebrows lifting a little more with each expensive model she recognised, but in spite of the fact that there were two other BMWs, neither was silver with a black interior.

'So much for my idea of seeing whether there was any damage on her car,' she grumbled as she made her halting way back to Dan's vehicle. But if it wasn't here, where could it be? Zara certainly hadn't driven herself to the hospital in it.

'Sara, what's the matter? Why did you get out of the car?' She hadn't even heard the lift coming down but there was Dan hurrying towards her across the oil-stained concrete.

'Um…I had a touch of cramp and needed to get out to move about a bit,' she invented clumsily, hating not to tell the truth, but how could she make such an accusation without a single shred of proof?

'Are you ready to get back in or would you rather change your mind?' he offered. 'It wouldn't take me five minutes to put clean sheets on the bed.'

Dan and bed in the same sentence weren't the ideal combination to ensure she had a good sleep. 'I'd rather go where I'm surrounded by my own things,' she said, while her brain was trying to find a way to get the answers she needed.

Finally, there was only one way.

'I couldn't see Zara's car in the garage,' she said, hoping it sounded like idle conversation while he steered them out of the garage and back onto the street.

'You wouldn't. It's usually parked in the slot next to

mine, but apparently she had an argument with a bollard the other day and dropped it off at the garage to have some scratches repaired…not for the first time, I might tell you,' he added with a chuckle.

'So, when did she take it to the garage?' Sara asked, and the frowning glance he threw her way told her that she'd pushed too far.

'Sara, what's all this about?' he asked as he drew up in front of the converted Victorian house she lived in. He turned to face her. 'Why so many questions about Zara's car? What do you *really* want to know?'

Sara swallowed hard when she met his gaze, knowing the frightening level of intelligence contained behind those green eyes. There would be no point insulting that intelligence with a half-baked invention.

'I wanted to know because…' She swallowed again, afraid that this was going to be the moment when she lost all semblance of friendship with the man she'd never stopped loving. 'Because the car that ran me down was a silver BMW with dark-coloured upholstery and I'm almost certain that it was driven by a woman with long blonde hair.'

To say he looked shocked by the implied accusation was an understatement, and the longer she looked at those eyes and the way they widened and darkened endlessly with the repercussions had her hurrying into speech again.

'I can't believe that *anyone* would want to do such a thing deliberately, least of all Zara, but…but I needed to know…about her car, and about the damage she did to it. Then I'll have the proof that it *wasn't* my sister who tried to…to…' She choked on the press of tears and couldn't say another word but, then, she'd already said more than enough if his expression was anything to go by.

There was an agonisingly long silence in the car while she tried to concentrate on keeping the tears back. Crying was one of Zara's favourite weapons and all her life Sara had consciously fought against them for just that reason.

'Well, then, there's only one thing to do, isn't there?' Dan said suddenly as he released his seat belt. His voice was so frighteningly devoid of any emotion that Sara felt sick.

'W-what?' she stammered as he threw his door open and prepared to slide out. 'What *are* you going to do, Dan?'

He didn't answer until he reached her side of the car and pulled the passenger door wide. 'Find some answers, of course,' he said briskly. 'Now, leave your crutches in the car because they're no use to you till your shoulder's a good deal less painful, and let me give you a hand out of there. You need to get some proper clothes on if you want to travel in my car again.'

Her startled grin must have been the reason he'd added that last proviso, and it had worked. In fact, it had worked so well that she didn't even think of objecting when he virtually carried her up the four flights of stairs that led to her little flat up under the eaves.

'Hop to it,' he joked as she did just that with one hand against the wall on her way to her minuscule bedroom. 'Give me a shout if you need any help.'

'As if,' she growled as she unwrapped herself from the grubby coat and shed the hospital scrubs in short order.

Clothing for her upper half wasn't a problem, barring the twinges from multiple bruises and pulling scabs while she put them on. All she had to remember was to put her injured arm in first because the strapping didn't allow for very much mobility.

Unfortunately, her underwear didn't come with a tie waist and the cast wouldn't fit through the appropriate hole when she did manage to get her foot through it and pull it up with her other toes, even though it was a pair designed for halfway-through-pregnancy mums.

'Damn, damn, damn,' she muttered as she pushed the stretchy fabric off with the other foot and heaved herself up off the end of the bed for another trawl through her underwear drawer.

'Sara, I'm not being funny but… You must be very stiff and sore this morning and I can imagine that it's almost impossible to manoeuvre things over that cast,' Dan said at the very moment that she unearthed the black lacy thong that she'd bought to cheer herself up shortly after Zara had made that fateful visit to A and E. It was testament to how well it had worked that it still sported a dangling price tag.

Well, she thought with a fatalistic shrug as she tugged the tag off and flicked it towards the bin in the corner, it was probably the only underwear she possessed that would work. As for outer clothes, the only ones to hand that were wide enough to encompass the cast without having to resort to splitting a seam was a pair of heavy silk loose-fitting palazzo pants with a drawstring waist, not unlike the scrubs she'd just taken off, now that she came to think about it.

'I could keep my eyes closed and take directions if you need a hand,' he offered, and the suggestion was so sensible, so helpful, so considerate, so *Daniel* that she felt the threat of tears again. And he wouldn't even have to see her bruises, scabs and bulges if he kept his eyes shut.

'You promise to keep your eyes shut?' she demanded as a strange thrill of excitement shot through her that he would offer to do such an intimate thing for her.

'I promise,' he said firmly. 'Now, is it safe to come in?'

'No! Wait!' she shrieked as she saw the door start to swing open, and grabbed for the nearest thing to cover her naked lower half. 'Now it's safe,' she announced, all too conscious of the slight quiver in her voice and hoping like mad that Dan couldn't hear it.

'So, what do you want me to do?' he offered, and suddenly a whole X-rated scenario leapt into her head and she could feel the heat of a deep crimson blush move up her throat and over her face. 'Which bit do you want to do first and how do you want to play it?'

Her imagination leapt into overdrive and it was only the patient expression on his face and the interrogative eyebrow sending creases over his forehead that reminded her he was waiting for an answer.

'Um, if I put my…my underwear on the floor and step into it, could you pull it up for me—just as far as my knees?' she added hastily, and was treated to one of Dan's most devastating grins.

'Spoilsport!' he complained with a long-suffering air. 'OK, where is this…underwear?' She knew his hesitation was a deliberate copy of her own but was determined to ignore it. It was enough that she had to sort out which way the thong needed to be placed on the floor without having to cope with the soft wolf-whistle Dan gave when he caught sight of them.

'Well, well, well!' he murmured as he bent to position the scrap of fabric at her feet. 'Who would have thought it?'

'And why shouldn't I wear something pretty?' she demanded, stung by his reaction.

'These aren't just pretty,' he said, his voice sounding strangely husky as he began to slide them up past her ankles and on towards her knees, every inch a sensual torment as her eyes followed them all the way. 'Pretty is lace and flowers and pink and white. *This* scrap of nothingness is something else entirely!'

'That's far enough,' she said hurriedly, embarrassed all over again when her voice ended on a squeak. 'I can manage from there,' she assured him, and he gave another sigh and shook his head.

'What's next, then?' he asked, nearly catching her settling the slender elastic straps over her hips.

'Those trousers, please.' She pointed at the silky pile on the corner of the bed. 'You might need to feed them up my legs a little way before I can stand up without treading on the bottoms of them.'

'Hey,' he said brightly as he got the job right the first time. 'I've just realised that this is good practice for when I'm helping those children in there to learn how to dress.'

And that was just the reminder she'd needed, she told herself when she was sitting in his car a few minutes later.

It had been absolute agony to try to keep some distance between them on the way down the stairs when she had needed his help every step of the way, but that was what she'd *had* to do. It had been so wonderful to slip into the light-hearted banter that had been so much a part of their relationship, even in those early days, but that was all in the past.

She couldn't believe what the two of them had been doing up in her room. They'd almost been flirting with each other and there was no excuse for that. Dan was a married man and he was married to her sister. To allow anything to happen between them would be the worst sort of betrayal and she just couldn't be a part of it.

The trouble was, her love for him hadn't died when he'd married Zara, no matter how much she'd prayed that it would. Yes, he was the father of the babies she carried and, yes, she would love nothing better than that he would be at her side as together they guided them through childhood and into adulthood, but it wasn't going to happen.

'Because he's married,' she whispered fiercely as he circled the front of the car. 'He's married to your sister and the only thing he wants of you is what you're carrying in your womb—the babies that Zara can't give him.'

Something in her expression must have told him that her mood had changed because the atmosphere in the car that could have been too cosy and intimate was all business as he put the key into the ignition.

'So, what *do* you remember of your accident?' he asked as he joined the stream of traffic heading back into town.

Too much, was the first thought that came into her head,

but she knew he needed a logical answer from her. She was just overwhelmingly grateful that he hadn't angrily brushed her suggestion off as the ravings of someone who'd had an unfortunate random accident. He could have accused her of using the incident to get some sort of petty revenge against Zara or…

'Sara?' She'd almost forgotten he was waiting for an answer, so lost had she become in her thoughts.

'I always walk home the same way…out of the back of the hospital and past that little parade of shops, just in case I need to pick anything up on the way.' She glanced across briefly and saw the tiny frown pulling his dark brows together, the way they always did when he was concentrating. Afraid she'd lose her train of thought if she looked any longer, she stared straight ahead and continued.

'I'd gone over the crossroads and was just crossing one of those little turnings that seem to lead round to the back of the shops, for deliveries or something…not a real residential road, if you know what I mean?'

Out of the corner of her eye she saw his brief nod but he didn't say a word to distract her—she could manage to distract herself without any help.

'I heard a car coming and glanced towards it and I remember thinking that it wasn't the sort of vehicle I expected to see coming out of there, then I realised that it didn't seem to be slowing down and I realised that I was too far away from the kerb to get to safety and when I tried to turn away so that the impact wouldn't hurt the baby, my foot slipped on the wet cobbles and then the car hit me and I went down and my head hit the kerb and…and I woke up in A and E.'

'So, what made you think it might have been Zara?' he asked, his white knuckles clenched around the steering-wheel testament to the fact that he wasn't nearly as calm as he sounded. 'It sounds as if it all happened pretty quickly…too quickly to have seen anything much.'

Sara knew he was right, but she also knew what she'd seen. 'Well, I can now tell you from firsthand experience that when it looks as if you're going to die, there is a split second that's imprinted indelibly in your mind. It's so clear that if I were any sort of an artist, I'd be able to draw it for you with the accuracy of a photograph.'

'Tell me,' he prompted softly. 'What do you see in the photo in your mind?'

'The cobbles are wet and shiny, and there's a skinny cat running towards the shadows of a pile of cardboard boxes and his fur's all wet from the rain, and the light is gleaming off the car as it comes towards me…off the paintwork and the chrome and the windscreen as it's getting closer… And when I realised that it was going to hit me, I realised that it might hurt the baby…this was before I knew there were two of them,' she interjected in a crazy non sequitur. 'But when I put my hand over my bump—as if that would protect it from half a ton of car—the person in the car pressed their foot down on the accelerator and I heard the engine roar in response.'

Dan muttered something under his breath but the scene inside her head and the emotions she'd been feeling at the time were so strong that she paid him no heed.

'I was staring at it in disbelief, so sure that the person would put the brakes on, but she was staring straight ahead—straight at me—and her hair was long and blonde and down over her shoulders and her face... At first I thought it was *my* face reflected back at me and that could *still* be what I saw but...' She drew in a shaky breath and continued, 'Her hands were gripped round the steering-wheel...up at the top of the wheel so that her thumbs were nearly touching...and I have the impression that her nails were really long and painted with a dark varnish, but I can't be sure what colour...' She closed her eyes for a moment in the hope that it would help her to focus, but it didn't get any clearer so she went back to her narrative, to the part that still made her feel guilty that it had happened at all.

'Dan, I really did try to get out of its path,' she assured him fervently, desperate that he should believe that she'd done her best to protect his child, 'but it was coming at me far too fast and then my foot slipped but the car still hit my leg and I spun round... Actually at the time I thought it was the streetlight that was spinning round me...but I was falling and falling and I couldn't stop myself and then my head hit the ground and everything went black.'

He was silent for so long that she wondered if he was ever going to speak to her again. What was he thinking? That she was crazy? That he'd made a monumental mistake in asking her to carry his children in case she passed her craziness on to his innocent offspring?

'So, what part of the car would have hit you?' he asked, his voice sounding more like a rough growl until he cleared his throat, and tears threatened when she realised that his question meant he hadn't dismissed what she'd told him out of hand. 'Would it have been the front, the wing or both?'

CHAPTER SIX

DAN and Sara stared down at the broken light on the passenger side of the BMW while the mechanic wiped his hands on a rag so black and oily that it couldn't possibly be doing any good.

'It's not the first time she's brought it in but, then, that's women drivers for you,' he added with blatant chauvinism and a knowing wink for Dan.

Sara didn't have the breath to argue this slur on her half of mankind. She was still devastated by the evident damage to her sister's car.

'You say she's brought it in for repairs before?' Dan questioned, and from the tone of his voice that fact was news to him.

'Oops! Sorry if I'm dumping you in it, love,' he said to Sara, 'but last time it was the back bumper. She said she'd managed to reverse it into a bollard somewhere up near the London Eye.'

'And what did she tell you about this?' Dan pointed to the recent damage.

His uncomfortable look in her direction, not quite

meeting her eye, made Sara suddenly realise that he thought *she* was Zara, being taken to task by a far-too-calm husband. He probably thought her rapidly developing black eye and the dressing on her forehead were signs of wife abuse, she realized with a crazy urge to laugh.

'Actually, she didn't say anything because she didn't drop it off until after the garage closed. And last night, that was six o'clock because we were waiting for a customer to come and pick his vehicle up and settle his bill—you don't mind staying open a bit longer when it's for a good customer bringing you money, do you?'

His attempt at comradeship fell flat as Dan leant forward to take a closer look at the damaged light, reaching out to fiddle with the shattered remains for a second before he straightened up again.

'Well, thank you for your time,' he said politely. 'Let me know when the vehicle's ready for collection, won't you?' He wrapped a supportive arm around Sara's waist and helped her to hop the couple of steps to his car.

'So, it could have been any number of things that caused the damage, if she's in the habit of bumping into things,' Sara said almost before he'd closed his door, trying to find a logical reason why the damage they'd seen had nothing to do with her injuries.

She hated the thought that her sister might have wished her ill, although that long-ago episode with the piece of wood and the 'accident' that hadn't been accidental at all. Still, she was desperately afraid that she'd set something in motion that couldn't be stopped.

But, then, did she want it stopped? If her sister *had* tried to hurt her by driving that car straight at her then it was important to find out why or she might never be safe. And what if it had been the pregnancy that had been Zara's target? Sara couldn't bear the thought that her precious babies might be put at risk if she handed them over to her sister.

Had Zara been taking some of the more exotic designer drugs that her colleagues brought back from their foreign photo shoots? If so, they could have disturbed the balance of her mind and caused her to do such an outrageous thing.

But there hadn't been any evidence of strange chemicals in any of her blood tests—at least, nothing beyond the sleeping tablets and paracetamol that they already knew about.

She shook her head, at a loss to know what to think. It was already aching enough with out this mental stress, but that was probably because she'd been on her feet far too much already today. It certainly wasn't what she would want a patient of hers to do after such an incident.

Into the silence of the car came the unmistakable sound of Dan's pager and he cursed softly under his breath as he tried to find a break in the busy traffic to pull over to the side of the road.

Once there, it only took seconds before he'd used his mobile phone to call the unit and Sara suddenly realised that it was the first time she'd heard him speak since they'd left the garage.

What had he been thinking while her brain had been strangled by conflicting ideas? Had he dismissed her claim that she'd recognised Zara as her assailant now that he'd seen that there was no real evidence or was he, too, worried about the ramifications for the children she was carrying if their mother-to-be had really tried to injure them?

'That was your mother,' he announced as he ended the call and pulled back out into the traffic. 'She says that we need to go back to the hospital straight away. Zara's next set of tests results have come in.'

'Is she worse?' Sara demanded anxiously, because, no matter what she'd done, Zara was her twin and she loved her.

'Your mother didn't say. All she told me was that we had to go straight to the hospital, so…' He shrugged, his eyes never leaving the road as he navigated the quickest route.

'Mum. Dad. What's happened? What's the problem with the latest results?' Sara asked as soon as Dan pushed her into the unit in a hastily purloined wheelchair and found her parents just inside the doors, as though they'd been waiting impatiently for them to arrive.

'What took you so long?' her mother demanded, whirling to hurry up the corridor. 'Mr Shah has got the results in his office and he needs to have a word with us.'

Sara suspected that the consultant was waiting to have a word with Dan rather than her parents. After all, as her husband he was legally Zara's next of kin.

'Daniel, come in, come in,' the dapper gentleman invited, but it was Audrey who pushed in ahead of the wheelchair and took one of the two available chairs, closely followed by her husband. Daniel was left to prop himself up on the wall beside Sara to wait for Mr Shah to open Zara's file sitting on his desk.

'The nurse said you've had some more results, and I want to know when we're going to be able to take our daughter home,' Audrey said with the air of a general firing the opening salvo in a war she fully intended winning.

An expression of annoyance slid briefly across the consultant's face, probably at the knowledge that a nurse had been giving out more information than she should have. Sara could imagine that before the shift was over her superior would be having a sharply worded conversation with whoever was responsible.

In the meantime, the man's face had settled into the sort of bland expression that always preceded less-than-welcome news.

'Unfortunately, the news isn't good enough for us to be able to give you that sort of information,' he said quietly. 'Her liver function tests are giving us more cause for concern and it looks as if there may be more necrosis than we'd expected.'

'Necrosis?' Audrey pounced on the word. 'What's necrosis?'

'It means that sections of her liver have been damaged and are dying, so they are no longer able to perform their proper function.'

'So it's the same as what you found on the last tests,' she summarised for herself.

'Yes and no,' he prevaricated. 'Yes, it's the same condition but, no, it's not the same as before because the condition has worsened.'

'So, what are you going to do about it?' Frank asked, and Sara wasn't surprised to see how pale he was looking at the thought that his precious daughter's health wasn't improving the way they'd hoped.

'I'm afraid we can't do much more than we're already doing as far as infusing the antidote into her system and supporting her and keeping an eye on the concentration of various components in her blood. It's still very much a case of wait and see, but I thought you would want to be informed of the results so that you would know to prepare yourselves in case—'

'Would a transplant cure it?' Audrey interrupted, clearly unwilling to hear that particular eventuality even as a theory.

'Well, yes, we can do liver transplants in some conditions—for example, in people with cirrhosis or hepatitis and also in some cases where the patient has had medication toxic to the liver—but the success rate is not as good as for kidney transplantation and there's still the problem of finding a compatible liver donor while there's still time to do the operation.'

'Well, that's not a problem, then…not for Zara,' her mother announced with a beaming smile. 'Sara will give her one of hers. I've seen it on television and they said that identical twins are a perfect match. Once you operate, Zara will be as good as new.'

'No,' Sara said sharply, and her mother turned on her with a look of utter disbelief on her face.

'What do you mean, *no*? Sara, you *can't* refuse to help your sister if she needs one of yours.'

'Mother, I've only *got* one liver, so I can't give it to her. The operation would mean chopping a chunk of mine away and that's major surgery. Anyway, I doubt if you'd find a surgeon willing to do it because I'm pregnant and it wouldn't be good for the babies.'

'Well, then, you'll have to get rid of the babies,' her mother announced with a breathtaking lack of feeling for the unborn lives nestling inside her. 'You can't refuse to help save your sister's life. She could die.'

'But you would be quite happy for me to murder *my* babies to save *your* baby?' Sara couldn't believe the pain that thought caused, her heart clenching inside her chest as though every drop of blood had been wrung out of it.

Ever since she'd seen those two hearts on the ultrasound screen, beating so valiantly in spite of the recent trauma, it had brought the reality of her pregnancy home to her the way no amount of reading pregnancy books had done. She felt so connected to those tiny beings, so protective, that the thought of deliberately scouring them out of her womb and flushing them away was anathema.

'So.' She lifted her chin and stared her mother right in the eye. 'What if I refuse to do it?'

'You *can't* refuse because they're not *your* babies, they're Zara's, and if she needs them to die so that she can live—'

It was Sara's turn to interrupt and she did so without a qualm.

'They might be babies I'm *carrying* for Zara, but they're growing in *my* body and from *my* eggs…and what's more, it's *my* liver you're talking about and *no one* can have it if I don't want to give it.'

Her mother broke into noisy sobs and no matter what her father said she wouldn't be consoled.

Sara felt dreadful.

She now knew firsthand just how fiercely a mother would defend her child and couldn't really blame her own mother for wanting to do everything she could to give her daughter a chance of being well again.

But she was a mother, too—at least while those two helpless innocents were still inside her—and she was going to fight every bit as hard for their survival.

Poor Mr Shah didn't seem to know what to do for the best. Her parents were clearly beyond listening to anything he said, even though he repeatedly tried to reassure them that Zara's condition hadn't yet reached the point of no return.

While Dan…

Suddenly, Sara realised that the one person with the most to lose in this whole disastrous situation was the only one who hadn't said a single word.

A single glance in his direction was enough to tell her that he'd retreated behind what she'd privately dubbed his 'stone' face. There wasn't a single emotion visible, until she happened to see the way his hands were clenched into tight fists inside his trouser pockets.

As if her mother had sensed that her attention had wandered she turned a tear-ravaged face to her son-in-law. 'Danny, do something,' she pleaded. 'You have to tell Sara to save my precious girl… You must *make* her give Zara a new liver!'

'No,' he said quietly with a reinforcing shake of his head. 'It's not time for that discussion, Audrey. Listen to what Mr Shah's been trying to tell you. Eighty per cent of patients with even severe liver damage eventually recover on their own, so it's just a case of waiting to see if Zara's liver is going to do the same.'

'But the transplant,' she persisted. 'Because they're identical twins it would be a perfect match and—'

'And it might only give her another year of life,' Dan finished brutally, and literally robbed her of the breath to argue any further, her mouth and eyes open like a gasping fish. 'That's the average survival rate for liver transplants at the moment,' he told her with an air of finality.

Sara knew from reading medical journals that some patients had survived considerably longer. It was probably the poor survival rate of liver cancer transplant patients that brought the overall rate down, but it wasn't accurate statistics that she cared about, it was the fact that he had managed to take her completely out of the firing line…for the moment at least.

'Now,' said Mr Shah, looking unusually flustered by the open warfare he'd just had to witness, 'I think it would be best if you were all to go home and have some rest.'

'Oh, but we haven't seen—' Audrey began, but was totally ignored as he continued inexorably, drawing a line in the sand.

'You may come back at visiting time this evening, but no more than two of you may visit at a time. That will ensure that my patient will have what remains of the day to rest and hopefully give her body a chance to start to recover.'

It was beautifully done, Sara acknowledged wryly as they filed silently out of the consultant's office, but it had left all of them in no doubt who was wielding the power in *his* unit.

'Would you like a lift?' Dan offered quietly, when they'd watched her parents scurry out of the unit before he began to push her in the same direction.

'Don't you have to go to work today?' she asked, desperate to spend what time she could with him but knowing it wasn't a sensible idea. 'You don't have time to keep ferrying me about.'

'Actually, I've got all the time in the world, having just been banned from visiting until evening visiting hours,' he contradicted her as he pushed the button for the lift that was just taking the Walkers down to the main reception area.

All Sara hoped was that it would deliver the two of them to the ground floor before it returned for Dan and her. She didn't think she could bear to be shut up in such a small space with her parents, even for the short time it would take to travel a couple of floors. Mr Shah's office had been bad enough with all that animosity flying around.

'Anyway…' Dan continued, breaking into her silent replay of the moment when her mother had glibly talked about aborting the precious pair already making their presence felt under her protective hand, the curve of her belly already noticeably bigger than it would have been for a single baby at the same number of weeks. 'As I'm on compassionate leave until we know what the situation is with Zara, you can just name your destination.'

'You're going to regret that offer when you find out where I need to go,' she warned, suddenly immeasurably grateful that the rest of the day didn't stretch out in front of her like an arid desert.

'Don't tell me!' Dan said with a groan as he pushed the chair into the waiting lift. 'You need to go shopping!'

'All right, I won't tell you…but that doesn't mean that I don't need to go.'

'All right,' he said with an air of long-suffering that caused several smiles on the faces of the people sharing the lift. 'I offered so I'll take you. Just tell me where you need to go and let's get it over with.'

'What is it with men that they don't like shopping? Is it a genetic thing?' Sara mused aloud, drawing a few smiles of her own, then relented. 'It shouldn't take very long because I only need to do some grocery shopping while I've got someone to carry the bags for me,' she added with a grin, then another thought struck her.

She hesitated for a moment, wondering if there was some other way she could achieve what she wanted and feeling the increased warmth in her cheeks that told her she still hadn't grown out of the habit of blushing. 'I'm sorry but I'll also need to do a bit of clothes shopping.'

He groaned as he waited for their companions to exit first then pushed the wheelchair out into the spacious reception area, thronged as ever by a constantly changing stream of visitors going in and out of the hospital. 'My absolute favourite occupation…not!' he complained in tones of disgust. 'If you're anything like your sister, that will take the rest of the day.'

His assumption stung her more than she had a right to feel and loosened the leash on her tongue. 'Apart from the obvious physical resemblance, over which I have *no* control, I am absolutely *nothing* like my sister!' she snapped. 'And furthermore, far from taking the rest of the day, my shopping should take me no more than five minutes because I only need some comfortable underwear that I can pull on over my cast.'

The words almost seemed to echo around the whole reception area—probably right around the whole of the hospital if the gossip grapevine was operating in its usual mysterious way.

'Oh, good grief!' she moaned, and covered her face when she saw just how many inquisitive faces were turned in their direction, *and* how many of them were sporting broad grins. 'Just get me out of here,' she ordered through clenched teeth, hoping that her long curtain of her hair was hiding the furious heat of her blush.

Dan didn't make the situation any better when he leaned forward and murmured in her ear, '*Comfortable* underwear, Sara? Is that what they call black lace thongs these days?'

'Shut up!' she hissed. 'Just shut up and get me to the car.'

'Ah…in just a second,' he promised as he veered the chair towards the policeman who had just entered the reception area. Then he abandoned her in the middle of the floor to hail the man and the two of them stood talking earnestly for several minutes.

Sara was puzzled when Dan reached into his pocket to pull out a disposable glove, especially when the two of them peered at something inside the glove.

They both had serious expressions on their faces but she was far too far away to hear a single word either of them said, especially with the constant hubbub of passing humanity around her.

'Right! To the car!' Dan announced as he came back to her with the air of a man pleased with a mission accomplished. 'Which would you rather do first—groceries or underwear?' he demanded cheerfully, and the chance to ask what that little episode had been about was lost in the return of her embarrassment.

The grocery shopping was done and they were standing in front of an embarrassing display of female underwear in her favourite high-street shop when Dan's mobile burst into the opening bars of the 1812 Overture.

Grateful for the fact that he wouldn't be looking over her shoulder for a moment, Sara grabbed a packet containing some very definitely non-sexy underwear in a size several larger than her usual one, in the hope that the leg opening would be loose enough to accommodate her cast. But she couldn't resist grabbing another containing a rainbow mix of coloured thongs, telling herself that at least she knew that they were relatively easy to get on. The fact that they were far sexier than the 'old lady' pants in her other hand had absolutely nothing to do with her choice.

There was a frown on his face when he turned back to her.

'That was the hospital,' he began, and her heart leapt into her throat.

'Zara?' she said, immediately feeling guilty that she and Dan were out shopping for her underwear when he should have been waiting for news of his wife. 'Is she worse?'

'No, Sara, no,' he soothed, looking contrite that he hadn't realised that she'd immediately panic. 'It was nothing to do with your sister. It was A and E, asking if I could possibly go in. With the two of us out and two others called in sick—that flu bug that's going around has finally felled Derek when he was only boasting the other day that he never catches anything—they're desperate for another doctor.'

'Desperate? As in…they're building up a logjam of patients and the waiting time's becoming unacceptable?' she asked as she handed over the two packages and had to submit to the indignity of having Dan pay for her under-wear, too. He'd already paid for her groceries when she'd belatedly realised that sneaking out of the ward meant that she hadn't collected the purse that had been given into Sister's safekeeping.

'That, and the fact that the traffic lights are on the blink at one of the crossroads and there's been a whole series of prangs as people take the law into their own hands. Pedestrians, cyclists and car-drivers, some more serious than others.'

'Ouch!' She pursed her lips as frustration swept through her. She was certain she would be able to work if she'd only injured her leg. Having a doctor working away in minors, doing the bread-and-butter jobs of stitching and re-trieving foreign bodies from various apertures, wouldn't be too taxing as she would probably be able to sit down for much of it, and it would definitely take some of the load off the rest of them. But with her shoulder strapped to prevent her using anywhere near the full range of motion and with the rest of her body complaining whenever she moved a bruised portion, she'd be more of a liability than a help.

'Stop brooding,' he chided as he pushed her back towards his car at a far faster rate than the companionable stroll with which they'd started their outing. 'You're in no fit state to work, so don't even think about it.'

'Hmm! I see you've added mind-reading to your diagnostic skills,' she sniped, uncomfortable that he'd been able to tell what she was thinking. She hadn't realised that she was so transparent and now worried just how many of her other thoughts he'd been privy to. 'Was that the Masters course in Mind-reading or just the Diploma?'

He laughed. 'Nothing so low-brow. I found I was so good at it that I went all the way to PhD.'

He quickly had her settled in the blissful comfort of the passenger seat and they were on their way—at least, they should have been on their way. The journey from the car park to her flat was only a matter of two streets but they weren't even able to join the stream of traffic on the first one because nothing was moving.

'This isn't going to work,' he said aloud as, with a careful look around, he put the car into a swift U-turn and went back the way they'd come. 'I'm sorry, Sara, but if I'm going to arrive at the hospital in time to do any good I'm going to have to drop you off at our place instead.'

She wanted to object because she really didn't want to spend any time at all in the place that her sister shared with the man *she* loved, but logic told her that she didn't have any other option. Even if she were to ring for a taxi, that would still leave her with the insurmountable obstacle of getting herself and her groceries up four flights of stairs with only one leg and one arm in any sort of usable state.

'I'll come back as soon as the panic's over and deliver you and your goods and chattels as promised,' he assured her as he deposited her shopping bags on the pristine work surface in his kitchen. The journey up in the lift had been a breeze in comparison to the struggle it would have been to install her in her own flat.

'Sling your perishables in the fridge so they don't succumb to the central heating,' he ordered briskly, his mind obviously already racing ahead to what he was going to find when he reached A and E.

'And make yourself at home,' he added, almost as an afterthought, with one hand already reaching out to the front door. 'It shouldn't take more than a couple of hours to sort through the worst of it.' And he was gone.

'Make myself at home?' Sara said into the sudden emptiness of Dan's home and knew it would be impossible.

And it wasn't just because this was the home he shared with Zara. It would have been just as bad *whoever* he was sharing it with because she'd hoped that any home he lived in would have been *her* home, too.

It was because she'd started to dream at one time that it would be her future for the two of them to choose the home they were to share together, to decorate it and choose the furniture and accessories together and… She looked around her, able to see into each of the rooms from her position in this compact central hallway. To the kitchen with the clean-lined Scandinavian cupboards trying desperately to soften the over-abundance of cold stainless-steel appliances and work surfaces; to the bathroom with what should have been a stylish art-deco-inspired combination of black and white that had been made overpowering with the excess of black on floors, walls and paintwork; to the bedroom with the oversized four-poster bed that was totally out of place in such a modern setting and whose voluminous floral drapery looked more like something a pre-schooler would prescribe for a fairy-tale princess.

In fact, the only room in which it looked as if Dan had finally put his foot down was the living room. That alone was an oasis of calm understatement with restful neutral colours a backdrop for the stunning views out of the wide uncluttered windows.

The furniture, when she finally made her way to it, was deliciously comfortable, particularly the reclining chair that was in reach of everything she could need, from the remote control for the television and another one for the stereo system to a wall of bookshelves that had everything from Agatha Christie to massive tomes on emergency radiographic diagnosis.

She quickly realised that this was the one place in the whole flat where she might be able to feel at home, but it wasn't until she turned her head and caught a hint of the shampoo that Dan used that she understood why.

'This is *Dan's* chair,' she said, and cringed as she heard

the words coming back to her sounding like the sort of reverential tones of a besotted fan of her favourite idol.

Disgusted with herself for mooning about like this, she forced herself up onto her feet—well, onto her one weight-bearing foot and her single crutch—and struggled her way into the kitchen.

'It's not your home, so don't go criticising it,' she told herself sternly as she sorted through her shopping to put the perishables away in the enormous American-style fridge. 'And don't go getting comfortable in it either…not even in Dan's chair. You're only going to be here for a short time—just until the panic's over in A and E—and then you'll be back in your own place.'

Her own place with the little poky rooms that were too small to have anything bigger than doll's-house furniture and the old draughty windows and iffy heating.

'But it's mine, everything in it is something I've chosen and it suits me,' she said aloud, even as she silently wondered who she was trying to convince.

It was two hours later that Dan phoned her.

Of course, she didn't know that it was Dan until the answering-machine kicked in and she heard his voice projected into the room.

'Sara, pick up the phone…it's Dan,' he announced—as if the sound of his voice wasn't imprinted on every cell in her body.

'Dan?' she said, furious that she sounded so breathless when she'd only had to reach out her hand to pick up the phone. Pathetic!

'Sara, I'm sorry to do this to you, but they really need

me to stay on till the end of the shift. Arne's had to go home with this wretched flu, too. He was nearly out on his feet and we could just about fry eggs on his head.'

Sara chuckled at the mental image painted of her colleague. Arne Kørsvold was an enormous gentle Swedish doctor who disguised the fact that he was rapidly losing his natural platinum-blond hair by shaving his whole head.

'Anyway, if you're OK with it, I'll stay on and work the rest of the shift, then call in for an update on Zara. I promise I'll take you back as soon as I can get away.'

What could she say? A and E's needs were far more urgent than her own so she resigned herself to several more hours of sitting on the chair that faced Dan's recliner and tried not to imagine what it would be like to spend her evenings sharing this lovely room with him.

Sara had no idea when the television programme finally lost her attention and she drifted off to sleep but she was completely out for the count by the time Dan let himself in.

She didn't know how long he stood in the doorway to the living room, watching her sleep; didn't see the way he frowned when he saw the shadows around her eyes that spoke of her exhaustion or the way his eyes softened as they traced the swelling curve of her belly.

The first thing she knew was a hazy realisation that Dan was there and that she was in his arms as he lifted her off the settee. Then he was laying her gently down again and she couldn't help giving a little whimper of disappointment when he took his arms away again.

'Shh,' he whispered softly as he stroked a soothing hand

over her head, and as she drifted off to sleep again, comforted by the fact that he was close to her, she imagined that she felt the butterfly brush of his lips on her forehead.

CHAPTER SEVEN

'I'M GOING to go mad if I have to stay here any longer,' Sara told the four walls of her borrowed bedroom.

She was spending yet another day in Dan's spare room…Dan and *Zara's* spare room, she corrected herself, although it was getting harder and harder to make herself remember that fact.

Because of the continuing staff shortages, Dan had returned to work full time. He was, however, being allowed time to go up at intervals to visit Zara.

Each evening, when he returned to the flat, Dan gave Sara a full report on the latest test results, but Zara's body seemed to be struggling to rid itself of the toxic metabolite of the paracetamol she'd taken.

'No doubt it's because her liver had reduced glutathione stores as the result of her years of drastic dieting,' he said soberly.

'But the liver can regenerate itself,' Sara reminded him. 'Surely the paracetamol hasn't done that much damage that it can't be repaired.' She shook her head and pushed her plate away, unable to eat any more even though it was her favourite tagliatelli carbonara.

'Oh, Dan, I'm in such a muddle. Half of me desperately wants her problem to be the result of taking the drugs earlier in the afternoon, which would mean Zara couldn't possibly be the person driving the car that hit me. But the other half wants just as desperately for it to have been her in the car, because that means the drugs hadn't been in her system so long and she's more likely to recover.'

There was a strange shadow in Dan's eyes but he didn't comment on her dilemma, choosing instead to tell her about one of the department regulars who'd turned up again after an absence of several months showing all the usual signs that she'd fallen off the wagon again.

'Somebody hadn't remembered to flag her name, so the new junior registrar went sailing into the cubicle to find dear old Alice lying there with all her worldly goods piled around her on the bed and snoring her head off.'

'Oh, dear! He didn't touch any of her bags, did he?' Sara chuckled. 'And she woke up and yelled the place down?'

'She started shouting "Fire!" then realised it was a male doctor in the cubicle with her and changed it to "Rape!" with all-too-predictable results.'

'Poor chap!' Sara laughed even louder, remembering her own noisy introduction to Alice and her obsession with her bags. 'I bet he got an even bigger shock when it took less than thirty seconds for the cubicle to fill with half the hospital's security personnel.'

'He was shaking and as white as a sheet and looked as

if he couldn't decide whether he was going into cardiac arrest or giving up his medical career on the spot.'

'The trouble is, rules and regulations are so tight these days about what you can write on a patient's notes, it's difficult to leave a message on them saying, "Treat with extreme caution. Liable to explode," or the hospital legal department would go into orbit. I take it you managed to smooth things over?'

'Well, eventually,' he said, and she was intrigued to see a wash of colour travel over his cheekbones.

'What did she do *this* time?'

'Oh, she was just her usual outrageous self,' he said with a self-conscious shrug.

'You may as well tell me,' she pointed out, her imagination in full flight. 'It will only take a single phone call to find someone else willing to spill the beans, and who knows how much bigger the story has grown in the meantime?'

'Don't remind me,' he groaned. 'I was counting on the fact that you're not fit to work at the moment so that particular bit of gossip would pass you by.'

'So?' she prompted, ignoring the comment about her fitness to work in pursuit of the punchline of the story. Her upcoming return to work was a topic she didn't intend to discuss with him. 'Tell me, tell me. What did she do?'

'It wasn't so much what she did as what she said,' he muttered, looking seriously uncomfortable. 'In front of half the damn department and heaven knows how many patients and relatives she told me she loved my green eyes and invited me into the cubicle to give her a damn good... um...bit of passion.'

Sara burst out laughing. 'Knowing Alice, I bet she didn't use such a genteel phrase.'

Those gorgeous green eyes were sparkling now. 'You'd win that bet,' he conceded. 'The trouble is, I'm never going to hear the end of it.'

'Oh, you will,' she reassured him. 'As soon as the next juicy bit of gossip comes up, that little proposition will all be forgotten…by the rest of your colleagues, at least.'

And it was relaxed conversations like that one last night that were making life so difficult for her. It was becoming harder and harder to stop herself from doing or saying something that would reveal her secret…the fact that she was falling deeper and deeper in love with him the longer she shared his flat.

'Well, enough is enough,' she said firmly as she pushed herself up onto her one good foot and reached for a single crutch.

She'd been practising getting around over the last couple of days. There had been so many empty hours while she'd waited for Dan to return that she'd worked out for herself how she could manoeuvre without needing a pair of them because her shoulder was still too sore to take the weight, even with elbow crutches.

It wasn't an elegant way of getting around, more of a stumbling lop-sided lurch, in fact, and definitely required the presence of a nearby wall as a last resort to stop herself losing her balance completely. The one good thing about it was that she'd almost perfected a way of getting around unaided, and that meant she could leave the danger zone of Dan's spacious flat and take herself back to her own far humbler one.

'It will probably take me a couple of hours to go up all four flights of stairs,' she muttered, feeling exhausted just thinking about it. She stuffed her belongings into a carrier bag, resolutely ignoring the fact that the packet of granny knickers hadn't even been opened, tied the handles to her crutch, then phoned for a taxi. By the time it arrived, she was waiting in the entrance with just a short hop across the pavement left to do.

'Hang on a minute, love,' called the cabbie and heaved his considerable bulk out of the driving seat to give her a steadying hand to climb inside. 'You're in a right mess, aren't you?' he commented soothingly, his eyes meeting hers in the rear-view mirror once he was back in his seat. 'Finally decided to get away from him before he does any worse? You've made the right decision, love. I've got no time for men who think it's OK to knock women about. Need someone to give them a bit of their own medicine.'

'Oh, good grief, no!' Sara laughed. 'It was a car that did this. I nearly got run over the other night.'

'That's right, dear. Get a good story ready to tell people so they won't twig what's really going on. Most of them will probably believe you, but me?' he shook his head and drew in a breath through his teeth. 'I've seen too much of the rough end of life and I can tell the difference, but don't you worry—even if he gets the police out looking for you, I'll never tell where I take you.'

He straightened up in his seat and put the engine into gear. 'Right, now, where do you want to go? To one of the refuges?'

'That's very kind of you, and I'm so glad that there are

people like you who will help battered women, but I've been staying with my sister and brother-in-law—' she didn't see the harm in stretching the truth a little, just to put the man's mind at ease '—ever since I came out of hospital. If you could drop me off at my flat, that will be great.' She gave him the address and was certain that he was quite disappointed he wasn't going to be a brave knight coming to the aid of a maiden in distress.

Except when he drew up outside the multi-storey Victorian building, all his protective instincts seemed to re-surrect themselves.

'I hope you're on the ground floor, love,' he said as he lent her a hand again.

'I wish!' she joked, and looked right up towards the very top windows. 'That's me, all the way up there.' And then, no matter how much she tried to reassure him that she could manage, he insisted on keeping her company all the way up all four flights, carrying her bag of belongings in case they unbalanced her and steadying her when her poor overworked leg began to tremble with overuse.

Sara was close to collapse when she finally got the key in the lock and swung the door wide, screwing her nose up at the shut-in smell that seemed to gather even in the space of a couple of days. Then she had a battle to make the man accept the proper fare for bringing her home, and when she tried to add a tip to thank him for spending the time to help her all the way up the stairs he drew himself up with an air of injured dignity.

'I didn't do that for money, love. I did that because you were someone who needed a helping hand. Now, you take this.' He handed her a business card. 'If you need to go anywhere, you ring that number and ask them to send George.'

'Oh, that's just perfect,' she said with a little quiver. 'Just like St George killing the dragon, you came to the aid of a lady in distress.'

He snorted and went a bit pink. 'I don't reckon my missus thinks I'm any sort of saint, but I know what you mean. Now, you take care of yourself.'

He was just about to shut her front door behind him when she remembered what she'd planned to do that evening.

'Oh, George,' she called. 'You don't go off work before seven, do you? Only I'll be needing a taxi to get to the hospital for visiting hours.'

'I told you, love, you need me, I'll be here,' he said with a broad grin. 'Will a quarter to seven be early enough for you?'

'Perfect. I'll see you then.'

It was just after seven o'clock when the lift chimed to announce its arrival on Zara's floor.

This time, thank goodness, she wasn't trying to get about with her single crutch because as soon as she'd arrived in A and E, courtesy of George, she'd been whisked off by a bevy of colleagues and given the loan of a wheel-chair.

'At least my immediate welcome in the department seemed to put his mind at rest,' she mused as she wheeled her awkward one-handed way towards Zara's room, then an alternative suddenly struck her. 'Or perhaps he took it as proof that they know me well because I'm always in here for treatment.'

She was still smiling at that thought when she tapped on Zara's door and began to push it open.

'There she is!' Zara announced, her face twisting into an unattractive scowl. 'And look at that smirk on her face. She just couldn't wait to get her foot in the door, could she? All this time she's resented the fact that Danny chose me and she waited until I'm too ill to do anything about it to move in with him and—'

'Zara!' Dan's voice cracked over her increasingly hysterical rant like a whip. 'That's enough! You're talking nonsense.'

'It's *not* nonsense!' she argued fiercely. 'How could you have let her move into my home after all the trouble she's caused? Didn't you read my note? It's all her fault. Everything is Sara's fault.'

'Ah, yes. The note,' Dan said, and Sara seemed to be the only one who noticed a strange edge to his voice.

'You mentioned it before,' he continued. 'Remind me, when did you write it and where did you put it?'

'I wrote it the afternoon I took the tablets, of course, and I put it on my bedside cabinet, where you'd see it when you came in… And I'm so sorry for doing that to you, but if you'd read the letter you would know how desperate I was…that I just couldn't cope any more with Sara wanting to keep the baby and…'

'Shh, sweetheart,' Audrey soothed, reaching for one of her daughter's flailing arms. 'It can't be good for you to get in such a state. Perhaps it would be better…' She turned with a scowl on her face to send a meaningful glance between Sara and the door.

Sara hadn't known whether to leave so that her sister didn't upset herself any more, but Dan had already drawn the wheelchair fully into the room and shut the door for some semblance of privacy so she was completely trapped when he drew a slightly crumpled piece of paper out of his jacket pocket.

'I take it that this is the letter you're talking about?' he said, and Sara felt sick when she saw the malice in Zara's glance across at her.

'You found it!' she exclaimed. 'So now you know exactly—'

'"My darling Danny,"' he read flatly, interrupting her without an apparent qualm. '"I can't bear it any more. You know how hard we tried to have a baby and what a wrench it was for me to have to have my sister being a surrogate for us. I know that she's always wanted you for herself and I'm just so afraid that she's going to steal our precious baby and there's nothing I can do about it. I just can't bear it any more, Your loving Zara."'

Sara felt the blood drain from her face then flood back in a scalding blush when he read the note for all to hear. Didn't he realise how humiliating it was for her to have her unrequited love spoken about like that? Didn't he realise that, even if she hadn't loved him, she would still have loved the children she was carrying because they were an intrinsic part of her?

And the letter was a complete lie because even though

she desperately wished that she was carrying Dan's babies for the two of them, there was no way that she would have broken her promise to him to give him the family he wanted. He was going to be a wonderful father and Audrey would spoil her grandchildren at every opportunity and provide the feminine touch that Zara would probably be too busy for.

She really didn't need all this extra emotional stress, to say nothing of the embarrassment of having her private feelings paraded for all, not when all the pregnancy books advised calm and serenity for the sake of the baby. After all, she was still recovering from her injuries and had, admittedly voluntarily, just gone through the exertions of moving out of his flat and back into her own.

And going from mind-blowing topics to the merely petty, there was the fact that she wasn't certain her smart-enough-for-work trousers would ever recover from her decision to come all the way down four flights of stairs on her bottom.

'Look at her face!' Zara demanded shrilly, pointing straight at Sara. 'At least she has the honesty to look guilty.'

With everyone's eyes directed at her, Sara had felt the heat of embarrassment flooding into her face. She was unused to being the centre of attention at any time, least of all when she was in the same room as her twin.

She hated what Zara was doing to her but she had known for far too many years that there was no point protesting her innocence. Zara's position as everybody's favourite was unassailable. The thing that hurt worst was the fact that Dan was privy to all Zara's spiteful lies. At least in the past it had been kept within the family.

'You ask her, Danny,' her sister demanded, with every evidence of being on the verge of tears. 'You ask her if she hasn't been thinking about keeping the kid for herself.'

Of course she'd been thinking about it, Sara admitted silently as she reached for the rim of the wheel to turn herself around. She was carrying the babies of the man she loved so it was obvious that she would long for the chance to bring them up with him, and there was no way she was staying in this room to allow her sister to make something shameful about a normal human response.

'Sara, stay,' Dan said in a low voice, his lean fingers resting on her wrist to dissuade her from opening the door. 'Please?'

There was something in those amazing green eyes that told her she could trust him, that he wasn't asking her to stay to have more humiliation heaped on her head. And even though she had no idea where this dreadful conversation was going, she knew that she *could* trust him, implicitly.

She missed the warmth of his touch when he took his hand away, but then he reached into his pocket again and pulled out a plastic bag.

Walking over to the side of Zara's bed, he tipped out a piece of plastic onto her lap.

'Do you know what that is?' he asked in a quiet conversational tone.

Sara almost gave herself away with a gasp of surprise. The last time she'd seen a piece of plastic like that had been in the garage when they'd been asking about the damage to Zara's car.

'Of course I don't know what it is,' she said with a dismissive shrug. 'It's just a bit of scrap plastic.'

'Actually, it's a bit more than that,' he said with a noticeably sharper edge to his voice as he retrieved it and put it back in the bag, without touching it with his fingers. 'It's part of the light from your BMW—the one you broke when you ran your sister down and left her lying in a side street, not caring whether she was alive or dead.'

'That's a lie!' Audrey gasped, clearly shocked out of her unaccustomed bystander's role. 'That's a wicked, wicked lie. Danny, why are you doing this to Zara? She's your wife and she's ill. You should be supporting her, not spouting this ridiculous nonsense that Sara's been feeding you.'

'Audrey—' Dan said forcefully, trying to break into her tirade.

'*I* know why you're doing it,' she continued, condemnation in every stiff inch of her. 'The two of you have got your heads together and made the whole thing up to cover up the fact that you've got a thing going between you. *You're* an adulterer and *she's* no better than a…'

'Mrs Walker,' Dan barked, apparently reverting to formality as nothing else seemed to be getting through. 'If you dare say one derogatory word against Sara, I shall assume you're hysterical and slap you.'

'What?' Her eyes and mouth were wide with shock but she must have seen something in his face that made her believe he would do what he'd threatened because she subsided ungracefully into the chair on the other side of Zara's bed.

'As I was saying,' Dan continued, apparently calm

again, but from her position Sara could tell from the way his veins were distended that his anger must have sent his blood pressure up. She would have to suggest that he have it checked, but for now she was still amazed that he would have sided with her against the rest of her family. No one had ever done that before. 'Unfortunately, it's the truth. I took that piece of plastic from the BMW and gave it to the police because I saw that there were fibres caught in it. Their forensic labs have confirmed that they were strands of top-quality vicuna and that they were an absolute match for the fibres in Sara's coat—the one you gave to her and that she was wearing when you knocked her down.'

There were several seconds of horrified silence at the end of his recitation and Sara almost felt sorry for her parents when she saw the way they were staring at their beloved daughter…almost as if they didn't recognise her any more…as if she'd suddenly grown a second head, or something.

'All right!' Zara snapped. 'So it all went a lot further than I expected, but I *still* didn't get what I wanted, and that was to get rid of the kid.'

It was all too much for her mother to cope with and she burst into noisy tears, unwilling even to be consoled by her husband.

'Why did you have to go poking around? Why couldn't you just leave it alone? After all, bones heal and she's still carrying your precious baby… Oh, I'm sorry, it's *babies*, isn't it? There's two of the ghastly ankle-biters in there, gradually bloating her body until she's going to look like a hippo.'

'Why, Zara?' Frank demanded, obviously completely confused. 'What went wrong? You seemed so happy until you couldn't have children, but then Sara offered—'

'Sara didn't offer,' she interrupted rudely. 'Mum virtually blackmailed her into it because I said I couldn't get pregnant.'

'Well, there was very little likelihood that you'd be able to while you were taking the Pill,' Dan supplied dryly.

Zara blinked, as though surprised that he knew that she'd been lying to him, but he was already moving on. 'What I don't understand is why you went through the whole pantomime in the first place.'

'Typical man!' she scoffed, tossing her head in a well-practised move that sent her hair tumbling over one shoulder. 'It's obvious. It was all a game, just a bit of fun seeing how easy it was to take you away from Sara, especially when I could tell that she had already fallen head over heels for you. *I* didn't love you—never really wanted you, if you want the truth—I certainly never had any real intention of going as far as marriage.'

Her mother gave a little whimper of distress but that only seemed to enrage Zara further and she turned her fury on her parents. 'If you two hadn't been so bloody eager to put on the big flashy fairy-tale wedding, none of this would have happened. I'm a successful model and there's a possibility that I might get a part in a Hollywood film. The last thing I want is to be stuck at home, nothing more than a housewife with two brats.'

'So, let me get this right,' Dan said icily. 'Everything you've done—married me, almost killed your sister because she's pregnant with the child you said you wanted, *and* taken an overdose of drugs—which, by the way, you carefully timed so that, if I hadn't been taking care of Sara, I would have found you before they'd had time to get into your system—*all* of that is somebody else's fault and beautiful Princess Zara is the innocent victim? I think not.'

He took a step closer so that he positively loomed over her and his words had the precision of surgical steel.

'The police are waiting for me to report back before they charge you with the attempted murder of your sister and her unborn children. If you're found guilty…which I hardly think is in doubt…you can expect to be sentenced to a minimum of twelve years in prison, but it's more likely to be eighteen years.'

'Eighteen years!' Audrey wailed, but Zara didn't say a word, at last speechless now that she'd been confronted with the probable consequences of her actions. 'She didn't mean to do it.' Audrey turned pleading eyes on Sara, as ever protective of her favourite daughter. 'You couldn't possibly send your own twin to prison.'

'I really didn't mean to do it,' Zara said suddenly, the subdued tone of her voice and the ghastly pallor of her skin telling Sara that perhaps she really was telling the truth this time. 'I've had a couple of photo shoots on the West Coast—of America,' she added, in case they weren't following. 'And when the possibility of this acting job came up and then became a probability, I suddenly felt trapped because the baby…*babies*,' she corrected herself, 'weren't due until a couple of weeks after filming's due to begin.'

'That still doesn't explain why you would decide to

run your sister over. Why on earth would you want to kill her?'

'Why? Because she's too bloody perfect,' she snarled. 'She got all the brains in the family and just sailed through school and medical training, *and* she got the beauty as well.'

'That's why you did this,' Sara murmured as she traced her original scar, the one Zara had given her so many years ago. 'I thought it was because you wanted people to be able to tell us apart. I never dreamed it was because you hated me.'

'No!' It was the first time that her sister hadn't rushed to claim that it had been an accident and the fact that her first instinct had been to deny that she hated Sara thawed something deep inside her that had been frozen for a very long time. 'Oh, everything just got so muddled in my head, probably because of the tablets one of my friends gave me.'

'Tablets?' Dan demanded instantly. 'What tablets? Where did you get them from?'

'My friend said she got them from America, on the internet. They call them designer drugs. They're gone now,' she added hastily. 'I flushed them when I got back to the flat after I…after…' She shook her head and started to shed what were probably the first genuine tears in years. 'My friend and I were high on them when she said my only option was to get rid of the baby, then I wouldn't have to be stuck in England, and my head was so messed up that it seemed to make perfect sense. Then, when I was driving towards Sara in that lane and her first thought was to save the baby…I was just so angry that she always…always did the *right* thing that I…that I aimed straight at her and… Oh, God, I'm sorry, Sara,' she gasped. 'And I'm just so glad that I didn't…didn't k-kill you…'

One part of Sara's brain must have been registering the changing figures on the electronic monitors because somehow she wasn't in the least surprised when Dan reached for her sister's wrist to feel for himself just how fast her pulse was beating.

'What's wrong?' Audrey demanded. 'What's the matter with Zara?'

'Probably nothing more than too much stress in the last half-hour,' he said soothingly.

'It's not her liver, is it?' her father suggested fearfully. 'It's not packing up completely, is it?'

'It's unlikely that it will pack up.' This time his tone was reassuring. 'That was one of the reasons why I started investigating Sara's accident, because if it had been Zara responsible for running her over, then it meant the drugs probably hadn't been in her system long enough to do serious permanent damage.'

'So, what's the matter now?' That was her mother again, holding onto Zara's hand as though it was a lifeline. 'Why are the monitors peeping and pinging like that?'

That, in far more clinical terms, was Mr Shah's first question when he appeared in the doorway a few seconds later, obviously alerted by the member of staff at the unit's central monitoring station.

'Her pulse and respiration were probably elevated by a family discussion,' Dan said blandly.

'In that case, I think I will have to ask you to leave,'

the consultant said formally. 'There has been a slight improvement in my patient's condition and I don't want anything to reverse it. Please, if you could return at the next visiting hour?'

Her mother obviously knew from the man's quiet air of command that there was no point trying to persuade him to change his mind and she bade her daughter a tearful good bye before leaving the room with her husband's arm supportively around her shoulders.

She was so wrapped up in her misery that she barely glanced in Sara's direction, so nothing had changed there.

'You, too, please,' Mr Shah said to Dan and Sara. 'I know you are both doctors in this hospital so you will know how important proper rest is for a body when it is recuperating.'

'Of course, sir,' Dan said respectfully, and walked round behind Sara to take charge of the handles of her wheel-chair.

At the last moment before she left the room, Sara glanced back over her shoulder to meet the golden hazel eyes that were the absolute double of her own.

'The authorities will *not* be informed,' she said cryptically, and saw from the dawning relief on her sister's face that she had understood what Sara was trying to tell her.

'I take that you meant you won't be preferring charges against your sister,' Dan said in a low voice meant for her ears alone.

'I'm presuming that you didn't give those authorities enough information to work out what happened with the car?' she countered.

'So you're just going to let her get away with it?' he asked in a voice that was as unreadable as the face in front of her in the lift.

'As there was no permanent damage done…' she agreed, very conscious that they had a captive audience. 'The penalty seems out of proportion.'

'I wouldn't know,' he admitted with a fleeting glimpse of a grin. 'I made that bit up.'

Sara nearly choked trying to subdue her sudden laughter. 'Remind me not to play poker with you.'

'Shame,' he teased as he pushed her across the reception area. 'I was thinking of suggesting a game after we eat tonight. What do you think?'

What she thought was that she'd completely forgotten to tell him that she'd moved out of his flat today.

'Um… Actually, Dan, I've moved back into my own place, so I won't be—'

'What? When?' he demanded, clearly startled, and just for a moment she tried to persuade herself that he looked disappointed, too. 'And how did you get there?'

'St George rescued me from the dragon,' she said, opting for laughter rather than tears as she suddenly realised that she had absolutely no idea where she stood with him any more.

CHAPTER EIGHT

THERE had been no mistaking the expression on Dan's face that time, Sara thought while he drove her towards her flat in complete silence. That had definitely been more than disappointment on his face, it had been hurt.

'Can you manage by yourself from here?' he asked briskly, and she suddenly realised that he had pulled up outside the front of her house.

She sighed heavily, wondering when she was ever going to get anything right.

'Dan, you saw how difficult it was for me to get into the car once I was out of the wheelchair. There are only two ways of getting up the four flights of stairs once I get in there, and that's either on my bottom the whole way or if someone helps me.'

'So why did you move back here, then?' he demanded impatiently. 'My place is eminently more suitable for someone in your position because it's got a lift.'

Unfortunately, it had far more than a lift. It had Dan living there, too, and she just couldn't cope with staying with him any longer.

'And it's Zara's place, too, and with any luck it won't be too long until she's ready to come home to it.'

'And?' Those green eyes were far too astute. Sometimes she was convinced that he could read her mind.

'And there's no way that Zara and I can live in the same flat, not after what's happened,' Sara said bluntly. 'She said she's sorry and she didn't mean to do it, but she said the same thing about this...' She pulled her hair away from her race to reveal the first scar her twin had inflicted on her so long ago. 'And she's said it over and over again until... Well, let's just say I don't really trust her because the only one who matters to Zara is Zara.'

He reached his hand out towards her and gently laid it over hers where she'd unconsciously splayed it protectively over the hard curve of her pregnancy.

'You don't trust her to be too close to the babies?' he asked, but they both knew it wasn't really a question.

He closed his eyes and drew in a deep breath then opened them again and gave a brisk nod as if he'd just come to some momentous decision.

Rather than telling her about it, he released his seat belt and slid out of the car, leaving her feeling strangely dissatisfied.

'Come on, then, let's get you up those stairs,' he said, and hauled her unceremoniously to her feet.

'All I can say is it's a good job you're not coming into work for a few weeks yet, or you'd have to set off the previous day to get there in time for your shift,' he teased when they finally reached the top floor.

That's what you think, she mused as she lay in bed later

that night and contemplated the prospect of weeks of sitting around, twiddling her thumbs.

'It would drive me completely mad, just staring at the walls when I could be making myself useful at work,' she continued aloud.

She tried to remember a precedent for a member of staff coming in to work a shift while they were sporting a cast and couldn't, but… 'There's that doctor who uses a crutch on that American hospital drama!' she remembered. 'She can get up a fair turn of speed on it and still manages to take care of patients.'

She gave a quiet snort of laughter, trying to imagine herself using an actress in a fictional hospital to argue her case for an early return to work.

'Well, that character may be fiction but I'm not. This is reality and the hospital is chronically short of staff. And even if I have to put up with weeks of being stuck in minors until the cast comes off, that's what I'm going to do.'

An hour later she was still lying there wide awake, her brain going round and round the same scene, even now unable to believe that her sister could have wanted to harm the infant she was carrying. It was hard to drift off to sleep when all she could see in her mind's eye was the harsh glare of the headlights bearing down on her.

'Did I do the right thing in promising not to press charges?' she wondered aloud. 'Should I have made some sort of formal complaint so that, if at some time in the future something should happen to the babies, they'll investigate Zara first?'

That hadn't been the right thing to think about as she

was trying to sleep. She felt sick at the very thought of something or somebody hurting them.

But what would she be able to do about it once they were born and she'd handed them over? On that day she would officially become their aunt rather than their mother and would have no legal say in what happened to them.

A feeling close to panic started to fill her and for several mad moments she imagined herself grabbing her passport and slipping out of the country. There was a whole wide world out there and in almost every country there were people crying out for doctors to treat their sick and injured. Surely she would be able to find a way to support herself and the two precious lives inside her?

Then she imagined how Dan would feel, knowing that somewhere in the world there were two children bearing his genes and he'd never seen them…beyond a fuzzy ultrasound picture.

Just the idea of the man she loved gazing longingly at that image year after year was enough to bring the hot press of tears to her eyes and she knew she couldn't do it to him.

So, what was she going to do?

A strange sensation deep inside drew her attention away from that insoluble conundrum and she pressed her hand over the firm curve, remembering with a smile the way Dan had placed his hand over hers.

Oh, yes, he was going to be such a good father to this little pair. Kind and gentle and endlessly patient and…

What was that?

She froze into complete stillness and concentrated, aware that all the textbooks said it was far too soon but…

'There it is again!' she exclaimed aloud when she felt the faint fluttering, hoping it was something more than gas travelling through her gut.

When she felt it for a third time she was certain and wanted nothing more than to whoop with delight, no matter that it was pitch dark outside and everyone else in the flats was probably fast asleep.

But she couldn't just lie here in the dark and savour it all alone. She had to share the news with someone else or it wouldn't feel as if it was real. She had to speak to…

'Dan? Did I wake you?' she asked apologetically when he answered the phone.

'No. I'm in bed but I haven't gone to sleep yet. What's the problem? Is something wrong?'

'No. Nothing's wrong,' she reassured him quickly. 'It's just that I was lying there and…and…' Suddenly, it felt so wrong to be telling him such momentous news when he was on the other end of the telephone. These were *his* babies, too, and he should have been here with her to feel…

'There *is* something wrong,' he said decisively. 'I can hear you crying.'

There was the sound of a crash on the other end of the line and some muttered words that were probably unprintable, then he was back with her again.

'I'm coming over,' he announced in a don't-argue-with-me voice. 'I'll need you to drop a set of keys down to me out of a window, because you're *not* to come all the way down those stairs again.'

'Drive safely,' she said, worried about his state of mind, but he'd already broken the connection.

Suddenly, she remembered that he didn't live more than a few streets away and in that powerful car of his it would only take minutes to get there.

'Keys. Keys,' she muttered as she heaved herself out of bed, briefly registering that round about the time that she finally had her bulky cast removed it would also be the time when her pregnancy made moving about more difficult.

'So, this is what my life is going to be like for the next few months,' she grumbled, then subdued a shriek of horror when she caught sight of herself in the mirror on the back of the bathroom door.

'Talk about the wreck of the *Hesperus*,' she moaned as she dragged a brush through the tangles put there by her restlessness. At least she wasn't having to do it with her injured arm. If she'd dislocated her right shoulder she would have been strapped up and completely out of action for several weeks yet.

And as for what she was wearing…this old T-shirt hadn't just seen better days, it had seen better years, and was so worn out that it really *was* translucent in places.

Before she could strip it off, she heard the deep purr of one of the more expensive makes of car outside the front of the house and her heart did a crazy little tap-dance at the knowledge that Dan had arrived.

'The keys! What did I do with…? Ah!' She pounced on them and hobbled over to the window, steadying herself against the furniture. 'Catch!' she called in a stage whisper as she lobbed them in a gentle arc towards him, then fastened the window as fast as she could and went back to changing her clothing.

He must have taken all four flights two at a time because he was already at her front door and fitting the key to the lock before she'd pulled a fresh, slightly less disreputable T-shirt on while balancing on one leg.

'Very fetching!' he teased, and she knew he'd caught sight of one of the packet of thongs she'd bought with him the morning after her accident.

'A gentleman wouldn't have looked, and if he accidentally caught sight of something he shouldn't, he certainly wouldn't have mentioned it,' she said sternly.

'Whatever made you think that I was a gentleman?' he said with one of those cheeky grins that never failed to turn her inside out, right from the first time she'd met him.

Oh, how hard it had been, day after day, forcing herself to keep a strict distance between the two of them and making herself treat him the same as all the other A and E staff.

'So, tell me,' he said as he guided her back to the side of her bed, the rumpled covers mute evidence of her lack of sleep. 'What had you so upset that you were crying?'

'I wasn't upset,' she denied, then had to blink as her eyes began to fill with tears again. 'I was lying in bed and I was resting my hand on the bump—'

'You do that a lot,' he interrupted seriously, once more resting his much longer, much broader hand over hers. 'I've seen you doing it around the department, and when you're sitting having a break you sometimes stroke your hand backwards and forwards and round and round.'

For a moment she lost the power of speech. How had he managed to see so much when she hadn't even noticed him looking?

'I'm sorry. I interrupted you,' he said, sliding his fingers between hers so that their sensitive tips were stroking her, too. And even though there was a layer of soft stretchy fabric between them, his fingers were so warm that she could feel each one of them and the tracks they made on her skin as clearly as if she'd been naked under his touch.

'You were saying that that you were lying with your hand on your bump, and…' His voice was deeper and huskier than before, almost as though he was as affected by the contact between them as she was.

'And I felt them move,' she finished in a whisper, and saw his eyes flare wide in response.

'Are you sure?' Now he was staring down at the curve that was still almost small enough to be spanned by fingers as long as his. 'Surely it's still far too early?'

'That's what I told myself,' she agreed, 'but then it happened again, and a third time and…and I thought you would want to know and…'

He drew in a shuddering breath and she was stunned to see the bright sparkle of tears gathering in his eyes.

'Oh, thank you, Sara,' he said, so softly that she almost had to lip-read the words. 'I can't tell you how much…' He shook his head, obviously moved beyond mere conversation.

'I don't know if they're still moving, but do you want to…?' She slid her hand out from under his and lay back across her bed, leaving his much larger hand spread across her.

It was so silent in the room that she could hear the

numbers click over on the radio alarm beside the bed, so silent that both of them seemed to have forgotten to breathe while they waited for something to happen.

'What did it feel like?' he murmured so softly that it was almost as if he was afraid of frightening them, as if those tiny forms were timid wild animals.

She concentrated for a moment, recalling the movement deep inside her.

'It felt like a cross between a flutter and a squiggle,' she said in the end. 'It wasn't quite as delicate as a butterfly's wing—it was slightly too substantial for that. But it wasn't strong enough to be called a—'

'There!' he exclaimed with a look of awe on his face as he stared down at the place covered by his hand. 'Was that what you felt?'

Sara concentrated for several long seconds and was growing worried that they'd reached the end of the performance when she felt the strongest movement yet.

'Yes!' she agreed joyfully, overwhelmed to be sharing this special moment with him. 'That's exactly what I felt. What do you think?'

'What do I think?' he asked seriously, a hint of a frown drawing those straight dark eyebrows together. 'I think it's boys, because that was definitely the sort of kick that will score goals.'

'Idiot.' She chuckled, delighting in his nonsense, but when she thought he would take his hand away again, he didn't, propping himself on one elbow on the bed beside her so that he could leave it just where it was.

'I was being serious,' he said with a deliberately solemn

expression, then asked, 'What do you think they are? Identical or fraternal? Girls or boys?'

'Or one of each?' she suggested. 'I've never understood some people being adamant about the sex they want their baby to be. I've always believed that it's far more important that it arrives as healthy and as safely as possible.'

Their undemanding conversation had drifted from topic to topic, all loosely connected with pregnancy, labour and the care of newborns, and it was some time before Dan realised that Sara had fallen asleep.

For some while he lay there watching her, glad that the room was still warm enough so that he didn't need to cover her with the bedclothes just yet, not while he was enjoying looking at the changes this pregnancy was causing to her body.

She'd never been as artificially slender as Zara and the soft curves of her burgeoning breasts and the full curve of her swelling belly were so naturally sexy that he'd been hard from the moment he'd walked into her flat and caught a glimpse of that skimpy purple thong.

Oh, what a fool he'd been, to be taken in by Zara's spiteful games. How could he not have seen while he'd been reaching for the paste imitation that he'd already had a diamond within his reach? Sara wasn't just a gifted and hard-working doctor, she was also one of the most genuinely good-hearted people he'd ever met. And, unless some sort of miracle happened, he'd lost her for ever.

So you'd better make the best of this special time, then, said a stern voice inside his head, and he took the words to heart. It might be the only opportunity he ever had to spend the night with her and he wasn't going to waste a moment of it.

In the end, exhaustion got the better of him and the next thing he knew he was waking up with Sara's softly curvy form wrapped firmly in his arms as if he was never going to let her go.

'If only,' he mouthed, full of regret, and whispered a kiss over the crown of her head.

A casual glance towards her bedside cabinet brought her clock into focus and he had to stifle an oath when he saw what time it was.

He hated having to do it, but there was no way he could untangle himself from her without disturbing her sleep. Besides, her cast had been resting over one of his ankles and he didn't know whether he was even going to be able to walk on it. It felt as if the weight might have caused permanent damage to his circulation.

'Sara?' he called gently, hoping he might be able to rouse her just far enough to extricate himself. 'Sweetheart, I've got to go,' he said a little more firmly when she just tightened her hold on him. 'I'm going to be late.'

'Late?' she repeated sleepily, and blinked…then blinked again and stared at him in disbelief. 'Dan? What are you doing here?'

'You invited me. Remember?' He only meant to prompt her memory by stroking his hand over the curve of her belly but when he found himself stroking naked skin he pulled his hand away as swiftly as though he'd been burned.

'Sorry,' he muttered, mortified to feel the heat searing his cheeks as he rolled swiftly out of reach and leapt to his feet.

His shoes were scattered on the floor and his keys were…under the edge of her bed, and his brain was definitely lodged south of his belt while she was curled up in the middle of all those crumpled bedclothes like a sleepy cat.

'I'm sorry but I've got to run or I'll be late for my shift,' he apologized, and let himself swiftly out of her flat, then nearly tripped on his way down the stairs when his hormones reminded him that he'd never seen a sleepy cat with such long slender legs…even though one of them was temporarily encumbered with a clumsy cast…or wearing such an outrageous scrap of underwear.

To lessen the danger that his preoccupation might cause an accident in the early-morning traffic, he forced himself to concentrate on the evidence he'd seen of how well her injuries were healing.

It hadn't been many days since she'd cheated death by inches, but already some of the bruises were starting to fade, working their way through the colour progression that marked the body's reabsorption of the various constituents in the blood.

He'd only caught a glimpse of her shoulder and most of the injured area was still covered by the strapping that was providing stability and support while the internal damage to the structures in and around the rotator cuff were repairing.

The grazes on her arm were much better than when he'd last seen them. Then, she'd been with Rosalie, the technician, having an ultrasound to find out if the pregnancy had been compromised, and she'd looked as if she'd been flayed raw almost from wrist to elbow.

It was all scabbed over now, evidence that none of the damage had gone very deep, and within a few more days she would be left with nothing worse than a deep pink mark on her skin that would probably be completely un-detectable in a matter of weeks.

The rest of her skin had looked silky-smooth and perfect and he'd longed to explore every inch of it in great detail and…

Whoa! That sort of thinking wasn't the right way to keep his car safely on the road. For that, he needed to keep his thoughts on the straight and narrow, too, as befitted a married man.

And if *that* reminder wasn't enough to take the shine off a morning that had started so sweetly, with the mother of his unborn children wrapped so trustingly in his arms, then nothing could.

Sara was cross with herself that she hadn't remembered to set her alarm the previous night. This morning she'd intended getting up bright and early so that she could go in to the hospital to negotiate her partial return to work.

By the time she managed to get herself washed and dressed, she was going to arrive hours after the morning shift had started and was going to give the department manager grounds to doubt that she could cope with coming back to work so soon.

Ah, but she couldn't really find it in her to regret the

reason why her plans had become so disrupted. Feeling the babies move for the first time had been amazing, and it had been made even more magical when she'd been able to share it with Dan.

Waking up this morning to find that he was still with her and knowing that his body had been wrapped protectively around hers while she'd slept was a bonus she'd never expected, and she refused to feel guilty about it. To have heard that her sister had deliberately ensnared Dan purely out of spite and, worse, that she hadn't even loved him when she'd married him—the whole situation seemed an utter travesty of everything that a marriage should be.

'If he had married me...' she whispered wistfully, then gave herself a shake. '"If wishes were horses then beggars would ride," Granny Walker used to say, and I'm just wishing for the moon, too.' And nothing could come of those wishes because even though Zara might not have loved Dan, he must have loved her or he would never have proposed to and married her.

'And none of that will get this beggar a ride, but a phone call will,' she declared when she was finally as ready as she could be. She reached for her purse and the business card of her own personal knight on a white charger...or in a black cab if she really wanted to be pedantic.

'Sara! What on earth are you doing here?' called one colleague when he caught sight of her.

'You're supposed to be on sick leave, darlin', taking it easy while the rest of us soldier on,' added Sean O'Malley in his lilting Irish accent. 'Have you just come to gloat?'

Everywhere she looked there was the usual morning chaos, except it seemed even worse than usual—or was that just wishful thinking? If everyone was being rushed off their feet, would that mean that she would be welcomed with open arms or would she be seen as a liability and shown the door?

There was only one way to find out.

'Actually, Sean, I wanted to have a word with the department manager and—'

'Oh. Admin stuff,' he said dismissively. 'Well, while you're in those recently refurbished offices sitting on one of their ultra-expensive chairs, will you remind someone that they still haven't scraped the loose change together to find us any replacement staff, not even part-timers? And we're already two and a half doctors down. It's getting beyond a joke.'

The staff in the human resources office reminded Sara of an ants' nest that had just been given a vigorous stir with a big stick.

Not that any of them seemed to be moving with the same innate sense of purpose that you'd find among ants. In fact, as far as she could tell, there was interminable duplication of effort going on while they seemed to concentrate most of their efforts on finding reasons why things *couldn't* be done.

'Have you found the new staff for A and E yet?' she asked sweetly, then gave the nest a deliberate extra stir. 'I heard a rumour that if you don't find them soon, it may have to be shut down because it's dangerously under-staffed, and all the patients will be diverted to other hospitals. Doesn't the hospital get a massive fine if that happens?'

By the time she was shown in for her 'chat' with one of the more senior members of the department, the rumour she'd started seemed to have taken on a life of its own.

'Have you any idea exactly how long you're going to need to be on sick leave?' the man asked from behind a desk that was laden with piles of paperwork nearly tall enough to hide behind.

'That's what I wanted to talk about,' she said brightly. 'The only thing wrong with me is this cast on my leg.' After all, the strapping on her shoulder was invisible under her clothing. 'And the wheelchair is only for show and to give my arms a rest from using crutches.'

It was such a long way from the truth that she almost expected to feel the searing heat of a thunderbolt from on high, but what she got instead was an administrator almost grovelling at her feet when she offered to pitch in to do an hour or two in minors to help clear the backlog. There was absolutely no mention of health and safety regulations, at least not in relation to her own fitness to work. The poor man seemed far more worried about the national disgrace that would ensue if his accident department was summarily shut down due to lack of staff.

'What on earth are you doing here?' Dan growled when he finally had a moment free to get into minors.

All morning he'd been regaled with one after another of his colleagues telling him how good it was to see Sara looking so well, and what a good job she was doing, and what a clever idea it was to have her ploughing her way through all that time-consuming debriding of wounds and painstaking stitchery, leaving the more mobile staff to do the rest of the work in the department.

'You should be at home, in bed.' And with that one sentence there was only one thing that she could think about, and she hardly needed to see the way those green eyes of his darkened with awareness to know he was thinking exactly the same thing.

'Ah…it's purely a temporary measure,' she finally managed to say. 'Someone said that they might be forced to close the department if they didn't find a few more staff—health and safety or something—and you know what chaos it causes when you have new staff who haven't a clue where anything is or how our system works…'

Enough! she ordered herself. Don't babble! Just because you can't stop thinking about the way his face lit up when he felt the babies move, and how it felt to have his arms wrapped around you…none of that means that you have to develop verbal diarrhoea.

For just a moment the way he looked at her made her think that he was going to say something of a personal nature but then he shook his head and gave a sigh of resignation.

'Don't get overtired,' he said softly, and she knew his concern was genuine.

'Don't worry, I won't do anything to risk the babies,' she reassured him. 'They've had enough trauma already.'

She was tired by the end of the day but it was a good tiredness that came from doing a worthwhile job to the best of her ability, and just before Dan appeared to offer her a lift back to her flat, she was given official permission to turn up the next day, too, so the precedent was set.

'I'm still not sure that you should be doing it,' Dan grumbled as he steered around the road that circled the whole of the hospital grounds and aimed for the exit. 'You're entitled to paid sick leave.'

'I know I am, but I really don't see the point of being paid to go mad when I can make myself useful. Go on, admit it. It worked well today, having me restricted to the needlework department. I already know the system and the staff, and everybody's been willing to help me, doing things like fetching more supplies.'

He stopped arguing after that, obviously deciding that there was little point as she had permission, and she was grateful that he would never know the real reason why she'd wanted so much to come back to work so ridiculously early.

'Because that's the only place where I can legitimately spend time with Dan,' she whispered as she watched from her window while he climbed back into his car and drove away.

She'd only had to see the longing on his face when he'd looked at her belly just a few minutes ago to know that he was yearning to feel the babies move again…probably as much as she did. But their situation as nothing more than the genetic parents of those babies made the relationship between them too strained for such intimacy to take place again.

As for the possibility that Dan would wrap her in his arms again and cradle her all night long, she may as well cry for the moon.

CHAPTER NINE

THE wretched woman was driving him mad.

It wasn't enough that she was back at work long before she should have been, and that the whole of the rest of the department had welcomed her with open arms, or that she'd made herself virtually indispensable as she'd beavered away in minors.

Her bright idea was almost single-handedly responsible for the 'new initiative' that the bean-counters had come up with. This meant allocating one member of the medical team per shift to do exactly what Sara had been doing—clearing the department of the vast numbers of niggling minor injuries that, in the strict rotation of normal triage, would ordinarily clog the place up and ruin the hospital's performance figures.

If he were honest, he would have to admit that the new organisation had certainly raised morale among the A and E staff, with far fewer instances of abuse hurled at them from members of the public who had been forced to wait unacceptable hours before there had been anyone free to sort them out.

Not that their department manager was going to allow medical protocols to be buried by upper-echelon diktats. He was far too experienced a man not to know that there were times when victims brought in with major injuries took absolute priority over everything else, and he wouldn't have it any other way.

No, the thing that was driving him completely off his head was the careful distance that she'd been keeping between the two of them ever since that morning when he'd woken up in her bed.

It felt as if he'd been trying to speak to her for weeks but there was never a moment when she was alone. Each time he'd had a moment to go looking for her she'd either been with a patient or in the staffroom surrounded by other colleagues willingly fetching and carrying drinks or food for her, or asking about the progress of the pregnancy, or, worst of all, putting their hands on the rapidly swelling bump to feel the increasingly visible movement inside it.

Oh, he'd been so jealous of the fact that she was letting them do that, and his only consolation was that he'd been the very first one to feel that miraculous quickening.

Zara had left the hospital now, with Mr Shah's final words—telling her that she'd been far luckier than she deserved after doing something so stupid—still ringing in her ears. She had also packed up a substantial amount of her belongings and returned to the welcoming arms of her parents to complete her convalescence. As far as the rest of the world was concerned, this was because her mother would be available to keep her company, whereas *he* would be out at work for long stretches at a time.

In reality, there was another very different reason and he needed to talk to Sara about it…

Of course he'd thought about turning up at her flat, but all the while she was wearing that cast he'd felt too guilty about the idea of forcing her to climb all those stairs in both directions to let him in. He smiled wryly when he remembered the way she'd tossed her keys out of the window to him. If he'd known then what he knew now he'd have put them in his pocket and kept them. It would have made what he was trying to do so much easier if he could just let himself into the old Victorian house and corner her in her little eyrie. Then she would *have* to listen while he explained, apologised, did whatever he had to while he tried to persuade her to give him a chance to get close to her, because only if he could get close would he be able to judge if there was a possibility she would give him a second chance.

He was very aware that time wasn't on his side as far as her pregnancy was concerned, and he had so much to achieve before that day arrived… And then the brainwave had struck and here he was, standing on her front doorstep and ringing the bell on the ground-floor flat.

'Sorry to disturb you,' he apologised when the elderly lady cautiously opened the door with the safety chain firmly in position, 'but could you let me in so that it saves Sara coming down all those stairs?'

'Why doesn't she drop her keys down to you…like she did before?' the sprightly woman asked with a definite twinkle in her eye, and when she saw his surprise gave a chuckle. 'I don't seem to need as much sleep these days, lad, and it's amazing what I see happening outside my window.'

'I wanted to surprise her,' Dan admitted, knowing that it was nothing less than the truth. Whether Sara would see it as a good surprise he had yet to find out.

'And you brought her flowers,' his inquisitor said with a nod of approval before she released the catch. 'That's always a nice touch.'

'How did you know they were here?' he asked as he brought the bunch of freesias—Sara's favourite flowers—out from behind his back.

'The rest of me might be sagging and crumbling by the minute, but my nose is still working perfectly,' she said wryly, then a look of sad reminiscence crossed her face. 'Besides, they're my favourites and I haven't been given any since my Dermot died.'

While she stepped back and pulled the door wide, it took no more than a couple of seconds to slide several stems out of the large handful he'd brought.

'My name's Dan, not Dermot, but at least it starts with the right letter,' he said with a smile as he presented her with the sweetly scented blooms, hoping that one day Sara would have such lovely memories.

'Oh!' A shaky hand came up to cover her mouth and she blinked rapidly as though fighting back tears. 'Oh, my dear boy… Thank you so much, but you didn't have to…' She bent her silvery head to sniff the perfume before looking back up at him, her eyes misty with memories. 'You tell your Sara from me that she's a lucky young woman.'

'I couldn't possibly do that,' he said, wondering if there was a chance that Sara would ever agree with her. 'It would sound far too much like boasting. I'll leave it up to you to tell her yourself.'

She was still chuckling at his nonsense when he set off up the stairs, the flowers clutched tightly in her hand.

'Dan!' Sara gasped when she opened the door to his knock and saw him standing there, obviously the last person she'd expected to see. His heart sank when he wondered if he might be the last person she *wanted* to see.

'I come bearing gifts,' he said, suddenly remembering the flowers he was in danger of strangling to death.

'Oh, thank you!' she exclaimed, and threw him a smile that seriously weakened his knees before burying her nose in the delicate blossoms.

This time there was only the slightest hesitation before she stepped back and invited him in. 'Would you like a cup of tea? I'm afraid I've only got herbal now. Caffeine-free.'

He pulled a face and she chuckled, the simple spontaneity of the sound like balm to his soul.

'I don't much like it either, but it's better for my blood pressure and therefore better for the babies, so I have to put up with it.' She turned to lead the way into her compact kitchen and he stopped in the doorway, leaning one shoulder against the frame as he watched her bustling about.

Except she didn't bustle any more, not now that her pregnancy was advancing so rapidly. Well, rapidly wasn't quite the right word, as the duration of most pregnancies was the same, give or take a week or two. What he'd meant was that the size of her bump had increased rapidly over the last few weeks, and he hadn't really noticed the extent because she'd been spending so much of her time sitting down, working in minors.

But today had been the day that her cast had finally come off, and the first day in a long time since he'd seen her in anything other than the soft drape of a shapeless uniform dress or in a tunic top that only fitted where it touched.

Since she'd come home from work, no doubt ferried by her own personal taxi driver, she'd obviously had a bath and had donned a pair of stretchy trousers that did absolutely nothing to disguise her shape and size...and she looked wonderful, so ripe and womanly and sexy and...

'Whoa, boy! Down!' he muttered under his breath, grateful that she'd turned her back on him for a moment to give him a reprieve, and he dragged his eyes away from her lest he leap on her and carry her through to her bedroom.

'What did you say?' she asked as she turned to face him again with a steaming mug in each hand.

'I was just thinking how good you're looking, Sara.' Which was at least the polite way of voicing his thoughts as he stepped aside to allow her out of the kitchen and into her cosy little sitting room.

'It's such a relief to be out of that cast, I can't tell you.' She sank gratefully onto the settee and immediately raised her legs up onto the other seat.

He could applaud her sensible decision to rest her legs but there was no way that Dan was going to sit in the chair on the other side of the fireplace. That was much too far away for his purposes.

'Hang on to this for a second,' he directed as he held out his mug to her, and she automatically took hold of the handle. 'I'll just do this…and then settle myself here,' he said as he lifted her feet and slid onto the settee beside her before lowering her feet onto his lap.

'Dan…'

'That raises your feet slightly and improves postural drainage in your legs,' he pointed out quickly, afraid that she was going to object. 'It also means that I can do this,' he added softly, as he chose one foot and began the sort of massage that he'd learned she loved back in those days before he'd been so stupid.

'Oh! Oh…that feels so good it *must* be illegal,' she groaned as he worked on each individual muscle until he'd worked all the knots out of both feet.

'Oh,' she said again when he finally stopped, and this time it was in tones of disappointment. 'It would almost be worth getting married to have my feet massaged like that every night,' she added, and completely stole his breath away.

She'd been so relaxed by the time he'd finished that he was certain she hadn't really been thinking about what she'd said, but it was too good an opportunity to pass up.

'That could be arranged,' he said seriously, his heart beating so hard that it almost felt as if it would burst out of his chest.

He felt the tension return as if he'd flicked a switch, and he regretted that he'd spoiled her moment of rest.

'Dan, that's not funny,' she said stiffly as she started to struggle up out of the settee and he put his hand on her knee to stop her for a moment.

'I didn't mean it as a joke,' he told her, and leaned down to reach into the pocket of the jacket on the floor beside the settee.

He drew a swift breath and sent up a prayer that he'd be able to find the words he needed before he handed her the envelope he'd brought with him.

'That's a decree nisi,' he told her. 'In exactly six weeks and one day after the date on that, I can apply for a decree absolute and my marriage to your sister will be over.'

Wordlessly she stared at him then dragged her eyes down to the papers she'd withdrawn from the envelope.

'So soon!' she whispered, and he knew she'd seen the date.

'After that awful scene in her room at the hospital, I went back and had a long conversation with Zara,' he explained. 'The upshot was that our divorce petition papers had already been filed with the county court before she was discharged.'

'But…I thought you had to wait years, or for one of you to be caught being unfaithful or…' She shrugged, admitting her ignorance of such matters.

'I knew as little as you before I did some research on the internet and found out that there are five criteria but the two that applied to our situation were what they call "unreasonable behaviour"—and I would definitely class trying to murder my babies as unreasonable behaviour or…'

'You didn't tell anybody what Zara did?' she interrupted urgently. 'I promised that I wasn't going to press charges but if you've put it on the divorce papers…'

'Shh! Of course I didn't,' he soothed, taking her free hand in his and lacing their fingers together. 'But that doesn't mean I didn't use the threat of it to get what I wanted—her admission that she'd been carrying on with a man over in America. The one who's going to finance the film she's been offered a part in,' he added, although that was neither here nor there to *their* situation.

'And she admitted it? To adultery?' Her eyes were scanning the papers still clutched in her hand. 'Oh, Lord, I bet Mother wasn't happy about that.'

'I think "incandescent with rage that she wasn't going to be able to hold her head up in the neighbourhood" comes closer to the mark. I went down to see your parents to tell them in person what was going on as Zara's already gone back to the States.'

'What did she say?' There was an awful fascination in the question.

'She began by trying to forbid the two of us to divorce at all. Far too scandalous.' She'd also tried to persuade him to say that *he'd* been the one to commit adultery, but he'd been completely innocent, at least in fact if not in his head and his heart. Besides, he'd wanted to be able to come to Sara with the fewest blemishes on his character possible. He'd ruined things between them once—he didn't want to risk doing it again.

'When I finally left, after convincing her that the divorce was already a done deal, she was muttering, "Adultery!" and "The shame of it!" under her breath and your father was going to pour her a large medicinal brandy.'

'Oh, Dan, I know I shouldn't laugh, but…' Gradually,

her smile faded, to be replaced by a pensive frown, and he knew her thoughts had moved on. It was only moments later that she proved him right by asking, 'So what are you going to do now?'

It was time for another swift prayer for courage.

'My plans are already made,' he said, hoping he didn't sound as nervous as he felt. 'I've got two babies due in a matter of weeks now, and I need to find someone willing to be a mother to them, someone who will protect them as fiercely as any mother lioness defends her cubs and will love them to distraction—in fact, almost as much as she loves me.'

Sara's heart felt as if it stopped completely when she heard those words, and it seemed to take for ever before it stuttered into a proper rhythm again.

Dan was going to go looking for a good mother for his babies? But they were *her* babies, too, and...

This time she didn't let him stop her from getting up. This wasn't the sort of news she could absorb while she was lolling back on her settee with her feet propped on his muscular thigh.

Too furious to stay still, she started striding backwards and forwards in the limited space in her little living room while thoughts whirled around inside her head.

How *dared* he think of finding someone else to love her babies when *she* loved them enough to die for them—had already proved it by protecting them at the risk of her own health when Zara's car had come towards her.

She knew he didn't love her...he couldn't have if he'd

chosen Zara instead…but he'd only stipulated that the woman he wanted should love him to distraction. And she did!

But how could she tell him how she felt?

At this precise moment he was still married to her sister…or at least still legally connected so that he couldn't marry anyone else…

She stopped in her tracks as a sudden thought struck her.

Perhaps that was the problem! Perhaps the fact that he'd been married to her sister was the reason why he wouldn't even consider marrying her.

She stared out of the window into the late autumn darkness, a tiny corner of her brain telling her that she should have closed the curtains to keep the heat in, and had to concede that there would be many people who would think it creepy that he could switch allegiance from one twin to the other, as though they were as easily inter-changeable as a pair of identical socks.

'When, in fact, we're more like a pair of shoes,' she muttered under her breath as she began pacing again. 'Fit perfectly one way and complete agony if you put them on the wrong foot.'

Oh, but she and Dan would have been such a good fit, she mourned as her steps gradually slowed. If only she had been just a little more like her glamorous, confident sister instead of her quiet bookish self, perhaps Dan wouldn't have been so dazzled when Zara had deliberately set out to attract him. It was all too late now, she admitted with a sigh, and her feet were dragging as she started to make her way to the chair on the other side of the fireplace, too downhearted to sit next to Dan again.

'Uh-uh!' Dan shook his head as he caught her hand and pulled her back to his side. 'That's too far away when there's still so much to talk about.'

It wasn't worth fighting about so she gave in and sat down in her corner again, resigned to listening to his plans for the rest of his life then wishing him good luck.

'Are you ready now?' he asked, and used a gentle finger to turn her head to face him.

'Ready?' she repeated listlessly, her last forlorn hopes already faded to nothing.

'Ready to listen to the biggest most grovelling apology I've ever had to make in my life.'

'Apology?' She frowned. 'What have you got to apologise for? It was your marriage and it's your right to end it. It's got nothing to do with me.'

'Oh, but it does if it should have been *you* I married in the first place,' he said softly, the expression in those beautiful green eyes so sincere that her heart did that crazy stuttering thing again.

'I was a stupid, gullible idiot when Zara came on to me like that,' he said bluntly, shocking her with his brutal honesty. 'My only excuse is that she seemed to have tapped into the way I was wishing *you* felt about me—that you enjoyed my company, that you found me sexy, that you desired me—and the fact that it all came in a package that looked identical to the woman I was already attracted to seemed to completely scramble my brains and short-circuit any attempt at rational thought.'

He hesitated a moment before he picked up her hand, as though he was expecting her to refuse to let him hold it, but she couldn't refuse him, not when he wore an expression of such despair.

'I knew I was doing the wrong thing even as I was standing waiting for the ceremony to start,' he admitted in a defeated voice so at odds with the dynamic man she knew him to be. 'I saw you walk in looking like a princess, wearing that beautiful dress—'

'My grandmother's dress,' she interrupted briefly, so glad that at least he'd noticed her when she'd been looking her best. He'd seen all too much of her at the end of gruelling twelve-hour shifts.

'I knew what I was doing was wrong,' he continued, 'but I was convinced that I'd completely burned my boats with you…and, besides, I couldn't just walk out and leave Zara at the altar, so to speak. If *she* hadn't killed me, your parents would.'

'You're right there,' she agreed. 'My mother had moved heaven and earth to get everything organised so quickly. She was convinced that the reason Zara didn't want to wait was because she was pregnant.'

'Hardly!' he scoffed. 'Even when we were supposed to be "trying for a baby" she was on the Pill. Then, so I wouldn't "waste my energy", she started taking the packs consecutively so it seemed as if she never ovulated and I was never invited to go near her.'

'But…she seemed so heart-broken that she couldn't have a child with you.' This was one facet of Zara's deception that she hadn't known about before. If she had, her parents would have had no chance of browbeating her into acting as surrogate for her sister…except…

Except in her heart it had never been Zara's child she'd agreed to carry but Dan's. It had been *his* sadness she'd wanted to banish with her gift.

'Sara, there isn't really a socially acceptable way of bringing this up but…your sister and I haven't…haven't been intimate for a long time… About a year before you became pregnant or even more than that. It certainly wouldn't be as if I were leaping out of one twin's bed and into the other…'

'Leaping into…' Sara felt her eyes grow wide. She seemed to have missed part of the conversation somewhere along the line because it had almost sounded as if he was saying…as if he was asking… And to her utter shock he slid off the settee onto one knee in front of her, taking both her hands in his as he looked up into her face.

'Sara, I've had to live with the knowledge that I made an utter mess of everything when we were just starting our relationship…when I was falling in love with you. I'll never be able to forgive myself that I've completely wasted the years between when we could have been married, because it was all my own fault. Can you ever forgive me for being so stupid?'

Sara wasn't certain whether she was laughing or crying…probably both, with her emotions in such turmoil.

'Oh, Dan, if it means the difference between not having you in my life and being married to you and making a family with you…of course I can forgive you.'

She quickly realised that pulling her into his arms really wasn't a possibility with such a large bump getting in the way, but she'd loved him for so long that missing out on any more of his kisses wasn't an option.

'I want to hold you,' he murmured when they came up for air a while later, then smiled at her with that same boyish grin that had always set her pulse somersaulting. 'This settee definitely isn't big enough for the four of us.'

He helped her to her feet, the process taking far longer than it should have, in spite of the fact she no longer sported a cast, because neither of them could resist another kiss.

She was a little uncertain that this was the right time for them—after all, it hadn't been very long ago that she'd believed he was going to hunt for someone else to be a mother for his children. But she was wrapped in his arms and she knew that if she led him through to her bedroom she could trust him to be gentle with her because he loved her.

Then, almost at the foot of her bed, he hesitated, as though having serious second thoughts.

'Um, Sara…would you think me very strange if I said I'd rather we didn't make love yet?'

Disappointment had her heart plummeting to her feet. She'd honestly believed that he was just as aroused as she was, but, then, he was a handsome, fit man while she…she was a vast bulky blimp who would soon need a marquee to cover her enormous belly full of babies—definitely not anyone's idea of an ideal sex partner.

'It's not that I don't want to,' he said hurriedly, and squeezed her hand, apparently only realising that there must be something wrong when she hadn't managed to find the words to tell him she didn't mind the delay. 'You only have to look south to know that's not true.'

Her eyes followed his directions and she couldn't help blushing when she saw the evidence that he definitely found her desirable, despite her advanced pregnancy.

So why was she feeling a strange sense of relief that he wanted to take the decision out of her hands, that he wanted to wait for another time to become intimate with her? But she still had questions.

'So why don't you want to go to bed with me?' she asked, needing to hear him spell out his reasons so that she knew what she was going to have to deal with. If his time married to Zara had given him unreasonable expectations about how slim and elegant his wife was going to be…

'It just doesn't feel right to be together yet,' he explained quietly, and gave a self-deprecating shrug. 'I know it's not really logical and there isn't long to wait before I can apply for the decree absolute and I've been wanting to make love to you for so long that even my *hair* aches with it, but…'

Suddenly she realised exactly what he was saying and that she felt the same way, too.

'You mean, you don't want to make love with me until you're completely free of Zara, so that there's a…a separation between those two parts of your life and a real new start,' she suggested, and felt like the brightest pupil in the class when he smiled at her.

'Exactly,' he said with patent relief. '*Do* you mind?'

'How can I when I've just realised that I feel the same way?' she admitted. 'But I would feel more than disappointed if you were also putting an embargo on kisses and cuddles.'

'There's no embargo on those,' he reassured her as he finally guided her across to the bed and laid her down on it, quickly joining her there. 'You can have as many kisses and cuddles as you want.'

In spite of the fact that the hospital was very busy, due to a combination of increasing numbers of patients with seasonal ailments and the resulting staff shortages, the next weeks simply flew by.

Sara had shared a wry joke with Dan that almost as soon as she'd be signed off as fit to return to full-time work she would be eligible to start her maternity leave.

'And not a minute too soon,' Dan growled, when he saw how exhausted she was at the end of a full shift.

In a move that had become a daily ritual since she'd accepted his proposal, he pushed her gently in the direction of the bathroom and flipped the taps on full before he turned to help her out of her clothes. 'You've got to make allowances for the fact that you're carrying twins,' he scolded gently, his eyes already scanning her from head to foot as he searched for any external signs of problems such as pre-eclampsia.

'Nothing untoward?' she prompted when he'd finished checking, but she could already tell from his face that he'd found nothing new to worry about.

'Grab hold of me,' he directed as he offered her a hand to steady her while she climbed into the bath, but she opted to throw her arms around him and share a heartfelt kiss with him first.

Next in the ritual was a leisurely soak while he made

preparations for their evening meal, then an equally leisurely foot massage that, more often than not, resulted in
Sara falling asleep.

It was such a relaxing routine and so devoid of anything
stressful that at times she wondered if she was the only one
who was aware of the gradually building level of tension.
It was worse when they slept together, curled up on the bed
on a day off duty when he managed to persuade her to take
a nap, or latterly even in the bed when cramp and backache
made her nights misery and it was easier to have her own
personal physician close at hand to administer the relevant
massage techniques.

Finally came the day that he arrived with an even bigger
bunch of freesias and a mysterious parcel that he presented
to her with a smile from ear to ear.

CHAPTER TEN

'WHAT'S this?' Sara asked as she took in the fact that the parcel looked rather hastily wrapped…most unlike the meticulous way he'd wrapped the present they'd given to her parents when they'd visited them to announce their intended marriage. 'It's a bit early for a Christmas present. That's nearly a month away.' Although it didn't look very much like it because the paper wasn't in the least bit Christmassy.

'No, it's not for Christmas, but I'm hoping that what's in it will make this the best Christmas ever,' he said, managing to look as excited as a child on Christmas morning. 'And I hope you're not going to take for ever to unwrap it,' he added, clearly impatient for her to see what was inside. 'I can't bear it when people unpick each knot or peel off the tape.'

'Well, then, this is just for you.' She chuckled, infected by his air of excitement, grabbed hold of the wrapping paper in both hands and pulled.

He groaned as the contents of the parcel flew in two directions and he had to retrieve them one by one.

'These first,' he directed. 'I took that packet of ugly harvest festivals back and swapped them for the sexiest ones I could find,' he said with a grin, and waggled his eyebrows when she blinked at just how risqué the delicate lingerie was.

'Harvest festivals?' she repeated with warmth in her cheeks, remembering the vastly oversized knickers she'd bought to fit over her cast and then never worn.

'My grandmother used to call them that,' he said with a laugh. 'She said it was because they were so all-encompassing that they reminded her of that hymn that's always sung at harvest festivals, "All is safely gathered in".'

'Well, if *they* were harvest festivals, what are *these*?' She was almost embarrassed to look at them while he was watching for her reaction. She'd worn that thong out of sheer necessity when she'd first broken her leg, but these definitely had a different purpose if his expression was anything to go by. There was absolutely nothing utilitarian about them.

'Those are definitely Mardi Gras, or even Copacabana,' he suggested, 'and I can't wait to see you modelling them.'

The heat in his eyes was enough to send her temperature and pulse soaring and it wasn't something she was used to from Dan. While they had their agreement to wait until he was finally free of his marriage to Zara, she'd recognised that he'd been walking a torturous tightrope. On the one hand he'd been at great pains to make sure that she knew just how sexy he found her ripening body and how much he desired her while preventing the situation getting out of hand.

This, today, was so out of character that she scarcely…

'And *this* is the other "Happy Christmas" present we're going to share,' he said, more seriously this time, as he handed her the other half of the parcel. It was a bulky envelope and looked quite official…almost like…

'The decree absolute,' she whispered, hardly able to believe what she was seeing when she slid the document out. 'Oh, Dan, you're free.'

'Exactly,' he said with delight, flinging both arms around her. 'And tomorrow morning we're both going to present ourselves with all our relevant documents and information and we're going to book our wedding for twenty-one days later.'

'Twenty-one days?' she repeated, quite shocked that everything suddenly seemed to be moving so fast. 'But that's so close to Christmas and…and… Dan, you've been crossing off the days until you'd be free. Don't you want a little while to get used to the idea that you're not married to Zara before you tie yourself to—?'

'Sara, my love,' he said as he tightened his arms around her and settled her head on his shoulder, where it belonged, 'there's only one reason why I've been counting every last second until I could get this decree in my hand, and that's because I can't wait to be married to you.'

'But…'

He stopped her speaking with a hungry kiss, although that was becoming more difficult without some careful positioning as her bump grew ever larger.

'And don't you start trying to come up with all sorts of ulterior motives, such as "he's only doing it so fast because he wants to be married before the babies arrive to make sure they have his name." I can tell you categorically that, while it *would* cut down on a bit of paperwork, I'd be in just as much of a hurry to marry you if you weren't pregnant at all.'

He gave her another kiss that went a long way to convincing her just how much he desired her, then cupped her face in his hands and drew back, but only far enough for her to focus on green eyes that now blazed with all the love she could ever want. He drew in a noticeably shaky breath then declared fiercely, 'Sara, I just can't wait to be able to tell the world how I feel…that the woman I love to distraction has given me the best Christmas gift in the world and is finally my wife.'

In the end, it hadn't mattered in the least that she'd been feeling as if she was the size of a small house, because Dan had been right—all that mattered *was* that they were married at last, and there wasn't a dry eye.

With so few days to go before Christmas there was evidence everywhere from the beautiful display of scarlet and green poinsettia around the room to the fine streamers of red and green ribbon spiralling down from Sara's bouquet of Christmas roses.

Sara suspected that her mother probably hadn't been able to resist comparing this small gathering in the nearest registry office with Zara's elegant ceremony. No doubt she was regretting that neither she nor Dan had been willing to give her the chance to arrange something similar for them.

This was far more intimate and more meaningful, with just their closest friends in attendance to wish them well; and she didn't have to look much further than Sean O'Malley to guess who had suggested that they should all celebrate the unique time of year by wearing red or green.

But there was no way that even Audrey could miss the loving way Dan had ushered her into the room or the supportive arm that had encircled her throughout the proceedings.

Even the registrar had looked ecstatic when she declared them husband and wife, but that was probably because the poor woman was so relieved that she hadn't had to witness a precipitate delivery all over her brightly polished floor.

'Still, it's a bit of a shame,' Sean teased when he came up to congratulate them. 'It would have been so handy for registering the birth.'

Sara was the only one who didn't laugh.

All morning she had been feeling ominous tightenings and Dan hadn't completely been able to convince her that it was just more Braxton-Hicks' contractions. She'd been horribly certain that she would never get this far before going into labour.

'I told you it would be all right,' he murmured smugly when their little gathering had filed out of the office to make way for the next couple. He stroked a loving hand over her ivory silk-draped bump. 'I had a little word with these two in here and told them we had big plans for today, so they were to stay put just a little bit longer.'

'Dan? Sara?' said a hesitant voice behind them, and

there was Zara, looking almost unrecognisable from the sickly person Sara had last seen in a hospital bed. For just a moment the sight of her sister looking so vibrant and healthy reminded Sara all too forcibly that she must look like a hippo draped in a marquee by comparison, and her hand tightened reflexively on Dan's arm.

It only took one glance from those deep green eyes to restore her confidence that he was finally married to the twin he loved.

Standing beside Zara was a man at least twenty years her senior and not nearly as handsome as Dan, but it was obvious from the way he looked at her sister that he was completely besotted.

'This is Zach,' she said, almost shyly, and this new side to her otherwise confident sister took Sara by surprise.

'I'm the guy who's putting the finance together for Zara's film debut,' he announced in an unmistakable American accent, holding his hand out to each of them in turn. 'When she told me that her sister was getting hitched, I just had to do everything I could to make sure she was here.'

'That's very kind of you,' Sara said weakly, slightly overwhelmed by the man's ebullient personality. 'Have you been to Britain before?'

'Oh, many times,' he said with a broad smile. 'My plane could probably fly here by itself, it's been so often. So don't you worry about your sister missing out on being an aunt to those kids of yours.'

'Oh, that's very—'

'And don't you worry about anything,' he added,

dropping suddenly to a confidential tone, his shoulder turned so that neither Zara nor Dan were privy to what he was saying to her. 'First, I'm going to make sure she's fully recovered, then she's going to get her shot at stardom, but somewhere down the line I'm going to do my best to persuade her that she'd like to marry me and have some kids of her own.'

He stepped back and caught Zara's hand to tuck it in his elbow. 'Now, I know this is only a flying visit, but you just send us the pictures when these two decide to arrive and let us know when the christening is. We'll be back for it.'

Sara's last secret fear—that because she'd agreed to carry these precious babies as a surrogate for her sister, Zara might have a claim on them—had just been completely demolished.

She met Dan's eyes to ask a silent question and his smiling nod gave Sara the answer she needed.

'She'll have to come back for the christening,' she announced softly, knowing her next words would send her sister the signal that all had been forgiven, 'because she's going to be their godmother…if she wants to?'

The hug they shared was awkward but heartfelt and Zara took advantage of the closeness to whisper, 'Oh, Sara, I'm so, so sorry for everything. I was such a blind fool.'

Stepping back, she managed to find a tremulous smile. 'Rather their godmother than their mother,' she joked, but Sara caught the gleam of determination in Zach's eyes.

The next day Dan and Sara had just finished decorating their very first Christmas tree together and were about to settle down to tea when there was a phone call from someone in Human Resources.

'That's ridiculous!' Dan muttered impatiently when the call ended. 'There are some papers I've got to sign…something about insurance cover for you and the babies now we're married…and they want me to come in to do it today.'

'Today?' Sara's heart sank with disappointment. They'd had some rather interesting plans for the rest of the day and some of them involved stoking up the fire in the fireplace and just leaving the lights on the Christmas tree while they… *Later*, she reproached herself, silently. *We've got all the time in the world.*

'Well, I suppose it's good that they're getting everything sorted out now, rather than later,' she conceded. 'It shouldn't take you long, should it? We'll still have the rest of the evening…and night.'

'You needn't think you're staying here, tucked up all cosy and warm. There are some things for you to sign, too, so you'd better get something warmer than that robe on.'

Sara groaned and held her hands out so that he could help her to escape from the embrace of his blissfully comfortable settee. Unfortunately, it had never been designed for an easy exit for a woman heavily pregnant with twins.

They were just walking into Reception when Sean hailed them from the other side, his red hair a beacon in spite of all the tinsel and glitter on the enormous tree beside him.

'Hey, you two! Have you come to say hello to the gang?' he asked as he came across to kiss Sara's cheek.

'Several of them were asking how you were after I saw you at the wedding. They were complaining that haven't seen you since you started your maternity leave.'

'We've actually got to see someone in Human Resources about some paperwork,' Dan said with a grimace. 'Can you believe they phoned us on a Friday afternoon *this* close to Christmas?'

'Ah, sure they can wait a few minutes,' Sean said dismissively, beckoning them in the direction of A and E. 'The department's quite quiet at the moment so you'd better take advantage of it. By the time you've finished with the paper-pushers, we could be rushed off our feet.'

Dan and Sara both knew just how true that was, so they didn't need any more persuading, but they hadn't realised that the whole thing was a complete set-up until they walked into the staffroom to a shower of confetti and a united chorus of 'Surprise!' and found the room packed with waiting colleagues.

'They couldn't be there for the ceremony but they weren't going to miss out on the reception, even if they had to lay it on for themselves,' Sean told them with a broad unrepentant grin. 'Can't have A and E missing out on anything this special!'

'And the appointment with Human Resources?' Dan asked wryly, wondering how they could have been so gullible.

'That was the only ploy we could think of to get you out of your love nest,' Sean said with a teasing wink that had Sara blushing, remembering just what they'd had planned for the rest of the day. 'Now, has anyone got a spare suture trolley somewhere? Because you look as if you need it to carry some of that weight around for you.'

The thought of Sara wheeling her bump around in front of her on one of the department's trolleys... 'Suitably decorated for Christmas, of course,' Sean had added...was enough to have them all laughing.

It wasn't until Sara and Dan had circulated for an hour, greeting each of their colleagues as one after another they managed to snatch five minutes between patients, that they finally felt they could reasonably make their farewells.

'A final toast,' Sean announced, holding up a plastic goblet of something fruity and strictly non-alcoholic that almost exactly matched the carroty colour of his hair, apparently having appointed himself master of ceremonies. 'To paraphrase an old Irish toast—May the road rise up to meet you, the rain fall soft upon your head, the wind be always at your back, and may you get to heaven half an hour before the devil knows you're gone! To the bride and groom!'

'The bride and groom,' the rest chorused amid laughter, saluting them with similarly colourful glasses, but when Sara went to raise her own glass in return, she felt a sharp pain somewhere deep inside and gasped.

'Sara? Are you all right?' Dan asked, and tightened his hand around her shoulders, instantly aware that something had happened.

The sudden cascade of fluid onto the tiled floor told him everything he needed to know.

'They're over two weeks early,' she whimpered as she gingerly sat in a wheelchair that had appeared from nowhere.

'That's par for the course with twins,' Dan said reassuringly, then bent closer to whisper in her ear. 'And it's probably due to our enthusiastically thorough consummation of our marriage. They say that the application of male hormones can set things going. And, anyway, Christmas is the perfect time for the very best gift of all…new life.'

Sara hoped it was that same delightful application of male hormones that had been responsible for an absolutely textbook-perfect delivery, with one healthily squalling little boy following the other out into the world in perfectly normal cephalic deliveries.

'Oh, Dan, look! They're beautiful!' she sobbed as she lay there in the specially subdued lighting of the delivery room with one precious dark-haired baby in each arm. 'They're identical and they look just like you.'

'You're the beautiful one,' he argued as he stroked her joyful tears away with gentle fingers. 'You're amazing, Sara Lomax, and I could never tell you how much I love you in a million years. As for you two,' he said as he turned his attention to two little boys that were so perfect that any man would be proud to be their father.

He leaned a little closer, and under the cover of the activity still going on around them said, 'I need to have a word with the two of you for spoiling things. I had big plans for your mother tonight, involving a certain black lacy thong.'

'You idiot!' Sara laughed, knowing she'd had some similar plans of her own.

She loved Dan all the more for teaching her to have confidence in herself as an attractive woman, confidence that

she'd never developed when she'd always felt herself to be
in Zara's shadow.

'We'll just have to remember what we had planned and
save it up for later,' she suggested, her heart so full of love
that it felt as if must be overflowing. 'After all, we've got
the rest of our lives to love each other.'

EXPECTING A CHRISTMAS MIRACLE

LAURA IDING

CHAPTER ONE

"SLOW down, Ben," Alyssa Knight called, tightening the red wool scarf around her neck and pulling her black jacket over her pregnant belly in an effort to block the chilly wind as she followed her charge down the path toward the Lake Michigan shoreline. "I can't move that fast."

"But I want to see if the water is frozen," Ben protested, with six-year-old logic.

"The lake is too large to freeze. Ben, I mean it. Stop right there and wait for me," Alyssa said in a firm, you'd-better-listen tone.

Ben let out a heavy sigh and stopped in the middle of the path. She smiled and shook her head. Ben was Kylie Germaine's active son, and she'd agreed to watch him for a few hours. Kylie was spending this Saturday afternoon doing some last-minute Christmas shopping, along with a final fitting for her wedding dress, in preparation for her New Year's Eve wedding to Seth Taylor, one of Cedar Bluff's Emergency Department physicians.

Kylie would make a beautiful bride, she thought with a pang of envy. The couple radiated happiness. When

Alyssa had been young, she'd always wished for a big family. Kylie and Seth were planning to have more kids, and Seth already treated Ben like his own son.

She was glad to help out, even for a couple of hours.

There was an inch of snow covering the ground and she was looking forward to a white Christmas. In spite of the chill in the cold December air, she'd thought a trip to Cedar Bluff Park would be a good way to keep Ben occupied. Much better than sitting around in her small apartment.

An apartment too small for her expanding family.

The dark, heavy clouds overhead indicated more snow might be on the way. She picked up her pace, more so to keep warm than to catch up with Ben.

"When are your babies going to be born?" Ben asked as she met up with him on the path. There was an upper path leading to the top of the bluff overlooking Lake Michigan, but they'd taken the lower path leading directly to the lakeshore. Climbing the upper path in her current condition had been too daunting.

"Not for another eight weeks," she told him, smoothing her hand down over her stomach. At least she hoped she wouldn't have them too early. With twins, nothing was certain. Not only was she facing the fact she was pregnant with twins, but that she'd need to raise them alone, since their father, an emergency department physician named Jadon Reichert, had vanished in a disappearing act over four months ago.

She'd tried to call him, to let him know she was pregnant, but after the first couple of messages his cell phone had announced the number was out of service. According to Seth, Jadon was on an extended personal leave of absence from Cedar Bluff Hospital. In her opinion, a personal leave of absence was nothing more than a euphemism for gone and never coming back.

Which meant she was on her own. Exactly how she would manage to raise two kids alone was something she hadn't quite figured out yet. But, no matter what, she was determined to succeed in providing her babies with a secure, loving home.

"Mom says you're gonna need our help when the babies are born," Ben said, skipping up the path. He picked up a large stick and poked it into the snow.

She was going to need help all right. And lots of it. Luckily the close-knit, family-like atmosphere of Cedar Bluff, the town and the hospital where she worked as an ED/trauma nurse, meant she was surrounded by friends. People like Kylie and Seth had already offered their support.

Alyssa knew she wasn't alone. Not really. But having friends who were willing to chip in and help wasn't exactly the same as having a full-time father for her babies.

Wishing for the impossible was a waste of time, so she quickly pushed thoughts of Jadon aside. She'd gone into the affair knowing it wasn't going to last, so it was her own fault if her heart had gotten bruised when he'd left. If he didn't want to be a part of her life, fine. Her focus needed to be on taking care of herself and the babies.

Besides, her favorite holiday of all, Christmas, was only a few weeks away.

The path opened into a small clearing near the lake-front. Ben dashed forward, heading straight for the rocky shore.

"Don't go near the water," she warned.

"I won't," he hollered over his shoulder.

She told herself not to worry so much. Kylie brought Ben down to the lakefront all the time; surely he would abide by his mother's limitations. The wind kicked up, blasting frigid air into her face, whipping her long dark hair over her eyes and stealing her breath.

Jiminy Cricket, it was cold.

She turned to face the wind, pushing her hair out of her eyes. She pulled the scarf around her neck a little tighter and looked for Ben. Where had he gone? Impatiently she scanned the area, finding him standing precariously on the rocks above the water.

What part of *Don't go near the water* hadn't he understood?

"Ben? What are you doing?" she called in exasperation. "Get down and come back here."

He didn't seem to hear her, poking intently at something between the rocks. She had no idea what he'd found—surely all the marine wildlife was in hibernation by early December. She quickened her step, intent on dragging him back to safety, when suddenly there was a loud crack and a shrill cry. His walking stick had snapped in two, throwing him off balance. His small arms made windmill motions as he hung for mind-numbing seconds poised above the water.

"Ben!" Alyssa broke into a run just as his body toppled into the icy lake with a horrifying splash.

She scrambled up and over the rocks, helplessly scanning the water for his body. Could he swim? Had he hit a rock? Could he survive in the dangerously cold water?

There, his tiny head bobbed in the water, his arms flailing as he tried to stay afloat, his heavy winter coat dragging him down. Quickly, she shrugged out of her coat and pulled off her scarf. Remembering some of her old lifeguard skills, she wound one end of the scarf around her left hand and leaned out as far as she dared before tossing the other end into the water toward Ben.

"Grab the scarf!" she shouted. "I'll pull you in."

Ben reached for the end of the scarf, but missed. Her heart lodged in her throat when his head disappeared beneath the water for a couple of long seconds. Thankfully, the tide pushed him a little closer as his head cleared the surface again.

"Ben!" She reeled in the scarf and this time took careful aim before throwing it again, hitting him in the chest. "Grab the scarf!"

In slow motion, his numb fingers grasped the end and she nearly wept with relief as she towed him the short distance to shore. "I've got you. It's all right, I've got you."

When he was close enough to the edge, she reached down to pull him up.

Her center of gravity shifted. She'd forgotten all about her pregnant belly and her miscalculation made her lose her balance. She plopped with a thud into the water next to Ben.

Her babies!

Shockingly cold water surrounded her, sucking her down into the murky depths. For precious seconds she couldn't move, stunned by the cold water, and she idly wondered if she and Ben were both going to drown. The thought spurred her into action. Frantically she strove toward the surface, her fingertips brushing against something soft. Ben. Her head cleared the surface and she coughed, grabbing hold of the boy and holding him upright in the water.

"I've got you," she repeated, gasping and clenching her jaw to keep her teeth from chattering. Poor Ben had already been in the frigid water too long for a child his size. She tried not to think about the potential harm to her unborn children as she shucked off Ben's water-soaked coat so he'd weigh less and then used every ounce of her strength to lever him upright, literally pushing him up and out of the lake, onto the rocks. "See my coat up there? Use it to get warm."

Ben crawled over the rocks, falling facedown onto her coat. He may have been out of the water, but he still wasn't safe. Hypothermia was deadly. He needed to get warm, and soon.

Alyssa struggled to follow him out and over the rocks, but her fingers slipped and she fell back into the water, her strength seeping away. Desperately, she lunged upward, clutching a boulder while also trying to find a toehold so she could climb out. The task seemed impossible. She didn't have the upper-arm strength to pull herself out of the water.

Her legs were numb. She focused on Ben's too-still body lying on her coat and on the survival of her babies to give her the energy and willpower she needed to pull herself out of the icy water. She had to do this. She had to! She found a toehold and inched her way up, willing the quivering muscles in her arms to support her.

Finally she broke free of the icy prison, dragging herself up, over the rocks to safety.

"Ben." She collapsed next to him, beyond shivering

as the cold wind hit her wet body. She recognized the numbing fatigue for the danger it presented. They needed help. Fast.

Her fingers didn't move very well, but she managed to pry her cell phone out of her coat pocket and fumbled to flip it open. Pushing the buttons for 911 wasn't easy, but she had to try. She couldn't rest, not until she'd told someone where they were.

Dimly she realized the connection had been made. The dispatcher wanted to know the nature of her emergency. "We're on the rocks by the lakeshore in Cedar Bluff Park. We fell in the water. Hypothermia. Hurry…"

The woman dispatcher on the other end of the line continued talking, but Alyssa couldn't hang on to the phone, uncaring when it clattered against the rocks, disappearing from view. Help was on the way, all they had to do was wait. She pulled Ben against her rounded stomach, sharing what little warmth they possessed between them and doing her best to use her coat to shelter his body from the dangerously cold wind.

"Don't worry, they're coming to get us," she whispered, closing her eyes, the need to sleep nearly overwhelming. "They're coming…"

Bright lights. Blurred faces. Unintelligible voices.

Warmth. Lifesaving warmth.

Exhaustion. Her arms and legs felt like dead weights. Even her head was too heavy. Tired. She was so very, very tired.

Time had no meaning. She vaguely realized she was probably at the hospital. Maybe still in the emergency department. The people around her were a blur. She needed to know if Ben was all right, but couldn't find the strength to ask.

"Alyssa? Can you hear me?"

She frowned, blinking against the light, recognizing a familiar face hovering above her.

Jadon?

No, it must be her mind playing tricks on her. Jadon was gone. He'd left.

He was on a personal leave of absence. Gone for months. And never coming back. He didn't know she was pregnant. He didn't know he was soon to be the father of twins.

"Alyssa? Look at me. Can you hear me?"

No, she didn't want to do this. She didn't want to keep having dreams about Jadon. They were too painful. She closed her eyes and turned away, seeking peace.

Allowing the precious warmth to draw her down into blessed oblivion.

Jadon Reichert clutched Alyssa's limp hand in his and willed her to open her eyes, to talk to him.

"We need to get her moved up to the OB unit," Kim Rayborn was saying. She was the OB doctor on call, responding to emergencies as needed, but had informed him that she was also Alyssa's regular OB doctor.

Pregnant.

Alyssa was pregnant.

With twins. His twins.

The irony of the situation didn't escape him. He was certain, without talking to Alyssa, that the babies were his. The timing was right, for one thing. He'd thought they'd been careful, but obviously not careful enough. How could this have happened? With everything else in his life falling apart, he hadn't even considered the possibility he'd left her pregnant.

Even now, when faced with the reality of Alyssa's round belly, his mind couldn't seem to grasp the news. He'd told Alyssa from the start he wasn't looking for a long-term relationship, and she'd agreed that she wasn't either. But things had quickly gotten intense between them. When he'd received the emergency call from his mother, he'd left Cedar Bluff, figuring the timing was for the best, since he'd been starting to care about Alyssa a little too much.

Now he was back. And Alyssa was pregnant. She and Ben had been rushed into the ED by the paramedics, both requiring immediate treatment for hypothermia on the same day he was being reoriented to the ED by Simon Carter, one of the other ED physicians.

He'd soon learned that Ben was Kylie and Seth's son. Kylie was relatively new to Cedar Bluff so he'd never met her, but he'd worked with Seth Taylor. The boy had been dangerously chilled after his dunking in the icy lake water, but he'd be all right. Seth had been home sleeping after his night shift, but he'd rushed in to be there for Ben, with Kylie showing up a little while later.

The boy would be fine. And so would Alyssa.

Kim Rayborn hadn't made a similar commitment regarding the survival of Alyssa's twins yet.

As much as he'd never considered being a father, he was oddly protective of his unborn babies now.

"We need to move her upstairs to the OB unit," Kim repeated, as if he were a dimwitted child.

"I know," he said, in a hoarse voice. "But I'd like to stay with her."

Kim's expression held uncertainty. "Jadon, Alyssa has been through a terrible shock. Maybe it's best for now to give her some time, some space. Why don't you let her get through this immediate crisis first?" Before disrupting her life, was her unspoken implication.

She was right. Logically, he knew Kim was right. Yet he didn't want to let go of Alyssa's hand, to let her be taken upstairs without him. The OB specialist had already confirmed his fear regarding the possibility of premature labor. Alyssa had nearly lost her life. Right now, she needed to conserve her strength.

Clearly, she wasn't ready to talk to him.

Alyssa had looked directly into his eyes when he'd called her name. The way she'd turned from him, deliberately closing her eyes to shut him out, had stabbed deep. But at the same time he understood she had every right to be angry.

Heaven help him, he hadn't known she was pregnant when he'd left.

And what in the heck were they going to do about it now that he knew? He couldn't even imagine how they'd move forward from here.

"All right," he said, prising his fingers from Alyssa's and taking a step back. "But please keep me updated on her progress."

Kim nodded. "As much as I can. You already know she's starting to have mild contractions. We're going to see if we can stop them from getting any worse. But I have to be honest, once she's awake, it will be up to her to decide how much information you'll receive."

He clenched his teeth, wanting to protest, but held his tongue. The health-care privacy laws had been in place for several years. As a physician he knew them well, had explained them to many a distraught family member.

But he'd never been on the receiving end of their restrictions until now. He tamped down the helpless anger at how government rules could keep him away from Alyssa and their unborn babies.

Kim snapped orders and the nurses scurried to prepare Alyssa to be transported up to the OB unit. Standing in the middle of the ED and watching her go was difficult.

"Are you all right?" Simon asked, clapping a hand on his shoulder.

"Sure," he lied, glancing around the ED. Now that Alyssa and Ben had been cared for, the activity level had returned to normal. Almost as if nothing had ever happened. The staff were already getting things cleaned up in preparation for the next emergency. "Is there anything else we need to review?"

Simon's gaze rose questioningly, not entirely believing he was fine, as he shook his head. "No, I think you've got it covered. You're cleared to be placed on the physician schedule."

"Great." Jadon was relieved. Work was what he'd wanted, what he'd craved during the months he'd been gone. He'd known he'd have to work with Alyssa again, and that probably things would be awkward between them after the way he'd left abruptly. But her pregnancy changed everything. He couldn't pretend their passion had burned itself out and he'd decided to move on without her. "Thanks."

"Maybe you should head home for a while," Simon suggested. "I'm sure you have plenty of other things to get caught up with since you've been gone."

He did, but nothing as important as Alyssa and her unborn children, fighting for their lives upstairs in the OB unit. For a man who hadn't wanted a family, he couldn't seem to get Alyssa and her babies out of his mind.

"Nah, I think I'll hang around here for a while." He couldn't make himself leave. Not yet. "Maybe I'll grab something to eat in the cafeteria." He didn't have anything to eat in his house anyway. The place had been closed up for months.

Simon nodded. "See you later, then."

Jadon wandered down to the cafeteria, not really hungry but desperate for something to do. He stared at the various meal selections before finally deciding upon a bowl of steaming hot chili. He'd barely sat down with his meal when he heard his name over the loudspeaker.

"Jadon Reichert, please report to the OB unit. Jadon Reichert, please report to the OB unit immediately."

Alyssa!

He jumped up, abandoning his food, and headed for the stairs. He ran all the way up to the fifth floor, his heart pounding from exertion as much as fear.

"I'm Jadon Reichert. You paged me? About a patient, Alyssa Knight?" he said to the clerk seated at the front desk.

"Yes, Dr. Rayborn was looking for you." The clerk picked up the phone and dialed. "Dr. Rayborn? Jadon Reichert is here."

Within moments Kim appeared, dressed in scrubs

and an ultra-serious expression. He clenched his hands into fists and braced himself for the news.

"I've started Alyssa on a continuous infusion of terbutaline in an attempt to stop her contractions," Kim explained. "They're getting less severe, but haven't stopped yet. If I'm not successful in halting her labor over the next twenty-four hours, you need to know there is a good chance Alyssa will end up delivering her twins prematurely."

CHAPTER TWO

WAITING was pure, interminable hell.

Jadon paced the small waiting room located near the delivery suites. Kim had insisted on keeping Alyssa in the labor and delivery area until she was certain she could stop Alyssa's labor. Especially since Alyssa hadn't fully recovered from her hypothermic episode.

Not knowing what was going on behind the closed doors was killing him. He was a man who liked to be in control. He didn't know how to be patient. After he'd practically worn a path in the carpeting, he finally sat, dropping his head into his hands with a low groan.

There was no reason to dwell constantly on the potential complications. Alyssa would be fine. And even if the babies came early, they weren't too small. Kim had estimated one twin to be about three pounds, the other about three and a half pounds.

About the same size he and Jack had been.

He closed his eyes on a wave of despair. He didn't want to think about his twin brother, or about Jack's problems.

Especially since he hadn't been entirely truthful with Alyssa. She knew he had a brother, but she didn't know Jack was his identical twin.

The lie of omission had stuck in his throat, even back then. But he'd gotten so used to hiding the truth over the years, especially where women were concerned. The stress of coping with his brother had destroyed too many relationships. The breakup of his own brief engagement was bad enough, but the failure of his parents' marriage had driven the lesson home. Relationships didn't work for someone in his situation and covering up the truth made it easier to avoid lengthy explanations.

No matter how much he wished otherwise, his life wasn't his own. Jack would always have to come first. It wouldn't be right to bring anyone else into his messed-up family.

But then he'd met Alyssa. He'd told himself to stay away, but he hadn't seemed to be able to resist her. He had broken their rule of no strings by falling for her.

And now Alyssa was pregnant with his babies.

With twins.

Worry gnawed a hole in the lining of his stomach. If he could go back and do things differently, he would. He wouldn't have left so abruptly, responding instantly to his mother's panicked phone call the way he always had before. He would have talked to Alyssa first, taken the time to formally break things off between them.

But he still would have left Cedar Bluff.

Jack had needed him. There'd been no choice but to leave.

"Jadon?"

Hearing his name, he glanced up and rose to his feet. Kim's gaze was warm, and relief flowed over him as he sensed good news. "Yes?"

"Alyssa's labor seems to have slowed down significantly and her membranes are still intact. I'm fairly confident we won't have to deliver the babies for a while yet, although we're going to continue to watch her closely overnight, just in case."

Thank God. Relief was overwhelming. "Alyssa's awake? She's feeling fine?"

"Well, she's still pretty sleepy. I don't know that she's fully recovered from her ordeal."

"I'd like to see her," he said firmly.

Kim hesitated. "Jadon, Alyssa confided in me that you were the father of her babies, which is why I've kept you in the loop about her condition. But now, since it seems she's stabilized, I think it's best if we hold off on any confrontations until she's stronger."

Confrontations? "Give me a little credit, Kim. I'm not going to argue with her. I just want to know how she's doing." And let her know he was sorry he'd left without saying goodbye.

"Wait until tomorrow," Kim advised. "Alyssa's been through enough of a shock for the moment. It's better if you give her a little time to rest."

Leaving Alyssa without seeing her went against every instinct he possessed. Yet clearly Kim felt she was acting in her patient's best interests. Knowing further arguments weren't going to get him anywhere, he let out a deep sigh and nodded.

"All right, I'll wait. But if she does wake up, please let her know I'm anxious to see her."

Kim pursed her lips thoughtfully. "And if she doesn't want to see you?" she asked.

Panic gripped him by the throat. Obviously he

couldn't force Alyssa to see him. To talk to him. To let him explain. And even if she did, what could he offer her? Nothing but heartache. Yet he had to help take care of his babies. "She will." He forced a confidence he was far from feeling.

"All right, Jadon. We'll see what tomorrow brings."

He could tell Alyssa's OB doctor wasn't convinced. Heck, neither was he. All he could do was hope Alyssa would give him a few minutes of her time to explain, as best he could, without going into too much detail.

He didn't want to add to her stress by disclosing the entire truth. She had enough to worry about at the moment.

He couldn't believe she would ignore him completely, not when they both knew he was the babies' father. They hadn't wanted a future, but here they were anyway. Somehow they needed to find a way to get along, at least enough to provide a secure, loving environment for their children.

Feeling grim, he was forced to acknowledge it was a task much easier said than done.

Alyssa awoke feeling groggy and disoriented, as if she'd slept for days instead of mere hours. What time was it anyway?

She scanned the room, looking for a clock, but quickly realized she wasn't in the ED. The bright yellow walls and the warm decor, including the snowflakes and "Merry Christmas" written on the windows in white spray-on snow, didn't look at all familiar. She lifted her head, trying to find a nurse, instinctively placing a hand over her swollen abdomen.

She smoothed a hand over her stomach, searching for the familiar movements from deep within her womb. After a few moments relief washed over her as she felt the babies moving. She and the babies had managed to survive their swim in Lake Michigan.

And Ben, too?

Panic made her suck in a harsh breath. What about Ben? What had happened to Ben?

"Is someone there?" she called out, searching in her bed for her call-light. No wonder patients felt so helpless when they didn't have their call-lights within reach.

"Yes, I'm here." A pretty nurse entered the room and Alyssa recognized her as Marla, one of the labor and delivery nurses whose husband was also one of the anesthesiologists on staff. "Don't worry, you're doing well. And your babies are doing fine, too. We've been monitoring them through fetal heart tones."

Good news about her babies. "But what about Ben?" Alyssa couldn't relax, not until she knew what had happened.

"Ben?" Marla looked perplexed for a moment, and then her expression cleared. "Oh, yes, Kylie and Seth's son, Ben. He's doing fine. I believe they kept him overnight for observation as well on the pediatric unit."

She relaxed against the pillows. "I'm so glad."

"Alyssa, it's good to see you're finally awake." Dr. Rayborn came into the room, standing beside Marla. "And of course you've been asking about Ben."

"I don't remember much once I called 911," Alyssa admitted. "I must have been out of it for a while."

Kim raised a brow. "You were. In fact, you've been sleeping all night. But don't worry, Ben woke up much quicker than you did, and he's been telling everyone who'll listen how you saved his life."

She flashed a tired smile, very glad to hear Ben was okay. She hoped Kylie would forgive her for putting Ben's life in danger in the first place. It was her fault he'd needed saving.

Now that she knew her babies and Ben were safe, she relaxed against the pillows. Through her open door she could hear the lyrical sound of hospital carolers singing "Joy to the World", one of her favorite Christmas songs. Just hearing the uplifting music made her smile.

"Alyssa." Kim's expression changed to one of concern as she reached for her hand. "There's something I need to tell you."

Her muscles suddenly tensed and her smile faded. "What?"

"Jadon's here."

"Jadon is here? In Cedar Bluff?" She stared, confused. She vaguely remembered dreaming about Jadon. Was it possible the image of his concerned face hovering over hers hadn't been a dream?

"Yes. And he wants to see you," Dr. Rayborn said. "He's back from his leave of absence, and was actually doing an orientation shift in the ED when the paramedic crew rushed you and Ben in."

Jadon was back. She hadn't been dreaming his face near hers after all. She could hardly comprehend the news. Why had he returned? And why hadn't he called, especially after she'd left him a message? Why hadn't he at least bothered to let her know he was planning to come back?

Useless questions, as only Jadon could provide the answers.

She glanced at Kim. "I assume he knows about the babies?"

Kim nodded. "You told me he was the father. Is that true?"

She momentarily closed her eyes, wishing things had been different. For her and for Jadon. Resigned, she nodded. "Yes, it's true."

"He was extremely upset when you were brought in," Kim said gently. "He was literally glued to your side during the rewarming process as we struggled to get your core temperatures up to normal. He was also very shocked to learn you were pregnant."

"Yeah, well, all he had to do was answer my messages and he would have known about my pregnancy a lot sooner." She couldn't hide the note of bitterness that crept into her tone.

"I know you're upset, but it might be good to at least hear his side of the story," Kim pointed out.

His side of the story? There was a part of her that didn't really want to know. She and Jadon hadn't spoken much about their pasts. The last thing she wanted to hear was about some wife, or ex-wife, or ex-girlfriend. While he'd been gone it had been all too easy to think the worst. And it was very hard to believe Jadon had been glued to her side in the ED, especially when he'd left four and a half months ago without a word.

No, she couldn't do it. She wasn't ready to face him. Wasn't sure she'd ever be ready.

Besides, what difference would it make to talk to him? She and Jadon didn't have a future. Things had changed during the time he'd been gone. She'd grown accustomed to being without him. Had already planned on raising her babies alone. She didn't need a man to be happy; she was more than content to focus her life on her children.

She wasn't the same person who'd loved recklessly and lost so painfully. She'd gone into an intimate relationship with Jadon, thinking she could keep things light and fun. He was handsome and charismatic, reminding her very much of her father. And he'd told her up front that he wasn't interested in anything long term either. Another factor that had reminded her of her father.

Which was exactly why she'd suspected Jadon wasn't ever coming back.

So why was he here now? Maybe he needed to see her first, before he walked away one last time. Surely discovering the news about the twins would scare him away. Did he know they were his? Or would she have to convince him through blood tests? If so, she wouldn't bother. If he didn't want to acknowledge them as his, it was fine with her.

"I'll see him later," she said, avoiding the inevitable but unable to help herself. "Are you going to discharge me soon?"

Kim hesitated and slowly shook her head. "I can't discharge you yet, Alyssa. I've had you on a continuous infusion of low-dose terbutaline to help stop your premature contractions. Once I wean you off the medication, we'll see how you do. I may be able to discharge you within the next twenty-four hours, but I'd like you to stay on bed rest for a few days."

Bed rest? Alyssa tried to hide her dismay. "I understand you're trying to prevent premature labor, but I can't work if I'm on bed rest."

"I know." Kim's warm gaze focused on hers. "I realize you need to support yourself, but the health of your unborn babies must be the highest priority."

Of course it was. Chagrined, she nodded. "You're right. I'm sorry. I'll stay on bed rest as long as you tell me I need to."

"Well, let's plan on a couple of days at least," Kim clarified. "Then we'll see how it goes. You are fairly far along in your pregnancy, but every week you carry the babies, the better their chances of survival without complications."

Alyssa knew her doctor was right. She'd make ends meet, somehow. "Okay, so when are you going to start weaning me off the medication?" she asked.

"Right now," Kim said with a smile. "Marla? Start lowering the drip rate, a few milliliters per hour, while monitoring for contractions."

"Okay." Marla made her way to make the first adjustments on the IV pump.

"Dr. Rayborn?" Alyssa called when Kim moved as if to leave.

"Yes?" She turned back toward Alyssa.

"If Jadon shows up this morning, I'll see him."

Kim raised a brow. "Are you sure? I don't blame you for needing some time."

There wasn't enough time left in all creation for her to be ready to face Jadon, and that was the God's honest truth. So she'd be better off facing him now, since she fully expected he wouldn't be sticking around much longer. He was reminding her more and more of her father, who certainly hadn't stuck around for very long. Some men just weren't meant for long-term relationships.

Once he understood she wouldn't force him into playing the role of loving father to her unborn twins, she suspected he'd do his all-too-familiar disappearing act once again.

"I'm sure."

"Jadon?"

At the sound of his name, he glanced up to find Kim standing in the entryway of the waiting room. He flashed a crooked smile. "Hi."

She raised a brow and shook her head, raking a gaze over his rumpled clothes. "Don't tell me you slept here all night?"

"Okay, I won't tell you." He stood and stretched, trying to work the kinks out of his back. "What's up?"

"Alyssa is being weaned off the terbutaline, and so far the contractions haven't returned. She'll be in the labor and delivery area for a while yet, but she's ready to see you."

She was? Alyssa was willing to see him?

He'd waited so long he'd assumed she'd decided against it.

"She knows I'm here?" he asked, suddenly extremely nervous about seeing her.

Kim nodded. "Yes, although I didn't tell her you slept here all night. But she did confirm you're the father of her babies, although if you need a formal paternity test, that can certainly be arranged."

"No. No tests. Unless Alyssa wants one." He almost blurted out the truth, about how now that he thought about it, he knew exactly when they'd conceived. The one time he and Alyssa had gotten carried away and hadn't used protection.

But this wasn't the time, or the place, or the appropriate person with which to have this conversation. He needed to talk to Alyssa first.

No matter how difficult.

"She's in Labor and Delivery room number five." Kim smiled again. "Take your time. I have patients to see in clinic this morning so I won't be back until later this afternoon, unless something changes."

He nodded, feeling nervous. He made his way back down the hall of the labor and delivery suites. The door to Alyssa's room was closed. He knocked, and then, when he couldn't hear anything, opened the door. "Alyssa? May I come in?"

"Yes." Her voice was weak, and he hesitated, wondering if his timing was bad. Maybe he should wait until she was fully recovered from her hypothermia episode.

Don't be a coward, he told himself, pushing the door open and entering her room.

Her face was pale, framed by a cloud of her dark, curly hair spread out over the pillow. She looked better than she had when the paramedic unit had brought her icy-cold, limp body through the trauma room doors.

He'd never been so scared.

"How are you feeling?" he asked, tentatively coming closer.

She lifted a shoulder and smoothed a hand over her

belly, as he'd often seen pregnant women do. There was something innately caring in her gesture. "Fine. They're telling me the babies are doing well, which is all I care about."

He didn't necessarily agree, since her well-being was very important to him, but nodded anyway. She was so beautiful, especially now, with her body soft and round with child. His gaze dropped to her lush breasts, not entirely hidden by the shapeless hospital gown she wore. They were fuller than he remembered.

He swallowed hard and dragged his glance away. What was wrong with him? Alyssa wouldn't appreciate his lustful thoughts. Especially after the way he'd left her so abruptly.

"Look, Jadon, I know you weren't expecting this." Alyssa, always direct, cut right to the heart of the matter. "But you need to know, I tried to call you. I left a message, but then the next time I called, your phone was disconnected."

"I'm sorry," he apologized, knowing she had every right to be upset as he pulled out his new cell phone. "My old cell phone was stolen." And he wasn't about to share the details of that story. At the time, he'd been lucky to have escaped with a mild concussion and a few cracked ribs. His cell phone and wallet had been the least of his worries. "I know it's not an excuse, but I didn't get your messages. See? New phone, new number."

She stared at him with wide, solemn blue eyes. "You had a right to know about the babies, but please understand that, other than some financial support, I don't expect anything from you."

He scowled, annoyed with the way the conversation was going. "What do you mean? I'm their father."

Her unblinking gaze bored into his. "Can you honestly tell me you're here to stay this time? That you'll be here for me and the babies no matter what? You'll never need to take another unexpected personal leave of absence?"

For long moments he debated lying to her and reassuring her he was here to stay. But his life wasn't his own. He had responsibilities. If his mother called, he'd have to drop everything to leave again.

And he couldn't lie to Alyssa, even by omission.

Not about this.

"No, I can't tell you that I won't ever leave Cedar Bluff. But if I do have to leave, I'll make sure to let you know first. And you can rest assured that, no matter what happens, I have every intention of being there to help support you and the twins. Emotionally support them, as well as financially."

Her eyes widened in surprise, as if she hadn't expected him to say that. "But you made it clear you weren't interested in a serious relationship," she protested, her eyes full of barely hidden anxiety.

"So did you," he shot back.

She stared at him, unable to refute his claim. They'd blithely jumped into an intimate relationship, never considering the possible consequences of their actions.

"Obviously things have changed, for both of us," Jadon continued. "I plan to be a part of my children's lives, so you'd better get used to the idea." She wasn't going to get rid of him that easily. "I'll give you some space now, because I don't want to cause you any more stress while you're supposed to be resting, but you can be certain I'll be back later."

She didn't utter a word as he turned and walked away.

CHAPTER THREE

ALYSSA had no idea bed rest could be so boring. It seemed all she could think about were the things she couldn't do. The next twenty-four hours crawled by painfully slowly. Daytime television was pathetic. She searched and searched for some Christmas-themed programs but didn't find a single one. Where were all the wonderful Christmas shows she'd remembered watching as a kid? Didn't they air them anymore?

She hoped the hospital carolers would come back. Or maybe the music channel on the television? She picked up the remote and turned it on, taking a deep breath when the lyrical sound of Christmas music filled the air.

She closed her eyes and hummed along, trying not to dwell on the four hospital walls holding her captive.

The problem with having nothing to do was that her thoughts kept going back to Jadon. He hadn't made good on his threat to return, and she wasn't certain if she was relieved by the lapse or disappointed. She tried to convince herself his absence was for the best. She needed time to get over the shock of knowing he was back. Somehow, she simply couldn't believe he'd meant what he'd said.

He wanted to be a part of their children's lives? Supporting them emotionally as well as financially? What exactly did that mean?

Was he envisioning some sort of joint custody agreement? Dual parenting? The thought of giving up her babies on alternate weekends made her feel sick.

So she tried not to think about their dubious future at all. Especially since Jadon hadn't been able to promise he wouldn't leave again. Maybe his definition of emotional support was different from hers. Once he understood the amount of work twins entailed, he'd likely disappear for good, just like her father had. She needed to keep her heart safe. No way did she want to be hurt like that again.

Several of her coworkers stopped by to see her, giving the occasional break in the monotony. Susan, her coworker in the ED, brought her a beautiful red poinsettia plant, which provided a cheerful, festive feeling to her room. Seth had popped in very briefly to assure her that Ben was indeed doing fine and that he'd be discharged the following morning.

Alyssa could only hope an early morning discharge was in her future, too.

As she hadn't done a thing all day except lie in bed watching television, sleep didn't come easily. She spent far too much time thinking of Jadon.

Remembering their last night together.

The way they'd made love, urgently, as if knowing, instinctively, the heat and passion between them couldn't last.

The desolation she'd felt once she'd realized he was gone.

At the time, she'd told herself she was better off without him. They'd met during a very complicated trauma resuscitation, two victims of a multiple motor-vehicle crash. From the very beginning, she'd realized Jadon was an excellent physician. She'd admired the way he kept calm in a crisis, yet treated the distraught families with dignity and respect. His charisma was like a beacon, drawing her near. She'd warned herself to ignore the attraction she felt for him, but it seemed like every time she glanced up at him, he was staring at her.

When their fingers had touched that first time, pure electricity had sizzled between them.

Eventually, they weren't able to stay away from each other. He asked her to come home with him after a late shift they'd shared, and against her better judgment she agreed.

She knew better than to fall for a handsome guy like Jadon. Her mother had harped on the inability of handsome men to remain faithful. Alyssa had seen a few of the early photographs of her parents together, realizing her father had indeed been a good-looking guy.

And he'd left a week before her third birthday, leaving her mother to raise a young daughter all alone.

All her life Alyssa had tried to avoid ending up like her mother. Her mother had been forced to go from job to job, always seeking better pay, which hadn't been easy since she didn't have a college degree or any specialty training. It wasn't her mother's fault that she'd spent more time working, or obsessing about working, than paying attention to Alyssa.

So Alyssa had vowed to make something of her life.

To never be dependent on any man. She'd taken out student loans to attend college, to have a career as an ED nurse so she'd never have to worry about not having a steady, reliable job.

She'd also avoided being hurt by men, like her mother had been, keeping her relationships light-hearted and fun. Especially if the guy she was with seemed like he wasn't exactly father material.

Like Jadon. Yet here she was, pregnant and alone. With twins, which put a big crimp in her plan to stay independent.

And as much as she wanted to blame Jadon, she knew the truth of the matter was that she had no one to blame for her situation but herself.

Jadon was exhausted; he'd been called in early for his night shift because the ED had been flooded with trauma calls. He hadn't slept very well in the first place, and being called in early meant he'd missed going back up to L & D to check on Alyssa. During the night, he'd had a few minutes of downtime, but obviously then wasn't the appropriate time to wake her.

When he finished his shift at eight-thirty in the morning, he took a few minutes to swing by to see how she was doing.

He helped himself to more coffee, double-strength to keep the fatigue at bay. With less than three hours of sleep, and a physically demanding endless stream of patients, his entire body ached, as if he'd been run over by an eighteen-wheeler.

As he stepped off the elevators on the fifth floor labor and delivery area, he ran into Seth, Kylie and

Ben. He quickly realized they were making their way down to see Alyssa as well.

"Jadon," Seth greeted him coolly. The silence stretched for a long moment before Seth grudgingly made formal introductions. "This is my fiancée, Kylie Germaine. And her son, soon to be our son, Ben. Kylie and Ben, this is Dr. Jadon Reichert, one of the ED physicians here at Cedar Bluff."

"Good to see you both again," Jadon said, forcing a smile. He'd noticed Seth hadn't introduced him as a friend, but only as a colleague. He turned his attention to the boy. "Especially you, Ben. You're doing much better than yesterday."

"Yes, well, he's finally been discharged, but has also refused to leave without seeing Alyssa," Kylie commented dryly.

"Alyssa can't come to visit me because she might have her babies too early," Ben announced in an all-important tone.

Jadon's lips twitched with the need to grin. "Yes, that's right," he agreed. "She needs to rest. But I know she'll be glad to see you, as she's been very worried about you."

"I love Alyssa," Ben said very seriously. "She risked her life for me."

"I think she's special, too," Jadon said, his chest feeling tight with emotion. He thought Ben's case of hero worship for Alyssa was sweet. Not that he blamed the kid.

He'd heard the story yesterday, about how Alyssa had fallen into the icy water, trying to rescue Ben. She'd gotten the boy out first, but then almost couldn't make her way out of the water. When he thought of how things could have ended very differently, he felt sick and shaky all over.

"Come on, Ben," Seth said, interrupting them. "Let's go and visit Alyssa, shall we?"

Jadon told himself he was overreacting to Seth's abruptness, but the way Kylie dodged his gaze only confirmed it wasn't his imagination. With a flash of annoyance he tried not to obsess about how he didn't even know Kylie on a personal level—she hadn't been here in Cedar Bluff when he'd left—so there was no reason for her to carry a grudge against him. She'd obviously picked up on Seth's disdain.

Part of their attitude might be because they were afraid he'd leave Alyssa again, he acknowledged.

But even more, he suspected Seth didn't think he was good enough for Alyssa. A fact he couldn't argue.

Even aside from the problem of sustaining a relationship, what did he know about being a father? Or having a normal family? Nothing. His family had been anything but normal.

He stood where he was, watching them make their way down the hall to Alyssa's room, a closely knit family unit, regardless of the lack of formality of marriage. Clearly they were good friends with Alyssa.

Maybe this wasn't a good time to visit after all. His presence in the room with Seth, Kylie and Ben would only make things awkward.

Coward, his subconscious jeered.

With a muttered oath he continued down the hall to Alyssa's room. He stood in the doorway, watching her smile and laugh while hugging Ben.

He swallowed the hard lump in his throat and stepped farther in the room.

When Alyssa saw him, the light in her eyes dimmed. "Hi, Jadon."

"How are you feeling?" he asked, avoiding Seth's none-too-subtle glare. "You look much better this morning."

"I am better," Alyssa said. "Dr. Rayborn has written my discharge notice. I'm free to go home."

"That's wonderful news." He was very glad to realize that Alyssa was stable enough to go home. At least he didn't have to worry about the twins being born too prematurely.

"I have to stay on bed rest for a few days," Alyssa explained, including all of them in her earnest gaze. "But Dr. Rayborn told me to come back to see her on Wednesday. If all goes well, I might be able to return to work after that."

He bit back a protest, knowing his opinion on her working this late in her pregnancy wouldn't be welcome. He wanted to reassure her about how he planned to help her to financially support the babies but at the same time he didn't want to invite an argument, especially in front of Seth and Kylie.

"Don't rush things," Kylie warned, and he wanted to kiss her in gratitude for saying exactly what he was thinking. "Remember, stay healthy so you can carry those babies to term."

"I know. I've already heard the same lecture from Dr. Rayborn," Alyssa protested, holding up a hand with a wry smile. "I won't rush things, but you know as well as I do that the longer I work before the delivery, the more time I can take off after the twins are born."

Again, Jadon had to bite his tongue to keep from interrupting. If he had his way, Alyssa wouldn't have to work for a long time after the twins were born. He might not know much about being a father, but he refused to let her struggle to make ends meet either.

Yet he understood they had a long way to go before she'd lean on him. So he'd be patient, taking one day at a time.

"Do you need a ride home?" Seth asked. "We're happy to stop by your place since Ben's officially discharged, too."

"That would be great," Alyssa said gratefully. "The nurses have already done the discharge teaching. All I need is a prescription for the oral terbutaline Dr. Rayborn wants me to continue taking and I'll be ready to go."

Jadon frowned, thinking her condition didn't sound too stable to him. "I can give you a ride home, Alyssa. That way Kylie and Seth don't have to wait."

Seth flashed a grim smile, crossed his arms over his chest. "Oh, it's no bother. We don't mind waiting, do we, Kylie? And besides, you worked graveyard last night, didn't you? I heard the ED was crazy. Might be better for you to hurry home and get some sleep. You look exhausted."

The dismissive note in Seth's tone put Jadon's teeth on edge. Silently, Jadon glanced at Alyssa, giving her the final word. She hesitated, and then grimaced as she nodded. "Jadon, I didn't realize you've just finished working the night shift. I'll go home with Kylie and Seth. You do look like you could use some sleep."

Her choice to go with her friends, rather than with him,

stung. Maybe he'd made mistakes but, dammit, it wasn't all his fault. He hadn't left knowing Alyssa was pregnant.

When the nurse didn't immediately return with Alyssa's prescription, he knew he'd lost the battle. Swallowing a heavy sigh, he turned and left, trying to be happy that Alyssa was doing well enough to go home.

But if she thought she could avoid him forever, she was wrong. Maybe he did need some sleep, but he and Alyssa needed to talk. Soon.

Preferably without an audience.

Alyssa sat on her sofa, staring morosely at her crooked Charlie Brown Christmas tree standing in the living-room corner of her apartment. She'd thought the ornaments would help fill in the sparse gaps between the branches, but instead the branches slumped beneath the weight of even her smallest ornaments.

Her apartment manager, Mr. Worthington, had brought her the tree and hauled her ornament boxes out of her storage bin located in the basement. Mr. Worthington was a sweet man; he'd been a devoted fan ever since the night he'd had crushing chest pain and she'd stayed by his side during the ambulance ride to the hospital.

So she couldn't complain about the tree. Instead, she should be glad she had at least something Christmassy to look at. Christmas had always been her favorite holiday even while she'd been growing up. It had been the one time of the year when her mother had gone all out, lots of decorations and celebrating to make their time together special. In recent years, though, since her mother had passed away, the holiday spirit had been more difficult to find. Now, with the babies coming, she'd grown excited about Christmas again.

However, bed rest did not include putting up Christmas decorations, or baking Christmas cookies. Heck, she couldn't even scrub the floors or really do anything to relieve the boredom of her apartment.

When the doorbell buzzed, indicating she had a visitor, she crossed over to the intercom system, expecting her coworker from the ED. "Susan? Is that you?"

"No. It's Jadon."

Alyssa closed her eyes and momentarily rested her forehead on the wall. She'd known Jadon wouldn't leave her alone for long, especially after she'd turned down a ride with him earlier that morning. She'd seen the flash of hurt in his eyes when she'd agreed to go home with Seth. She'd felt guilty.

But she wasn't any more ready to continue their discussion now she had been earlier in the day.

Since avoiding him hadn't worked, she pushed the button to release the door lock of the apartment. In moments he knocked on her door.

She ran her fingers through her hair and opened it, all too aware of how awful she looked wearing maternity sweats. Not that she should care.

But she did.

"Alyssa, are you supposed to be up off the sofa?" he asked, his brow furrowed with concern as he shut the door behind him.

She suppressed a sigh, telling herself it was natural he was worried about the babies. They were his babies, too.

"Yes, I can make simple meals for myself, walk to

the bathroom and back. I'm to keep a log of any contractions I have and to call Dr. Rayborn if they become at all regular or sustained."

Jadon nodded and thrust his hands deep into his pockets. "I'm glad. Kim seems like a great doctor."

"Yes, she is." Alyssa made her way back to the sofa. "Help yourself if you want something to drink."

"I'm fine." Jadon followed her into the living room, taking a seat on the chair across from her. If he noticed her pathetic little Christmas tree, he didn't say anything. "Alyssa, I'm sorry. I shouldn't have left all those months ago without saying anything. Give me a chance to explain."

She swallowed hard and shook her head. "Jadon, if this story involves some other woman, like an ex-wife, a fiancée or a girlfriend, I really don't want to hear the gory details."

"What?" His startled expression would have been comical if she hadn't felt so sick to her stomach to be having this confrontation. "Is that really what you think? That I left you for some other woman?"

She rubbed a hand over her stomach, hoping she could calm the babies, sheltering them from her tension. "What was I supposed to think? Why else would you leave without a word?"

"There isn't another woman, Alyssa. Not now, or during the time we were together." His low tone and the seriousness in his gaze made it difficult to doubt him. "But you're right, I haven't been entirely truthful with you. About my past."

She licked suddenly dry lips, suspecting she wasn't going to like this. "To be fair, Jadon, neither one of us talked much about our pasts." Their physical attraction had overridden most of the normal let's-get-to-know-each-other small talk.

"Alyssa, I left Cedar Bluff a few months ago because of a family crisis."

"A family crisis? One of your parents?" she asked in concern, remembering the few sketchy details they'd shared about their backgrounds.

Slowly he shook his head, letting out a heavy sigh. "They're fine, well, sort of, but that wasn't the problem. It was my brother who needed help. I know this isn't fair, but I'd rather not go into all the details right now because it's complicated."

"Complicated," she repeated, trying not to feel hurt. She tried to tell herself that whatever had happened wasn't her business, but it was difficult. "I guess I can understand." Even though she really didn't. Then again, she shouldn't be surprised. Jadon had always tried to keep his distance from her emotionally. This was just another example.

"I'll tell you the entire story sometime, but right now I'm more worried about you. And the babies."

"There isn't anything to be worried about. I'm fine and so are the twins." She gave a small shrug, hiding her true feelings. Jadon had never confided in her before, and obviously he didn't see a reason to start now. Maybe he hadn't left her for another woman, but that didn't change the fact that he wasn't open to a future. "All I can do is follow doctor's orders and hope for the best."

"Yes. But I'd really like to help."

"Help?" she repeated, trying to figure out where he

was going with this. "Like with what? The babies haven't been born yet."

"Do you have everything you need?" he asked. "It's going to be rough as you need two of everything. So what about cribs? Car seats? Strollers?"

The thought of Jadon buying baby things almost made her smile. "Seth and Kylie threw me a shower, inviting all the ED staff, so I have most of what I need, thanks."

He swept a skeptical glance over her apartment. "You'll be crowded in here, don't you think?"

She raised a brow. "For now maybe we'll be a little cramped. But I won't be living here forever." At least, that was her plan. She had some small savings that she hoped to use as a down payment for a house, depending on how things went after the twins were born. If she could work enough hours to afford a small mortgage.

"Alyssa, I have a three-bedroom house. There's no reason you can't move in with me for the rest of your pregnancy and then even after the babies are born. Between the two of us, we should be able to help care for the twins, keeping our child-care costs down."

Her eyes widened in shock. Was he crazy? Was he really suggesting they live together for financial reasons? As if the babies were nothing more than a business arrangement? "I don't think that's a good idea."

In fact, she was pretty sure it was a really bad idea. His emotions may not be involved, but hers would be.

"Please, think about it." He didn't back down as she half expected he might, but stood awkwardly in her living room, looking like a fish out of water. "I know things have been rough for you, and I'm sorry you had to go through this alone. But right now we need to focus on the babies. Having you move in with me, even temporarily, is best for them."

CHAPTER FOUR

LONG after Jadon had left, Alyssa found herself replaying their brief conversation over and over again.

He'd asked her to move in with him. As a business arrangement. Because there was extra room in his three-bedroom house. A temporary solution to solve her child-care needs.

Typical of Jadon to gloss over the emotional side of things. Did he ever think about their time together? Did he have any feelings for her at all? Other than as the mother of his children? Children he'd never planned on having?

Logically, she knew his offer had some merit. She'd always sworn not to end up like her mother, struggling to make ends meet. And now here was Jadon, offering a solution to at least part of her problems. But at what cost?

Emotionally, sharing a roof with Jadon would risk her heart, a huge price to pay.

Yet didn't her babies deserve a safe and secure childhood? And would she really be able to provide that on her own? For one baby, yes, but for two? Doubtful.

She hadn't given him an answer, simply telling him she'd need to think about it.

For a long time she stared at the pretty, bright star

topping her lopsided Christmas tree, as if seeking divine guidance. What on earth should she do? Maybe moving in with him would be best for the twins, but what about her?

If only her pulse didn't leap so erratically whenever Jadon was nearby. If only she didn't still feel that spark of attraction whenever he spoke to her. If only she didn't wish so much that things were different.

She'd gone into a relationship with Jadon planning to keep things light, but she'd been hurt more than she'd realized when he'd left. Maybe he'd left for a family crisis but, still, he hadn't called to let her know he was coming back. Clearly he hadn't anticipated renewing their relationship. Because they hadn't *had* a relationship.

She didn't want to be hurt again. Jadon had already proved himself to be too much like her father. She'd be better off to stay away from him.

Except he was the father of her babies.

Avoiding him would be impossible. Somehow she had to find a way to work with Jadon, to meet the needs of her children, without becoming emotionally dependent on him.

Could she do it? Live with him as a business arrangement, to help share the trials of providing feedings for two infants every two to three hours, without getting emotionally involved?

The four walls of her apartment were closing in on her, especially the way she couldn't do anything. She longed to leave. Yet the idea of moving in with Jadon seemed too much like simply exchanging one type of prison for another.

* * *

Jadon figured he'd botched things with Alyssa for good. He hadn't intended to bring up them moving in together, yet suddenly it had seemed like such a great idea. Obviously, by her horrified expression, she hadn't shared his enthusiasm.

And her wishy-washy, gee-let-me-think-about-it response hadn't been promising.

Seeing Alyssa in her cramped apartment, with her crooked Christmas tree, had bothered him. He couldn't imagine how she'd possibly take care of two babies in the single-bedroom apartment. Especially as she didn't have anyone to lean on for support. Her mother had passed away a few years ago and she was an only child.

The rest of Alyssa's past was sketchy. He knew she was estranged from her father, but that was about it. They hadn't made an attempt to know each other on a deeply personal level.

Their relationship had been physically intimate. He'd realized how much he was starting to care for her at the same time his family crisis had torn him away. He'd thought the distance would help.

But he'd missed her. Had thought about her a lot. Had missed their physical closeness.

A closeness he'd considered resuming once he'd returned, since he'd learned a lot about his brother's illness while he'd been gone. He'd spent time with Jack's doctor, who'd put some of his old fears to rest.

And, truthfully, he'd liked their hot, steamy nights together.

Alyssa's pregnancy changed everything. He didn't know anything about being a father. The idea of raising children, twins on top of it, secretly scared him. He knew, only too well, how things could go wrong.

With a sigh, he rubbed his aching temple and then decided to head for the shower. He was on for another night shift tonight, then had only one day off before working again on Wednesday night. At least he had Thursday and Friday off before being back on for the weekend. He'd been assigned the less-desirable grave-yard shifts and weekends, but since the physician team had covered for him while he'd been gone for the past four and a half months, he couldn't exactly complain.

Even though he personally would have rather stayed here, he understood there were feelings of resentment among the others.

Simon Carter had been pretty decent toward him. And there was a new guy, Quinn Torres, scheduled to start soon, to replace Ed Cagney, who'd just retired. But Seth Taylor had been another story. Seth couldn't have made his feelings any clearer.

Monday night started out fairly quiet. He had to admit he was glad of the chance to ease back into the work he'd loved and hadn't been able to do for so long.

At midnight, a woman carrying a small infant rushed in.

"He aspirated and started turning blue." The woman was talking fast, but with the way she used medical ter-minology, he thought she was probably a doctor or a nurse. "I didn't do any CPR, but used the bulb suction to keep his airway cleared."

"Okay, let's take a look." They must not have called

911, but had driven here themselves. He reached for his peds stethoscope. "How old is the baby?"

"Ten days old." Her voice shook as he gently took the baby and placed him on the infant table. Melanie, one of the nurses, placed a pulse-ox device on his forehead and then stripped off his little outfit to put tiny EKG patches on his chest.

"Pulse ox 86 percent," Melanie said in a low tone. She fiddled with the heart monitor. "Heart rate 176."

He nodded and used his stethoscope to listen to the little guy's lungs. He definitely must have aspirated as Jadon could hear rales in the bases of his lungs.

"Did you witness the aspiration?" he asked the visibly upset mother.

She nodded. "It was my fault. All my fault. I had him propped on his side after his feeding, but I couldn't have tucked the blanket securely enough behind his body. Next thing I know, he's lying on his back, turning blue." She momentarily closed her eyes. "It was awful."

He gave her a reassuring smile. "Well, his pulse ox is coming back up, he's almost at 90 percent. And his heart rate was pretty tachy, but that's coming down, too. So far he's not running a fever, but that probably won't happen until tomorrow. Who's your pediatrician?"

"Dr. Piterle, in the Pediatric Care Group."

Jadon gave Melanie a nod and she left to get in touch with whichever pediatrician in the group happened to be on call. "Are you a nurse?"

"Yes, although I haven't worked since having my daughter."

"I thought so. What's your son's name? We need to get him admitted into the system."

"Never mind, Dr. Reichert." Wendy, the night shift

admitting clerk, came into the room. "Dad's here and gave us all the information we need. This little guy is Aiden Crosby."

"My name is Diane and my husband is Steve." Diane introduced her husband, who came into the room with a cute toddler in his arms. "And my daughter, Katie."

Melanie returned. "Dr. Piterle was on call and he didn't think Aiden needed to spend the night, but he does want to follow up with the baby tomorrow morning."

Diane nodded with relief. "Okay, that's fine."

"Now, remember, if he runs a fever tomorrow, he'll probably need a full course of antibiotics," Jadon warned. "IV antibiotics since he's so young. But for now his pulse ox and heart rate are back to normal, so he should be in the clear."

"Thank you," Diane said gratefully.

Jadon was glad the ten-day-old Aiden would be all right, but seeing the tiny baby only made him think about Alyssa and their twins. He was more convinced than ever that it would be best for her to move in with him. He took his responsibilities seriously. He needed to convince Alyssa to let him support her.

In the morning, he decided to stop at the grocery store for her, since she obviously couldn't do it on her own. Rather than guess what she wanted to eat, he headed over to her apartment to get a list.

But when he pulled up, he saw Kylie, Seth and Ben hauling some grocery bags out of their car and trooping up to Alyssa's apartment building. He was too late.

Alyssa didn't really need him after all.

* * *

The ED was unusually quiet on Wednesday night when he entered the arena. When Jadon saw Alyssa standing near Susan, the charge nurse assigned to the night shift, discussing the various patient assignments, he was shocked.

How was it possible she was back at work already? Sure, she'd mentioned something about only being on bed rest for a few days and being scheduled to see Kim Rayborn today, but to already be released to work? It had to be too soon.

What if she started having contractions again?

"Hi, Alyssa," he greeted her, careful to keep his tone light. "I see you're back at work."

"Jadon." Her smile was fleeting. "It feels good to be back. I was going crazy sitting at home."

He nodded, barely refraining from pointing out she didn't have to be at her apartment all alone. He'd wanted her with him.

"Who wants to cover the trauma room?" Susan asked.

"I will," Alyssa volunteered. She smiled at the new nurse, Maureen, who was learning the ropes. "Maureen can work with me."

"Okay, I'll put you guys down as first trauma coverage." Susan scribbled on her clipboard.

"Did you see the full moon out there?" Alyssa said to Susan and Maureen. "It was so beautiful."

"Yeah, beautiful." Susan let out a loud snort. "You know what a full moon means—more work for us. The crazies will be out in full force."

"Is that really true?" Maureen asked with wide eyes.

"You bet," Susan said. She turned to Alyssa. "Remember last month, Alyssa? When the police brought us that guy who'd stripped down to his bare butt while standing right in the middle of Main Street? Like, what were we supposed to do with him? Other than put his clothes back on." Susan rolled her eyes at the memory.

Alyssa nodded and let out a chuckle. "Yeah, he was a strange one all right."

Jadon clenched his jaw at their slightly derogatory tone. He wanted to snap at them to shut up because obviously people couldn't help having emotional illnesses, but he also knew they didn't mean any harm. Alyssa and Susan were excellent nurses.

He was just being overly sensitive. He turned away, to focus his attention on the two patients who were still waiting to be transferred up to inpatient floor beds. He needed to make sure these patients were placed before new ones began to arrive.

They received their first trauma call about thirty minutes later, a car versus tree. The driver was a young man who luckily didn't have severe injuries. Jadon and Alyssa fell into a familiar rhythm, working together as if he'd never left. When she handed him a chest tube insertion tray, the slightest brush of her fingers sent an unexpected yet familiar tingle of awareness zipping through his system.

"Thanks," he managed.

The way she avoided his direct gaze convinced him she might have felt it, too. This sizzling attraction had drawn them irrevocably together the first time they'd met. Tonight was proof the passing of time hadn't lessened the attraction.

He still wanted her.

There wasn't time to dwell on the knowledge because as soon as they managed to get the patient stabilized, it was as if a dam had burst, the way the patients flooded in.

Loud screaming erupted from the ED waiting room.

Jadon glanced up in alarm. "Stay here," he told Alyssa as he dashed through the doors into the waiting area to see what was going on.

"Don't touch me! Leave me alone! I can't listen— Don't touch me!"

A man stood in the center of the room, his eyes wild, his clothes disheveled, a three-day growth of beard covering his face. He grabbed at the hair on his head with one hand, while waving a butter knife clutched in the other. While the butter knife wasn't sharp, it could still be used as a weapon and the few people in the waiting room were pressed against the back wall, giving the guy a wide berth.

"Easy, now," Jadon said, waving a hand at the others to indicate everyone should stay back. He prayed Alyssa hadn't followed him in. She was pregnant. He didn't want her anywhere near this guy. "No one is going to touch you. I promise, no one is going to touch you."

"I can't. They won't stop— I can't listen. Don't touch me." The man was clearly in distress, and Jadon knew that if he didn't help this man calm down, he might quickly turn violent.

And violence meant someone would get hurt.

Not Alyssa. Please, keep Alyssa safe from harm.

"No one is going to hurt you. You can relax now. I can help you. You're safe here." Jadon understood, only too well, that while this man seemed crazy, his wild actions were the result of a deep fear.

Fear of what, he wasn't sure. Something the rest of them couldn't see but that was very real to this man, nonetheless.

He continued to talk to the man holding the butter knife in a calm tone, reassuring him he was safe here. No matter how much he wanted to turn around and look for Alyssa, to make sure she was safe, Jadon didn't break eye contact with the patient. And as he continued to talk him down, he hoped the hospital staff, including the security guards, were busy getting the other patients and their families out of the waiting room, just in case.

Psych crisis de-escalation techniques didn't always work the way they were intended to. It paid to be prepared for anything.

"I'm here to help you. You're safe here. My name is Jadon. What's yours?"

"Mitch. Mitchell Park Conservatory. I'm Mitch, but I'm not crazy. I don't have to listen."

Jadon wasn't sure if this guy's name was really Mitch or not, as the Mitchell Park Conservatory was actually three horticultural domes that served as a local tourist attraction in Milwaukee, but he decided to go with it. "It's nice to meet you, Mitch. You're here in the safe zone where no one can hurt you. It's my job to keep you safe. You're not crazy. I think you're scared. But you don't have to be afraid. You're safe with me."

The more he repeated himself, and key phrases like *You're safe here with me*, the better chance he had of convincing Mitch to calm down enough to let go of the butter knife. Jadon suspected Mitch was suffering from some form of schizophrenia, especially if he was really hearing voices in his head.

He wanted to hurry and get the guy some treatment, but rushing him would only make things worse, so he forced himself to take his time, to remain calm and to keep his gaze trained on Mitch, hyperaware of his every movement.

It took him nearly twenty minutes, but Mitch eventually gave up his knife and agreed to go into an examination room. Jadon steered him toward the opposite end of the emergency department where they could isolate him to a certain extent from the other patients.

"Nice job," Alyssa said in a quiet voice, once he'd given Mitch a mild sedative, a similar dose, they'd discovered in going through his old records, to the one that he should have been taking at home.

"Thanks. I'm glad you stayed far away," he admitted.

She frowned. "Of course. I'm not stupid."

He winced. "I didn't mean to say you were. I was just worried about you."

Alyssa stared at him for a long moment and he wanted to pull her close and kiss her, but they didn't have that kind of relationship. Not anymore. Finally she turned away and he heard her calling the psych crisis center for Mitch.

"See?" he heard Susan say to Maureen. "You thought we were kidding, didn't you? I told you the crazies would be out. Mitch is a true nutcase."

Her derogatory tone caused him to spin around, pinning her with a fierce glare. "He's not crazy, he's sick," he said in a low, furious tone. "His illness isn't any different from having diabetes or congestive heart failure. And I don't want to hear you call him a nutcase again, do you understand?"

Susan's eyes widened and she took a hasty step back, making him irritated all over again, especially when he realized Alyssa was staring at him with troubled concern. "Sure. I'm sorry, Dr. Reichert."

Only slightly mollified, he turned away, continuing to see patients one after the other as the full moon kept its promise of keeping them busy.

Mitch had brought all Jadon's old fears to the surface. He should stay far away from Alyssa, yet he couldn't make himself. When he realized he was creating excuses to be near her, he knew Mitch wasn't the crazy one.

He was.

Because it was crazy to want something he could never have.

CHAPTER FIVE

ALYSSA waited patiently until the respiratory therapist finished giving Mr. Waverly a breathing treatment for his pneumonia, then she placed the peripheral IV he required for his full course of antibiotics.

She couldn't help wondering about Jadon while she worked. It was very unusual for him to snap at anyone the way he'd jumped on Susan. In fact, she'd never seen him as uptight as he'd been during this shift.

Although facing wild Mitch who'd been armed with a butter knife would put anyone on edge.

Had he always been somewhat protective of patients with emotional illnesses? She thought back to those first few weeks they'd worked together, but couldn't really remember.

Ashamed, she realized she hadn't taken the time to really understand Jadon. She'd settled for a physically intimate relationship, enjoying the sheer thrill of being with him. And working with him tonight brought the intense feelings of attraction back again. She was aware of him at every moment. It was hard to concentrate when he was near. Yet she also missed him when he was gone.

When he'd left, she'd been upset because she'd started falling for him, even though she'd told herself she wouldn't, and then later because she'd discovered she was pregnant.

The latter was her fault—to a certain extent—as much as his.

A mere touch from Jadon while they were caring for their patients made her remember the hours they'd spent together making love. Yet there was so much about him she didn't know. Who was Jadon, really? And what past experiences had molded him into the man he'd become?

Ironic that she knew as much about Jadon as she did about her long-absent father.

They'd become intimate, agreeing they weren't looking for a long-term relationship, but here they were, about to be parents of twins. What a tangled mess.

She put her troubled thoughts aside, refusing to allow her personal life to interfere with her professional one. As the night wore on, Alyssa became more and more fatigued. There wasn't much downtime during the night thanks to the full moon hanging over the hospital like a large, yellow-orange bad-luck charm.

She started Mr. Waverly's antibiotics as Jadon had ordered for his pneumonia and stifled a yawn as she trudged slowly back to the main desk. Every room was full and she knew there would undoubtedly be additional patients assigned to her.

"Alyssa, take a break," Jadon murmured in a low tone as he came up behind her. "Put your feet up and relax for a bit."

Jadon's concern was touching, but she shook her head. "There are still patients who've been waiting almost two hours to be seen. I'll take a break once we've gotten caught up." Which, at the rate they were going, might be never.

"Alyssa, please." He put his hand on her arm, stopping her from walking away. "Maureen can cover for a bit."

She looked at his strong hand and wished he'd cared as much about her before she'd become pregnant, and was now not just focused on the babies. She missed being held by him more than she'd realized.

"Soon," she said, regretfully pulling away. She missed the warmth of his hand when it dropped to his side.

She only had to hang on a few more hours as the oncoming shift started at seven in the morning, yet she also knew that if there were still lots of patients she couldn't just leave when her shift was up.

A trauma call came in at five forty-five in the morning, giving her a badly needed spurt of adrenaline. A young twenty-one-year-old man had fallen asleep at the wheel, crossed the center line and hit an oncoming car. The woman in the other vehicle was in her mid-forties, and had been having significant abdominal pain at the scene of the crash. The airbag had saved her from a serious head injury, thank heavens.

"Get a trauma surgeon down here," Jadon ordered. He glanced at Alyssa. "I want to know her hematocrit and hemoglobin. I suspect she's ruptured her spleen, bleeding into her belly."

Alyssa nodded. She quickly finished her initial set of vitals and then proceeded to draw the labs he'd requested. She handed them to the runner and then turned back to her patient. The woman's name was Elaine Sansone, and the way she moaned in pain on the gurney made Alyssa privately agree with Jadon's assessment. Elanie's abdomen was hard and painful to the touch.

"I need a CT scan of her belly stat. Where the heck is Trauma Surgery?"

"I'm here," Leila Ross said, entering the trauma bay. She was a petite woman with exotic Oriental features and beautiful straight long black hair. "What do you have?"

Alyssa continued checking Elaine's vital signs, not entirely surprised when her blood pressure dropped dramatically, confirming Jadon's assessment of bleeding into her belly. "Blood pressure is down to ninety systolic. Do you want me to give more fluid?" she asked.

Jadon nodded. "Give a liter bolus of normal saline. Leila? What do you want to do?"

"A CT scan would help, but if her pressure is that low, I think it's better if we simply take her up to the OR. I can explore her belly up there."

"Alyssa?" Jadon glanced at her. "Get Elaine transferred up to the OR."

"What about the other patient?" The young twenty-one-year-old, by the name of Curt Neilson, had suffered multiple fractures, especially in his forearms and his right leg. His injuries weren't as critical, so she'd allowed Maureen to handle his care.

"I'm sending him for a slew of radiology films. The orthosurgeon is on his way in. There isn't much more we can do other than manage his pain."

Alyssa nodded and began to connect Elaine to the

portable monitor so she could transport her to the OR. Leila jumped in to assist and between the two of them they wheeled Elaine up to the OR suites. When the OR nurse took over, Alyssa returned to the ED to help Maureen.

It took a while to get Curt's X-rays but just as they finished and returned to the trauma bay, he lost his blood pressure, too. But on the monitor his heart rate still looked as if it was doing all right.

"Check his pulse," Alyssa said sharply.

Maureen put her fingers on his carotid artery, her eyes wide. "I don't feel anything."

Alyssa muttered a curse under her breath and double-checked for herself, although she suspected he was in PEA. "Start CPR," she told Maureen. Raising her voice, she called, "Jadon? We need your help over here."

Jadon rushed over and immediately knew what was going on. "His last set of labs were fine, right?" he asked.

Alyssa nodded. "He does have cracked ribs. Do you think he has a tension pneumothorax?"

"Stop CPR." Jadon picked up an eighteen-gauge needle and inserted it in Curt's fourth and fifth intercostal space. Within moments his pulse returned.

Maureen's eyes were wide. "Wow. It worked. It really worked."

"Yes, it did," Alyssa said in relief. A tension pneumothorax was life-threatening, yet also relatively simple to treat, once you had the correct diagnosis. A glance at the clock told her the day shift would be coming in soon. Thank heavens.

"I love this job," Maureen said reverently.

Alyssa had to laugh. Normally, she loved it, too.

Most of the time. She'd love it tonight if she weren't so darned tired.

They waited a long time for Curt to be accepted as an ICU admission. Once she and Maureen wheeled him upstairs and handed over his care to the ICU team, they were pretty much free to go.

Alyssa punched out at the time clock, and then headed into the staff lounge for a few moments. Whoever had hung the Christmas decorations must have gotten interrupted halfway through. There was red garland strung along the ceiling, but an artificial tree stood in the corner, bare of any ornaments. If she had the energy she'd finish the decorations herself.

Her feet ached terribly, so she plopped in a chair and lifted them up on the table. The soreness in her legs eased and she leaned her head back with a sigh and closed her eyes. She longed to rest, for just a few minutes.

"Alyssa?"

She pried her eyes open, surprised to see Jadon. For a moment she was confused. Where was she? Then she remembered that she'd sat in the staff lounge for a few moments before heading home. "I'm awake," she said, wincing a little as she set her feet back on the floor.

"You're exhausted," Jadon said mildly. "You'd better let me drive you home."

"I'm fine," she protested. "I didn't mean to fall asleep, it's just the first time I've sat down in hours. And I'm more tired these days than usual."

"I know." Jadon's grim gaze met hers. "You earned the right to rest, Alyssa. Heck, I was surprised to see you back at work tonight anyway. Please let me drive you home. It's been snowing for the past hour. You don't want to end up like Curt and Elaine, do you?"

He was right, she was exhausted. But she didn't live that far from the hospital. "They were on the highway," she stubbornly reminded him. "They crashed at high speeds. Different situation altogether."

"A crash is still a crash, regardless. And it doesn't matter, because I'm not taking no for an answer," Jadon said firmly. He bent to take her hand, helping her to her feet. "Come on. It's no trouble. Much better to be safe than sorry."

She gave in, knowing that arguing with Jadon was useless. He was as obstinate as a mule when he wanted to be. That was one area where they'd butted heads in the past—each of them liked having their own way. But for now she was too tired to argue anyway, so she reached for her coat, surprised when Jadon took it from her grasp and held it for her.

"Thanks," she murmured.

Outside, snow fell from the sky in large, thick flakes. An inch of fresh snow covered the ground, and she knew the roads would be slippery.

Much better choice to sit back and let Jadon drive.

"In you go," he said, opening the passenger door of his car and helping her in. Her stomach tended to get in the way, so she backed into the seat and then swung her legs around.

Jadon tucked her in, closed the door behind her and then slid into the driver's seat. He started the car and then went back out to brush the snow away from the windows.

Shivering a little, Alyssa huddled in her coat, remembering how cold she'd been the afternoon she'd fallen into Lake Michigan. At times like this the cold seemed to seep into her bones, making her wonder if she'd ever be warm again.

She'd always been warm in Jadon's arms, she thought with a sigh, putting her head back and closing her eyes.

Somewhere along the route home she fell asleep. When Jadon gently shook her, she lifted her heavy eyelids, blinking against the bright snow. "Where are we?"

"My house. Don't argue. Two cars were sitting sideways in the road leading to your apartment complex because the hill was too slick for them to make it up, so I came here instead."

She let out a heavy breath. "I don't want to argue, but I hate to cause trouble," she said weakly.

He sent her a narrow glare. "Don't be silly. You're no trouble, Alyssa. At least here I can keep an eye on you."

An eye on her for what? Because she needed a caretaker? At least before they'd been equal partners in their intimacy. Now he was treating her more like a responsibility.

She didn't like it. She wanted to mean more.

"Wait for me. The driveway is very icy."

Since she couldn't lever herself out of the car without help anyway, she waited. Jadon tugged her out of the car, and then wrapped his arm around her waist, supporting her as they gingerly made their way across the slick, snowy sidewalk up to the house.

This close to him, his familiar musky scent filled her head, bringing back memories of the nights they'd spent together. Did he think about those times at all?

She glanced up at him as he unlocked the door, irrationally wishing she could force him to remember. Large, fluffy snowflakes covered his dark hair, clinging to his eyelashes. For a moment their gazes locked and she could tell their closeness affected him, too. But then he stepped back, helping to take her coat off as if she couldn't perform the simple task herself. And suddenly she wanted to prove she wasn't weak or helpless.

"Jadon." He froze when she placed a hand on the middle of his chest. His eyes darkened and his heart beat erratically beneath her fingertips and she knew she finally had his full attention. Keeping her gaze locked on his, she gripped his shirt, lifted herself up on her toes and pressed her mouth against his.

Stunned, Jadon couldn't move, absorbing the heady taste of her kiss. The intense heat that simmered beneath the surface didn't take long to ignite and within moments he'd clutched her close, her round belly pressed intimately against him as he deepened the kiss.

She tasted so sweet, he couldn't get enough. How long had it been since he'd touched her? Held her? It seemed like forever.

"Jadon," she whispered on a moan, and suddenly he realized what he was doing. This couldn't happen. He broke off the kiss, breathing heavily.

"I'm sorry," he muttered, trying to regain his equilibrium. "I shouldn't have done that."

Alyssa stared at him with an oddly hurt expression. "I'm the one who kissed you."

She had, and he wasn't sure why. Unless she was

under the delusion they could simply pick up where they'd left off before? Impossible.

"I shouldn't have let things get out of control. This wasn't why I brought you here."

"No. I'm sure it wasn't." She turned away, leaving him to pick up her coat he'd dropped on the floor, putting it away in the closet.

"Are you hungry?" he asked, when she made her way into his living room.

"Not really. And I don't need you to wait on me. I'm going to stretch out on the sofa to rest."

"Alyssa, don't." He quickened his pace so he could reach out to grab her arm. "Take my bed. I insist."

She tugged her arm away as if she couldn't tolerate his touch and crossed her arms over her chest. "I can't take your bed."

"Why not? I can't let you sleep on the sofa." He had two spare bedrooms, one he used as an office and the other just a junk room. When he'd invited her to move in with him, he'd intended to buy a bedroom set for the second bedroom. "Please, just this once, humor me."

She cocked a brow. "Just this once? I thought I'd been humoring you all along."

He couldn't disagree. "Maybe you have, but give me a break, will you? What if you tried to roll over on my sofa and fell to the floor, landing on your stomach? I'd never forgive myself."

Her mouth curved in a reluctant smile but then quickly faded. "Fine. I'll take your bed. But if you wake up with a sore back, don't blame me."

Better him having a sore back than her, but he didn't say anything. He headed down the hall and gestured to the bedroom, feeling somewhat awkward. "I'm, uh, sure you remember where everything is, right?"

Avoiding his gaze, she nodded. "Yes."

He tried not to remember the last time she'd been at his house, the night they'd made love several times, staying awake until dawn.

Pulling his gaze away from his bed, Jadon grabbed a pillow and a blanket from his linen closet. "Goodnight, Alyssa. Sleep well."

She didn't answer but closed his bedroom door with a loud click. He stared at it for a long moment before he turned and headed back into the living room to stretch out on his sofa.

The cloudy, snowy day should have made it easier for him to get some rest.

But even though he was dead tired, he couldn't sleep.

Images of Alyssa, in his bed, tortured him. He'd never made love to a pregnant woman before, but kissing Alyssa had been pure heaven. He found he was enthralled by the changes in her body, especially when he discovered she was still as responsive as ever. There must be something wrong with him to see Alyssa as more sexy than ever while soft and round, carrying his children.

From a medical perspective, he knew sexual intercourse wasn't dangerous during pregnancy. Alyssa had seemed to be as involved in their kiss as he'd been.

So why had he broken things off? Because sex didn't solve anything. They couldn't go back to being the carefree lovers they'd been. He didn't have a normal family, a normal future to offer her. He couldn't let himself fall for her. He had responsibilities. Obviously he'd help support her and the twins, but that was all he could do.

Knowing the truth didn't ease the ache in his groin. If he hadn't let his conscience get the better of him, they'd be sharing his bed right now.

He had no one to blame for his restlessness but himself.

CHAPTER SIX

About five hours later, Jadon woke up to the sound of his stomach growling. As he struggled upright on the not-so-comfortable-for-sleeping sofa, wincing against the light streaming through the living-room window, he wondered if Alyssa needed something to eat as well.

After all, she was eating for *three*. And working night shifts really messed up your body's normal rhythms. If he was hungry, she had to be starved.

Yawning widely, he shuffled down the hall toward the bathroom, pausing outside the closed door to his room and listening intently for any signs that she was up and awake. When after several moments he didn't hear a thing, he turned away. After spending a few minutes in the bathroom, he headed back to the kitchen.

Pursing his lips, he stared inside his fridge. Cooking wasn't exactly his strong suit, but he had eggs and milk. He opened a drawer and found cheese and a few green onions. He thought he still had some bacon bits, too. Just enough ingredients to scrape together an omelet. And some French toast if she wanted some.

He'd made both of the breakfasts for her before, he remembered, during those brief months of their steamy affair, and she'd seemed to enjoy them. So which one should he go with now?

Both, he decided. Couldn't go wrong with a choice.

He made a small pot of coffee, feeling a little guilty for drinking the brew in front of Alyssa but needing some caffeine to help clear his fuzzy, sleep-fogged brain.

He downed two cups of coffee, feeling more human afterward as he set about cracking eggs into a small bowl. He rather liked cooking for Alyssa.

Just as he finished preparing the meal, he heard the bathroom door close. Alyssa was awake, no doubt making one of her all-too-frequent trips to the bathroom.

He grabbed a rather beat-up metal TV tray left over from his college and medical school days, and loaded up the two plates he'd prepared. He added a tall glass of milk for Alyssa and then carried them out to the living room, just in time to catch her coming out of the bathroom.

She wore a pair of his old navy blue sweatpants and a sweatshirt, looking sleepily adorable despite the baggy clothes. He had to clench his teeth against a wave of desire.

"Alyssa? Are you hungry?" He hoped his voice didn't betray his lustful thoughts and he avoided her gaze by staring down at the food on the tray. "I have French toast and omelets."

She paused, and then nodded, showing no sign of her earlier ire. "You know, I am hungry. Thanks, it sounds great."

As she came closer, he noticed her face was pale and drawn, her earlier exhaustion still evident on her features.

Obviously, she needed a few more hours of sleep.

"Sit here on the sofa where it's more comfortable," he said, shoving aside the pillow and blanket he'd used. "Put your feet up and relax."

She walked slowly into the living room, gingerly sitting on one end of the sofa. She rested her feet on top of his coffee table with a muffled sigh.

He frowned in concern. "What's wrong?"

"I've been having some episodes of contractions," she admitted. "But they seem to be getting less frequent."

"Contractions?" His heart clenched and he stared helplessly at her rounded stomach. "Shouldn't you call Kim Rayborn?"

Alyssa bit her lip. "Yes," she agreed. "But I'd like to eat first. Last time this happened, they stopped on their own."

Last time? When? During the night? Or before she'd even gone to work?

Dammit, she had no business going back to work so soon.

He clenched his jaw and gently set the TV tray on her lap. Then he took the pillow off the sofa and tucked it beneath her ankles to protect them from the hard edge of the coffee table.

"Thanks," she murmured. She dug into the omelet and French toast meal he'd created with obvious enthusiasm. "Hmm. This is fantastic."

"I'm glad you like it." He sat beside her with his own plate, eating mechanically but not tasting a thing as he kept darting worried glances at Alyssa. When he realized his plate was clean yet he didn't remember tasting any of it, he set it aside with a grimace. "Alyssa, having contractions isn't good."

"It's not that bad. I've been timing them," she said defensively. "They're not regular and they don't last long."

He wanted to shake some sense into her. "You were on your feet the entire night—don't you think you might have overdone things just a bit?"

"Maybe," she said, avoiding his gaze.

He stifled a sigh. "Are you going to call Kim? She should be the final judge as to whether or not you should continue working."

Alyssa was silent for a long moment, before she finally looked at him. "I already called off work for tonight. I just don't think I can do another night shift like the one we had last night and I wanted to give them plenty of time to find someone to replace me."

"Thank heavens," he said, overwhelmed with relief. Finally she'd come to her senses. Now, if only he could convince her to stay here at his house where he could watch over her. "Your health, along with the babies', are your two main concerns. I'm sure they'll find someone to work your shift."

"I hope so." She frowned. "I don't like to leave them short-staffed. Look how busy we were being fully staffed."

"I know, but they're going to be working without you soon enough," he pointed out. "Especially if you deliver early. So pushing yourself isn't going to help."

She simply nodded as she ate the last bit of eggs and

toast on her plate. When she was finished, he stood and took the tray from her lap.

She frowned a little. "You cooked, so I should clean up."

Yeah, over his dead body she would. "Are you still having contractions?" he asked warily.

"Not in the last fifteen minutes," she said dryly. "Stop hovering, Jadon. The only thing Kim would tell me to do right now is go back on bed rest, which I can do on my own. I know my body well enough, and these few contractions aren't anything to worry about."

Maybe, but he didn't like it. He preferred having control of the situation, not waiting to see what might happen. He carried the dirty dishes back to the kitchen.

When he returned to the living room a few minutes later, she was lying back against the cushions with her eyes closed. He didn't want to disturb her but suddenly she opened her eyes.

"Jadon, this isn't going to work. You keep acting as if I'm going to fall apart. I think it's time you took me home."

"No." He stared at her for a long moment. "I'm happy to go to your apartment to pick up your things, but I'm not taking you home and leaving you alone."

Her eyes widened in surprise at his blunt response. "Excuse me?"

"You heard me. Don't ask me to do it, Alyssa, because I can't. Look at you! You're exhausted. You need to rest and you can't do that if you have to do everything for yourself." He rubbed the back of his neck, wishing he knew what to say to convince her. "Please. Stay here with me. At least until you deliver."

"Because you want to take care of me," she said, her tone laced with a hint of bitterness.

He didn't understand why that made her mad, but knew he had to step carefully. "No, it's not just that. I've missed you. And we have a lot to work through before the babies are born, don't you think?"

He sensed she liked that answer a little better, because she didn't immediately jump into another argument.

After what seemed like a lifetime, she slowly nodded. "All right, Jadon. I'll stay for a short time." His relief must have been obvious, because she hastily added, "But only if you bring my bedroom set here so that we both have a place to sleep. I refuse to kick you out of your bed."

Logically, he knew sharing his bed with her was out of the question. Still, that common-sense thought didn't stop his body from reacting at the possibility.

This move was for Alyssa and the twins, not for him.

"It's a deal," he said quickly, before she could change her mind.

Alyssa had truckloads of doubts regarding the wisdom of her decision to stay with Jadon, especially the way he sprung into action, calling Simon Carter for help and making a list of everything he needed to bring over from her apartment. He left so quickly when Simon arrived to pick him up she didn't have time to voice her concerns.

He'd said he'd missed her. And unfortunately he was right when he'd said they had a lot of details to work through before the twins were born. No matter how much she wanted to remain independent, she couldn't be foolish about it. And despite how she'd reassured him, the contractions worried her. What if she couldn't work anymore? She didn't want to end up like her mother, obsessed with making ends meet. Hadn't that been the real reason she'd insisted on going back to work so soon?

And now look at her. She'd overdone it, big-time. With slow, deep breaths she performed the relaxation techniques she'd learned in Lamaze class. The contractions came and went, but were much less now that she was resting quietly.

She'd missed her last session thanks to her hospitalization. It wasn't that big a deal, the last class being to watch a video of a birth, and she'd seen one during her nurse's training. Kylie, too, had not only had Ben but as a paramedic had also seen a birth. Kylie would be a great birthing coach.

Would Jadon mind knowing Kylie was her birthing coach? Maybe, although it wasn't as if he'd been around to attend classes with her. She remembered Megan, the birthing instructor, telling them there was a DVD version of the class available, too. Jadon would probably be more than willing to watch it.

Wait a minute, was she seriously thinking of asking Jadon to be her birthing coach?

Yes. She was.

She closed her eyes with a weary sigh. Moving in with him was definitely a mistake. They were soon-to-be parents without the benefit of a loving relationship. And she was beginning to care about him, too much. And what did he want from her? Nothing. He'd been the one to break off their kiss. He'd been clear about how much he wanted her to stay here with him, but only because she needed help. Not because he was interested in pursuing an intimate relationship. That much was obvious.

Her cheeks flushed and her breath shortened as she relived the kiss. For some strange reason—maybe an excess of hormones—she was burning with pent-up sexual frustration. She'd never realized how easy it was to get sexually stimulated while pregnant.

She'd wanted Jadon.

Had practically thrown herself at him.

Only to be turned down.

She opened her eyes and gazed morosely at her large belly. Of course Jadon hadn't been interested, why would he? She was the size of a house!

Before she could wallow too deep in her pool of self-pity, Jadon and Simon returned with the first load of stuff from her apartment. Jadon hauled in the mattress from outside, laughing and shaking snowflakes off his dark hair as he entered the house. She couldn't tear her gaze away from him, especially the way his muscles flexed as he maneuvered the mattress down the hallway to the spare bedroom he'd already cleared out for her.

So far, Jadon certainly didn't look as if he minded the extra work. Or that he was regretting asking her to stay. Did he really want to talk about the possibility of a future? And could she trust him if he did? How could she know if Jadon would really stick around for the long haul? Especially with the stress of raising not just one baby but two?

"Hi, Alyssa," Simon greeted her, coming in behind Jadon, lugging a large suitcase she hoped was full of her maternity clothes. She felt like a lost waif in Jadon's sweats. "How are you and the babies feeling?"

"We're fine," she said with a smile. Simon was a nice guy—in fact, they'd gone out on a couple of dates prior to her meeting Jadon, but there just hadn't been any spark. She was glad they'd been able to remain friends. "Thanks for moving all my stuff."

"No problem. I think it's very good that you're staying here with Jadon," Simon said in a serious tone. "You shouldn't be alone, not with all the complications you've had."

"I only had complications because I was silly enough to fall into Lake Michigan," she protested. "Not because of my pregnancy in general."

"It wasn't silly to save Ben's life," Jadon said, walking back through the living room.

"No, but I should have been able to get Ben out of the water without falling in." She wrinkled her nose. "I didn't factor in how much larger and lower my center of gravity is."

"All that matters is that you're both safe," Simon said.

"Come on, Simon." Jadon clapped him on the shoulder. "Help me carry her bed frame inside."

"How did you get all this stuff over here?" Alyssa asked with a puzzled frown.

"Jadon rented a truck," Simon answered over his shoulder. "And a good thing because the four-wheel drive sure helped us get up that hill on your street."

She vaguely remembered Jadon saying something

about the slippery, snow-covered hill on the street leading to her apartment. It was one of the reasons she'd ended up here with him in the first place. She didn't ask any more questions until they had everything moved in.

Including her small, lopsided Christmas tree.

"I can't believe you brought it along," she murmured as Jadon set it up in the corner of the living room, directly in her line of vision from her position on the sofa. Simon had left a few minutes previously, to return the rented truck.

He rocked back on his heels, flashing her a quizzical, sideways glance. "Well, I couldn't just leave it there in your apartment, the poor thing looked lonely enough as it was. And since I didn't have any Christmas decorations up of my own, I figured this would cheer you up better than nothing."

"Thanks, Jadon." She was foolishly touched by his consideration. "I've been really looking forward to Christmas this year."

"Yeah?" His smile was infectious.

"Yeah. So, uh, do you have to work tonight?"

"No, I'm off the next two nights." He spent more time making adjustments to the tree, until he finally stood and put his hands on his hips in disgust. "I swear I've done everything to straighten this tree. Nothing works. It's still crooked."

Her lips twitched at his vexed tone. She lifted her shoulder in a shrug. "I kind of like it that way."

He rolled his eyes. "Figures. Okay, I give up, then. The tree is up, and Simon helped me put your bed back together, so all we need to do is unpack your clothes. Do you want me to do that for you?"

"Ah, no," she said hastily. It was bad enough that her maternity clothes probably looked like giant tents, she didn't need him going through stuff any more than he already had. "I can do it."

"But you're supposed to be resting."

She took her feet off the table and struggled to her feet. "I've been doing nothing but resting." And despite the fact she'd already been up to the bathroom several times, she needed to go again. She paused long enough to put a hand on Jadon's arm. "Thanks, Jadon. I mean it. I appreciate how you went out of your way to bring everything over here."

"Hey, having you move in was my idea, remember?" he joked. But he placed his hand over hers, squeezing it gently. "Everything will be fine."

She wished, really wished that were true. If only he'd see her as a woman, and not as a burden to care for.

Jadon couldn't sleep. Across the hall he could hear Alyssa's bed frame creaking as she tossed and turned, and figured she wasn't getting much rest either. For long moments he stared at the ceiling, fighting the urge to check on her. She'd claimed he was hovering too much, and he supposed she was right.

He couldn't help it. The very idea of Alyssa delivering the twins early sent him into panic mode.

She'd be fine. The twins would be fine. He couldn't control her labor. He had to lighten up a bit.

He jerked upright when Alyssa cried out. In alarm, he leaped out of bed and dashed into her room.

She was moaning, thrashing in the covers, obviously caught in the throes of a bad dream.

"Alyssa," he whispered, putting a calming hand on her shoulder. "Wake up. It's only a dream."

He had to repeat himself several times before his low voice penetrated her subconscious.

"What?" She blinked at him through the darkness. "Jadon?"

"I think you were having a bad dream," he told her, sitting on the edge of her bed, wearing only his boxers. "Are you okay?"

She stared at him for several heartbeats and then slowly nodded. "It was a bad dream. Some guy was chasing me and being pregnant I couldn't run fast enough to get away from him. For some reason he wanted to hurt my babies. When he grabbed me I thought I was going to die. Sorry if I woke you."

"You didn't wake me. I wasn't sleeping." He was glad he'd come in. What an awful dream. "Do you want me to get you something?"

"No." She pushed up and propped herself on her elbows. "But now that I'm awake I need to go to the bathroom."

He chuckled and held out his hand. She took his hand, using his strength to lever herself out of bed.

"Thanks," she murmured, moving past him. Her hair brushed against his bare chest, leaving tiny shocks of awareness.

Jadon took a deep breath and rubbed the back of his neck, knowing he should go back to his own room. Alyssa was fine. He wasn't needed here anymore.

But he waited until she returned. Her white nightgown left her sexy shoulders bare and he had to swallow hard not to show his reaction. "Are you sure you're okay?"

"Yes." Her nightgown rose a bit as she swung her legs back into bed. "The dream was far too real, though."

He didn't want to leave, but forced himself to move toward the door. "Call me if you need me."

"I will. Uh, Jadon?"

He swung back toward her. "Yes?"

"You don't think my dream is some sort of a premonition of something bad happening to the babies, do you?"

"No, of course not." He came back and sat next to her.

She shivered. "It was just so real."

"Do you want me to stay with you for a while?" He didn't want to leave her like this. "I'll hold you until you can fall asleep."

She must have been more shaken than he'd thought because she nodded. "Maybe, just a few minutes, if you don't mind."

All of his senses went on red alert. Lying beside her didn't sound like much, but he was already half-aroused; he wasn't sure he could trust himself to be so close to her.

But his thoughts didn't make it to his mouth. "Sure," he heard himself say. "I don't mind."

"I'm sorry to be such a problem," Alyssa said as he slid beneath the covers on the opposite side of the bed. She lay on her side, facing away from him.

"You're not," he promised, gently snuggling up behind her. He slid his arm under her pillow so he could hold her closer.

"That feels good," she murmured on a sigh, relaxing

against him. "It's hard to get comfortable. My back aches constantly."

With her bottom pressed firmly against his groin he could relate, since he was anything but comfortable. Yet he wasn't about to complain.

Not even when she slipped into sleep, leaving him rock-hard and wide-awake.

CHAPTER SEVEN

ALYSSA woke up with the vague sensation of being nestled in a cocoon. Safe and warm. A sleepy smile curved her mouth. Jadon had stayed with her all night and the nightmare hadn't returned.

How sweet was that?

She enjoyed listening to Jadon's deep, even breaths as he slept beside her. Soon, though, she became aware of his body pressed against her. And she grew warm. Extremely warm. Hot. Very hot.

Aroused.

During the night, the lower edge of her nightgown had crept up around her waist. Jadon's erection pressed urgently against her bottom and his hand rested dangerously close to her breast.

Her breasts, especially her nipples, were hypersensitive. When his hand moved, cupping her breast, she sucked in a quick breath. His fingers lightly brushed the tip of her nipple and instantly her body grew ready. Her breath came in short gasps as she became fully awake. Moisture gathered deep between her thighs and she instinctively arched against him, pressing her bottom more fully against the hard ridge of his desire, wanting him to touch her. Everywhere.

Maybe the reason she yearned for this intimacy with Jadon was because she was pregnant and hadn't felt very attractive these past few months. Despite the twins growing in her abdomen, she was more than a mother-to-be.

She was a woman. And she hadn't been with a man in months. Since the last time she'd been with Jadon.

Obviously meeting men when you were pregnant wasn't easy, but it wouldn't have mattered anyway because she hadn't wanted any other man but Jadon. How could she have convinced herself it was nothing more than an affair?

He groaned, a low raspy sound near her ear as he caressed her breast again. She couldn't see his face to know if he was awake. Or still half-asleep.

She wasn't sure she cared, except for the possibility that if he woke up and realized what he was doing, he might pull away again, like he had after their kiss. And if he did that, she'd probably scream with frustration.

His knee pressed between her legs and she eagerly parted her thighs, opening herself to him. His hand left her breast, lightly caressed her round belly and then moved lower still, until he reached the juncture of her thighs. She held her breath with anticipation as he moved her silky panties out of the way and touched her where she needed him the most.

With his fingers caressing her from the front and his hard erection behind her, Alyssa was trapped in pleasure and didn't want to move. Yet at the same time she ached with the need to have him inside her.

"Please," she whispered, subtly lifting her hips to press against him again.

"Are you sure?" he murmured near her ear, before trailing a string of heated kisses along the side of her neck.

Was he kidding? He was finally treating her like a woman he was attracted to and he thought she had doubts?

"Yes. I'm sure." She pressed urgently against him.

"Easy now," he said, kissing her again and gently stroking her cleft, sending shock waves of pleasure through her body. "Relax. Let me do all the work."

Fine with her if he wanted to do all the work, but could he get on with it? Relaxing when you were aroused was impossible. And he was treating her like she was fragile spun glass instead of a woman who knew exactly what she wanted. She didn't want him to hold back. Reaching around, she tried to pull him closer. She was more than ready. Like ready right now.

He brought her close to the edge of an orgasm before he managed to get rid of her panties and push his boxers out of the way. Her body offered no resistance as he slid deep. The feeling of his thickness inside her, skin against skin, without the barrier of protection, was exquisite.

"Yes. Finally," she gasped.

He pressed another kiss below her ear and pulled her over so that she was lying more fully on top of him. This position not only gave him more access to thrust inside her but also freed up his other hand to caress her breasts.

The sensation was dizzying.

"Jadon," she moaned, wanting the pleasure to last forever yet striving for more.

"Alyssa, tell me if I hurt you," he said between careful thrusts.

"You're not." He was holding back again and that wasn't what she wanted. Then his fingers found the super-sensitive spot between her legs and she gasped, arching her back.

Her climax hit hard and she cried out with pleasure as Jadon crested his pinnacle seconds later. For long moments, the only audible sound in the room was their heavy breathing.

Jadon slid her over to the side, yet held her close. She was happy they'd made love but wished Jadon could have let himself go, the way he once had.

"Alyssa, are you all right? I didn't hurt you or the babies, did I?"

Exasperated, she swiveled her head around to look at him. "Why would you have hurt me? Do you think I'm the only pregnant woman in the world to have sex?"

He propped his head up on his elbow, gazing down at her, a frown puckering his brow. "No, but you were having contractions yesterday. I should have used more restraint."

His gaze was so serious, she knew he was really bothered by the idea that he might have caused some harm. Yet he acted as if he wished they hadn't made love. "Are you always going to treat me like I'm fragile?"

He was taken aback by her sharp tone. "You almost died. Every time I think of you delivering the babies early, my gut gets tied up in knots."

Surprised by his revelation, she arched a brow. Jadon didn't talk about his feelings, ever. "I'm fine. I wish things could go back to the way they were before."

"You can't go back. You're a mother now."

So she wasn't a woman? "And you're a father."

"I know." His expression turned grim. "That wasn't exactly part of my plan."

She tried not to take offense at his honesty. "Is that the real reason you left?"

"No." Jadon pulled away, reaching for his boxers. Apparently his brief display of emotion was over. "I didn't know you were pregnant."

"Would it have mattered?"

He paused, before continuing to pull his boxers on. "Of course it would have mattered. I would have stayed in touch with you while I was gone."

He still would have left. Even now, he was putting distance between them. They'd made love, but nothing had really changed. He was still holding her at arm's length, keeping himself emotionally apart.

And she wasn't satisfied with that. Not anymore.

"Why don't you take a shower? I'll make breakfast."

"Don't wait on me." She didn't hide her annoyance. "I'm perfectly capable of making my own breakfast."

He hardly glanced at her when she slid from the bed to find her clothes. "I'm cooking anyway, so it's no bother."

He had an answer for everything. Discouraged, Alyssa showered, using the hot water to wash away her disappointment. Afterward, she pulled out the first maternity outfit she found. It didn't matter what she wore. Jadon wouldn't notice anyway.

Stop it, she admonished herself. So maybe she and Jadon weren't a happy couple. Too bad. He was the father of her babies and she just had to find a way to deal with it.

She walked to the kitchen, where Jadon had made steamy bowls of oatmeal, topped with cinnamon, brown sugar and raisins. As she sat down, a contraction tightened her abdomen.

Hard.

Worse than she'd experienced the day before.

She mentally ticked off the seconds until the contraction eased, noting that it lasted for over a minute.

Hmm. Not good. She continued eating her breakfast without saying anything to Jadon. He'd only start worrying again. And she wasn't in the mood to be coddled.

But clearly she'd have to give Kim a call. Maybe she'd be lucky and the contractions would stop.

Jadon watched Alyssa eating her oatmeal and mentally talked himself out of taking her back to bed for an encore.

Did she have any idea how much he wanted her? She looked so beautiful, with her dark hair falling in waves around her shoulders, the bright pink long-sleeved maternity top emphasizing the plumpness of her breasts and her gently curved stomach.

Just looking at her made him sweat. He shouldn't have stayed the night in her bed, but he couldn't find the energy for regrets. Not when their morning had started off so great.

He'd been half-asleep that morning when she'd moved against him, silently urging him to touch her. At some level he'd known exactly what he was doing, yet he hadn't been able to make himself stop.

Especially when Alyssa had clearly been egging him on.

But then they'd argued and the time of closeness had

gone. He didn't understand what she wanted from him. No, he hadn't planned on being a father, but he was here with her now, wasn't he? Didn't that count for something?

They couldn't go back. They had to figure out how to move forward. And no matter what, he couldn't give her the happy, close-knit family she wanted. His fault, not hers.

Alyssa rose from her seat at the table, moving stiffly. "Are you all right?" he asked, sure he had hurt her.

She rolled her eyes. "I'm going to sit on the sofa. Do you mind?"

"Not at all." He needed to clean up the kitchen and take a shower, too. "What do you want to do today? Christmas shopping?"

Her annoyance faded and her eyes brightened. "Yes. I'd like to pick up something for Kylie and Seth, and a special present for Ben."

"Good. Let me clean up and shower first."

On his way to the bathroom he heard his cell phone ringing. So he turned back, searching through his pile of dirty laundry, another task he'd have to tackle soon, for the device.

His mother's number was on the display screen. Dread squeezed his intestines and twisted, hard. God, no. Not again. Wishing he could ignore the call, he slowly opened the phone and lifted it to his ear. "Hi, Mom. What is it? What's wrong?"

"Nothing," she swiftly reassured him. "How are you?"

He frowned, not understanding. "Nothing is wrong? You're sure? Jack is doing okay?"

"Yes, actually Jack seems to be doing better. This

new doctor has started a whole new medication regimen and so far Jack is going along with it. He likes the new doctor anyway."

The new doctor he'd pulled strings for his brother to see was a female, which might explain why Jack liked her but he didn't care since Dr. Elizabeth Cranberg was also a renowned expert in treating patients like Jack.

"Good. I'm glad." He knew Jack probably had a long way to go but maybe this was a turning point for his brother. Maybe there was a chance for Jack to lead a relatively normal life.

Foolish hope swelled in his chest. Maybe someday he'd have a normal life, too. "Will you keep me informed on how things go?"

"Of course." His mother didn't sound tired and exhausted like she had before. Instead, it seemed like things were cautiously optimistic with Jack. "Anyway, I called because I'd like to make some plans for the holiday. Do you know when you might be coming home to visit?"

Oh, boy, he'd forgotten his mother's request to have the whole family together for Christmas. Including his father, whom he hadn't seen in years. The stress of Jack's problems had ruined his parents' marriage and his father's subsequent second marriage, too. He needed to tell his parents about Alyssa and the babies, but if he did that, they'd expect her to come along.

He sank down on the edge of his bed, trying to figure out the best way to handle things. He didn't want Alyssa exposed to his problems. She hadn't signed on to be Jack's caretaker, that was his role. He didn't want her involved.

"I have to work Christmas," he reminded her. "I'll see if I can get a couple of consecutive days off, all right?"

"Okay." He could hear the disappointment in his mother's voice. "Are you sure you can't get off for Christmas?"

"I was off work for over four months," he reminded her. "At this point, I'm not in a position to ask for favors."

"I understand," she said hastily, knowing very well why he'd needed to take that time off in the first place. Things had been bad. Jack had gotten completely out of control. "We can celebrate whichever days work best for you."

"All right, I'll be in touch."

"Bye, Jadon. I love you."

Guilt swelled his throat. "I love you, too, Mom."

After he hung up the phone, Jadon realized he couldn't keep the truth about his twin brother a secret from Alyssa for much longer. Alyssa needed to know about Jack, so she'd understand when he had to leave again. And why he couldn't give her what she needed. What she deserved.

He needed to explain everything.

From the very beginning.

Alyssa sat on the sofa, taking slow, deep breaths while waiting for Kim to return her call. She hoped Kim would call while Jadon was still in the shower, but already she could hear him leaving the bathroom and making his way to his bedroom.

The contractions hadn't eased very much. They hadn't gotten any worse, but they certainly hadn't gotten any better either.

She nibbled on her lower lip, wondering what to do. She didn't want to rush to the hospital, yet the medication to prevent contractions didn't seem to be working very well either.

If she didn't hear from Kim in a few hours, she'd go in. Better to be safe than sorry.

"So, have you thought about where you'd like to go Christmas shopping?" Jadon asked, striding into the living room.

"Uh, actually, I'm feeling a bit tired. Do you think it's okay if we do a little online shopping instead of going out?"

His eyebrows rose in surprise. "We can, but are you sure? I thought you'd be ready for a change in scenery." He glanced toward the window. "It's not snowing."

"It's not the weather. I've had a couple of contractions," she admitted, knowing he was going to ask in a minute anyway. "And, yes, I've already called Kim Rayborn but she's busy with a delivery so I left a message for her to call me back."

"Dammit," Jadon muttered. "We shouldn't have made love."

"You don't know for sure sex caused the contractions." She removed her feet from the top of the coffee table and struggled to stand.

"Where are you going?" Jadon asked in alarm, jumping over to her. His strong hands lifted her from the soft sofa cushions without difficulty. "Stay put. I'll get my laptop computer if you want to shop online."

She sighed. "I'm going to the bathroom. You can't help me with that."

"Oh. Okay." His expression was sheepish. "I'll turn on the computer while you're gone."

"All right." She took a few steps but then stopped as

another contraction hit. Moisture gushed down between her thighs and for a horrified moment she thought she'd lost control of her bladder. But looking down, she realized there was a lot of fluid. Clear fluid. Amniotic fluid.

"Um, Jadon? You'd better forget about the computer. I think my waters just broke."

CHAPTER EIGHT

ALYSSA tried not to show her panic as one of her ED coworkers, Susan, wheeled her upstairs to the third-floor labor and delivery area.

Kim crossed over to greet her as she rolled in. "Alyssa, how are you? I just picked up your message and suddenly you're here. What happened? Have your contractions gotten worse?"

"My waters broke." She kept a hand on her stomach, forcing a smile for Jadon's sake. "And yes, the contractions have gotten worse. Not only are they coming more frequently and regularly at seven minutes apart, but they're lasting longer, too."

"Well, it's clear those twins are not going to wait any longer to be born," Kim said. "Looks like we'll be getting you ready for delivery."

"They're still pretty early, aren't they?" Jadon asked, concern evident in his tone.

Kim nodded. "A bit. But they're thirty-one weeks along now, which is one more week's worth of growing. I'm sure everything will be just fine."

A week's worth of growing didn't sound like very much. And she wished more than anything she could believe everything would be fine. Reality set in as another contraction tightened her abdomen.

"Neenah?" A nurse hurried over when Kim called, a young woman Alyssa didn't recognize. "Let's get Alyssa settled into room six. I'd like to get her twins hooked up to the fetal monitors to see how they're doing."

"Of course," Neenah said, taking over behind the wheelchair. "Alyssa? My name is Neenah Burnes and I'll be your nurse for today."

Alyssa nodded, but her mind was struggling to come to grips with what was happening. She was in labor. She was going to deliver her babies. Twins. Jiminy Cricket, how on earth was she going to manage? What if she couldn't handle the pressure of raising a baby? Two babies? Her mother had struggled with the demands of single parenthood.

At least Jadon was here, so she wasn't nearly as alone as her mother had been. And even though she wanted more from him at the moment, she'd take what she could get.

Neenah helped her move from the wheelchair onto the bed, shooing Jadon out so she could change into a hospital gown. He'd been suspiciously quiet and Alyssa couldn't help wondering if he regretted being here with her. She suspected the prospect of fatherhood scared him.

Would he stay with her during the delivery? Or should she call Kylie to be her coach?

When she was settled in bed, the fetal heart monitors in place, she took several deep breaths, trying to relax. Stress was not good. Especially not now.

"Jadon?" she called.

"I'm here." He came in, and took her hand in his. They'd given him scrubs to wear. "What's wrong? Another contraction?"

"Yes." They were coming even more frequently now. "Kylie was supposed to be my labor coach. But I'd rather have you. If you don't mind."

He stared at her for a long moment. "I don't mind. They're my babies, too."

"I know." She sucked in a harsh breath as the contraction crested, sending shock waves of pain through her whole body. "Oh, boy, that was a strong one," she whispered as it finally eased.

Jadon cradled her hand in both of his. "It's okay, Alyssa. I'm here. I'll help you through this."

He wasn't going to leave, or call Kylie. He was going to stay.

"I need to do a quick exam, to see how far along you are," Kim said, coming into the room dressed in fresh scrubs and pulling on a pair of gloves.

Alyssa couldn't help it, she tightened her grip on Jadon's hand, full of apprehensive fear. He pulled up a chair with his foot and sat right next to her bed, staying close.

Kim lifted the sheet and Alyssa's hospital gown and then gently eased her thighs open. "Good heavens, you're already five centimeters dilated. I suspect these babies are going to be born very quickly."

"Good." Another contraction tightened her abdomen and she glanced over at Jadon. "Don't leave me," she begged through clenched teeth.

Not just for now, but forever. She didn't want Jadon to leave her alone ever again, but as the contraction grew tighter and tighter, she didn't have a chance to explain.

"I won't," Jadon promised.

She wanted nothing more than to believe him.

Watching Alyssa suffer through one contraction after another was enough to make him swear off sex forever. Sweat beaded on his forehead, trickling in rivulets down his back, and he wasn't even the one doing all the work.

This was all his fault, for not having enough self-control to protect her from becoming pregnant in the first place all those months ago. And, again, for allowing his desire to overcome his common sense that morning.

He was about to become a father.

Panic tightened his throat. Juggling his responsibilities with Jack had been hard enough before, but the twins' impending birth just made it that much more complicated.

He'd promised Alyssa he'd stay, and he'd sensed she meant more than just during the delivery. But what if Jack needed him again? He couldn't abandon his mother. If Jack needed him, he'd be forced to leave.

He turned his attention to Alyssa, and within moments the entire labor room had been converted into a delivery suite, complete with a neonatal team on standby in case the twins needed them.

He was a doctor, had seen births a couple of times before, but nothing could have prepared him for the miracle of watching his children being born.

"Come on, Alyssa, one more big push," Kim was saying. "You're almost there. The first baby is crowning."

Tears streaked Alyssa's cheeks but she didn't sob or cry out. She simply gritted her teeth and pushed, nearly crushing all the bones in his hand in the process.

"Wonderful! Perfect. Congratulations, you have a beautiful daughter."

Jadon's grin almost split his face. "Can you see her, Lys? She's absolutely beautiful."

Alyssa nodded. "Is she okay? How big do you think she is?"

"We'll get her weighed and measured in a jiffy," Kim promised, handing the infant over to Renee, one of the neonatal ICU nurses who was part of the resuscitation team. She took the baby to the first isolette and began the exam with the help of the neonatologist.

Jadon knew they needed to do an Apgar assessment on the baby, along with placing the proper identification bracelets, so he didn't leave Alyssa's side, even though he was anxious to meet his daughter.

He was a father. He could barely wrap his mind around the concept. More responsibility. Double the responsibility.

"Oh, no, another contraction," Alyssa whimpered.

"This might be the placenta," Kim warned. "I know it's tough, Alyssa, but hang in there. You're halfway there."

"Only halfway," she groaned, panting through another contraction. "Doesn't seem fair."

Jadon leaned down to press his lips to her forehead. He shared her pain. "I know. I wish I could do this for you."

"You and me both," she said with a groan.

"Knight baby girl number one weighs in at three

pounds, nine ounces," Renee announced for everyone to hear. "And she's seventeen and a half inches long."

Alyssa smiled. "Three pounds nine ounces is pretty good, right? Is she breathing on her own?"

"Yes, so far she's breathing fine. Don't worry," Kim told her. "Your job is to deliver this next baby."

As if on cue, another contraction caused her to grab Jadon's hand again. Her determined gaze met his. "I think baby number two is on his or her way."

Jadon wasn't sure what to expect. He was an identical twin, but women Alyssa's age were prone to fraternal twins. Either way, he didn't care. He was still in awe about having a daughter. "Slow, easy breaths," he instructed. "Don't think about the pain, think about the baby."

The second birth went faster and within another minute Alyssa was pushing again.

"Congrats, you have another beautiful daughter," Kim announced with a laugh. "Beautiful twin girls."

The second baby girl was passed on to the neonatal team as well and from where he stood, Jadon could tell the second baby was slightly smaller than the first one. They didn't look identical, but they were pretty small so it was difficult to tell. Although a little more than three and a half pounds was not a bad size for a preemie.

And if both babies could breathe without any help from a mask or a ventilator, that was a minor miracle in itself.

"You did a great job," Jadon said, kissing Alyssa lightly on the mouth. "I'm proud of you."

"Thanks." This time she smiled through her tears. "I can't believe we have daughters."

"Beautiful twin daughters," Kim corrected with a smile. "Have you thought of names yet?"

Alyssa nodded. "I've chosen Grace Aubrey for the older baby and Gretchen Louise for the younger one." Her gaze darted to his. "I, uh, hope you don't mind."

What could he say? It wasn't as if they'd been together these past few months, planning for this day. Alyssa had been on her own. Of course she'd picked names for the babies.

"Grace and Gretchen are beautiful names." A part of him wished their last names would be listed as his, rather than Alyssa's last name of Knight, but that wasn't meant to be.

"My grandmother's name was Grace and my mom's name was Louise, so I wanted to include both their names in their memory if the babies were girls," she explained, as if expecting some sort of argument.

"Alyssa, the names are fine," he reassured her. "I love them, don't worry."

She nodded and relaxed. "When can we hold them?" she asked Kim. "I'm anxious to see my babies."

"Just a few more minutes and the neonatal team should be finished with them." Kim began cleaning up the delivery area. "One good thing about having small babies is that you didn't need an episiotomy and there are no vaginal tears either. You should heal up very nicely."

"One bright spot as I'm trying to breast-feed two babies," Alyssa said with a dry laugh. But then she caught the doctor's hand, giving it a grateful squeeze. "Thanks, Kim. For everything."

"My pleasure." Kim glanced at Jadon, including him as well. "Congrats to both of you."

"Knight baby girl number two is three pounds, three

ounces, and is seventeen and a quarter inches long," Renee announced. "She's breathing on her own, too."

Three-three wasn't bad at all. Jadon grinned as the tight knot in his stomach relaxed a bit. "Gretchen Louise. The younger, smaller baby is Gretchen."

"And the older one is Grace Aubrey," Alyssa chimed in. "Can we hold them now?"

"You sure can. Here's Grace for you, Mom. And Gretchen for you, Dad." Renee and another nurse handed each of them a tightly wrapped pink bundle. "We don't want to keep them out of the isolettes too long. We still need to keep a close eye on them, but bonding is important, too."

Jadon gazed at Gretchen's small, perfect face, her tiny lips, her button nose and her tiny, tiny eyelashes with an overwhelming sense of awe.

He glanced at Alyssa and in that moment they shared a special intimacy, a bond that shook him to the soles of his feet.

Together, they'd created these baby girls.

Looking at Alyssa holding Grace and the way Gretchen slept so peacefully in his arms, he realized what he'd told her earlier was true. There was no turning back. He was a father now.

This new, precious family was a part of his future. His and Alyssa's future.

If only he knew how in the world he was going to make it work.

Alyssa rested for a few hours after the birth as the process had totally worn her out, but when she awoke she was alone in her room. She missed her babies. On the bedside table were two photographs, so she picked them up to gaze at the small pictures of Grace and Gretchen that the neonatal resuscitation team had given her.

The babies were small, but doing amazingly well. Kim had explained that the stress of her labor over the past few days had helped the babies develop enough surfactant in their lungs to enable them to breathe on their own.

At least, so far they were breathing on their own. The girls might need some help from a CPAP machine, which wasn't as invasive as a breathing tube and ventilator, if they didn't maintain regular breathing patterns, keeping an acceptable level of oxygen in the blood.

Renee had explained the concerns about intermittent apnea, a common phenomenon with preemies. They could breathe on their own, but it was almost as if they exerted so much energy to do the work they got tired out and stopped breathing for a few seconds.

So the baby girls would need to be on the heart and apnea monitors for a while, not to mention kept warm since their tiny brains weren't fully developed yet to keep their temperatures stable. Hence the pictures, since Alyssa couldn't have the babies housed in her room.

She was relieved they were doing so well.

Yet she didn't want to look at pictures, she wanted to hold her daughters, touch them. Cuddle them.

Was Jadon in the neonatal nursery with them now? She was fairly certain he was. She bit her lip, anxiety creeping back into her chest. He'd been so wonderful through all this, taken on the role of being her birthing coach without making her feel guilty.

Her baby girls were seven weeks early. What would

she do once they were big enough to come home? She knew she shouldn't just plan on going back to Jadon's house but if she didn't, how would she manage to nurse them both while still managing to get some rest?

Was Jadon's invitation to stay with him still open? She didn't want her babies to suffer in any way. What if after a few weeks of no sleep he changed his mind?

Stop looking for trouble, she warned herself. Take it slowly, one day at a time, and the future would sort itself out when it was ready.

Sage advice. Now, if only she could heed it.

She swung her legs out of the bed and stood, feeling only a slight twinge of discomfort after her delivery. Reaching for a robe, she put it on, then walked out into the hallway to get directions to the neonatal intensive care unit.

"Right here," Amanda, a helpful nurse, informed her. "We actually don't call them neonatal ICUs any more, we call it a level-three nursery. But it's right next to the level-two and level-one nurseries. As your babies progress, they'll move down to the less acute area."

"Good to know," Alyssa admitted. Neonatal was not her area of expertise.

In the level-three nursery, most of the babies lying in their isolettes looked extremely tiny. She was somewhat relieved to realize her daughters were the largest babies in the group.

She stood in front of their isolettes, surprised to note Jadon wasn't there. One nurse approached with a warm smile.

"Hi, my name is Carla. I'm the second-shift nurse taking care of Grace and Gretchen."

"Hello, I'm Alyssa, the proud mother of these two. Oh, look, Gretch is waking up," she said, leaning over when Gretchen began to stir.

"She is waking up. It's about time as she's been sleeping quite a bit. What a wonderful early Christmas present you have, hmm?"

Alyssa smiled weakly. "A better Christmas present would be to have them home with me."

"True, but if they grow nicely and don't run into trouble, that is a distinct possibility. Now, would you like to hold them? Both at once or one at a time?"

"Maybe just Gretchen, since she's awake." Alyssa figured she'd need to learn how to manage both babies at the same time eventually, but for now she thought easing into the process of learning about her daughters might be the better approach.

"Okay. Both girls have apnea monitors on, so we can watch their heart rates and breathing. I'll fetch a warm blanket." Carla hurried off, returning with a warm fuzzy pink blanket.

She opened the isolette and competently lifted Gretchen with one hand, taking care not to disturb the wires connecting the patches to the infant's chest or the tiny IV as she slid the warm blanket underneath with the other hand. After tucking her cozily inside, she gently lifted Gretchen out and set the bundle in the crook of Alyssa's arm. "Here you go."

"Oh, she's so adorable." And tiny, especially being the smaller of the two. She clutched the baby protectively to her chest, infused with a wave of love. She'd do anything for her children. Anything.

Gretchen moved her head toward her breast in a

rooting movement, her tiny mouth making sucking motions. Alyssa drew a quick breath of excitement and glanced at Carla. "Look, do you think she'll be able to nurse?"

"It's possible," Carla agreed with a smile. "Your milk hasn't come in, but the colostrum they'll receive is even more healthy than milk. And worth a try, don't you think?"

"Yes." She was a little uncertain how to go about the whole process but Carla was great, helping her with techniques to encourage Gretchen to latch on. The baby only suckled for a few minutes before stopping.

"Don't worry, preemie babies do tire easily. Once your milk comes in more fully, we'll give intermittent feedings of your breast milk as often as the babies need it."

"But what if they're not strong enough to drink as much as they need?" Alyssa asked.

"We'll give feedings through a nasogastric tube."

A nasogastric tube didn't sound good, but she tried not to show her discouragement. Carla tucked Gretchen back in her isolette and then drew Grace out for her turn. Gracie latched on to her nipple a little quicker than Gretchen, but also seemed to get tired quickly. Alyssa wasn't sure either of the babies got any nourishment at all from the attempt.

"How am I going to keep up with breast-feeding both of them?" she asked, after she'd finished with Grace. The responsibility was daunting and she suddenly doubted her ability to be a good mother to the twins. "At this rate, they might need to be fed every hour."

Carla put a reassuring hand on her shoulder. "Nursing is a wonderful experience, but the nutritional value of your breast milk is what's most important for these little ones. Even if they can't nurse for lengthy periods, they can get the nourishment they need if you pump your breasts and freeze your milk. We can feed them through a nasogastric tube if need be and then through a bottle. At least with bottle feedings, Dad can be more involved, too."

Jadon. The image of his strong, large hands holding and feeding their daughters filled her with a mixture of longing and trepidation. Would he stick around for the long term? Or would he get tired of the responsibility of having a family and leave, like her father had?

At least now he could stop being so protective of her. Although she suspected he'd shower the babies with his concern instead.

"Was Jadon here?" she asked Carla.

"Yes, he spent a lot of time with the girls. He asked Dr. Downer, the neonatologist, lots of questions. I think he left about an hour ago, maybe a little more."

An hour ago? He hadn't been in her room when she'd woken up.

Her stomach clenched with anxiety. So where was he?

CHAPTER NINE

So THIS was it. The beginning of the end. Jadon was gone. Alyssa walked back to her room, trying not to feel overwhelmed by the concept of raising the girls all by herself.

When she crossed the threshold, she stopped, startled to see a huge bouquet of more than a dozen pink roses in a vase on her bedside table. There were also two pink "It's A Girl" balloons tied to the side-rail of her bed.

She read the small card tucked between the roses, feeling ashamed for doubting him when she realized the flowers and balloons were gifts from Jadon.

"Arranged some extra time off work, then ran home to get your suitcase. Be back soon, Jadon."

He hadn't left unexpectedly, other than to talk to his boss about having time off and to buy flowers and balloons. Ashamed, she realized she'd jumped to conclusions. He hadn't left her. He wasn't like her father. They must have just missed each other.

She counted eighteen blooms, stroking the velvet-soft petals with the tip of her index finger. Another first. Not quite as monumental as giving birth to twins, but she'd never received pink roses before. Or any other color roses. Not from Jadon or from anyone else.

He'd been so sweet and so supportive during the few hours she'd spent in labor, and afterward when they'd both been given the chance to hold their newly born daughters. She found it difficult to reconcile this new Jadon with the emotionally distant man who'd made love to her and then left without saying a word.

Let it go, she told herself. There's no reason to keep dwelling on the past. Jadon was here now, had gone as far as to ask her to move in with him. Maybe there was still some hope for them. Maybe he'd learn to show his feelings. Maybe she could trust him with her heart.

She was glad he'd gone to get her things.

Because she wouldn't mind wearing something other than the shapeless hospital gown to help her look a bit more attractive.

Jadon returned right after she finished with her dinner tray. "Do you want me to call the nurse to bring another tray for you?" she offered.

"No, thanks, I'm fine. I grabbed something quick right after I left." He set her small suitcase on the floor beside her bed.

"Thanks for the roses and the balloons," she said. "They were a nice surprise when I returned to my room after seeing Grace and Gretchen."

"You're welcome." He pulled up a chair beside her bed. "I spoke to Louis Downer, the neonatologist assigned to Grace and Gretch, and he really feels like the girls are doing amazingly well for being seven weeks early."

"I'm glad. Although I did try breast-feeding earlier and neither of the girls suckled for very long." She blushed when she noticed Jadon's gaze dropped to her breasts. Was he imagining how large and full her breasts were now? "The nurse told me the girls might need tube feedings."

Jadon nodded. "Yes, Louis mentioned that possibility to me as well. But tube feedings aren't the worst thing in the world. As long as they get nourishment and continue to grow, that's what really matters. Do you plan to, ah, continue nursing?"

She knew he was dancing around the issue of asking if she planned to pump her breasts to provide breast milk if the girls couldn't nurse on their own. "Yes, because at this point they need every possible advantage they can get."

"Very true." Jadon looked relieved at the news. "Louis warned me that both girls will likely need to be placed under the bili-lights, too. Even full-term babies sometimes need the bili-lights, but preemies even more so as their livers aren't fully developed yet."

"I know, I pretty much expected that." She'd learned a few things during her nursing school rotation through OB, but was hardly an expert.

"Alyssa, I think we need to talk about the future, maybe not right now but soon. Once you're discharged and back home." His serious, earnest gaze warmed her heart.

Home as in back at his house? She thought so. She saw his willingness to talk as a good sign. "I know."

"So that's settled," he said with satisfaction. "How about if we go and visit our daughters again?"

"I'd like that." She threw aside the blanket and

grimaced a little when she swung her legs over the side of the bed.

"Are you all right?" Jadon asked, noticing her discomfort. "Do you want me to get you a wheelchair?"

"No wheelchair, I'd rather walk." She bent down to grab the suitcase he'd brought in. "But first I need a few minutes in the bathroom."

"Sure." He relaxed in his chair, not seeming to be in the least bit impatient. "No rush."

In the bathroom she quickly changed into her own nightgown and robe, feeling a little better wearing her own things. The nightgown had a lace-tie in the front that would help if she tried nursing the girls again.

Jadon lightly clasped her hand as they walked down to the level-three nursery. Jadon led the way straight to Grace and Gretchen's isolettes.

"Are you here to hold your babies?" Carla asked, crossing over to them. "Let me grab a couple of warm blankets for you, all right?"

"Okay." Alyssa leaned forward, dividing her attention between both babies. "Aren't they cute, wearing those little pink hats?"

"They're adorable," Jadon agreed in a husky voice. "Beautiful, just like their mother."

Her heart swelled with love as she gazed at her daughters. Jadon had created these wonderful miracles with her. "Which one do you want to hold?" she asked him.

"I'll take Grace this time. I feel like we should alternate so we don't play favorites."

"I think it's a little early to worry about playing favorites," Alyssa said with a small laugh.

Carla returned with the warm blankets and quickly

wrapped up both babies and handed Grace to Jadon, and Gretchen to Alyssa.

They sat in side-by-side rockers, content to simply hold the babies.

"Lys?" Jadon said, glancing up at her. "You are going to come back home with me after you're discharged, right?"

"Yes." She frowned a little because she'd thought that was what he'd meant earlier.

"I knew you'd be discharged in the next day or two, but I also know that Louis thought the babies would be here for maybe a couple of weeks," Jadon explained. "So I wanted to make sure."

"A couple of weeks?" It was hard to hide her dismay. "He really thinks they'll need to stay that long? I was hoping we'd have them home by Christmas."

"Christmas is just over two weeks away, so don't be discouraged. We may get to take them home by then. Depending on how much weight they gain. And how well their breathing progresses."

"Alyssa?" Denise, her postpartum nurse, came into the nursery. "You have a couple of visitors, and there's one little boy especially who would like to see the babies."

"Kylie and Seth must have brought Ben," she said to Jadon before turning to Carla. "Do you think we could hold the babies up in the window for Ben to see? I'd hate to disappoint him."

"No problem," Carla said. "We'll just have to momentarily disconnect them from the monitors." At her panicked expression, Carla hastily reassured her. "Don't worry, we do that from time to time anyway, like to give them a bath. It's not a big deal for a few minutes."

"I'll bring the group over to the window," Denise said as she turned to leave the nursery.

Carla disconnected the twins from their monitors so that Alyssa and Jadon could hold the babies up in the window for Seth, Kylie and Ben to see.

"Wow, they're so tiny!" she heard Ben exclaim.

"Very tiny," Kylie agreed with a wide grin. "They're beautiful, Alyssa," she called through the glass.

"Thanks." She and Jadon only stayed for a minute, before turning back so that Carla could reconnect the babies to their monitors. Then they tucked the girls back into their isolettes and headed out to visit with Seth and Kylie.

"Hey, congrats to both of you," Seth said when they met up in the hall. He held out a hand to Jadon, who looked somewhat bemused as he accepted the handshake. Seth then turned to give Alyssa a hug. "You didn't call us," he complained in a light, teasing tone. "I had to hear the news from the ED staff."

"Yeah, and I thought I was supposed to be your birthing coach?" Kylie added, giving both Alyssa and Jadon a hug. "Looks like you did fine without me."

"I'm sorry, Kylie," Alyssa said. "Everything happened so fast."

Kylie rolled her eyes. "I'm only kidding, it's not a big deal. I'm just glad they're both doing all right."

"How come I can't hold the babies?" Ben wanted to know.

Alyssa reached down to give him a hug. "They're too little yet. We need to restrict visitors until the babies grow bigger and get stronger."

Ben looked disappointed.

"Ben, don't forget to give Alyssa the card you made for her," Kylie reminded him.

"Oh, yeah." He looked down at the rather crumpled piece of paper that he'd been clutching in his hand as if he'd forgotten all about it. "Here." He thrust it at Alyssa.

"Thank you, Ben. It's beautiful." He'd written a crooked "Congratulations, Alyssa" on the front with what she assumed were two babies in cribs and not tiny people in jail drawn on the bottom of the page. Inside the card he'd painstakingly penned a short message that she read out loud. "'Thanks for saving my life. I love you, Ben.'"

For a moment the words swam in her vision as her eyes misted. She drew him close for another hug. "This is my favorite card in the whole world, Ben. Thanks so much."

"Welcome," he muttered, giving her a tight hug and then breaking away, his attention already moving to the next thing. "Can we get something out of the vending machine, Mom?"

Seth and Kylie exchanged a questioning glance and when Kylie nodded, Seth dug several quarters out of his pocket. "Sure, here you go, sport."

"Cool!" Ben dashed off.

"Jadon, I picked up your Saturday-night shift for you," Seth informed him.

"Thanks." Jadon looked pleasantly surprised. "I appreciate it."

"No problem." Seth shrugged it off but Alyssa knew the gesture was a peace offering. She and Kylie exchanged knowing grins.

Shortly after Ben returned, Kylie and Seth prepared to leave. After they left, promising to return for another visit soon, Jadon stood, too. "I'd better let you get some rest."

She masked her disappointment, knowing there was no reason for Jadon to stay overnight. She was fine. Gracie and Gretchen were fine. He deserved a good night's sleep, which he wouldn't get sleeping on a recliner in her room.

"All right. Get some sleep," she told him.

"You, too." He leaned over and kissed her. For a moment their lips clung and then he deepened the kiss, exploring her mouth in a way that made her breathless when he finally lifted his head.

"See you tomorrow," he promised in a husky voice.

She relaxed against the pillows, her lips tingling from his kiss, and nodded.

This time she believed him.

"Simon, are you off work yet?" Jadon demanded over his cell phone. It was late, eleven-thirty at night, and he'd been waiting impatiently for Simon's call. "I need your help."

"Yes, I just finished, we had another busy night. Why? What's up?"

"I'm at Alyssa's apartment. I need your help to move the two cribs, the baby swings, the dressers, and every-thing else that she has here in her storage bin to my place."

Simon let out a heavy sigh. "Where in the heck are you going to put all that stuff?" he asked.

"At my house," Jadon repeated as if he were a tad slow. "I rented the truck again this afternoon so I have most of the stuff loaded in there already, except those two baby dressers because they're darned heavy."

"I'll be right there," Simon said in a resigned tone.

Jadon knew he'd set an almost impossible task, getting the bedroom totally painted and the furniture all set up as a surprise for Alyssa once she was discharged from the hospital. Yet he also knew he'd get it done, even if he had to stay up all night.

Simon arrived and they carried the two baby dressers down to the truck. Once they arrived at Jadon's house, he elicited Simon's help to take apart Alyssa's bedroom set.

His friend placed his hands on his hips. "But if we take Alyssa's bed down, where is she going to sleep?" he asked with feigned innocence.

Jadon sent him a narrow glance. "Ha, ha. Very funny. Give me a hand, will you?"

"Okay, but remember it was only a couple of days ago that you asked me to help you put it together in the first place."

He grimaced. "I know. But we didn't plan on having the girls seven weeks early either."

"Listen to you," Simon said as he took a screwdriver and attacked the bed frame. "You sound like an old married man."

His words made Jadon's stomach clench. He still wasn't sure how he was going to handle things, but somehow he'd make it work. He didn't really have a choice. "Alyssa's going to be thrilled to see this," he said. "I'm painting the walls pink."

"Pink?" Simon's gaze was skeptical. "You might reconsider. You're going to get sick of pink with two girls."

"Never." Jadon grinned as he hauled the mattresses

out of the room. He was going to store Alyssa's bedroom set down in the basement for now. Simon had already helped him haul all the baby stuff inside, so maneuvering through the living room with the mattresses wasn't easy.

He didn't mind. He already had everything all planned out. Once Alyssa had been discharged from the hospital he'd bring her here to see the nursery he'd made for their daughters and then he'd tell her the truth about his brother.

The answer to his problems was simple. He could keep his dysfunctional family separate from his new one. With this arrangement, he could minimize the stress of Jack's illness for Alyssa and the girls.

This could work.

The next day Jadon didn't show up until almost noon, and even then he looked awful, ragged and exhausted as if he hadn't gotten much sleep.

"What happened?" Alyssa asked in alarm. "Did you get called in to work?"

"No, I just had trouble sleeping, that's all." He yawned widely, but then opened his eyes wide as if to prove he was really awake. "It's not a big deal. I'm fine."

She wasn't so sure. What on earth had kept him up all night? It wasn't as if there was anything to worry about or to stress over.

Except being a father.

Her stomach tightened. That had to be it. Was he having second thoughts about asking her to stay with him? Was the stress going to eventually get to him, making him leave? Did Jadon really want a fully committed relationship? Or was he already backing off?

She needed to stop imagining the worst.

"Have you seen the babies yet today?" he asked, changing the subject.

"Yes. I tried to nurse again this morning, but they didn't do very well again. So I learned all about the breast pump." She made a face.

"I thought it took a few days for your milk to come in?" he asked, as if having a detailed conversation about breast-feeding was perfectly natural.

Which didn't give the impression he was having second thoughts.

"It does. But the colostrum that's there before the milk comes in is very good for the babies, too, and my milk won't come in unless I nurse." Darn it, she could feel her cheeks getting warm again. Why was she embarrassed? Their tentative relationship seemed to be going well; there was no reason for her to overreact like this.

"And they're still breathing fine on their own?"

She nodded. "Yes, even Gretchen, although she seems to be having more of that apneic breathing that they're so concerned about. Grace has it, too, but I guess Gretchen's percentages are a little higher."

"Hmm. Something to ask Louis about, I guess. Do you mind if we go down to see them again?" Jadon asked. "Or if you're too tired, I can go myself."

"I'm not too tired," she assured him, getting up out of bed. She was moving much better today and, as Kim had promised, was hardly sore at all. She'd spent over two hours in the level-three nursery that morning, but she didn't mind going again.

Soon the babies would be her responsibility, full-time. Jadon would help, but she'd still better get used to it.

"Do you realize the girls are now a little more than twenty-four hours old?" Jadon announced as they made their way down the hall.

She had to smile. "Yes, I know. I was there, too, remember?"

"It's just so amazing." He took her hand again and she reveled in the closeness as they made their way through to the nursery.

This time she took Grace and Jadon took Gretchen. Although Gretchen was very sleepy, they traded off after a while.

Louis Downer came in to make rounds while they were there. "Hi, Jadon. Alyssa, how are you feeling today?"

"I'm fine, although I'm a little worried about how the girls still aren't suckling very much," she admitted.

"I know. But we'll give them tube feedings so they'll still grow fine." He glanced at the babies they held in their respective grasps. "Which one is Gretchen?"

"I have Gretchen," Alyssa said. "Why?"

"I'd like to examine her first. Her chest X-ray didn't look as good as I would have liked this morning."

Alarmed, she glanced at Jadon as she handed the infant to the neonatologist. "Do you think she's sick?"

"Just something to keep an eye on," he assured her, as he took the tiny twin. He gently set her back in her isolette, and then unwrapped the blanket from around her chest so he could listen. After he'd removed the stethoscope from his ears, he picked up her clipboard and reviewed her vital signs.

Alyssa craned her neck, so she could see, too.

"Well?" Jadon asked, when Louis set the clipboard aside and turned back toward them.

"She's started to run a slight fever," Louis admitted. "I'm going to treat her with IV antibiotics because I suspect she's showing early signs of pneumonia."

CHAPTER TEN

JADON wanted to reassure Alyssa that Gretchen would be all right, but it was difficult to put aside his own fears. She was so tiny, it was hard to imagine how her immune system would fight off something as serious as pneumonia. And there was the additional concern about how well her premature kidneys would tolerate the antibiotics. Not to mention how she'd maintain her oxygenation levels with lungs full of infection.

There was no doubt the next twenty-four hours would be critical for Gretchen.

And there was nothing he could do to help her.

Alyssa refused to leave. Watching her keeping vigil over Gretchen was difficult. After several hours Jadon had had enough. "You need some rest," he pointed out in a low tone. "And it's close to dinnertime. Let's go back to your room."

"No. I want to stay here." Alyssa had been staring at the monitor over Gretchen's isolette for so long she was starting to look like a zombie. It was as if her emotions had completely shut down. He understood how she felt—he'd always done the same thing when faced with one of Jack's crises, shutting away the pain so it couldn't hurt. Still, he didn't like the idea of Alyssa sitting by the girls' isolettes all night long.

"Alyssa, look at me," he demanded in a sharp tone, breaking through her zombie-like stare.

Reluctantly, she turned to meet his gaze, her eyes dull with resigned acceptance.

"Wearing yourself to the brink of exhaustion isn't good for you or for Grace. We have two daughters, remember? You need to eat, to keep up your strength and your nutrition, as you've told me you want to continue to provide breast milk for them."

Alyssa slowly nodded, as if agreeing with him. But she didn't move to leave.

He intended to keep pushing, to do what was best no matter what it took. He reached down, grasped her hand and tugged her to her feet. "Let's go. We need to head back to your room."

For a heart-stopping moment Alyssa looked as if she might burst into tears, but she allowed herself to be drawn upright. "You're right. I know you are. But I just can't bear to leave her. What if something happens while we're gone?"

He understood her angst because he felt it, too. He pulled her into his arms, enfolding her in a warm hug. "I know it's difficult to leave, but she'll be okay."

Alyssa didn't push him away as he half expected, but clung to him, burying her face against his chest, as if she couldn't stand under her own power. He could feel the dampness of her tears soaking his shirt. He held her close for countless minutes as he silently offered his strength and support, drawing strength from her closeness as well.

It was much easier to face the hardship together.

Although hardships also had the power to drag people apart, too.

Finally she drew a ragged breath and lifted her head. "Do you think Carla will call us if anything changes?"

He lifted his hands to cradle her face, using his thumbs to wipe away her tears. "Yes, I know she will. But I honestly think Gretchen is going to be fine. Louis Downer is a good doctor. Our daughter is getting the best care available. Besides, Gretch is a fighter. She'll be fine, you'll see."

"She barely weighs three pounds," Alyssa murmured, swinging around to stare down at Gretchen lying in her isolette. Both babies had lost a few ounces after the delivery, which was completely normal.

"I know," he soothed, despite the grim certainty of knowing there were no guarantees. "But think about all these other tiny babies, most of them less than three pounds, and they're doing all right."

Alyssa's mouth turned up in a watery smile. "They are all very tiny, aren't they? You're right, Gretchen is one of the larger babies in here. She'll fight this and win."

"Of course she will." He slid his arm around her waist, turning her slowly away from the babies and encouraging her to walk along with him out of the nursery.

"How did she get pneumonia so quickly?" she fretted as they made their way back to her room.

"She was in utero longer than Grace," he reminded her. "Maybe she aspirated during the delivery."

He'd heard the story about his and Jack's birth and the circumstances were eerily similar to those of Grace and Gretchen. Except he'd been the smaller, younger baby, in fact, much smaller than Gretchen.

He slammed a door on those wayward thoughts. The last thing he wanted to do was to draw comparisons between his daughters and how events had unfolded between him and his brother. There were plenty of neonates who got sick. A little pneumonia wasn't the end of the world.

And no matter what, he was going to pay attention to both of his children—focusing on their strengths and offering encouragement no matter how different their personalities.

He managed to keep Alyssa resting in her room for a full hour while they ate dinner, but when they'd finished, she insisted on returning to the nursery.

He accompanied her back to see Grace and Gretchen, noting the nursing staff had been required to change Gretchen's IV site already because her other one had blown. Knowing it was a common occurrence for infants didn't make looking at her bruised yet delicate skin any easier.

"Poor Gretch," Alyssa murmured.

"Let me hold her for a while," he said to the nurse. "I'll keep her in the isolette as she's getting another dose of antibiotics, but I'll cradle her in my hands for a bit."

"Of course," Carla said, gesturing to the isolette. "Go right ahead. The more you hold her, the more she'll become used to your scent and your touch."

"I know." He gently lifted a listless Gretchen off the blanket, drawing the tip of his finger down the side of her cheek in a slight caress.

He'd tried to be strong for Alyssa, but as he stared down at Gretchen, he silently prayed his tiny daughter would make it through unscathed. That she'd not only make it over this hurdle of pneumonia but also over all the other hurdles she'd face throughout her life.

There were some things he couldn't do for her. And fighting off this infection was one of those things. There would be others as well.

The responsibility of fatherhood weighed heavily on his shoulders.

Alyssa had to bite her lip hard to prevent herself from crying out as Dr. Downer placed a tiny CPAP mask over Gretchen's face, the device totally engulfing her cute button nose and perfectly formed mouth. The apparatus seemed overly large and invasive against her tiny, dainty features.

Her daughter was sick. Very sick. And she couldn't simply tell herself Gretchen would get through this, because she wasn't certain she would.

How could such a small baby fight off a life-threatening infection?

And why wouldn't Jadon talk about his feelings?

Later that night, she followed Jadon back to her room. He stayed for a while, but then went home for a bit. When he left, she slipped out of bed and went back to the nursery.

The neonatal nurses looked at her with kind empathy, suggesting she needed to get some sleep, but she ignored their advice.

What if the mask didn't work? She was too afraid Gretchen was going to need a breathing tube in her lungs and be placed on a ventilator.

"It's after midnight, Ms. Knight," Evie, the night nurse, said in her soft, quiet voice. "You really should go back to your room to get some rest."

"Are you telling me I have to leave?" Alyssa asked sharply, annoyed by the nurse's prodding. "I was under the impression I could stay for as long as I wanted."

Evie's eyes widened at her vehement tone. "Not at all, but wearing yourself out isn't good for you either. I'm only concerned about your welfare."

Alyssa closed her eyes and took a deep breath. She shouldn't have snapped, but in that moment the night-shift nurse had sounded so much like Jadon she hadn't been able to help her response.

"I'm sorry," she murmured to Evie. "I'll leave, soon."

Her anger wasn't really aimed at the nurse but toward Jadon. Over the past few hours she'd realized she resented how easily he'd gone home, leaving her here all alone. Granted, he'd been exhausted, and she'd noticed how he'd tossed and turned in the recliner. Still, she'd wanted him to stay.

Slowly she rose to her feet, understanding Evie was right. If she didn't get some rest, she wouldn't be any help to Grace or Gretchen.

If only Jadon were still here with her. Maybe then she wouldn't have felt so alone.

The next morning, the uncomfortable tautness in her breasts confirmed her milk was coming in.

Good news that she'd be able to provide healthy nourishment for Gracie and Gretchen.

Especially Gretchen, who needed the extra boost now more than ever.

She went to the nursery for more attempts at nursing, and Grace did suckle for almost ten minutes, a record for the little one, but Gretchen was still wearing her mask, so nursing wasn't an option.

She used the breast pump to provide milk for Gretchen's tube feedings, taking time to hold the baby close for some additional bonding.

Kim showed up in her room after she'd finished with the girls.

"Good morning, how are you doing today?" Kim asked.

Alyssa's smile was strained. "Fair, although I'd be much better if Gretchen's pneumonia would clear up."

"I know." Kim's expression softened as she continued, "You know, according to hospital policy, I'm supposed to discharge you today. However, considering Gretchen's tenuous condition, and the fact that you're breast-feeding, I could probably extend your stay one more day."

She sucked in a quick, hopeful breath. "Really? You could do that for me?"

"Yes. I think I could make it work so your insurance will cover the extra day, too."

"That would be wonderful," Alyssa admitted. "Not that I'm thrilled with the idea of staying here in the hospital rather than being home in my own bed, but I really want to be close to the girls for a little while longer."

"I understand," Kim said with a smile. "Leaving your babies here while you go home is probably going to be difficult. And I can only promise one more day. Just remember you can come in to visit anytime."

"Thanks, Dr. Rayborn," she said gratefully. "I really do appreciate the extra time."

"No problem. Please pay attention to your own body, too, though. You did just give birth and we need to make sure you're fully healed as well. How have you been doing? Everything all right? No aches or pains, or problems that you might not have paid attention to?"

She hid a wince, knowing all her attention had been centered on Grace and Gretchen. She thought back over the past few days. "Well, now that you mention it, I did notice a little burning last night when I emptied my bladder."

Kim arched a brow. "Hmm. Maybe you have a bladder infection. We'll send a sample to the lab and start you on antibiotics."

"Antibiotics?" she echoed in alarm. This was exactly why she hadn't said anything right away. "But I'm breast-feeding. I don't want to take anything that will harm the babies. Why don't we wait to see if the infection will clear up on its own? I'll drink extra cranberry juice, I promise."

"Cranberry juice is a good idea, but I don't want to take any chances. The antibiotic is very mild and it won't hurt the babies at all," Kim reassured her. "Don't worry."

"Okay," she reluctantly agreed.

Jadon returned to the hospital earlier than the day before and at least he looked better, not nearly as tired and exhausted as the day before.

"Good morning," he greeted her with a smile. "Has Kim been in yet? Are you officially discharged?"

"Kim has been in, but I'm not going to be discharged

today," she told him. "Turns out I have a bladder infection, for one thing. And she thought as Gretchen is so sick, she could work it out so that I can stay for another day."

"Oh." Was that a flash of disappointment in his eyes? "Well, it's good that you can be close to Grace and Gretchen for another day."

"Are you ready to see the girls?" she asked, swinging her legs out of bed. "My milk has come in, so I was able to nurse Grace this morning, but Gretchen had to settle for tube feedings."

"Sure." He smiled again, and took her hand as they went down the hall toward the nursery.

When they arrived, though, Dr. Downer was standing in front of Gretchen's isolette with his stethoscope dangling from around his neck, discussing something intently with a nurse. Her stomach clenched in warning.

"Something's wrong," she murmured.

Jadon gave her hand a reassuring squeeze. "Maybe not. It's possible she's doing better and they're discussing taking off the mask."

"Maybe." But she didn't think so. For one thing, Dr. Downer's expression seemed too serious. And so was Renee's.

"Hi, Alyssa, Jadon," Louis greeted them when they came closer. "You're just in time. We've been discussing Gretchen's breathing."

Alyssa's mouth went dry. "Is there something wrong? Isn't the CPAP mask helping her lungs?"

"It's helping," Louis said hesitantly, "but I'm not sure it's helping enough. Her chest X-ray this morning doesn't look much better and her pulse ox is hanging in the low nineties." He shook his head. "I'd like to see her oxygen percentage up higher than that."

The knot in her stomach tightened. "How?"

"First we're going to give her a few breathing treatments and another dose of IV antibiotics."

"And if that doesn't work?" Jadon asked.

"Then we'd need to place a breathing tube in her lungs and put her on a ventilator," Louis admitted. "We'll try to hold off, using the breathing tube as a last resort. And if we do put it in, we probably won't need to keep it in very long. I promise we'll take it out the moment Gretchen doesn't need it anymore."

Alyssa didn't know what to say. She didn't want Gretchen to have the breathing tube; she knew there were all sorts of potential complications that went along with it. Yet not having enough oxygen in her blood available to all her vital organs like her heart, brain and kidneys could also create problems.

"Can I hold her for a while?" she asked Renee.

"Sure, but keep her in the isolette if you can."

Holding Gretchen in the palms of her hands wasn't nearly as rewarding as holding her against her heart, but she was determined to spend as much time with Gretchen as possible.

Renee and Louis left them alone. Alyssa found she couldn't tear her eyes away from Gretchen, her brain already imagining what she'd look like with a breathing tube in.

"You can't ignore Grace," Jadon chided. "I know Gretchen is sick, but Grace deserves your love and attention, too."

His slightly accusing, brusque tone grated on her

nerves. "I was here this morning, nursing Grace. You're the one who went home last night. Don't lecture me. If anyone hasn't been spending enough time with Grace, it's you."

For a long moment antagonistic tension shimmered in the air between them.

Jadon turned away first, letting out a harsh breath and plowing his fingers through his hair. "I'm sorry. You're right. I have no right to lecture you."

His apology caught her off guard, and she realized this was their first fight. Ever. When Jadon had left so unexpectedly, she hadn't been given a chance to argue with him. You had to care about something, have feelings to argue.

She was inexplicably encouraged by his outburst. He'd proved he wasn't as emotionally distant from the situation with Gretchen as she'd thought.

"It's okay," she said slowly. "I shouldn't have snapped. I guess I've been on edge lately, too."

Jadon nodded. "We both have. Obviously there's been a lot to deal with in a very short period of time."

They took turns holding the girls, switching the babies, declaring a wordless truce to support each other during this time of crisis. Jadon seemed less remote after their disagreement.

Alyssa hoped that surviving their first fight was a good sign of their evolving relationship. Fighting meant having feelings.

Maybe there was hope for their future after all.

CHAPTER ELEVEN

ALYSSA and Jadon both stayed in the nursery until almost midnight again, relieved when Gretchen seemed to be holding her own on the CPAP mask.

So far she hadn't needed a breathing tube and Alyssa could only hope and pray that Gretchen was on the cusp of doing better, her pneumonia clearing up so she soon wouldn't need assistance with her breathing at all.

She was glad Jadon had decided to stay with her this time, instead of going home. Even if the recliner did look awfully uncomfortable.

When she finally awoke the next morning, she was distressed to see Jadon was already gone. Was he visiting the babies? Or had he left to run home?

She missed him. Sleeping beside him, being held by him when she'd been upset about Gretch. He'd been a rock during this very emotionally draining time. So far he wasn't giving her the impression he was going to cut and run when things got tough.

How on earth had she imagined she'd be able to raise these two girls by herself? Especially given that she'd had the twins prematurely? Who else would she have leaned on when Gretchen had got sick?

Her friends? Seth and Kylie? Maybe, but not likely. Not the way she'd leaned on Jadon.

And how had her mother managed?

She had no idea. Her mother was more of a saint than she'd given her credit for.

After climbing out of bed, she hurried down to the nursery to attempt to breast-feed Grace. She'd expected to see Jadon there, but he'd been in and had already gone. Trying not to be disappointed, she rocked and fed Grace, silently acknowledging that maybe she hadn't been entirely fair in her assessment of her mother's ability to adapt to being a single mother.

It wasn't exactly her mother's fault that she hadn't attended college. Her mother had fallen pregnant during her first year of college and had been forced to drop out of her classes. She'd tried going back for evening sessions, but had stopped altogether when Alyssa's oh, so charming father had disappeared from the picture for good.

Maybe they hadn't had a lot of money while she'd been growing up, but certainly they'd had love. Maybe her mother hadn't shown love as much as she'd wanted, but they had shared some wonderful, very special Christmases. And if they'd moved around a lot, from one seemingly better job to another, at least Alyssa hadn't gone hungry.

Constantly making new friends hadn't been easy, and that had been why once she'd come to Cedar Bluff she'd immediately fallen in love with the town. The people were exceptionally nice and friendly. From the very first she'd felt as if she'd come home.

If she hadn't experienced the nomadic upbringing she had, she might never have found Cedar Bluff.

Or Jadon.

She smiled down at Grace, who'd suckled hungrily that morning at her breast. Grace was by far the stronger and healthier of the twins. Gretchen still wore the mask, but Alyssa told herself that was better than coming in to find her on a ventilator.

Once Grace had taken her fill, which admittedly wasn't a lot, Alyssa used the breast pump so she could freeze the extra milk for both twins and then spent some time holding Gretchen.

Leaving the nursery, she returned to her room to eat her own breakfast and to wait for Kim to come and formally discharge her. While she knew this would mean spending less time with the girls, she was anxious to get back home.

Not to her apartment, but to Jadon's house.

"Good morning," Kim greeted her cheerfully as she entered the room. "Are you ready to go home?"

"Absolutely," she agreed, although she thought it was odd that Jadon hadn't returned. Where was he?

"And how is your bladder? Are you still experiencing some burning when you go?"

"Nope, that's all fine."

"Good. That means the antibiotics are helping." Kim made a few notes on her clipboard. "All right, then, you're free to leave. I have a prescription here for your antibiotics. You can get it filled right here at our outpatient pharmacy."

"Sounds good." She took the prescription Kim held out. "Thanks again for everything."

"You're very welcome," Kim said with a smile. "Don't forget, no sexual activity for a while, until you feel up to it. And you'll need to come and see me in six weeks."

"I will." Alyssa put the prescription near her purse and reached for her suitcase. Once Kim had left, she changed out of her nightgown and into the clean clothes Jadon had brought for her.

She was disappointed that she still needed to wear her maternity clothes. All the nurses had assured her she'd lose the extra weight faster if she breast-fed the babies and she really hoped they were right. Not that Jadon had said a word about her pudgy shape, but she still wanted to get back into her old clothes.

And where was Jadon? She frowned and then decided there was no need to sit here and wonder about Jadon. She should spend every minute she could with the girls instead.

On the way to the nursery, though, she abruptly stopped as an idea occurred to her. Maybe Jadon had been called in to work. He'd been off for several days already so she certainly understood if he needed to pick up a shift.

She turned and headed down to the emergency department to see if he was there, working. The charge nurse on duty would know which attending physicians were scheduled to work.

The ED was bustling with activity when she walked into the arena. Muted Christmas music was playing through the loudspeaker, but the tunes could barely be heard through the normal sounds of monitors beeping, staff talking and the occasional patient yelling.

Wistfully, she glanced around, realizing she missed the place. As soon as a few of her nursing colleagues saw her, they rushed over.

"Alyssa! How are you? How are the twins?" Susan asked, reaching her first and giving her a quick hug.

"We heard you have two girls," Melanie added, coming up behind Susan.

"I'm fine and the twins are fine, too," she said with a laugh. "Their names are Grace and Gretchen, and of course they are the most beautiful babies in the whole nursery."

"Of course they are," Susan agreed staunchly. "What are you doing down here? Looking for Theresa?"

Theresa Williams was their nurse manager and with a shock Alyssa realized she hadn't exactly kept her boss informed of the events surrounding her delivery.

"I should probably talk to Theresa," Alyssa agreed, glancing around the arena. "Do you know where she is?"

"I think she's in her office," Melanie said helpfully. "But if not, we can have her paged."

"Thanks. I'll chat with you both later." Alyssa hurried to her boss's office, spending a few minutes going over the terms of her medical leave of absence. She felt a sense of relief when she'd finished all the paperwork, including the form she needed to complete in order to add her infant daughters to her health insurance plan.

Considering the bill they were running up in the nursery, it was a good thing she'd stopped by or she might have forgotten all about it.

"By the way, which physician is on duty tonight?" she asked her boss.

"Let me check." Theresa pulled up her computerized physician schedule. "Unless there have been any changes, Dr. Carter is on for the second shift and Dr. Taylor is on for third shift."

So Jadon wasn't on the schedule, not even on third shift. Unless either Simon or Seth had called him to cover their hours at the last minute.

Trying not to dwell on where Jadon might be, she left Theresa's office. As she walked past the trauma bay, she noticed there were two trauma resuscitations going on at the same time, and curiosity caused her to stop to watch for a few minutes. It quickly became apparent that the two victims had been involved in the same crash.

"Here's the chest X-ray you asked for, Dr. Torres."

An attractive, tall, dark-haired, rather European-looking doctor glanced at the computer image of the film and turned back to the patient. "This guy's left lung is collapsed," he said in a sharp tone. "I need to insert a chest tube, stat."

Maureen, the new trainee she'd worked with a week ago, was rummaging through the trauma resuscitation cart, anxiously looking for the chest tube he'd asked for.

Alyssa didn't recognize Dr. Torres, but as Maureen was looking in the wrong places for the tube, she darted in and opened the correct drawer. "Here," she said, pulling out the chest tube and handing it to her. "Drawer six for chest tubes and instruments."

"Thanks," Maureen said in obvious relief. Evidently, the new physician had her on edge. "Here you go, Dr. Torres."

He took the chest tube, but then his attention centered on Alyssa. "Who are you?" he demanded. "If you're not a part of this resuscitation team, get out or I'll call Security."

Alyssa glanced around, but realized with a shock

that he was actually talking to her. Not that he didn't have every right to question who she was, as she obviously wasn't wearing the proper attire or her ID tag, but his threat to contact Security seemed a bit extreme. Hadn't she just helped out a coworker? What was his problem?

"I'm sorry," she started to apologize, but Leila Ross, one of the trauma surgeons, quickly came to her rescue.

"Alyssa Knight is one of our ED nurses—there's no reason to call Security." By the acid contempt in her tone, it was easy to deduce that Leila didn't particularly care for the new physician. "Thanks for your help, Alyssa. We're fine now."

"Sure," she murmured, taking the hint and stepping out of the trauma area. She glanced at Dr. Torres, but he'd apparently already forgotten about her, his attention centered on placing the chest tube in his patient.

She headed back toward the arena, where she ran into Susan. "The traumas are two snowmobile riders who hit each other head-on. I bet you're glad to be out of here for a few months, huh?" Susan asked, coming up beside her. "Good way to escape the craziness around here."

She thought dealing with premature twins would have its own element of craziness, but didn't respond. Susan brushed past, heading into the trauma room to offer more help, and Alyssa watched, wishing she had a chance to ask about the new doctor on staff.

Not that it mattered much, since, as Susan had pointed out, she'd be off for a few months. Hopefully by the time she was scheduled to return, Dr. Torres would have forgotten all about this little incident.

She turned and left, heading back upstairs to the

nursery, knowing she'd miss the excitement of the ED to a certain extent. Taking care of patients had always been her passion. Yet she was also a mother now, and her precious, tiny, preemie daughters had to come first.

Half expecting to run into Jadon, she was disappointed to note he wasn't waiting for her in the nursery. Where in the heck was he? Surely he hadn't forgotten she was being discharged today?

Her ire faded when she looked at Gretchen and noticed the CPAP mask had been removed from her daughter.

"Renee?" she called to the day-shift nurse, who was standing nearby. "Why is Gretchen's mask off? Is she doing better?"

"Yes, Gretchen is doing much better," Renee confirmed, crossing over to her with a reassuring smile. "As a matter of fact, Dr. Downer was just here looking for you and Jadon. Why don't I page him?"

"Please. I'd love to talk to him." Alyssa wished Jadon was here, too, so the doctor could talk to both of them.

They should be able to share the good news along with the bad.

"Alyssa, I'm glad you're here. Gretchen's chest X-ray looks remarkably improved so we're doing a trial to see how well she's oxygenating with the CPAP mask off." He glanced at the monitor over Gretchen's isolette and waved a hand at the pulse ox reading. "She's at ninety-five percent, which means so far she's holding her own."

"Really?" She was almost afraid to hope. "You really think she won't need the mask again?"

"I think between the antibiotics and the extra nutrition she's been getting, little Gretchen is going to be just fine," he assured her. "But we'll watch her closely, just in case."

Hope swelled, filling her heart with joyous relief. She knew they would keep a close eye on Gretchen, and on Grace. She was lucky to have such a great team of caregivers for her babies. "I'm so glad."

"Me, too. I understand you're going to be discharged today, is that correct?" he asked.

"Yes, but you can contact me on my cell phone if there's any changes with Grace or Gretch." She recited the number, patting her pockets and belatedly realizing the device was still in her suitcase. Jadon had thought of everything when he'd packed the bag for her, including her cell phone. "And I'll be here for a little while yet." Thankfully Jadon lived close to the hospital, so she could come and visit the girls often.

"Great. For now there isn't much else for us to do except to take good care of the babies and watch to be sure they don't have any other complications while they gain weight," he said.

"Sounds good." Excited, she took Gretchen out of her isolette to hold her close to her breast for the first time since the mask had gone on.

It seemed like forever. But after she'd held Gretchen, she gave Grace a nuzzle, too, unable to stop smiling.

Gretchen was doing okay. Soon the girls would be able to come home.

Which meant she needed to get ready for them.

After visiting for another hour, Alyssa walked back down to her room, becoming more vexed with Jadon.

It was past noon. Why wasn't he back by now? What on earth could be so important?

"Alyssa?" Denise flagged her down. "Jadon has been trying to get in touch with you."

"He has?" she asked with a frown. "Where is he?"

Denise lifted her shoulder in a slight shrug. "I'm not sure, but he would like you to call him on his cell phone. I wrote the number down for you."

Good thing, as she didn't have Jadon's new cell-phone number. She didn't even have his old cell-phone number anymore. She took the slip of paper and returned to her room. Picking up her phone from her suitcase, she saw there were several missed calls.

And the battery was almost flat, so she used the phone in her hospital room to call him. "Jadon, it's Alyssa. I just got your message," she said when he answered.

"Alyssa, I've been trying to reach you. I won't be able to take you home today."

A warning chill snaked down her spine. "Why not? Where are you?"

There was a slight pause, as if he was trying to figure out exactly what to say. "I had to leave early this morning for another family crisis. You were sleeping, so I didn't want to wake you. I should be back later tonight. Traffic is awful so I can't get into it now. I promise I'll explain later."

She sank onto the edge of her bed, staring out her window at the snow-covered trees surrounding Cedar Bluff Hospital. Looking at the wintry landscape, it made her all the more aware of the coldness she felt inside. "You left town," she said dully.

"Yes. But not for long. I'll be back soon."

Now it was soon, when earlier he'd claimed he'd be home later that night. So which was it?

She had a bad feeling he didn't know.

"So what am I supposed to do? Go back to my apartment and sleep on my couch?" Her bedroom set just happened to be set up at Jadon's house.

"I left a key to my place with Simon. He's working second shift tonight, and he's going to stop by the hospital to give you the key. If you want him to give you a lift to my place, I'm sure he will, but if you're going to sit and visit with the girls anyway, you may as well wait there for me. It's your choice."

Her choice? What if she wanted option number three—none of the above? What if she wanted Jadon to forget about his family crisis because they were having their own family crisis here?

There wasn't any choice. Jadon had already made it by leaving.

"Fine," she said woodenly, unable to hide the depth of her disappointment and discouragement. She wasn't sure she could stand going back to Jadon's house under these circumstances, although the idea of going to her small apartment wasn't much better. "Call me when you get back into town."

"I will." There was another pause, as if he wanted to say something more, but he only added, "Take care."

She closed her eyes and whispered, "You, too," before hanging up the phone.

The bitter taste of resentment nearly choked her. She buried her face in her hands to stave off the threat of tears burning the back of her throat. She should be glad he'd called her this time, instead of simply taking off without a word, but she wasn't.

Because Jadon hadn't mentioned anything about either of his daughters.

He'd been to the nursery earlier that morning but had left without knowing Gretchen had taken a turn for the better. From the way Dr. Downer had found her to give her the update on Gretchen, she knew he hadn't already talked to Jadon over the phone.

For all Jadon knew, his tiny daughter could still be fighting for her life.

And she couldn't believe his family crisis could be more important than his own daughter.

CHAPTER TWELVE

JADON closed his cell phone, feeling sick to his stomach. Could his brother's timing be any worse? Alyssa was upset, not that he could blame her. He should have discussed everything with her sooner.

Although reliving the past hadn't been much of a priority, not with everything going on in the present.

He'd gotten up early and had gone to the nursery to check on Gretchen, but then his mother had called. He didn't want his mother to be hurt by Jack's outbursts like she had in the past, so he'd promised to come, even though he'd wanted to stay with Alyssa and Gretchen. But what choice did he have?

Jack needed him. He'd wanted to refuse to rush to the rescue, but he couldn't ignore Jack's problems.

Not when they were inadvertently at least partially his fault.

His mother lived in the same small house they'd grown up in, located in the rural part of Madison, Wisconsin. She'd stayed after she and his father had divorced. The trip took a couple of hours by car. When he finally pulled into his mother's driveway, he was shocked to discover there were several cars there. Jack's for one. But what about the others?

When he strode up to his house, he was even more surprised to recognize his father standing beside his mother. From the way they were talking, his father had just arrived, too.

His parents had split up when he and Jack had been teenagers, the strain of Jack's illness having been too much to hold their marriage together. Jadon hadn't seen his father in years, especially after he'd remarried. His new stepmother hadn't liked dealing with Jack's illness either.

So why was he back? He wasn't sure, but he didn't have time to sort it all out now. His mother stood in the kitchen, obviously upset, wringing her hands.

"Where is he?" he asked, barely glancing at his father.

"Upstairs. He's locked himself in your old bedroom."

He raked her with a gaze, searching for any sign of injury. "Are you all right? Did he hurt you?"

"I'm fine." His mother's strain was evident in her falsely positive tone. "But I'm worried about him, Jadon. He seemed to be doing so well, and now this."

"I know. I'll go up there to try talking to him, but you'll have to call the police, just in case."

Clearly his mother didn't like that idea. He'd told her to call the police earlier, too, when she'd first called him, but she hadn't listened.

"I don't want him to be arrested again," she protested in a low voice.

He suppressed a sigh. "Neither do I, but we may need them to help control him." Last time Jack had almost killed himself, which was bad enough. But his unpredictable behavior was also a threat to those around him. Jadon wasn't taking any chances.

His father was surprisingly silent during their brief conversation, but now he stood and headed for the phone. "I'll call the police."

Grateful, Jadon gave him a brief nod and then headed upstairs, hearing thuds coming from their old bedroom as Jack paced. His brother always paced when he was upset. Jadon heard Jack talking to himself, sounding agitated and making threats.

A wave of helplessness washed over him. None of this was Jack's fault, not really. His brother was sick with a mental illness. It just didn't seem fair that some people struggled with so much inner turmoil while others didn't.

There was a crash as something hit the floor. Oh, boy. He drew a deep breath and knocked at the door. "Jack? It's me, Jadon. I'm here to help. Unlock the door and let me in."

Jack's voice got louder. "No. Leave me alone. Just leave me the hell alone."

Jadon pressed his palm flat against the door, knowing he could break through the flimsy frame with a solid kick if he had to. But that would only rile his brother, putting him on the defensive. He maintained his calm approach. "Jack, please. I want to help. Let me in."

There was no answer, but then the door swung open and his identical twin stood there regarding him with bloodshot eyes. Jack looked awful. He obviously hadn't shaved in days, and his wrinkled clothes looked as if he'd slept in them. Yet there was enough of a resemblance that it was like looking at himself in the mirror, except for the tortured expression branded deep in his brother's eyes.

"You can't help. You're never here to help."

Bull's-eye. The barb hit deep. Guilt clogged his throat. Jack was right. He did keep leaving, returning to Cedar Bluff because he wanted a normal life. At his brother's expense. "I'm sorry, Jack. I'm here now. I can help you." Jadon kept his tone calm and reassuring. "Everything is going to be fine."

"It's not fine." Jack spun away, his movements jerky and agitated. "It's bad, Jadon. The voices are bad. Telling me to do bad things."

His heart sank. The voices were back. The same voices that had told Jack to set his apartment building on fire four months ago. He couldn't imagine how awful it must be for Jack to be tormented like this. What had happened to the new medication regime that had been working so well?

"You're not a bad person, Jack. You're tired and scared. I'm here to keep you safe. Come with me so we can go back to the hospital and get some help."

"No!" Jack swept his arm across the top of the dresser, sending various picture frames and sports memorabilia crashing to the floor. "You don't under-stand what it's like. I'm not going back to the hospital."

Once the police arrived his brother would have no choice. It was a pattern that had repeated itself too many times to count. He tried to hang on to his patience, knowing he'd pushed too hard, too fast, because he'd wanted this to be over so he could head back to Cedar Bluff.

To Alyssa and his daughters.

"I thought you liked Dr. Cranberg?" Jadon asked, keeping his tone casual, nonthreatening. "I thought things were going better with her?"

"I do like Dr. Liz. She's nice." For a moment uncertainty shone in Jack's eyes. "She doesn't think I'm crazy."

"You're not crazy, Jack." Man, he hated that term. "Let's go see Dr. Liz. I'll go with you." Jadon kept his voice calm even as he inched closer, knowing he'd take his brother down by force if he had to. One reason he always told his mother to stay out of the way, calling him instead.

Jack clutched his hair with both hands, his face twisting into a mask of anguish. "Make them stop, Jadon," he pleaded in a low, tortured tone. "Make the voices stop."

"I will, Jack." He reached his brother, sighing in relief. He took Jack's arm, giving his brother a sideways hug, knowing the worst of the confrontation was over. "I will. Come with me."

Jack's shoulders drooped and he followed Jadon down the stairs to the main floor of the house. When Jadon saw the police had arrived, he warned them back with a shake of his head, leading Jack to his own car instead.

He'd drive Jack to the hospital. The cops could follow if they wanted to. He wanted to discuss Jack's care with Dr. Cranberg. For now this was the best he could do for his brother.

For himself.

How selfish was he, to want a normal life with Alyssa and their daughters when it was clear Jack would never have anything close to that kind of future?

Bleakly, he watched as Jack muttered to himself, curled in the corner of his passenger seat. Maybe Jack was right. Maybe him leaving to go back to Cedar Bluff wasn't helping.

But what could he do? Move to Madison? He'd considered that option before, but not now. Not with having Alyssa and the girls to consider. Gretchen was doing better the last time he'd called in, but they still needed him.

Yet so did Jack.

Thankfully, this episode had ended without violence. But they hadn't all ended this peacefully. Even so, the situation had been stressful, which was exactly why he still hadn't told Alyssa the truth.

There was a small, selfish part of him that didn't want her to meet Jack. To see what his life with his twin brother was really like. She didn't need any more stress. If he had his way, he'd keep Grace, Gretchen and even Alyssa in a protective cocoon, safe from the harsh realities of life.

Jack moaned and mumbled something under his breath and Jadon prayed his brother would stay calm until they'd been able to see Dr. Liz.

At the hospital, the staff quickly admitted Jack for an inpatient psychiatric stay. The police had followed with his parents, doing the necessary paperwork to keep Jack under strict observation for his own safety.

"The new medication was working," his mother said in a low voice a while later, once they'd finished and were waiting in the lobby. "For a while he was doing better. I don't know what happens to him, why he suddenly stops taking his pills."

He didn't know either. Just more proof that his mother and his brother needed him. "Jack needs to stay in the inpatient program where they regulate his medication closely," he said, drawing in a deep, heavy sigh. "But he has to stay voluntarily, we can't force him. At least this episode wasn't as bad as the last one. Has he been staying away from those useless friends he'd been tangled up with?"

"I don't know for sure, but I think so," his mother said. "He seemed to be doing everything that Dr. Liz asked of him."

Jadon hoped so. His brother had gotten mixed up with a bad crowd, and under their negative influence Jack had become much worse. In fact, his brother had owed some of them a lot of money, which Jadon had figured out after he'd been jumped and robbed the last time he'd come home.

He'd suspected at the time they'd thought he was Jack. Just like when they'd been kids, Jack's troubles had often rubbed off on him. Because people couldn't tell them apart.

He'd suffered more than once for Jack's sins. Yet he couldn't hold his brother responsible for being sick either.

"He'll stay an inpatient now for a while, won't he?" his mother asked, drawing Jadon out of his reverie.

"Yes, he'll be an inpatient for a while." Probably not long enough. Psychiatric programs were losing money and government funding, making the inpatient programs few and far between. And in most cases the patient had to agree to stay.

"Will you stay for a few days and talk to his doctor?" his mother asked. She glanced at his father, and he wondered why there were together. Had his father officially divorced his second wife? Were his parents thinking of getting back together again?

"I can't. I have to get back to Cedar Bluff."

His mother's eyes widened in surprised dismay. "You can't! What if something happens?"

The old familiar guilt made him waver. Should he stay? His mother deserved to have a normal life, too. Heaven knew, she'd given up a lot. Didn't he owe Jack and his mother at least some of his precious time?

Yes, but so did Alyssa. He had other responsibilities now and the two were tearing him apart. He'd wanted to keep them separate but maybe he was deluding himself.

Thinking of Alyssa, Grace and Gretchen waiting for him at the hospital made him shake his head. "I can't. Mom, there's something you need to know. You're a grandmother, grandparents," he amended, including his father in the announcement. "I have twin daughters, Grace Aubrey and Gretchen Louise. They were born just a few days ago."

"Twins?" his mother repeated in stunned surprise. She couldn't have looked more shocked if he'd announced he'd been kidnapped by wild monkeys. "My goodness, you're married?"

"No," he said grimly. Marriage was not an option. Convincing Alyssa to stay with him on a temporary basis was hard enough. And what more could he ask? Jack's difficulties weren't easy to handle. Some families weren't meant to stay together. "The babies were born prematurely and the smaller one, Gretchen, has had some complications. We haven't had time to really think about the future."

"I see." His mother fell silent and he knew she was upset and hurt that he hadn't brought Alyssa over to meet her. Or that he hadn't invited her to Cedar Bluff to meet Alyssa.

How could he explain a relationship he wasn't sure he had?

"Look, a lot has happened. Alyssa is being discharged today from the hospital. I need to get back. I'm sure you'll meet Alyssa soon, maybe at Christmas." His voice lacked conviction, but he couldn't help it. He didn't really want Alyssa to be a part of his problems with Jack.

"All right." His mother looked a bit forlorn, but he noticed his father stepped closer, adding his support. Seeing his parents together again after so many years made him wonder what would be different the second time around. Did his parents have what it took to stick together this time if things went bad with Jack again? Love couldn't solve everything.

"Dad, it was good to see you again." He made an effort to mend the rift of the past, thinking about how he'd feel if his daughters remained angry at him for years on end. Not good. He forced a smile. "I'll be in touch with both of you about our plans for the holiday."

"Bye, Jadon." As he turned to leave, he heard his mother exclaim, "Grandparents! Can you believe we're actually grandparents, Josh?"

"Good news," his father agreed. "And about time."

Jadon felt bad, knowing he should have asked them right then and there to come back with him to meet their grandchildren.

But first he needed some time alone with Alyssa.

* * *

Outside, it had started snowing again. Good thing his parents hadn't come with him to meet Alyssa after all. The roads were slick, forcing him to drive much more slowly than he wanted to. At one point a woman spun out in front of him, hitting the median of the interstate and coming to a jarring stop. He'd gone over to help her, to confirm she wasn't badly hurt, and had waited with her for the police to arrive before going back out on the highway again.

He headed to the hospital first, even though it was late, nearly eight o'clock at night by the time he made it back to Cedar Bluff. He'd called Alyssa's cell phone, but it had gone immediately to voice mail, indicating she didn't have her phone turned on. He pulled into the hospital parking lot and shut off the engine.

The hospital wasn't a white building, like so many of them were, but had been structured with a dark brown cedar wood which made it stand out starkly against the snow-covered trees. In the summer the building meshed with the wooded landscape, but not now. A brightly lit Christmas wreath hung over the front door, a welcoming beacon through the swirling snow.

Inside, the warmth and the muted Christmas music engulfed him. Odd that being in the hospital felt very much like coming home.

Alyssa wasn't in the nursery. He spent a few minutes with Grace and Gretchen, amazed and relieved at how well Gretchen was doing without her mask.

She looked so much better without it.

As much as he wanted to stay and hold his daughters, he really needed to find Alyssa. No doubt Simon had driven her to his house. Braving the snow-covered streets once again, he headed home.

But the house was dark. Not a single light shone through the windows. Frowning, he glanced at the clock. Had she gone to bed already? It was early, but she was no doubt exhausted.

Inside, he flipped on the lights as he walked through the kitchen and into the living room. He expected her to be on the sofa, since he'd taken down her bedroom set, but she wasn't. If she'd made herself at home in his bed, she couldn't be that upset with him. Treading softly, he opened the door to his room.

Empty.

Alyssa wasn't here, waiting for him.

He tried not to become alarmed. If she wasn't at the hospital and she wasn't here, where was she? At her apartment, without a bed? Or staying with Seth and Kylie?

He called her cell phone again without a response. Then he called the hospital to get Seth's number. Kylie answered the phone and confirmed that Alyssa wasn't with them.

"Sorry to bother you," he mumbled, hanging up before Kylie could ask all sorts of questions. Questions he couldn't answer.

Feeling panicky and desperate to find Alyssa, he drove to her apartment building. The snow-covered hill made things tricky, but he managed to get up to the top. He noticed Alyssa's car in her parking space and stared at it for a moment, thinking back.

She'd worked on Wednesday night, and had driven herself to work. Then he'd taken her home to his place, where she'd stayed until she'd gone into labor.

Her car shouldn't have been here, unless Alyssa had found it in the parking garage and had driven herself home.

Relieved to have that mystery solved, he went up to the main door and pressed on her buzzer. When there was no answer, he delved into his pocket, finding the keys she'd given him when he'd moved her things.

Letting himself inside, he took the stairs two at a time to get up to her second-floor apartment. He didn't bother knocking at the door but used the key to get in.

Alyssa was asleep on her sofa. Breathing a sigh of relief, he crossed over to her, reaching down to gently shake her awake.

"Alyssa? I'm back."

"Jadon?" She opened her eyes and blinked at him. "How did you get in?"

"I still had your key. How did you get in?"

She swung up to a sitting position, pushing her hair out of her face. "Mr. Worthington let me in."

He swallowed hard and dropped down beside her. "I'm sorry about this morning. Remember I told you about my family crisis?"

Warily, she nodded. "Yes. You didn't want to go into detail at the time," she said.

"I know. Partly because I didn't want you to worry or to be stressed out." He knew he was botching up the explanation. "Let me start at the beginning. Remember I mentioned I had a brother?"

When she nodded, he braced himself. "Jack is more than just my brother. He's my twin. My identical twin."

CHAPTER THIRTEEN

ALYSSA stared at Jadon, trying to comprehend what he was saying. Half-asleep, she was certain the neurons in her brain weren't working properly.

Because she could have sworn he'd just told her he had a twin brother.

"I know it's a shock, and I'm sorry I didn't tell you sooner," Jadon was saying. "But Jack has a few…emotional problems. Rather serious problems."

A deep coldness washed over her body, seeping down into her bones. She felt slow and somewhat confused, very much like the day she'd slipped and fallen into Lake Michigan. "A twin," she repeated carefully. "With emotional problems."

Jadon's Adam's apple bobbed nervously in his neck. "Yes. I can't lie to you. My parents divorced before Jack and I started high school. The stress of coping with Jack's illness eroded their marriage."

Her mouth went dry as she thought of little Grace and Gretchen. Was Jack's problem hereditary? Was that why he'd kept it a secret? "What illness does he have?" she asked, dreading the answer.

Jadon lifted a hand, his tone pleading. "I know what

you're thinking and there's no reason to suspect that our daughters will also inherit Jack's illness. No one in my family, or in my extended family, has the same problems as Jack. No one."

She wanted to believe him. More than anything, she wanted to believe her daughters would be fine. But he still hadn't answered her question. Her fingers curled into her fists, her nails digging into her palms, although she was oblivious to the pain. "Jadon, what sort of illness does he have?"

"Paranoid schizophrenia." At her stunned expression, he rushed on. "Jack's been getting treatment from a variety of doctors over the years, but this newest doctor, Elizabeth Cranberg, is the area expert in managing this illness. And Jack seemed to like her. But for some reason, like so many other patients with a chronic illness, once he feels better he stops taking his meds. And then he tends to suffer a bad relapse."

Jiminy Cricket, she never would have suspected Jadon's brother had paranoid schizophrenia. She swallowed hard, hearing the exhaustion in his tone. She couldn't even imagine how hard it must be to live with someone with such a debilitating condition.

No wonder Jadon had been so protective of their psych patient Mitch. She understood now why he'd snapped at Susan that night.

He'd lived with someone who was just like Mitch.

"But, Jadon, schizophrenia does tend to run in families," she said, her stomach tied up in knots. She'd learned that much in her psych class. "I'm worried about our daughters."

Jadon's expression was grim. "Normally schizophre-

nia does run in families. But I researched this exten-
sively the first time I left, and I discovered there are
other reasons people come down with a form of schizophrenia. Jack was a wild child when we were young.
He got mixed up in a rough crowd during middle school
and began experimenting with drugs. That's when we
first noticed his behavior had changed. We put him in
treatment several times. Even years later, when his drug
screens were finally negative, his behavior was still
erratic. I got him in to see Dr. Elizabeth Cranberg and
she confirmed that his case didn't show the classic signs
of schizophrenia. She thought it was more likely related
to his drug use, especially as there is no family history."

Had Jadon worried about coming down with the
disease, too? Being Jack's identical twin, he must have
thought about the possibility. She couldn't imagine how
he must have felt, watching his twin and wondering if
he might be next.

"Is that why you told me you weren't interested in a
long-term relationship when we first met?" she asked.

Jadon momentarily closed his eyes, his expression
pained. "Yes. I didn't tell you the truth from the very
beginning because I was embarrassed. Maybe a little
ashamed. I've had to live with the stigma of mental
illness my whole life. My family has struggled for a
long time. Jack's illness ruined my parents' marriage
and then, when my father remarried, his second wife
couldn't cope either. You can see why I'd never planned
on making a commitment."

The truth still had the power to hurt. Obviously if she
hadn't fallen pregnant, they wouldn't be sitting here,
having this conversation.

She felt nauseous. The last thing she'd planned to do was to trap Jadon into something he didn't want. Something he'd gone to great lengths to avoid.

The same way her mother had inadvertently trapped her father. Who'd left once the novelty of being a parent had worn off. She knew comparing Jadon to her father wasn't fair—he at least accepted his responsibilities. But she wanted more.

"I always thought you didn't care about me, as you never once talked about your feelings."

"I do care about you, Alyssa. Very much. I missed you more than I ever would have imagined. But then Jack needed me and I used him as an excuse to leave. I came back, thinking of getting in touch with you, only to find out you were pregnant."

"And me being pregnant meant more responsibility for you," she guessed in a low tone.

"Not just that," he argued. "Alyssa, I'm trying to protect you, to keep you and our daughters away from the stress of dealing with Jack's illness."

After seeing Mitch, she could somewhat understand what he meant. "Are you saying he's violent?"

"Psych patients are unpredictable. They're really not violent very often, unless provoked. Jack and I were in an argument once and a former girlfriend of mine got in the middle of it, making things worse, and he shoved her, knocking her right off her feet." Jadon's lips thinned. "I didn't blame her when she broke off our relationship."

Dear heaven. She could only imagine. Yet she didn't like his fatalistic attitude. "So where does that leave us?"

He slowly shook his head. "I don't know. Jack is my

responsibility, not yours. I don't want the same thing that happened to my parents to happen to us."

She wanted to be glad Jadon had finally opened up about his feelings, admitting he at least cared for her, but her thrill of hope was overshadowed by his news.

Could she really live with the stress he described? On top of having preemie twins? She honestly wasn't sure.

"I stopped by the hospital on my way home," he said. "Gretchen looks so much better with her mask off."

Alyssa nodded, grateful for the change in subject. "Yes, she does. I'm relieved both girls are doing well. If they don't have any more complications, and continue to gain weight, Dr. Downer thought they'd probably come home by Christmas."

"The perfect Christmas present," Jadon said with a smile.

She couldn't smile back, already thinking of how Jadon would want to go home to see his family for Christmas. Without her and their daughters. Deep down, she could admit that while she'd been determined to be happy raising the girls alone, she'd also secretly wanted a traditional two-parent family. But Jadon wasn't free to be a part of her family. Not the way she wanted. The magnitude of their problems seemed greater and greater.

"Alyssa, I know I don't have much to offer you, but I'd still like to take you back to my house."

Earlier, she'd wanted nothing more than to go back with Jadon. Had been upset that he'd left her again. But now she wanted more than their half relationship.

She wanted it all. She wanted love and commitment.

"I'm sorry, Jadon. But I can't. Not right now." Maybe not ever, if he wasn't willing to try.

He stared at her for a long moment. "Alyssa, you don't even have a bed to sleep in. At least come back to my place so you can get some rest."

She shook her head. "I'm fine here, really. And I have my car, too. Please understand, I need time. Time to assimilate what you've told me."

He dropped his head in his hands in apparent defeat. "All right. But please call me. No matter what you need."

"I will."

Jadon slowly stood and moved toward the doorway. He stopped, glanced back at her as if he wanted to say something, but then remained silent as he let himself out of her apartment, gently closing the door behind him.

Alyssa stretched out on the sofa, feeling overwhelmed and exhausted. A twin brother with emotional disturbances. No wonder Jadon rarely talked about his feelings. He'd probably learned early on to repress his emotions when his brother was acting out. She'd fallen in love with him, but Jadon hadn't said anything about love. He was certainly a pro at handling responsibility, though.

She and the babies were just more responsibilities for him to deal with.

Jadon drove back to his house, feeling sick again. His idea of keeping his two families separate had seemed like a good compromise, but the anxious expression in Alyssa's eyes when he'd told her about Jack's problems convinced him he'd been right all along. The stress would be too much.

Deep down, he knew it was better that he'd come clean with the truth.

He cared about her too much to expose her to the same problems his parents had faced.

And as much as he wanted nothing more than to be with Alyssa, to watch Grace and Gretchen as they grew, he couldn't renounce his brother.

Jack was his responsibility, too.

Did he have to give up one family to care for the other?

He pulled into his driveway, trudging up to the cold, empty house.

An impossible situation, no matter which way he looked at it.

Jadon didn't get much sleep. Using his palms to rub the grit from his burning eyes, he staggered to the bathroom, hoping a shower would make a difference in how he felt.

No such luck.

On the way out of the shower, he stopped outside the new nursery, a wave of hopelessness overwhelming him. Would he and Alyssa have to agree to some sort of joint-custody arrangement? He couldn't imagine she'd do that willingly, and how could he push the issue when the twins were still so small?

He turned away from the smiling ballerinas in the pictures hanging over the two cribs, set against pale pink walls he'd painted late into the middle of the night as a surprise for Alyssa. It hurt to remember how excited he'd been, how he'd agonized over the decor, hoping and praying Alyssa would like what he'd done. For her. For their family.

Talk about being in a state of denial. Fantasizing about having a family with Alyssa had been nothing more than an idealistic dream. How could he have forgotten, even for a moment, the impact of Jack's illness?

He turned away from the cheerful nursery to head into the kitchen. His appetite had disappeared so he settled for a cup of coffee, sipping out of his mug and staring sightlessly outside. The snow from last night had stopped, and the warmth of the sun had burned away the clouds, glimmering brightly off the newly fallen snow.

If only the sun could warm his heart, too.

As he was scheduled to work nights, he decided to go to the hospital early to visit the girls, figuring he could try to get some sleep later.

The drive to Cedar Bluff Hospital was short and within fifteen minutes he walked into the nursery, not entirely surprised to see Alyssa had already arrived. The rapt expression on her face was so poignantly serene as she rocked back and forth, nursing Grace, it stopped him in his tracks.

His chest tightened painfully, making it difficult to breathe. She'd never looked so beautiful.

So content.

He loved her. The knowledge hit like a truckload of Christmas trees. Good grief, he loved her. Loved Alyssa with all his heart and soul. Had begun to fall in love with her even before he'd had to leave to rescue Jack all those months ago. The idea that he could be intimate with her and yet keep his heart isolated from her was laughable.

She was everything he'd wanted in a wife, a mother for his children.

And in some dark region of his mind he realized the best thing he could do for her, and for Grace and Gretchen, was to provide for them financially while keeping them far away from the impact of his messed-up family.

Which meant keeping them distant from himself, too.

Alyssa felt Jadon's gaze and glanced up from where Grace was successfully nursing to look at him.

The admiration in his heated glance made her mouth go dry. For a moment they stared at each other, but then he broke the connection, looking away, and the expression was gone.

Had she imagined it? She didn't think so.

She swallowed hard and glanced back down at Grace, confused all over again. She'd pretty much made up her mind to accept losing Jadon and the family she'd always wanted.

But now she wasn't so sure.

"Gracie is nursing better, isn't she?" Jadon asked in a low voice, as if to not disturb the baby.

She nodded. "Gretchen still doesn't nurse very much, but Grace is becoming a pro. She doesn't nurse for long, but as long as she's gaining weight, I'm happy."

"Has she?" Jadon stepped closer. "Gained weight, I mean."

"Yes, two full ounces." She never would have realized just how important the smallest accomplishment was for a preemie. But gaining two ounces was a very big deal.

Gretchen hadn't gained weight—in fact, she'd lost another ounce, probably a result of her time wearing the CPAP mask and battling pneumonia.

Although the mask was off, Alyssa knew Gretchen wasn't completely out of the woods yet. The tiny twin wasn't nearly as strong as Grace.

"Wonderful. And Gretchen?" he asked.

She shook her head. "No, down another ounce."

For a long moment Jadon stared down into Gretchen's isolette. The baby was getting a tube feeding, so they couldn't hold her until the feeding was finished.

"Jack is older than me by about two and a half minutes," Jadon mused. "But he was much larger than I was, almost a full pound. The doctor said that sometimes one twin can actually steal nourishment from the second twin, especially in cases where the twins are identical, sharing one placenta."

"Really?" She hadn't known that. Good thing Grace and Gretchen hadn't been that far apart in weight, although they were also fraternal and not identical twins. "How big were you?"

"Only two and a half pounds," Jadon said. "My mother said I was in the neonatal ICU for a full week longer than Jack. And because I was so small, and needed so much more care, both she and my dad focused all their attention on me."

She began to see where Jadon's bout of reminiscing was going. "Do you think that's why Jack went a little wild when he was older? Because he was always competing for your parents' attention?"

Jadon tucked his hands in his pockets and lifted a shoulder. "I imagine that could be one theory. Despite my small size, and being delayed as a baby, doing all the normal milestones of sitting, crawling, walking and so on, I always did well in school."

"Better than Jack?" she guessed.

He nodded. "Yeah. It wasn't that Jack wasn't smart, but he certainly didn't try as hard."

"So you feel guilty? Like it was your fault your parents paid too much attention to you and not enough to Jack?" she asked, already suspecting the answer.

"Isn't it?" he countered. "Not that I did it on purpose, obviously, but it's something I always wonder about. Let's face it, if I had been the older twin, and Jack the younger, smaller twin, don't you think it's possible our lives would have been different?"

She swallowed hard, hating to admit he might have a point. No wonder he'd been so adamant that she pay attention to Grace, too, during Gretchen's illness. Even now, despite his reassurances otherwise, he was worried that history might repeat itself with Grace and Gretchen.

Glancing down at Grace, who'd fallen asleep, Alyssa traced the tip of her index finger over her daughter's dainty features, and vowed not to let that happen.

"At least now that we know, we won't make the same mistake as parents," she said slowly.

Jadon didn't answer as she stood and placed the sleeping Grace back into her isolette.

"I know you said you needed time," Jadon said in a low voice. "But I want you to know the offer of staying with me, at least for a while, is still open. I'm concerned about your ability to manage caring for the twins without help."

Alyssa wavered. He was being the responsible one

again. Jadon had opened up about himself, more than he ever had. Which offered some hope. Yet she knew, once she took that step of going home with him, it would be very hard to go back.

Should she fight for her love? Or would that be a constant uphill battle? And was she strong enough to handle the impact of Jack's illness on top of caring for Grace and Gretchen?

"At least think about it," Jadon advised. "I'm working night shift tonight and tomorrow night, so it's not as if I'll be there much."

Reassuring her he wouldn't be there much didn't sound promising. Were they back to being parents in name only? Ironic that she'd already come to feel as if his house was a home.

Their home.

She missed Jadon. And she missed her lopsided Charlie Brown Christmas tree. She needed to take a chance, to see if she could somehow bridge the gap between them.

"All right," she agreed. "But only as a trial to see how well I can manage with the girls."

CHAPTER FOURTEEN

ALYSSA second-guessed her decision several times over as she followed Jadon's car through the streets to his house.

Yet when she entered the living room, surprised to find a variety of brand-new Christmas decorations, including a wreath over the fireplace, a nativity scene and tiny twinkling lights strung around the living-room windows, she realized how wonderful it felt to be there with him.

"Here, I'll take your coat," Jadon said, treating her as a guest rather than someone who might be living there. She hid a pang of disappointment.

"Thanks." She crossed over to her lopsided Charlie Brown Christmas tree and gave the drooping branches a welcoming pat. "I see you didn't toss him out for a bigger, better tree," she observed. "And you've been giving him water."

"Of course I've been giving him water. The needles are already starting to fall off. They don't need another excuse."

She smiled, knowing he was right. The poor tree would be lucky to last until the holiday.

"So why didn't you replace him, then?"

"Because this tree obviously held a special place in your heart, and that was more important than how the room looked."

A warm feeling filled her chest. Jadon did care. And if he cared, maybe he could learn to love. He certainly understood her better than she'd thought.

"I…uh, put all the baby stuff into the bedroom," Jadon said, coming up to stand beside her.

Surprised, she glanced up at him. "You did?"

He nodded and she brushed past him, filling her senses with his musky scent as she went over to investigate. In the doorway of the spare bedroom she stopped and stared, realizing he'd done far more than simply set up the baby things.

He'd fully decorated the entire nursery.

"Oh, my," she whispered, her heart melting at the obvious care and concern Jadon had put into every detail. Not only did he have the two cribs set up, and the dressers with changing tables across their tops strategically placed near each one, but he'd painted the walls a soft pink, had hung a border of tiny pink and white ballerina slippers around the entire room, and displayed two portraits of ballerinas on the walls above each crib. In one corner of the room he'd set a gleaming wooden rocker with comfy pink cushions, the perfect spot to rock and nurse the babies.

Completely overwhelmed, she didn't know what to say. The Christmas decorations were special, but this additional surprise was beyond words. Maybe he didn't talk about his feelings much, but his actions had definitely shown them. "Jadon, this is absolutely beautiful."

His smile didn't quite reach his eyes. "I hoped you'd

like it. And don't worry about the sleeping arrangements. I'd planned on putting a sleeper sofa into my office anyway, so I can sleep on the living-room sofa until it's delivered. In the meantime, you can have the bedroom."

Sleeping arrangements? She glanced at him, but he avoided direct eye contact, confirming her suspicions. He'd obviously planned on the two of them sharing the master bedroom.

Because he cared about her? Or was starting to love her?

Swallowing hard, she simply nodded, knowing she still wanted to share a bedroom with him, badly.

"So this is what you were working on while I was in the hospital," she guessed, changing the subject to something safer. No wonder he'd looked so awful those few days, as if he hadn't had any sleep. By the extent of the completed nursery, he couldn't have slept much if at all. "Not just the Christmas decorations, but the nursery, too."

"Yeah. I wanted it all to be a surprise." He looked uncomfortable for a few moments, then said, "I'm going to take a short nap as I'm working tonight."

"Of course. Use the bedroom. Don't argue," she interjected, as he opened his mouth to do just that. "It's going to be difficult enough for you to sleep in the middle of the day, especially with how sunny it is, without trying to do that in the middle of the living room."

He hesitated, but then acquiesced, murmuring, "Thanks," as he headed into the bedroom, gently closing the door behind him.

Alyssa felt curiously lonely without Jadon's presence. In fact, suddenly she felt very much like the guest and not someone who belonged here. She tried to rest for a bit in the living room, thrilled at the festive atmosphere, but then found herself going back into the nursery and picking up one of the matching pink elephants as she settled into the rocking chair. It was all too easy to imagine how cozy things would be once the girls came home.

But this arrangement was only temporary, wasn't it?

They couldn't just simply share parenting duties and nothing else. A family in name only? No, it would never work.

She loved him too much.

And she wanted a happy family. And Jadon's love, forever. She wanted it all.

For the first time in months, since the day she'd discovered she was pregnant and had been unable to get in touch with Jadon, she allowed tears to slip down her cheeks.

Her heart and soul ached for what she'd never have.

Jadon couldn't sleep. Sleeping in the middle of the day had never been easy for him but, with everything seemingly falling apart around him, rest was more elusive than ever.

He stared at the ceiling over his bed, trying not to relive the moment when Alyssa had seen the nursery, her eyes lighting up with excitement and pleasure.

He'd once hoped she'd feel as if she belonged here. With him. With the girls, too.

Marriage was such a huge step. One he hadn't planned on taking. Alyssa deserved marriage, full commitment. Because they'd made a family with Grace and Gretchen.

Yet Jack was family, too. His brother.

His cell phone rang, startling him badly, making him swear under his breath at how he'd forgotten to silence the ringer as he fumbled in his discarded clothes for the instrument.

His stomach twisted when he realized the caller was his mother. "Mom? What's wrong? Jack can't possibly be out of the hospital already?"

"No, nothing is wrong," she quickly assured him. "Ah, actually, we're here to see you."

"Here? In Cedar Bluff?" Jadon shot out of bed, frantically searching for his pants, imagining his parents were right now standing outside his front door.

"Yes, we're at a restaurant on Main Street. What's it called, Josh?" she asked his father. "Oh, yes, The Spinnaker. The food was excellent."

He tugged on his pants, cradling the phone between his shoulder and his ear, hardly able to believe his parents had shown up in Cedar Bluff. "Ah, okay. That's not far away."

"We were hoping we could come to your house and then visit the babies, Grace and Gretchen."

Momentarily closing his eyes, he let out a soundless sigh. Of course they wanted to visit the babies. He couldn't blame them. But he needed to talk to Alyssa about this, too. So much for keeping his two families separate. "Why don't you come here first to meet Alyssa?"

"That would be nice," his mother agreed, sounding excited.

He gave her directions that she repeated for his father. He hung up and sank down onto the edge of his bed, running his fingers nervously through his hair. He was nervous. What would Alyssa think?

His parents hadn't brought Jack, but what if Jack discovered the news about the twins? He'd want to see them, too.

There was no use dwelling on all the complications. He had to deal with his parents first.

He pulled himself together and finished getting dressed. He opened his bedroom door and hesitated, seeing the nursery door was still ajar, and went with his instincts to search for Alyssa in there.

He saw her sitting in the rocking chair, clutching one of the pink elephants to her chest, tears glistening in streaks down her cheeks.

"Alyssa? What's wrong?" Alarmed, he crossed the room to kneel beside her.

"Nothing. Everything." She swiped at her eyes, offering a pathetic attempt at a smile.

He couldn't stand it. Rising to his feet, he took her hand and drew her up and into his arms. "Shh, it's okay. Everything is going to be fine."

She buried her face against his chest, shaking her head as if she disagreed with him.

"Yes, it will. I promise." He kissed the top of her head, smoothing a hand down her back, offering comfort in the only way he knew how. He wasn't sure how he'd fix it, but he wanted to find a way. For her.

Slowly the tension eased out of her body and she melted against him in a way that caused his own body to harden in awareness. Knowing that intimacy was impossible for more reasons than just one, he forced himself to ignore the discomfort.

The doorbell pealed. Alyssa lifted her head from his chest.

"Someone's here," she said, rubbing her face as if to erase the evidence of her tears.

"My parents."

"Your parents?" Her gaze widened in shock.

"I'll get rid of them if you want me to."

Just that quickly, the shocked surprise turned into exasperation. She swiped the dampness from her face. "They're your parents. You can't just get rid of them. Not when they've come all this way to see you."

Still unsure, he nodded. Maybe one, slightly dysfunctional family was better than trying to divide his time between two families? There was only one way to find out. He held out his hand. "Come on, I'd like to introduce you."

She trustingly placed her hand in his. "I thought they were divorced?" she asked as they walked into the living room.

"They are, but I think maybe they're working on getting back together." Jadon still was a little surprised by that revelation himself. The absence of a wedding ring on his dad's hand and the way he seemed to be renewing a relationship with his mother had convinced him his dad had ditched his second wife. Or, more likely, she'd ditched him.

He opened the front door to find his parents anxiously waiting on the front porch. "Come on in, Mom. Dad."

His parents entered the house, their gazes immediately seeking Alyssa, who stood near the center of the living room.

"Alyssa, these are my parents, Janet and Josh Reichert," he said, performing the introductions. "Mom, Dad, this is Alyssa Knight."

Alyssa's tremulous smile betrayed her nerves. "It's nice to meet you," she said.

"It's so nice to meet you, too." His mother wasn't shy, but crossed right over to envelop Alyssa in an enthusiastic hug. "We're so glad you and Jadon found each other. And we just can't wait to see the babies. Twin girls."

Alyssa's smile faltered a little as she glanced over at Jadon, her brow raised questioningly. He tried to reassure her with his gaze that the decision was hers.

He'd abide by her wishes.

Alyssa found herself immediately warming to Jadon's parents. They were both so nice and friendly it was difficult not to like them.

And as they chatted, she began to hope that the fact Jadon had told his parents about the girls meant he was planning a future together.

"Of course you're welcome to see the babies," she told them.

They all climbed into Jadon's car, talking as he negotiated the short distance to Cedar Bluff Hospital, the brown building standing out starkly against the white snow. She told his parents about the labor and delivery, having to go back and repeat the entire story about how she'd fallen into Lake Michigan, which had sent her into early labor. They were horrified and thankful everyone was all right.

Inside the hospital, Jadon's parents commented

about how friendly the staff were when they were constantly greeted by people she and Jadon knew.

"That's why I like it here so much," Jadon explained to his parents. "It's like everyone is part of a family."

Up in the nursery, Jadon's mother started crying when she saw the babies. Jadon's dad held her with a sturdy arm around her shoulders and Alyssa's, though his own eyes seemed a bit moist as he gazed down at the two isolettes holding Grace and Gretchen.

"They're just beautiful," Janet said, reaching over to give Alyssa another hug as she sniffled loudly. "My granddaughters."

"Would you both like to hold them?" she offered, feeling very much like a proper daughter-in-law.

When they both nodded, she fetched warm blankets and wrapped Grace and then Gretchen, handing one baby to each of Jadon's parents. They settled into the two rockers, rapt expressions of sheer wonder on their faces.

"Thank you," Jadon murmured as they stood back, allowing his parents some time with the babies.

"For what?"

"Allowing them to visit."

"Did you think I wouldn't?"

He shrugged. "I wasn't sure."

She stared at him, realizing he would truly have stood by whatever decision she'd made. If she'd thought the situation would bring too much stress, he would have turned them away. Love shone from his eyes and she realized that with Jadon actions spoke much louder than words.

He'd shown her how much he cared in everything he'd done for her. Why had she been so hung up on the words?

He was offering her the family she'd always wanted.

Maybe it wasn't perfect, she knew there would be challenges to face with Jadon's twin brother, Jack, but did she really have anything to complain about? No family was completely perfect, and wasn't it their flaws, along with all the love and laughter, that made the whole package?

And worrying about illnesses of any kind, emotional disturbances, cancer, pick-the-disease-of-your-choice was ridiculous. There was no predicting the future. There was no point to living your life in fear.

"Jadon, I would never keep you or your family away from the girls. Ever."

"Really?" He didn't look sure.

"Yes. And I hope someday you'll allow us to be a part of your family, too."

Instead of closing down his emotions, a glimpse of hopeful surprise gleamed in his eyes. And she understood he didn't want to be the cause of distress, so she needed to convince him that when you loved someone, you made sacrifices for them.

Wasn't that what Jadon had done with Jack? He'd made many sacrifices, she was sure.

None of this was Jadon's fault. He'd done the best he could, considering the difficult circumstances.

"Alyssa, your girls are the most beautiful babies in the entire nursery," his mother gushed. "Don't you think so, Josh?"

"Absolutely," Jadon's father agreed.

"Thank you. Jadon and I feel the same way."

"Yeah, and we're thrilled they're doing so well," Jadon added, taking her hand in his.

His parents stayed a few more minutes, then stood to leave.

"Do you want to ride home with us?" Jadon asked.

"I think I should stay here, to see if they'll nurse a bit," she told him.

He nodded. "Okay, I'll take my parents back in my car and then come back to pick you up."

She watched them leave, and then turned to try nursing Gretchen, who'd woken up and started crying.

The baby actually latched on for a few minutes and Alyssa was thrilled with the small progress. She then nursed Grace, finishing just as Jadon returned.

"I don't think I've ever seen my parents so excited," he said, grinning broadly. "I think they've always secretly wanted a daughter."

She'd felt like a daughter with them, when she hadn't for a very long time. And it was time to put her fears to rest, fighting for what she wanted. "Jadon, there's something you need to know."

Instantly his smile faded and his gaze turned wary. "What is it?"

Gathering her courage, she blurted, "I love you."

He stared at her, his gaze reserved. "Alyssa, I know you think you love me, but Jack's illness isn't going to magically disappear. I don't think you understand the impact it may have on us. I'll always have to help when he's in trouble."

"Do you think I don't know that?" His comments hurt. "I love you, Jadon, because of who you are. The man who loves his family. The man who supports the people he loves. The man who will be the perfect father for our daughters."

He took a deep breath and let it out slowly. "I love you, too, Alyssa. But I'm afraid. I'm worried our love won't be strong enough to weather the stress of Jack's illness."

"Jadon, everything we've gone through has been easier when we've been together. We'll make it through the tough times. I believe in you and I believe in us. Our love is strong enough to get through anything."

He didn't answer but drew her into his arms for a deep kiss and she could tell he was showing her the best way he could, with actions and words. "I have to be there for Jack, but I promise to love and support you and the girls, too."

"I know." She believed him. And knowing he was committed to helping his brother only made her love him more. He wasn't anything like her father, who hadn't stood by anyone. Jadon was committed to his family. Their family was solid and would support Jack. She was optimistic that if Jack stayed on his medication, he'd be fine. "I think Jack will get better. And if there's anything I can do to help, I will."

Jadon's gaze was full of admiration. "What did I do to deserve you?" he asked.

She smiled, circling his waist with her arms and resting her head on his strong, broad chest. "We deserve each other. I love you, Jadon. With my whole heart. With love, we can do anything."

"I want to believe that, Alyssa. Very much."

His hesitancy didn't bother her. She had enough faith for both of them. She was confident the power of their love would make it work.

No matter what.

EPILOGUE

JADON gazed nervously down at the tiny babies, their faces barely visible through the blankets tucked securely around them in their respective infant car seats.

This was it. Grace and Gretchen were coming home. They wore tiny infant apnea monitors, but otherwise they were just fine. The realization that the two were solely dependent on him and Alyssa made him feel just a little panicky.

Alyssa's eyes were full of excitement. "It's Christmas Eve. It's a miracle that we're able to bring the babies home in time for Christmas."

He swallowed hard and nodded. He thought it was a miracle that they were going to have a family dinner this evening at his house. His mother had already prepared most of the meal so that everything would be ready to go when they arrived.

"Thanks for everything," he said to Louis Downer and Carla, the nurse they'd grown close to over the past two weeks. "Are you ready?" he asked Alyssa, grabbing Grace's car seat.

"Yes." Alyssa gave Louis and Carla quick hugs before picking up Gretchen's infant seat. "I'm ready."

Getting both car seats tucked into the backseat of the car wasn't an easy task, but soon they were on their way home.

"Are you sure about this?" Jadon asked, darting a glance over at Alyssa.

She simply smiled, looking far more relaxed than he was. "Yes, Jadon. I'm sure."

He couldn't seem to mask his own anxiety, but nodded anyway. When he pulled into his driveway, he saw that another car stood in the driveway, behind his mother's.

They were here.

He helped unbuckle the infant seats, which was much easier than getting them strapped in. He handed one of the babies to Alyssa and he took the other.

Inside the house, the scent of honey-roasted ham and cranberries filled the air. His father and his brother were busy setting gaily wrapped gifts beneath Alyssa's lopsided Christmas tree. By pouring gallons of water into the bowl at the base, they'd managed to nurture it along until Christmas. It seemed to fit right in with the rest of his family.

Alyssa's eyes widened when she saw his brother. Jack rose to his feet uncertainly, tucking his hands in the front pockets of his black slacks and gazing wistfully at the infant carrier seats.

His brother had cleaned up nicely, making his resemblance to himself all the more startling. Jack's most recent stay at the hospital had brought some great progress and it had actually been Alyssa's idea to have the entire family together for Christmas. He'd only agreed after discussing the possibility with Dr. Liz, who'd ensured Jack's medication blood levels were within therapeutic range to avoid any erratic episodes before giving her permission for the visit.

"Hi, Jack," Alyssa greeted his brother warmly. "It's great to meet you."

"It's good to meet you, too, Alyssa. Thanks for inviting me to dinner." Jack's earnest expression made Jadon relax a bit. Things were going to be fine.

Alyssa smiled and unbuttoned her coat. "Would you like to meet your nieces?"

"Sure."

Jadon set Grace's infant seat on the couch and took Alyssa's coat from her hands. She unbundled the babies just enough for Jack to see their peacefully sleeping faces.

"This one is Grace Aubrey. She was three pounds, nine ounces at birth. And this one is Gretchen Louise, who was three pounds, three ounces when she was born."

Jack stared at the baby girls in awe. "They're beautiful. Jadon is a very lucky guy."

"Well, I think I'm pretty lucky, too," Alyssa said with a tiny laugh, putting him at ease. Jadon noticed his mother and father exchanged a grateful look.

"Mom, do you need any help in the kitchen?" he asked.

"Nope, I have everything under control," she claimed before disappearing back into her haven.

His father had picked up Jack at the hospital to bring him to Cedar Bluff. Jack would only stay for a short while and then his father would take him back to the hospital.

"Would you like to hold one of the babies?" Alyssa was asking Jack now.

His brother's eyes lit up. "Yes, please."

"Take a seat on the chair over there. You can hold Grace." Alyssa gently drew the baby out of her car seat and carried her over to Jack, who took the precious bundle in his arms as if he were holding the most priceless piece of crystal in the world.

Jadon had to swallow hard and look away. Alyssa was doing everything right. She'd made his brother feel at ease and had trusted him with her most prized possession.

It was perfect, having his entire family together at last.

Later, after dinner was over and everyone had opened their gifts, which included lots of baby clothes for Grace and Gretch, it was time for his brother to leave.

Jadon walked with Jack and his father outside. His father slid inside the car to warm it up, leaving the brothers alone for a minute.

"You have a great family, Jadon," Jack said in a low voice.

"*We* have a great family, Jack," he corrected. "Remember, we're all in this together."

"I finally accepted what Dr. Liz has been telling me about taking my medication for the rest of my life," Jack said slowly. "I realize that if I stop, bad things happen."

Jadon nodded. "I'm glad you're following Dr. Liz's advice. She really cares about you, Jack. We all do."

A ghost of a smile flitted on Jack's mouth. "Yeah, I know. Maybe if I keep taking my medication, I'll have a chance at a normal life someday, too."

Jadon hoped so. He really hoped so. And maybe he and Alyssa together could help Jack better than he'd been able to do alone. Small, delicate snowflakes started to fall, and he threw an arm around Jack's shoulders, giving him a quick embrace. "Take care, Jack. We'll see you at the girls' baptisms in a few weeks."

"I'll look forward to it." Jack returned his embrace, before climbing into the passenger seat beside his father.

Jadon stood, watching them leave, barely feeling the cold snow-kisses as he stared at the spot where his dad's taillights had vanished in the dark night.

Alyssa came outside, shivering. "Hey, it's snowing! Jadon? Are you all right?"

"I'm fine." He turned and hugged her, knowing how lucky he was to have such a wonderful woman in his life. She'd given him such a precious family. "Let's go back inside."

"All right," she agreed.

He waited for her to take a seat near the Christmas tree before kneeling beside her. "I have a Christmas gift for you."

She gasped when she saw the black velvet box. "Jadon?"

"Alyssa, I love you so much. You've made me realize how much stronger we are when we're together. Will you please marry me?" He flipped open the ring box, displaying a dazzling pink diamond engagement ring with a matching wedding band.

Pink. Of course he'd bought her something pink. First, they'd brought the babies home, then they'd had a wonderful family dinner with Jadon's brother. And now a proposal.

Three Christmas miracles in one day. She smiled through happy tears. "Yes, Jadon, I'd be honored to marry you."

"Merry Christmas, Alyssa."

She smiled and kissed him, hugging him tight and vowing to never let go. "Merry Christmas, Jadon."

No Christmas had ever been as special as this.

TWINS UNDER
HIS TREE

KAREN ROSE SMITH

To my father-in-law, Edgar S. Smith, who served in World War II in Patton's army. We miss you.

For all servicemen who strive to keep us safe.

Thanks to Captain Jay Ostrich,
Pennsylvania National Guard,
who so readily and patiently answered my questions.
I couldn't have developed my hero's character
so deeply without his input.

Chapter One

Late February

Dr. Lily Wescott stood at the podium, peering through the spotlight into the sea of faces in the hotel ballroom. Many grinned and waved as she prepared to accept the Medical Professional Woman of the Year Award.

She brushed tears away, stunned and totally overwhelmed. These days, she blamed the rise and fall of her emotions on her pregnancy, though memories of the husband she'd lost in Afghanistan were never far from her heart.

Suddenly an odd sensation gripped her back and a cramp rippled through her stomach. As best she could, she fought to keep her shoulders back and a smile on her face. She couldn't go into labor now! She was only at thirty-three weeks.

But she was an ob/gyn—and she knew all too well that her twins would come when *they* were ready. Lily could only hope for the best.…

"Thank you," she said into the microphone. "I never imagined I'd win this award." She'd really expected one of her friends at the table to win. After all, they were all baby experts at the Family Tree Health Center in Lubbock, Texas. She went on, "At the Family Tree Fertility Center, we strive to help women who—"

A second cramp squeezed Lily's side and she caught the wooden podium for support. Out of the corner of her eye, she saw her friend and colleague, Dr. Mitch Catega, jump to his feet, concern on his face. He rushed to the stage and up the steps.

As she managed to suck in a gulp of air, hot liquid washed down her leg. *Oh, God—I am in labor!*

She was *not* going to panic. She was *not* going to crumple to the floor. She was *not* going to be embarrassed.

At her side now, Mitch's arm curled around her waist…his injured arm. *The one he never let anyone see,* she thought, needing something other than the pain to concentrate on. His arm was always covered, tonight by a well-cut black tuxedo that made his shoulders seem even broader than usual. She'd noticed that tonight… and it wasn't the first time…

"Can you walk?" he asked, his breath warm at her ear.

A murmur swept through the audience.

She turned, the side of her cheek brushing his chin. "I'm not sure."

Mitch's angular jaw tightened, his almost-black gaze held hers with…something she couldn't define. But then it was replaced by the empathy and compassion she'd felt from him many times before. "The twins are our main priority. Hold on to me if you can't stand on your own."

She really thought she could. The cramp faded away. If it weren't for the wetness between her legs, she could deny what was happening.

With Mitch's arm still around her, she took a couple of steps. Maybe she could even give the rest of her acceptance speech—

The lance of pain that pierced her back stole her breath and weakened her knees. She exhaled, "Mitch…"

And he was there…lifting her into his arms…carrying her down the dais steps.

"I'm driving her to the hospital myself," Mitch said, as Lily's friends and colleagues rushed toward him. "It will be quicker than waiting for an ambulance."

"And more economical," Lily realized aloud, trying to think practically. But that was difficult with Mitch's cologne reminding her of the last time he'd held her so close on the day she'd discovered she was having twins. His grip felt safe now as it had then…as if no harm could come to her while she was in his arms.

She must be delusional.

"I'll ride with you," Jared Madison offered as he jogged alongside Mitch and pushed open the ballroom door. "I'll be handy if the twins won't wait, since Lily's doctor is at a conference."

Jared had his own obstetrical practice at Family Tree but took turns covering with the doctors in *her* practice. Lily knew and liked Jared and felt comfortable with him. Still, she murmured, "They'd darn well better wait. It's too early. They'll be too small!" Her last words almost caught in her throat and her bravado deflated.

In the middle of the hotel lobby, Mitch stopped. Looking her directly in the eye, he said, "If you panic, Lily, you won't help the babies. Take calming breaths. You can do this."

Her heart felt lighter, as if Mitch was really part of this pregnancy, too. Not just because her husband had asked him to watch over her but because he *cared*. "If I'd taken the childbirth classes this month instead of next—" She'd been putting them off, maybe trying to deny the inevitable—that yet again, her life would be altered in an earth-shattering way.

"The twins would still come early," he reminded her. "They apparently want to meet their mom *now*."

Yes, they did. And she wanted to meet *them*. She couldn't wait to hold them and tell them how much she loved them. How much their daddy would have loved them...

Mitch's expression was gentle, as if he could read her thoughts, but his gaze didn't waver. His arms were so strong. For a moment, she felt a little trill of excitement in her chest. But that was because of the babies—wasn't it?

"Let's go," she whispered, shaken by the emotions she didn't understand.

Mitch paced the maternity floor waiting room and stopped when he saw Lily's friends watching him peculiarly. He didn't like the worried expressions on their faces. Raina, Gina and Tessa were all baby experts. Along with them, he knew premature babies often had problems—thirty-three weeks was iffy.

Trying to loosen up the tight feeling in his shoulder, arm and hand—injuries that reminded him all too often of his service in Iraq—Mitch flexed them, then sank down on one of the vinyl chairs.

Moving forward on the sofa, Tessa said gently, "It really hasn't been that long."

What was worrying Mitch was that they hadn't heard anything in the hour they'd been here. Closing his eyes, he remembered the day Lily had learned she was having twins. It had been the week before Thanksgiving. One of the techs in the office had performed the ultrasound. Mitch had just finished discussing fertility procedure options with a couple. As his clients had headed for the reception area, he'd noticed Lily exit the exam room, her complexion almost sheet-white, her blue eyes very bright.

"The ultrasound go okay?" he'd asked.

"Oh, Mitch, I'm having *twins!*"

He hadn't been able to tell if she was totally elated or totally terrified.

Clasping her hand, he'd pulled her into the office he'd just vacated. "What's going through your head?"

She'd stood at the chair in front of his desk, holding on to it for support. "The obvious. I'll be a single mom. My friends all say they'll help, but these babies will be *my* responsibility."

"Twins will always have each other," he pointed out. "They won't grow up lonely. They'll be able to play together." He hoped Lily could see the upside of this monumental news. "Girls or boys?"

"They're girls."

"Our techs are pretty good at distinguishing the difference."

Lily had actually blushed a little. Until he'd met her, he didn't think women blushed anymore. But she was blonde with fair skin and all of her emotions seemed to show in her complexion. Major ones had played over her face over the past few months—grief, fear, determination and the sheer loss of her husband.

"Troy would be so proud," she'd said, tears beginning to run down her face.

That's when Mitch had done something he *never* should have done. He'd taken her into his arms. She'd laid her head on his shoulder, crying. And he'd felt desire that had no place in that room.

Mitch had met Troy—at that time Troy and Lily had been engaged—when the Family Tree staff had planned a dinner to welcome Mitch into the practice. Since he'd once served in the Army National Guard and Troy still had, they'd developed an immediate rapport, becoming friends. After Troy and Lily married, Troy had even asked Mitch to watch over Lily while he'd served overseas.

But then Troy had been killed in action, leaving Lily pregnant and alone.

When Lily had finally looked up at him, Mitch hadn't been sure *what* he'd seen there. Yet he'd known damn well it hadn't been interest. Gratitude, maybe?

She'd pulled away, wiped her eyes and mumbled an awkward apology, and they'd gone their separate ways. They'd gone back to being colleagues. She hadn't really confided in him again.

That was okay. Being merely colleagues was safer for both of them.

Now, however, it was the last week in February and

she was in labor. When he'd seen her double over on that dais, he'd felt panic twist his gut.

"Mitch!" A male voice called his name.

When he opened his eyes, he saw Jared, gesturing from the hall.

He stood immediately. "What's going on?"

"She wants you."

"What do you mean, she wants me?"

"She's in labor, and she wants you to coach her."

Her friends all glanced his way. He knew they were wondering why and so was he. But he wasn't going to ask Jared his questions. He was going to ask Lily.

"Suit up," Jared advised him. "When you're ready, she's in delivery room two."

Five minutes later, Mitch had pulled sterile garb over his clothes. It would feel strange being back in an operating-room setting, even though he had to admit a delivery room wasn't *exactly* that. When he'd rushed through the ER with Lily, one of the nurses had waved at him. Years ago, she'd worked with him in trauma surgery.

Sometimes he itched to be doing that kind of work again. Reflexively, he bent his fingers, most of them not responding well. But he'd gotten used to limited use of his right hand, as well as insomnia and nightmares. At least the stiffness in his shoulder and leg could be relieved with the right amount of exercise. He was damn lucky he'd left Iraq with his life. There was no point in complaining about what might have been. Changing his specialty to endocrinology had saved his sanity.

When he pushed open the door of the delivery room, he forgot about whether he should or shouldn't be there. Seeing Lily on the table, her face flushed, her hands clenched tight on the sheet, a protective urge took over. She was hooked up to monitors that measured the frequency and intensity of contractions as well as the babies' heart rates. She looked small and frightened…and fragile. Yet he knew she was the strongest woman he'd ever known. She'd proved that since her husband had died.

He strode to the bed, hooked a stool with his foot and positioned it beside her. Glancing at Emily Madison, Jared's wife and a professional midwife, he asked, "Don't you want Emily to coach you?"

Lily pushed damp hair behind her ear. "She's assisting Jared."

He knew why he was fighting being here. Witnessing a woman in labor, watching a birth, was an intimate experience. Right now, bonding with Lily would be foolish.

He could see a contraction gearing up in intensity. Maybe she just wanted him here instead of one of her friends because he might be more detached yet professional about the births.

With a mental kick that he hoped would push him toward that detachment, he took hold of her hand, felt the softness and warmth of it.

Suddenly she squeezed his fingers so hard he lost any feeling he *did* have left. But the pressure reminded him he had a job to do. If he concentrated on coaching, maybe he wouldn't notice how her chin quivered or how her eyes grew shiny with emotion.

When the contraction eased, he admitted, "I'm not sure how best to help you."

"You worked with men in the field. You helped

them. Help me the same way. Just help me *focus* on something."

She was right. He had helped men before and after surgeries, with mortar blasts exploding, with rocket-propelled grenades shattering the air. Finally he really did understand why she wanted him here.

Realizing what he had to do, he smoothed his thumb over the top of her hand, telling himself his need to touch her was simply for her comfort. "Watch my nose," Mitch ordered Lily.

She looked at him as if he was crazy. "You're kidding, right?"

"I'm not. Use it as your focal point and listen to the sound of my voice."

She focused on his eyes instead of his nose. He saw so many emotions there—worry, hope and grief...the resoluteness he'd admired as she'd exhibited it each day, ready to go on with her life and care for her twins.

Mitch saw her tense and turned to the monitor. With another contraction coming, he squeezed her hand. "You can do this."

She was still looking into his eyes instead of at his nose. He felt as if his heart was going to jump out of his chest. He felt as if...he *shouldn't* be here. Again, he warned himself that he couldn't make such an intimate connection. He should just be watching over her.

But how could he watch over her without getting involved?

At this moment, he wished he'd never made that promise to Troy.

At the foot of the bed, Emily said, "Lily, you can start pushing now."

At that moment, neonatologist Francesca Fitzgerald came into the room with two nurses behind her.

Lily gasped, "Francesca."

The doctor patted Lily's arm and summed up the situation with a quick assessment. "My team's here. You do your part and we'll take care of the rest."

Lily's contraction peaked and her cry of pain sliced through Mitch.

Jared encouraged her. "Good one, Lily. Come on. I want this baby out."

"You can do this," Mitch reminded her. He held her hand as the tension built in her body again. Her face reddened and she gave another fantastically effort-filled push.

All at once he heard Jared say, "I've got one!"

"Is she all right?" Lily asked. "Please tell me she's all right."

A light infant cry came from the area where Francesca was standing. It was very soft, but it *was* a cry.

"She's a beauty," Jared told her. "We might have a few minutes now. I want to get her sister out, as quickly as I can."

"I don't think I have a few minutes," Lily gasped. "It's starting again." She practically sat up with the strength and pain of the contraction.

"Use it," Mitch said. "Go with it."

"Just one more push," Emily encouraged her. "She's your youngest. You're going to have to coax her a little harder."

Mitch realized Lily wasn't focusing on him anymore. She was breathing when she had to, breathing any way she could. She needed a different type of support, physical as well as emotional. Knowing exactly what he had to do, Mitch stood, went to the head of the birthing table and wrapped his arm around her shoulders. He warned himself he was only a substitute for Troy. But he didn't feel like a substitute. His arms around Lily, he knew he was doing this for himself as well as his friend.

Tears swept down her cheeks. Her bangs were plastered to her forehead. She pushed her shoulder-length hair away from her face and stared straight ahead.

As her contraction built, her body curved into it, curved around it. Mitch held her as she delivered a second little girl.

Jared announced, "And here's princess number two."

Again he passed the infant to Francesca who worked at clearing her airway, cleaning her eyes, checking her lungs, hooking her up to the ventilator to help her breathe. When Mitch saw that, a lump rose in his throat.

"I've got them," Francesca reassured Lily. "I'll be around to give you a report as soon as I can." Then she pushed the babies away, out another door before Lily even glimpsed them.

Reluctantly, Mitch released Lily as she collapsed onto the bed, murmuring, "Maybe I should have quit work sooner and stayed in bed. It's often recommended with twins. But I rested the past two weeks. I kept my feet up as much as I could."

Mitch knew he had to keep Lily calm after her ordeal. "You did everything you thought was best. That's all you could do."

Lily surprised him when she caught his hand again and held it tight. "Troy should have been here. He should have seen his girls born. He should have helped me name them. He should have…he should have…"

"He should have never died," Mitch filled in.

Lily bowed her head and finally let the tears fall unchecked. Mitch did the only thing he could—he held her in his arms until she simply couldn't cry anymore.

Lily had been settled in her hospital room for at least two hours and was growing anxious. Why hadn't Francesca come yet? Wouldn't they have told her if something had happened to either of the babies?

Her gaze landed on Mitch, who was standing at the window. He was as calm as she was agitated. Where did that calm come from after what he'd been through? He'd been presented a Combat Medical Badge, awarded a Silver Star and a Purple Heart, though he never spoke of them. All Troy had told her was that Mitch had been involved in an IED explosion.

"How do you do it?" she asked, following the train of thoughts in her head.

Minus his jacket and tie, his tuxedo shirt was rumpled. He turned to look at her. "Do what?"

"Stay calm under any circumstances."

He shot her a wry half smile. "It's a learned technique."

Interested in anything that would keep her mind off what was going on down the hall, she asked, "Like meditation?"

Even though she'd worked with Mitch for more than two and a half years, she didn't know much about him. Just the little Troy had told her. She knew he was forty-five, had been born in Sagebrush—the small town where they both lived about fifteen minutes outside

Lubbock—but he had no family there. He'd been deployed to Iraq, injured and changed specialties—from trauma surgery to endocrinology—because he'd lost the fine motor coordination in his hand that he needed to perform surgery. But that was about the extent of her knowledge of his background.

"I learned several techniques," he replied, running his hand through his jet-black hair. "Meditation was one. Guided imagery was another."

Her gaze went to his hand and the ragged scars there. She wanted to ask if he'd learned the techniques when he'd been hurt. Had they been his method of recovering? But that was such personal territory. If he didn't mention Iraq himself, she knew better than to jump into it.

In spite of herself, she still remembered gazing into his eyes rather than looking at his nose while he'd coached her. Every time since the day she'd told him she was having twins, she'd felt such an intense...

She wasn't sure what it was she felt. Mitch knew things. He'd *felt* things. She could just instinctively sense that. The compassion he showed her seemed personal, but maybe he was that way with everyone.

"You know, your friends wanted to stay," he said.

Yes, they did. But they all had children and husbands and practices to see to. "I told them there was nothing they could do here. I'm going to call them as soon as we find out about the babies. Oh, Mitch, what's taking so long?"

Leaving his pensive position at the window, he crossed to her bed. He was so tall...confident...strong.

She remembered being held in his arms—in the exam room at the practice, on the dais, in the delivery room. His cologne had wrapped around her as he'd given her his strength. That's why she'd needed him with her through the delivery—because he was so strong. Now when she looked at him she could hardly swallow.

With one push of his booted foot, the comfortable chair by the nightstand now sat beside her bed. He sank down into the chair. It was well after 1:00 a.m. and she knew he had to be tired after a full day of work. She should tell him to go home, too. But he seemed willing to see her through this and she felt she needed him here.

Though she realized her body was ready for a good long rest, she couldn't relax. Adrenaline was still rushing through her because she was so concerned about her twins.

In the labor room, Mitch had taken her hand. Now he didn't.

Why should it matter? she wondered. She quickly decided it didn't. After all, she was still in love with Troy. At times, she thought she heard him in the next room. Other times, she expected his booming voice to announce that he was home. She fought back sudden emotion.

Mitch's deep, even voice reassured her. "I have a feeling Francesca will only come to you after the babies are stabilized…after she can tell you something for certain."

"You're so honest," Lily blurted out. "I wanted you to say she probably had another emergency and that's why it was taking her so long."

"Do you believe that?"

His expression wasn't stern. His lean cheeks and high cheekbones just made him appear that way sometimes.

As his black brows drew together just a little, he looked expectant…as if he knew she couldn't lie to herself.

"It's possible," she murmured.

"Yes, it's possible," he agreed.

"Talk to me about something," she pleaded. "Anything."

She knew she might be asking for a lot. Mitch communicated, but only when he had something to say. Chitchat didn't seem to be in his nature. But now she would be glad for anything her mind could latch on to.

"When is Raina McGraw's baby due?"

Lily smiled, picturing her friend with her rounding stomach. "June fifth. Talk about having a lot on your plate."

"I understand Shep adopted three children before she married him."

"They're still in the process with Manuel, their two-and-a-half-year-old. Shep had started adoption proceedings, but then he and Raina married. It was almost like starting over. Their housekeeper, Eva, is wonderful, but Raina could be running from morning to night once the baby's born. I think she's going to take a leave from her practice."

"Have you decided yet how long you're going to stay out?"

"I'll make up my mind soon. Everything about my life is in flux right now."

"You don't have to decide right away. You might have to consider getting help with the twins."

"No, I won't need it. My roommate Angie—Gina's sister—says she'll help me. She's a nurse, away right now on the disaster relief team. But she should be back soon. Besides, there are lots of moms who take care of two babies."

"Not necessarily at the same time." His tone held a warning note that maybe she was being a little too Pollyanna-ish.

"I can handle it, Mitch. You'll see."

She was contemplating the idea of breast-feeding both babies when the door pushed open and Francesca walked in. She seemed surprised to see Mitch there, but didn't comment.

Lily hadn't known Francesca very long. But one evening, the women who'd lived in the Victorian house on a quiet street in Sagebrush had gathered there and just enjoyed a ladies' night of chatting and sharing backgrounds. All of them were connected in so many ways— through their professions, friendships or family ties.

Lily had felt so alone after Troy had died, but that night all of the women had made her feel as if she had a support network.

"Tell me," Lily said to Francesca.

"Your older daughter weighs four point two pounds, is seventeen inches long, and needs a little time to put on weight. We're giving her CPAP treatment. She's breathing on her own and is definitely a crier when she's unhappy."

The continuous positive airway pressure would help the infant breathe but not breathe for her. Lily's heart swelled with love for this tiny baby although she hadn't even laid eyes on her yet. "And my youngest?" Lily's voice shook a little bit when she asked.

"She weighs four pounds, is sixteen and a half inches and had trouble breathing." Francesca immediately held up both hands. "Now, don't panic. We have her stabilized. She's on a ventilator for now—"

"Oh my God!" Lily's chest felt so tight she could hardly breathe.

"I mean it, Lily. Don't panic. We'll wean her off it. Her lungs need to develop and, of course, she needs to gain weight, too, before she can go home."

"When can I see them?"

Francesca sighed. "I shouldn't allow it, but I know you're not going to rest or get any sleep until I let you visit them."

Lily nodded. She was happy, afraid and plain exhausted. But she had to see them.

"All right. I'll find a wheelchair. But you can only have a few minutes with them, and then I need to tuck you in. Childbirth is natural, but it's traumatic, too, and you need time to recover."

"I know," Lily said. "When do you think I'll be discharged?"

"You'll have to ask Jared that, but my guess is you'll be here until Sunday morning."

At least she'd be here so she could visit her babies. *Her babies.* Everything about their birth came rushing back, especially Mitch's presence and support. "Can Mitch come, too?"

Francesca hesitated and looked from one of them to the other. "This is just for a few minutes. You both have to wear masks and sterile gowns. I'll be right back."

Mitch looked troubled. "Are you sure you want me there, Lily?"

"You helped me bring them into the world. Of course, I want you there."

Maybe it was because of the letter Troy had left for

her. In it, he'd told her he'd asked Mitch to look after her if anything happened to him. He'd trusted Mitch, and that made it easy for her to trust him, too. He'd certainly come through for her tonight.

Ten minutes later, Lily and Mitch were in the NIC unit, staring at her two precious little girls. The babies absolutely snatched Lily's breath away.

Mitch stood behind her, his hand on her shoulder. "Have you considered names?"

"Now that I see them, I can name them." She pointed to her firstborn, saying lightly, "Sophie, I'd like you to meet Mitch. He helped me bring you into this world."

Her baby opened her eyes, seemed to gaze at them both for a few seconds before she closed them again.

Lily's heart overflowed with love as her focus turned to her youngest, who needed help to breathe.

Mitch's fingers tightened on Lily's shoulder and she was so grateful for his quiet strength, his stalwart caring.

"And this tiny angel is—" Lily's voice caught. Finally she managed to say, "Her name is Grace."

Mitch crouched down beside Lily so he could see her children from her vantage point. The slant of his jaw almost grazed her cheek as he reassured her, "They're going to gain weight and strength each day."

When Mitch turned to her instead of the twins, Lily's heart beat faster. "Thank you," she said simply.

"You're welcome," Mitch returned with a crooked smile. Just for tonight she'd let Mitch Cortega be her rock. Just for tonight, she'd depend on him.

Then she'd stand on her own two feet and raise her babies alone.

Chapter Two

Mitch stood in Lily's hospital room on Sunday afternoon. She was ready to go home and be a mom, but her babies couldn't go home with her. At least, not for a few weeks, and only then if no further problems developed. She didn't want to leave them, but she had no choice. She also couldn't drive herself home. Gina was in Houston again. Angie was still away, helping flood victims. And Raina, six months pregnant with a new husband and three boys to think about, had enough on her plate.

So Mitch had offered to drive Lily home, and she'd accepted. In fact, the thought of being with him again had made her feel...less worried. But now that he was standing in the room, dressed in jeans and a dark-green V-neck sweater, her pulse was speeding faster. She told herself she was just excited about leaving the hospital.

However, she snuck another peek at him and felt her stomach flutter.

Maybe she should have just paid taxi fare from Lubbock to Sagebrush instead of accepting his assistance so readily.

He seemed to read some of her thoughts. "I know you want to be independent, Lily, but I'm only giving you a ride home. You'll be driving again soon."

She did have to put this in perspective. "I just never expected to be going home without my babies and without—" She abruptly stopped.

"And without Troy," he filled in, not afraid to say it.

Blinking very fast she zipped the overnight case that Raina had dropped off for her. "I'm ready to get out of here and finish decorating the nursery. Everything needs to be perfect when my girls come home."

Mitch came up behind her, gently took her by the shoulders and turned her around. "You don't have to hide what you're feeling."

"I have to get *over* what I'm feeling, Mitch. I have two babies to take care of, to support. I can't think about Troy not being here and do what I have to do."

"You can't deny it, either. That will only bring you more heartache in the end."

Gazing into his deep brown eyes, she felt that unsettled sensation in the pit of her stomach again.

"I'm ready to go," she said firmly. She'd cry at night when she was too tired to do anything else. In the meantime, she was going to put a life together for her children.

Mitch dropped his hands from her shoulders and

picked up her overnight case. "Then let's get you home."

Their fifteen-minute drive from Lubbock to the small Texas town of Sagebrush was quiet for the most part. Mitch didn't seem to feel the need to talk and stared straight ahead as he drove. She had too many thoughts buzzing through her mind to want to be involved in conversation—including her unsettling awareness of the black-haired, broad-shouldered, protective man sitting beside her. Before her labor, hadn't she looked at Mitch as the person he was? Had she just seen him merely as a colleague? Simply a friend of Troy's? A person on the outskirts of her life but not really *in* her life?

He pulled into the driveway in front of the detached garage at the large blue Victorian-style house with yellow shutters, then turned to her with questions in his eyes, voicing one of them. "Who's going to be staying with you?"

"No one's staying with me."

Silence fell over the SUV as wind buffeted it.

"Isn't Angie back yet?" Mitch asked.

"No. When she's called away on the disaster relief team, there's no knowing how long she'll be gone."

"What about Raina?"

"I can't expect her to come over here and sit with me with all her responsibilities. Besides, I don't need a babysitter."

"As soon as you walk into that house, you're going to be surprised by how tired you feel. You can't stay here alone tonight."

Lily suddenly felt panicked without knowing exactly why. "What are you suggesting?"

"I'm not suggesting anything. I'm going to give you

two options. One, I can take you home with me and you can stay there for the night."

She was shaking her head already.

"Or, two, I can sleep on your couch."

She was still shaking her head.

"Is your refrigerator stocked?"

"I don't know."

"Do you feel like cooking supper?"

Though she didn't want to admit it, she did feel really tired. "I can make myself an egg."

"I seem to remember Jared ordering you to go home and rest today, for what's left of it, and turn in early tonight."

"He's just being cautious."

Mitch unbuckled his seat belt and shifted behind the wheel to face her. "I know as doctors we make the worst patients, but you've got to be sensible. When those babies come home in a few weeks, you have to be ready *physically* as well as emotionally. So, at least for today, accept help without argument."

Was she being unreasonable? *Was* she trying to be too strong? Why was that? Because she didn't want anyone helping her…or she suddenly didn't want *Mitch* helping her? The thought of him sleeping on her couch tonight made her stomach do something more than flutter. She felt as if she'd gone over the top of a Ferris wheel.

But she certainly wasn't going to Mitch's place. The gossips in Sagebrush would have a field day.

"Let's go inside and you can curl up on the sofa," he suggested. "I'll get you something to drink and we'll go from there."

"Don't you have other things to do today?"

"Repairing winter's damage to the patio? Sweeping out my garage?" He gave her one of his rare smiles.

Ever since Mitch had started with the practice, she'd noticed the long hours he worked, longer than any of the other physicians. He even scheduled consultations on Saturdays. He had rarely taken off work in the time she'd known him. Didn't he have a life outside of the fertility lab? Did he have friends other than the service buddies Troy had once mentioned? Mitch was an enigma, a puzzle she couldn't solve—one she shouldn't be interested in at all.

She nibbled on her lower lip for a couple of seconds and then asked, "Do you know how to cook?"

When he chuckled, she liked the sound of it. "I do. My mother taught me the basics," he said with fond remembrance. "I do all right."

The air in his SUV seemed stifling. She was relieved they were separated in the bucket seats because being physically close to Mitch now seemed…dangerous.

She asked in a low voice, "Why are you doing this, Mitch?"

"I made a promise to Troy. I keep my promises."

That's what she thought. This was duty for Mitch. He was a man who knew duty and honor well.

She let out a long breath. "All right, you can sleep on my couch. But just tonight. That's it. Tomorrow I'm on my own again."

"Deal," he agreed.

Even though he said it, she saw a considering flicker in his eyes. How long would his promise to Troy hold?

Minutes later they were escaping the blustery weather outside and walking into the old house that Lily now thought of as home. Last September she'd moved out of the apartment she'd shared with Troy because the memories there had been too painful.

She breathed in the scent of cinnamon emanating from the potpourri dish beside the Tiffany lamp in the foyer. Angie had filled it before Christmas. Her housemate had understood how difficult the holidays would be for Lily and had included her in her family's celebrations. So had Gina and, of course, Raina. They'd kept Lily too busy to think if not feel. At night, alone in her room, she'd faced her loss and spoken to her unborn babies about their dad and about what their first Christmas the following year might bring. She had to look toward the future.

"Where would you like your overnight case?" Mitch asked, stepping in behind her.

"Upstairs on my bed would be great."

"The steps won't be a problem?"

"Not at all. But I'll only do them once today."

"Which room is yours?"

A jolt of reality hit when she realized Mitch would be standing in her bedroom in a few minutes. He'd see the baby catalogs and magazines splayed across the chest at the foot of the bed, as well as the photo of Troy on her dresser. What else would he notice?

And why was the idea of Mitch standing in her bedroom so unnerving?

"What's wrong?" he asked.

"Nothing. My bedroom's the second one on the right. It's the one with the yellow rose wallpaper."

"Got it," he said with the flash of a smile that made her breath hitch a little.

Confused, she decided she was just tired from the trip

home and worried about her babies. She wasn't reacting to Mitch as a man. She absolutely wasn't.

When Mitch returned downstairs, she was pulling greens and carrots from the refrigerator.

He came up beside her and took them out of her hands. "Stop. Today you're not doing a thing. Wouldn't you be more comfortable in the living room in an easy chair?"

He was a doctor, too. He knew what her body had been through, though she was trying to deny it.

"Don't you have a good book you want to read?" he teased.

She supposed humor was better than anything else. Maybe it would make this jumpy feeling she had when she was around him go away. "I'm sure I can find something to read."

When she took a last glance around, he said, "Relax and trust me."

Trust him. That was the tall and short of it. She did. And trusting him formed a bond that she just didn't want right now. She'd trusted Troy because he was her husband. But now he was gone, and she shouldn't be able to simply turn around and trust another man so easily.

Should she?

"What's going on in your head?" Mitch asked with gentle persuasion.

Nothing he'd want to know about. Her doubts and questions and issues were all hers. None of it had anything to do with him. "I'm just…wired and tired at the same time."

He set the greens and carrots on the counter. Then he nudged her around and walked her toward the living room. He was a good six inches taller than she was and she felt petite beside him.

The heat of his palm on her shoulder seeped through her knit top. She should have worn a sweater. This old house could be drafty. If she'd worn a sweater, she wouldn't feel the warmth of his hand at all…or remember him holding hers as Sophie was born.

He released her as they reached the sofa. Then he stood there and waited and she realized he wanted her to sit. He definitely was a commanding male. Why would that change simply because he was trying to be her friend? Men in the military had a particular bearing, a straightness of their backs, a tautness of their shoulders, that made them seem *more* than ordinary men. Not that anything about Mitch today seemed military. His jeans, sweater and even his leather boots looked comfortable. She couldn't remember ever seeing him dressed so casually before.

She sank down onto the sofa.

"Put your legs up," he ordered.

She didn't usually take orders well. "I'll be bored," she muttered.

While he pulled the afghan from the back of the sofa and spread it over her, he asked, "Don't you knit or something?"

"Crochet," she corrected automatically, then pointed to the tapestry bag beside the easy chair. She knew if she made a move to get it, he wouldn't let her.

When he stooped to pick up the bag, she noticed the play of his shoulder muscles, the length of his upper torso, his slim hips. A tingle that she relegated to post-birth pangs rippled through her belly. Looking away, she pulled the afghan up higher.

He brought the bag to her and settled it in her lap. "What are you making?"

After opening the Velcro closure, she extracted a pink sweater that sported one sleeve. "I didn't know whether to make these both pink or not. You know, stereotypes and all. But then I thought, two baby girls. What could be cuter than matching pink sweaters?"

He laughed. "I'm sure Sophie and Grace will agree."

She turned the sweater over in her hands and then admitted, "I was an only child. I wanted a sister desperately. Sophie and Grace will always have each other." She looked up at him again. "Do you have brothers or sisters?" She really didn't know anything about Mitch's background or his childhood.

"Nope. No brothers or sisters."

"Troy and his sister Ellie were close," Lily said in a low voice.

"He talked about her often," Mitch responded, in the way he had ever since Troy had been killed. She was grateful he made it all right for her to speak about her husband and anything connected to him.

"She's in a tough situation right now," Lily said to Mitch. "She had a small store where she sold her own line of baby clothes. But her area of Oklahoma was hard hit by the economic downturn and she had to close the store."

"What's she doing now?"

"She's trying to take her business to the internet."

"Is she coming for a visit?"

"Ellie and Troy's mom, Darlene, both want to visit after the babies come home." She'd always gotten along well with Ellie and Darlene...with all of Troy's family.

She knew he'd moved to Texas because the construction market had been thriving around Lubbock, unlike Oklahoma. She'd often wished his family wasn't so far away.

An odd expression crossed Mitch's face, one she couldn't decipher. He said, "You'll have a lot of people to help with the babies. That's just what you need."

"*Is* that what I need, Mitch? I'm their mom. I want to take care of them myself."

"Sure you do. But twins are a lot of work. There was a kid in my neighborhood when I was growing up. His mother had twins. She was always run ragged. And when you go back to work, you're definitely going to need child care."

"I have to go back," she said. "Insurance money and savings will only go so far."

"You'll have Troy's benefits," Mitch reminded her.

"That money is going into a trust fund for the twins."

He didn't contradict her, or try to convince her otherwise. She wanted to give her girls the advantages she'd had growing up. Yet, most of all, she wanted them to appreciate the people around them who loved them. When she'd lost her parents, she'd realized how little material possessions actually meant, and she'd grown up quickly.

"Did you grow up here in Sagebrush?" she asked Mitch, curious about his childhood.

"Yes, I did."

Frustrated he wasn't more expansive, she prompted, "But you don't have family here."

"No, I don't."

"Mitch," she said, letting her frustration show.

"What do you want to know, Lily? Just ask."

Studying his collar-length black hair, his chiseled features, she let the question pop into her head. *Are you just here out of duty or do you care?* Instead she replied, "I *am* asking. But you're not telling me much."

"And why is this suddenly important?"

That was a good question. "I'm not sure. I guess talking about Ellie, thinking about how I'm going to raise the twins— It just made me wonder, that's all. At least give me something to think about while I rest and twiddle my thumbs."

"Crochet," he pointed out.

"Same difference."

The silence in the living room enveloped them for a few moments until Mitch said, "Your background and mine are very different."

"How do you know about mine?"

"Troy shared some of it when we played pool."

Lily's husband and Mitch had gone out and shared an evening of guy stuff now and then, the same way she shared time with her friends.

"Just what did he tell you?"

Mitch's shrug told her he was attempting to make the conversation casual. "That your father was a respected scientist and professor at Stanford. That your mother was a pharmacist who developed her own line of cosmetics and did quite well with them. Something about after your father died, she sold the formula to provide you with a college education."

"Yes, she did," Lily murmured, mind-traveling back to a time that was filled with bittersweet memories. "Daddy died of a massive coronary when I was in high school. My mom died of breast cancer when I was in college. Losing them both made me want to find a profession that gave life."

"If your father taught at Stanford, how did you end up *here?*"

"My mom had a friend who lived in Lubbock, so we moved here. But she and my dad had always planned I'd go to their alma mater. I was at Stanford when she got sick. I flew home as often as I could, but then took off a semester when we called in hospice."

"You've had a lot of loss."

"The people I love leave me." She stared at her hands when she said it, but then she raised her gaze to his. "I know. I know. I shouldn't believe that. If nothing else, I should think positive to change the pattern. But this negative pattern is awfully fresh again and it's hard not to wonder."

"You have two little girls now to love."

"I do. And you can bet, I *will* be an overprotective mom."

"I don't think there's anything wrong with that."

Somehow the conversation had rolled back to Lily again. Mitch was so good at deflecting. Why had she never realized that? But she was also determined to delve below the surface.

Hiking herself up higher against the sofa arm, she nodded toward the space at the end of the couch where her feet had been. "Tell me how you grew up."

He looked as reluctant to sit on her couch as she was to have him sleep there tonight. But in the end, he decided she wouldn't rest until he gave her something. So he sat on the sofa, his thigh brushing one of her stockinged feet. He looked terrifically uncomfortable. "There's not much to it."

She waited, her gaze on his rugged profile.

With a grimace, he finally said, "My father married my mother because she was pregnant when they were both eighteen."

She knew Mitch was probably going to need some prompting, so she asked, "Did it last?"

Mitch's brows drew together as he, obviously reluctant, answered, "He stuck around for a year, then took off on his motorcycle and bailed. She went to business school and became a medical transcriber, but she couldn't always find work. Other times she held two jobs, cleaned offices at night and saved for when times were thin again. I was determined to make life better for both of us."

"Did you always want to be a doctor?"

"Do you mean was it a lifelong wish from childhood? No. Actually, at first I thought I might become a stockbroker or an investment banker."

Lily couldn't help but smile. She couldn't imagine Mitch as either of those. She didn't know why. She just couldn't. "So why aren't you working on Wall Street?"

"I was good at sports…basketball. I won a scholarship to college. But during my sophomore year my mother got sick and didn't tell me. She didn't have insurance so she didn't go to the doctor. She developed pneumonia and died."

"Oh, Mitch. I'm sorry. That had to be awful for you."

Again he looked uncomfortable revealing this part of his past. "She'd been my motivator. After she died, I took a nosedive. I'd been a good student, but my grades tanked. Then one day, after a few months of drinking into the night and sleeping too late to get up for class, I looked out the dorm window and knew that campus wasn't *real* life. Guys hooking up with girls, frat parties, learning to play teachers for better grades. I thought about my mom's life, how hard it had been and how it ended, and I decided to make a difference. I wanted to help patients who didn't have much of a chance. I wanted to give life when it was hardly there any longer. So I juggled two jobs, got my B.S., and went on to med school. I decided on trauma surgery. In my last year of residency, September 11th happened."

Lily thought of Raina and her first husband, a firefighter, who had lost his life that day. Her knowledge of Mitch's character and her intuition where he was concerned urged her to ask, "And that's when you signed up for the Army National Guard?"

"Yes."

"When did you go to Iraq?"

"Two years later."

They were both quiet for a few moments.

Mitch flexed his hand and moved his fingers as she often saw him do, and she knew he was remembering something he never talked about...something that caused those deep fatigue lines around his eyes some mornings.

To break the heavy silence, she asked, "Are you happy being part of our fertility practice?" She and two other doctors had been in unanimous agreement, voting him into their partnership.

"You mean would I rather be performing surgery? Sure. But I like what I do. You and me, Jon and Hillary...we give the seeds of life a chance, as well as at-risk pregnancies. That's rewarding. What I miss is not being part of the Guard, no longer having that unique camaraderie and sense of spirit. Before deployment, it was tough trying to be a doctor as well as a guardsman. But it was what I wanted to be doing."

Abruptly he stood, his body language telling her that this conversation was over. He already knew Lily was the type who wanted to know more, who would ask questions until she got her answers. He was cutting that off before it could go any further. To her surprise, she already missed his presence at the end of the sofa.

"I checked your refrigerator and you have a couple of choices," he said with a forced smile. "Scrambled eggs, scrambled eggs with asparagus and bacon on the side, or... I think I saw sausage in there that I could turn into sausage and pasta of some kind, maybe with canned tomatoes."

"Are you kidding me?" Her eyes were open wide and she was staring at him as if she really didn't know him.

"I told you my mom taught me the basics. But in college I had an apartment with two other guys. I couldn't stomach pizza every night, so I cooked. I borrowed a cookbook or two from the library and they kept me going for the year."

"You're just full of surprises," Lily said, laying her head back against the arm of the sofa, suddenly tired and feeling weak.

"Is the adrenaline finally giving out?" he asked her.

"If you mean do I feel like a wet noodle, yes. Are you happy now?"

The corner of his mouth turned down. "Seeing you tired doesn't make me happy. But knowing that because of it you'll get some rest does." He took hold of the afghan and pulled it above her breasts. He made sure she was covered from there to her toes. Then he gave it a little tuck under her hip so it wouldn't fall away.

Mitch's fingers were strong and long. She felt heat from them with just that quick touch. He'd used his left hand. From what she'd heard, he didn't have much feeling in the fingers of his right hand.

She caught his arm before he moved away.

His gaze crashed into hers and they stared at each other for a few moments.

"Thank you for bringing me home."

"No problem," he responded, as if it was no big deal.

But it was a big deal to Lily. She'd never forget his friendship with Troy. She'd certainly never forget his kindness to her. But something about that kindness and her acceptance of it unsettled her. She had to figure out why it bothered her so much that Mitch would be sleeping on her couch tonight.

Chapter Three

Lily stared at the TV that evening, not really focused on the newsmagazine show that was airing. She was too aware of Mitch rattling the back screen door, fixing loose weather stripping.

Over supper they'd talked about the house and former tenants, needing dispassionate conversation. When they didn't stay on neutral territory, they seemed to wander into intensity...or awkwardness that came from being alone together. It was odd, really. For the past two and a half years while working with Mitch, she'd found him easy to be with. Now...

The phone rang and Lily picked up the cordless from the end table. When she saw Gina's number on caller ID, she breathed a sigh of relief.

"Hi," Gina said. "How are you and Sophie and Grace?"

"I called the hospital a little bit ago. They're doing okay. And I'm…good. I'm at home."

"So you said in your message. I'm sorry I just got it. My plane had a delay taking off. It was a whirlwind trip, leaving yesterday and coming back today. But I didn't want to be away from Daniel and Logan any longer than I had to be."

A baby development expert, Gina had received an offer from a Houston hospital to start her Baby Grows center there, too. Lily was sure Gina would someday not only have an additional Baby Grows center in Houston but many all around the country.

"So Mitch is keeping you company? How's that going?"

"It's okay. It's just…he's hovering. He insists I shouldn't be alone today. He gave me the option to sleep over at his place, or his sleeping on my couch. So he's sleeping here on my couch tonight."

"Are you okay with that?"

"Sure." But Lily knew her voice didn't sound sure. A man who wasn't her husband sleeping under her roof. Is that what was bothering her? Or was there more to it?

"Do you want me to come over?"

"No," Lily was quick to answer. "You need to be with your family."

"I was going to take off work tomorrow. Why don't I drive over first thing? Then Mitch can go to Family Tree."

"Are you sure you don't have other things you have to do?"

"I don't," Gina replied. "Tomorrow we can talk about Sophie and Grace, possibly visit them, and maybe I can get some things ready for you."

Seeing her twins. Baby talk. Girl talk. That sounded great to Lily. "I really appreciate this."

"No problem. Have you heard from Angie?"

Angie was Gina's sister, and Lily knew Gina worried about her when she worked on the team. "No. Have you?"

"No, not since she reached the Gulf. But the disaster relief team really doesn't have time for anything but helping the victims." After a short pause, she asked, "Why don't I stop at the bakery and pick up croissants on my way over?"

"I'm supposed to be losing weight, not gaining it."

"You don't have that much to lose. Besides, if you're going to pump milk and then breast-feed, you need some extra calories."

"The croissants sound good. That way I can convince Mitch he doesn't have to make breakfast."

"Did he make supper?"

"He did. And now he's doing some minor repairs on the house."

It must have been her tone of voice when she said it that made Gina ask, "That bothers you?"

"I don't want to be indebted to him. Do you know what I mean?"

"Oh, I know. But remember, Troy asked him to watch over you. That's what he's doing."

Last fall, Lily had shared Troy's letter with Gina, Angie and Raina. They also knew Mitch was simply fulfilling a promise. She should be grateful instead of uncomfortable.

Lily had just ended the call when Mitch strode into the living room. She told him, "Gina's coming over early tomorrow morning so you don't have to worry about me."

No change of expression crossed Mitch's face, but there was a flicker of reaction in his eyes that said he would worry anyway.

"I have a new client tomorrow who will be making decisions about in vitro fertilization and a few follow-up appointments after that. So if you need anything, I can try to rearrange my schedule."

She jumped in. "No need. I'll be sorting baby clothes with Gina and hanging decorations on the nursery walls. I wasn't prepared for an early delivery, which isn't like me at all!"

Mitch set the duct tape he'd carried in on an end table. "You wanted to stay in the pregnant zone as long as you could."

Although diplomatic, what he wasn't saying was obvious. She'd wanted to put off the idea of becoming a mother without Troy by her side for as long as possible. For once in her life, denial had definitely been more palatable than reality.

But now reality had smacked her in the face.

"You look lost," Mitch said, with a gentle edge to his voice.

That gentleness fell over her like a warm cloak. But then she had to ask herself, *did* she feel lost? Adrift? Alone? But she wasn't alone when she had good friends helping her. "No, not lost. Just off balance. I hate the unexpected. And my life has been one unexpected crisis after the other."

Rounding the coffee table, he approached her and she wished he'd sit beside her on the sofa. But he didn't.

"Sophie and Grace coming home will be grounding. You'll see."

His dark eyes didn't waver from hers and she felt sudden heat rising in her cheeks. Not from looking at Mitch! How many times had she looked at him in just that way?

No. Not just *this* way.

"The bedding for the sofa is upstairs," she said in a rush. "I'll get it."

"Are you staying up there?"

"I suppose." She produced a smile. "You'll have the downstairs to yourself if you want to watch TV or get a snack."

"I'll walk up with you."

There was no point in protesting. What would she do? Toss him the bedding over the banister?

When she swung her legs over the side of the sofa, Mitch was there, holding out his hand to help her up. She could be stubborn. Or she could accept a hand up when she needed it.

His strong fingers closed over hers, and her heart raced as her mind searched for something to say.

"Take it slowly," he reminded her as she rose to her feet.

Everything Mitch said today seemed to be full of deeper meaning. Although she longed to keep her hand in his, she slid it free and headed to the stairs.

A few minutes later in the hall on the second floor, Lily stopped by the linen closet and opened the door. Blankets lay folded on the shelf above her head. She reached up but she shouldn't have bothered. Mitch was there, behind her, easily pulling a blanket from the closet. His superior height and strength was obvious.

She could sense both, even though he wasn't touching her. Jittery, tired and anxious about what was going to happen next, she knew her hormones were out of whack. That was the best explanation she could think of to explain how she was feeling around Mitch.

He stepped away, bedding in hand. "This is great."

"Don't be silly. You need a sheet and pillow." And *she* needed something to do with her hands. She needed something to do with her mind. She needed something to *do*.

Choosing a pale blue sheet, she yanked a matching pillowcase from a stack. "The extra pillows are way up on the top shelf," she explained, moving away, letting him reach.

He easily removed one of those, too.

"I wish the sofa pulled out. You're going to be uncomfortable all scrunched up."

He laughed. "Believe me, I've slept on a lot worse. You worry too much, Lily. Did anyone ever tell you that?"

Her husband's name came to her lips, but she didn't say it. She didn't have to. Mitch knew.

He looked disconcerted for a second—just a second—but then he took the sheets from her arms. "Do you have a phone in your room?"

"My cell phone is in my purse. You brought that up with my suitcase. Why?"

"If you need something, call me. You might go to bed and an hour from now figure out you want a pack of crackers or a glass of milk."

There was only one way to answer with a man like Mitch. "I'll call you if I need you."

But somehow they both knew she wouldn't.

She went to the door to her room, which was only a few feet away. He didn't move until she stepped over the threshold and murmured, "Good night."

He gave her a slight nod, responded, "Good night, Lily," and headed for the stairs.

As she closed her door, she leaned against it and sighed. She wanted to make up the sofa for him so it would be comfortable.

How silly a notion was that?

"What do you mean you sent Gina home?" Mitch demanded as he stood in Lily's living room the following evening, a gift-wrapped box under one arm.

"She arrived before I was up this morning, as you know. She helped me ready the nursery. She took me to see the babies, and then I told her she should go home to her husband and son."

"And she just went?" He seemed astonished by that idea.

"She protested, but I plopped here on the sofa, told her I'd stay here, and she saw I meant it."

Lily was one exasperating woman! There was no doubt about that. But he had to admire her in spite of himself. "What did you do for dinner?"

"What is this, the third degree?"

He just arched a brow.

"Gina made a casserole for lunch and I had leftovers, with a salad and all that. What did *you* have?" she returned, almost cheekily.

All day he'd thought about eating dinner with her last night…saying good-night at the end of the day, spending the night on her couch in the strong grip of an insomnia he knew too well. Yet that was better than waking up in a sweat after too-real flashbacks or nightmares. Moments of sensual awareness when Lily had come downstairs this morning had been unsettling enough to push him on his way as soon as Gina had arrived.

Answering her, he said, "I went to the drive-through at my favorite burger joint." At her expression, he laughed. "Don't look so outraged. I have to do that once a week to keep fit."

Lily laughed then, even though she tried not to. That was the first real laugh he'd heard from her since before—even he had trouble saying it sometimes—since before Troy had died. He wanted to keep her spirits up. "So…how are Sophie and Grace?"

"Sit down," Lily said, motioning to the sofa. "I hate it when you loom. What's under your arm?"

"We'll get to that." He considered her comment. "And I don't loom."

"Whatever you say," she said too quickly, with a little smile.

Shaking his head, he set the box on the coffee table and lowered himself to the sofa. Not too close to her. Before he'd driven over here, he'd warned himself about that.

"The babies are so small," she explained, worried. "I can touch them but I can't hold them, and I'm dying to hold them."

"You'll soon be able to hold Sophie, if not Grace. How's their weight?" he asked, digging for the bottom line like a doctor.

"They're holding their own. My milk should be in soon and I'm going to pump it—" She stopped as her cheeks turned more pink.

"Don't be embarrassed. I'm a doctor, Lily. We talk

about this all the time with our patients." Right now he had to think of her as a patient so other images didn't trip over each other in his head.

"I know. But it seems different with…us."

Yes, something *did* seem different. Her perception of him? His of her? The fact that they'd been friends and maybe now something more was going on?

Nothing should be going on. It was way too soon for her. Maybe way too late for him.

"Can you tell them apart?" he asked, knowing conversation about her little girls would be comforting for her.

"Of course. Sophie's nose is turned up a little bit more at the end than Grace's. Grace's chin is just a little daintier, a tad more refined. They both have Troy's forehead and probably his eyes. It's a little too soon to tell. Sophie's a half inch longer than Grace, but Grace could catch up if she gains weight."

"She'll gain weight. They both will."

"Grace is still on the ventilator." Lily's voice trembled a bit.

Needing to fortify her with the truth, he asked, "What does Francesca say?"

"Francesca insists they're doing as well as can be expected and I have to give them time. I just feel like I should be doing something. Do you know what I mean?"

"Oh, yeah. Sitting still isn't easy for either one of us." He patted the box. "That's why I brought this along. Doing is always better than worrying."

"A gift?" Lily tore the wrapping paper off and read the information on the outside of the box. "Oh, Mitch, this is one of those new baby monitors."

"It is. The screen is small, but there's a portable handset you can carry with you to another room. So I'm also going to hook up a larger monitor you won't need binoculars to see. It's in my car."

"I can't let you—"

He shook his finger at her. "Don't even say it. You're going to be running yourself ragged when those babies come home. Having cameras in their cribs and a monitor down here so you can see them will help save a little bit of your energy."

"It will save a lot of my energy. Thank you."

Her blue eyes seemed to try to look inside him, into his heart...into his soul. That unsettled him. His soul was tormented at times by everything that had happened in Iraq. He hadn't been able to save his friend, and that, along with the PTSD symptoms, clawed at his heart. He quickly replied, "You're welcome. Why don't I get this hooked up? That way it will be ready whenever you bring the babies home."

"The cribs were delivered this morning. Gina supervised so I didn't have to run up and down the steps. But I don't know if she put the bedding on."

"Don't worry about it. I can position the cameras with the bedding on or off."

"Do you need my help? I can come up—"

"No." If Lily came upstairs, she would definitely be a distraction. "I brought along a toolbox and everything I might need. You drink a glass of milk and crochet or something."

"Drink a glass of milk?" She was smiling and her question was filled with amusement.

That smile of hers packed a wallop. It turned up the corners of her very pretty mouth. It seemed to make the few freckles across her cheeks more evident, her face actually glow.

Had he been attracted to Lily before Troy's death? If he was honest with himself, he had to say he had been. But attraction was one thing, acting on it was another. He'd shut it down when he'd learned she and Troy were to be married. He and Troy had become good friends and he'd congratulated them both at their wedding, always keeping his distance from Lily.

Being colleagues at their practice had been difficult at times. But not impossible. He kept their dealings strictly professional. They'd been cohorts, interacting on an intellectual level. He and Troy had been close. He and Lily? They'd just existed in the same universe.

Until…after Troy had died. When Mitch had hugged Lily that day after her ultrasound, he'd experienced desire and felt like an SOB because of it. That day, Mitch had realized that if he was going to keep his promise to Troy, he couldn't deny his attraction any longer. At least to himself. *She* didn't have to know about it.

But now—

Now nothing had changed. He had baggage. She had a world of grief and loss and new responsibility to deal with.

Turning away from her smile, which could affect him more than he wanted to admit, he muttered, "Milk's good for you and the babies. You've got to keep your vitamin D level up, along with your calcium. I'll go get what I need from the SUV and be right back."

Sometimes retreat was the best part of valor. Remembering that might save them both from an awkward or embarrassing situation.

* * *

Lily was emptying the dishwasher when Mitch called her into the living room. She'd been aware of his footfalls upstairs, the old floors creaking as he moved about. She'd been even *more* attuned to his presence when he'd come downstairs and she'd heard him cross the living room. She'd stayed in the kitchen. Somehow that had just seemed safer...easier...less fraught with vibrations she didn't want to come to terms with.

Hearing her name on Mitch's lips was unsettling now, and she told herself she was just being silly. Yet, seconds later when she stepped into the living room and found him taking up space in his long-sleeved hoodie and jeans, she almost backed into the kitchen again.

Making herself move forward, shifting her eyes away from his, she spotted the twenty-inch monitor on a side table. One moment she glimpsed one white crib with pink trim and green bedding. The next he'd pressed a button and she spotted the other crib with its pink-and-yellow designs. She could watch both babies by changing the channel.

"The wonders of technology." A smile shone in his voice.

She knew Mitch was good with electronics and especially computers. He was the first at the office to understand a new system, to fix glitches, to teach someone else the intricacies of a program.

"Are systems like this a side hobby for you?"

"Always have been. I'm self-taught. The skills come in handy now and then."

As long as she'd known Mitch, he'd downplayed what he did and who he helped. "You're a good man, Mitch."

He looked surprised for a moment.

She added, "If you can do something for someone else, you do."

"Lily, don't make so much of setting up a monitoring system."

Telling herself she should stay right where she was, she didn't listen to her better judgment. She advanced closer to Mitch and this time didn't look away. "You're not just helping *me*. It's sort of an attitude with you. If someone has a problem, you take time to listen."

Maybe he could see she was serious about this topic. Maybe he could see that she was trying to determine exactly how much help she should accept from him. Maybe he could see that this conversation was important to her. Nevertheless, by his silence he seemed reluctant to give away even a little piece of himself.

"Does it have something to do with being in Iraq?" she asked softly.

The flicker of response in his eyes told her she'd hit the mark. She saw one of his hands curve into a fist and she thought he might simply tell her it was none of her business. Instead, however, he lifted his shoulders in a shrug, as if this wasn't important. As if he didn't mind her asking at all.

"I survived," he told her calmly. "I figured there was a reason for that. I returned home with a new understanding of patience, tolerance and simple kindness."

Although Mitch's expression gave away nothing, Lily knew he was holding back. He was giving her an edited version of what he felt and what he'd experienced.

"Have you ever talked about Iraq?"

"No."

"Not even with your buddies?"

"They know what it was like. I don't have to talk about it."

She supposed that was true. Yet from the tension she could sense in Mitch, she understood he had scars that were more than skin deep.

With a tap on the control sitting next to the monitor on the table, he suggested, "Let me show you the remote and what the lights mean."

Discussion over. No matter what she thought, Mitch was finished with that topic, and he was letting her know it. She could push. But she sensed that Mitch wasn't the type of man who *could* be pushed. He would just shut down. That wouldn't get her anywhere at all. Why was she so hell-bent on convincing him that the bad stuff would only damage him if he kept it inside?

She'd let the conversation roll his way for now. For the next few minutes she let him explain the lights on the remote and how she could carry it into the kitchen with her and upstairs to her bedroom. When he handed it to her, their fingers skidded against each other and she practically jumped. She was so startled by the jolt of adrenaline it gave her, she dropped the remote.

She stooped over to retrieve it at the same time he crouched down. Their faces were so close together... close enough to kiss...

They moved apart and Lily let him grasp the control.

After Mitch picked it up, he handed it to her and quickly stepped away. "I'd better get going," he said. "Do you want me to turn off the system?"

"I can do it."

He nodded, crossing to the door, picking up the toolbox he'd set there.

She followed him, feeling as if something had gone

wrong, yet not knowing what. "Thank you again for the monitoring system. I really appreciate it."

"Are you going to be alone tomorrow?"

"No. Raina's coming to visit. She's going to drive me to the hospital so I can spend time with the twins while she makes rounds."

"That sounds like a plan. I'm glad you have friends you can count on."

"I am, too."

As their gazes found each other, his dark brown eyes deeply calm, Lily felt shaken up.

"If you need help when you bring the babies home, you have my number."

Yes, she did. But the way she was feeling right now, she wasn't going to use it. She couldn't call on him again when she felt attracted to him. That's what it was, plain and simple—attraction she was trying to deny. Oh, no. She wouldn't be calling his number anytime soon. She would not feel guilty believing she was being unfaithful to her husband's memory.

Maybe Mitch realized some of that, because he left.

Even though a cold wind blew into the foyer, Lily stood there watching Mitch's charcoal SUV back out of the driveway. When his taillights finally faded into the black night, she closed the door, relieved she was alone with her memories…relieved she might not see Mitch for a while.

Then everything would go back to normal between them.

Over the next few weeks Mitch didn't see much of Lily, though he stopped in at the hospital NICU almost every day. A few days ago, the twins had been moved to the regular nursery. This morning he'd run into Angie, who told him they'd gone home. Lily hadn't called him. Because she was overwhelmed with bringing the twins home and everything that entailed? Or because she wanted to prove to herself she could be a single mom and manage just fine?

He was going to find out.

When Mitch reached the Victorian, he scanned the house and grounds. Everything *seemed* normal—until he approached the front door. Although it was closed, he could hear the cries of two babies inside. New mothers had enough trouble handling one, let alone two. But where were Lily's friends?

With no response when he rang the doorbell, he knocked. When Lily still didn't answer, he turned the knob—no one in Sagebrush locked their doors—and stepped inside.

Immediately he realized the wails were coming from a room down the hall from the living room. Turning that way, he found the room that had been the women's exercise room. Now it looked like a makeshift nursery. There were two bassinets, a card table he assumed Lily used for changing the twins, and a scarred wooden rocking chair that looked as if it could be an antique. His gaze was quickly drawn to her. He knew he should look away from Lily's exposed breast as she tried to feed one baby while holding the other. Respectful of her as a new mom, he dropped his gaze to an odd-looking pillow on her lap, one of those nursing pillows advertised in baby magazines. But it didn't seem to be doing much good. Lily looked about ready to scream herself.

When she raised her head and saw him, she practically

had to yell over the squalls. "I couldn't come to the door. I can't seem to satisfy them," she admitted, her voice catching.

Without hesitating, Mitch took Sophie from her mom's arms, trying valiantly to ignore Lily's partially disrobed condition. He had enough trouble with the visions dancing through his head at night. Concentrating for the moment on Sophie, he flipped a disposable diaper from a stack, tossed it onto his shoulder and held the infant against him. The feel of that warm little girl on his shoulder blanked out any other pictures. Taking in a whiff of her baby lotion scent, he knew nothing in the world could be as innocent and sweet as a newborn baby. His hand rubbed up and down her little back, and miraculously she began to quiet. In a few moments, her sobs subsided into hiccups.

Lily, a bit amazed, quickly composed herself and tossed a blanket over her shoulder to hide her breast. Then she helped Grace suckle once more. This time the baby seemed content.

"Did your friends desert you?" He couldn't imagine them doing that.

"No, of course not. Gina and Raina were here most of the day. When Angie got ready for work and left, Sophie and Grace were asleep."

Mitch watched as Lily took a deep breath and let it out slowly. "But they woke up, crying to be fed at the same time."

"Do you have milk in the fridge?"

"Yes, but—"

"Breast-feeding two babies is something that's going to take practice. In the meantime, I can give Sophie a bottle." He gestured to her lap. "Nursing pillows and experts' advice might work for some people, but you've got to be practical. There is no right way and wrong way to do this, Lily. You just have to do what works for you and the babies."

"How do you know so much about babies?" Lily asked in a small voice, looking down at her nursing child rather than at him.

His part in the practice was science-oriented and mostly behind the scenes. "Training," he said simply, remembering his rotation in obstetrics years ago.

That drew her eyes to his. He added, "And...sometimes in the field, you have to learn quickly." In Iraq, he'd helped a new mother who'd been injured, returning her and her newborn to her family.

Before Lily could ask another question, he gently laid Sophie in one of the bassinets and hurried to the kitchen to find her milk. A short time later he carried one of the kitchen chairs to the nursery and positioned it across from Lily. Then he picked up Sophie again and cradled her in his arm. They sat in silence for a few minutes as both twins took nourishment.

"What made you stop by today?" Lily finally asked.

Lily's blond hair was fixed atop her head with a wooden clip. Wavy strands floated around her face. She was dressed in a blue sweater and jeans and there was a slight flush to her cheeks. Because he was invading private moments between her and her babies?

"I was at the hospital and found out they were discharged today."

Lily's eyes grew wider. Did she think he was merely checking up on her so he could say he had? He wished! He was in this because she'd gotten under his skin.

"Feeding these two every three hours, or more often, could get complicated. What would you have done if I hadn't arrived?"

"I would have figured something out."

Her stubbornness almost convinced him to shock her by taking her into his arms and kissing her. Lord, where had that thought come from? "I'm sure Gina and Raina never would have left if they knew you were so overwhelmed."

"Raina and Gina have families."

"They also both have nannies," he reminded her.

"They also both have—"

Mitch knew Lily had been about to say that they both had husbands. Instead, she bit her lower lip and transferred Grace to her other breast, taking care to keep herself covered with the blanket.

"I'm sorry I just walked in on you like that." He might as well get what happened out in the open or they'd both have that moment between them for a while.

"I'm going to have to get over my privacy issues if I intend to breast-feed them for very long. I sat down with the accountant last week. I can take a leave for seven or eight months and be okay financially. My practice is important, but I really feel as if I need to be with them to give them a good start in life."

Since she was the only parent they had, he could certainly understand that.

"Do you think the practice can do without me for that long?"

"We can manage. You know our client list is down because of insurance issues. This could work out to everyone's advantage. We can always consult with you from home if we need your expertise."

Suddenly remembering the need to burp Sophie, he set the bottle on the floor and balanced the tiny baby on his knee. His hand was practically as large as *she* was. What would life be like taking care of them every day? Being able to watch their progress and all the firsts? Keeping his palm on her chest, he rubbed her back until she burped.

Smiling at Lily he said offhandedly, "She's easy."

Lily smiled back.

In that moment, he knew being here with Lily like this was dangerous.

What he was about to suggest was even *more* dangerous.

Chapter Four

"Do you want me to sleep on the couch again to-night?" Mitch asked as he cradled Sophie in his arm once more and offered her the bottle again. He couldn't help studying her perfect baby features. He was beginning to recognize a warm feeling that enveloped his heart when he was around Sophie and Grace.

After a lengthy pause, he cast a sideways glance at Lily to gauge her expression. As long as she was upstairs and he stayed downstairs, he wouldn't worry her with the restlessness that plagued him at night.

She looked somber as she debated with herself about what to say. He could almost hear her inner conversation because he'd already had the same one. If he stayed, they'd connect more. If he stayed, they might get to know each other better.

Quietly, she responded, "If you stay, I think I can

keep Sophie and Grace happier. The two of us are obviously handling them better than *I* was handling them alone. I have to learn what works and what doesn't. That will just take time. In the meantime, I want to stay calm. I want to enjoy both of them. I can't go into a panic just because Grace and Sophie are crying at the same moment."

"Why *did* you panic?" Extreme reactions weren't at all like Lily. But she'd never been a mom before. She bit her lower lip and he found himself focused on her mouth much too intensely.

"I have these two little beings depending on me twenty-four hours a day, seven days a week," she attempted to explain. "I don't want to let them down. I don't want either of them to feel neglected."

It was easy to see Lily had already bonded with her daughters and she wanted nothing to interfere with those bonds, not even another willing pair of hands giving her aid. He attempted to be reasonable, realizing he wanted to stay more than he wanted to go. "Right now, they need to have their basic needs met—feeding, changing and cuddling. They'll learn to know you," he reassured her quickly. "They won't mind if someone else gives them what they need. In a few months, they'll both be more particular. They'll want you when they want you. So for now, take advantage of the fact that someone else can help."

"You make it sound so simple," she said with a wry smile. "And we know it isn't."

No, nothing was simple. Besides the sheer enormity of the twins' birth, other feelings besides affection for Sophie and Grace were developing between him and Lily. However, neither of them were going to mention those. No. They wouldn't be having that discussion any-time soon…which left the door wide open for his desire to cause trouble. Yet he still wanted to be close to her.

As he set Sophie on his knee to burp her again, he asked, "Will you take the babies upstairs to sleep tonight?"

"Yes. I want them to get used to their cribs. I've got to get the hang of breast-feeding both of them, but that might be easier to juggle during the day. I thought I might put a small refrigerator upstairs for night feedings."

"That sounds like a good idea. Maybe I can go pick one up for you tomorrow."

"But I'm paying for it."

"Okay, you're paying for it." He knew better than to argue.

With her gaze locked on his, he felt a turning so deep inside of him that he had to stand with Sophie and walk her back and forth across the room. She'd drunk three ounces of the bottle and that was good. Taking her to the card table, he unsnapped her Onesies so he could change her.

"Mitch, you don't have to do that."

He glanced over his shoulder while he held Sophie with one hand and picked up a diaper with the other. "I don't mind changing her. But if you'd rather I didn't, I won't."

Mitch guessed Grace was still locked on Lily's breast. Just imagining that—

"As long as *you* don't mind," Lily finally said.

He seemed to be all thumbs with the small diaper, but he hoped Lily wasn't noticing. The tiny snaps on the Onesies were a challenge, too, but his left hand had almost become as proficient as his right hand had once been—before shrapnel had torn into it.

Finally Sophie was ready for bed. Her little eyes were practically closed and her angelic face was peaceful. "I'll carry her upstairs and lay her in her crib. You can come up when Grace finishes."

"I have receiving blankets up there on the side of each crib. Can you swaddle her in one? They're supposed to sleep better if I do that."

"I'll try it."

"And you have to lay her on her back."

"I know, Lily."

She flushed.

"After I put her to bed, I'll pull out a blanket and a pillow for the sofa. I remember where you got them."

Lily nodded, but dropped her eyes to Grace and didn't look at him. If they didn't admit to the intimacy developing between them, then the intimacy wouldn't exist, right?

Right.

They were tiptoeing along a line in the sand, hoping neither one of them fell onto the other side.

He let out a pent-up breath he didn't even know he was holding when he left the downstairs nursery and headed up the steps, Sophie sleeping against his shoulder. The hall light guided him into the babies' room, where he grabbed the blanket and carefully wrapped Sophie in it on the changing table, murmuring softly to her as he did. Then he gently laid her in her crib and switched on the monitoring system.

After turning on the castle night-light by the rocker, he went to the hall for his bedding. At the closet, he glanced back at the room, almost ready to return and wish the little girl a good night. But he knew he couldn't become attached, not to the babies any more than to Lily. Nothing was permanent. Everything ended. He had no right to even think about Lily in a romantic way. He had no intention of making life more complicated for either of them.

After Mitch went downstairs, he made up the sofa and sat on it, staring at the monitor. Sophie did look like a cherub with her wispy blond hair, her blue eyes, her little body that seemed more heavenly than earthly. Her tiny face turned from left to right and he wondered if she missed Grace already.

He was so engrossed in his reflections that he didn't hear Lily come into the living room until the floor squeaked. She was holding Grace in a sling that kept her nestled against her chest.

"Is Sophie asleep?" Lily asked.

"Come see."

"I have to put Grace down, too."

"A couple of minutes won't matter. Come here."

Lily just stared at Sophie, her sweet sleep as entrancing as her little nose, long eyelashes and broad brow. "The monitor is wonderful, Mitch," Lily said in a low voice. "But they're so small. I'll probably be going in every fifteen minutes to check on them."

"You need your sleep. I'll be watching from down here. How about if I stay awake until the first feeding?"

"You need your sleep, too."

"I'm used to not sleeping. I was a trauma surgeon, remember?"

She remembered and unintentionally her gaze went to his arm and his hand.

Self-consciously, he moved it and balled it into a fist. Though he expected her to move away, she didn't.

"Do you think about what you used to do very often?"

"Often enough. But that was then and this is now. Why don't I walk you upstairs? We'll make sure both babies are settled."

Lily took one last look at the image on the monitor and then crossed to the stairway. Mitch waited a beat or so and then followed her.

Upstairs, by the glow of the night-light, Lily took Grace from her carrier and wrapped her in a blanket as Mitch had done with Sophie. After Lily laid Grace in her crib, she stooped over the baby and kissed her forehead. "I love you, sweet girl. I'm glad you're home."

Then she moved to Sophie's crib and did the same.

Aware Mitch hadn't come far into the room, Lily glanced at him as he stood by the chair, his arms crossed over his chest—watchful and distant.

When he'd arrived at the house earlier and come into the downstairs nursery, she'd felt so many emotions that they'd tumbled over each other. Yes, she'd been embarrassed. But she'd also felt a little proud. Only a few moments had passed until she'd realized she *should* feel embarrassed. And then she had.

As they'd put the babies to bed, though, the situation had seemed right. Mitch handled them so well… so comfortably…so like a father. Sometimes she could see the affection he felt for them. But other times, he removed himself.

Like now.

He fell into step beside her as she left the nursery

and walked down the hall to her bedroom. At her door, she was ready to say good-night, ready to fall into bed, exhausted from the stress, the worry and the joy of bringing the babies home today. Yet a simple good-night didn't seem adequate and when she gazed into Mitch's eyes, she couldn't look away.

He seemed to have the same problem.

There was something about him standing there, perfectly still, his shoulders wide enough to block the doorway, his height filling the space. Maybe it was the sight of him without his tie and with the first few buttons of his white shirt open. Maybe it was her reaction to the black chest hair peeking out. Maybe she thought about all he'd done for her. Maybe, for just a short time, she gave in to the thought that she might *need* someone to watch out for her. She only knew that thoughts weren't running through her brain as fast as heat was flashing through her body. She wasn't thinking at all when she leaned forward. Rather, she was feeling and wishing and hoping and remembering what it had felt like to be held by a man.

Her babies were so little. Her life had been torn apart. In the midst of caring for her girls and forging ahead, her attraction to Mitch seemed to be a living, breathing entity that at that moment she couldn't deny.

When his strong arms enfolded her, she felt safe. As he murmured her name, she felt cared for. He lowered his head and she lifted her chin. Their lips met.

Lily's senses whirled and she couldn't deny a longing that came from deep within. As Mitch's mouth opened over hers, she lost all sense of time and place. All she cared about was now, the rush of wanting, the scent of

Mitch that was new and exciting, the thrill of feeling like a woman again.

Suddenly her womb tightened as it did when she nursed the babies. Troy's daughters.

What in God's name was she doing?

As suddenly as the kiss began, she tore away. The expression on Mitch's face told her he knew why. She clamped her hand over her lips and tears rushed to her eyes. She saw that determined look come over Mitch and she couldn't face it, not tonight.

"Talk to me, Lily," he coaxed gently.

She shook her head. "I can't. Not now. Maybe in the morning."

"Do you want to let us both stew all night when what you need is sleep?"

"It was a mistake."

He sighed. "Maybe that's one of the things we need to talk about."

When she remained silent, he stroked a tear from her cheek, finally agreeing. "All right. Go to bed. I'll be here if you need help with the babies during the night."

"Mitch, I'm sorry."

He put his finger gently over her lips.

Backing into her room, she closed the door. She heard his boots on the wooden floorboards, his tread as he walked down the stairs. Then she collapsed on her bed, not even taking her clothes off, shutting her eyes and praying sleep would come quickly.

The following morning, Mitch made scrambled eggs while Angie and Lily fed the twins in the upstairs nursery.

He'd crossed the line last night. He'd known physical

contact with Lily was taboo. But it hadn't been until his lips had touched hers that he'd realized how truly vulnerable she was.

He'd damaged their relationship and he didn't know if he could fix it. But he had to get the old one back—he'd made a promise to Troy.

When Angie had arrived home after midnight, the twins had been starting to stir. She said she'd help him feed them so Lily could sleep. But Lily had heard them, come in, taken Grace from Angie and told her to go to bed. She'd hardly glanced at him.

They'd fed Grace and Sophie in silence. When the twins woke again at four, they'd both fed them again. Mitch had never actually appreciated how complicated this was for women. They hadn't recovered completely from giving birth and they had to use reserves they didn't know they had to combat sleep deprivation, fatigue and chores that seemed to multiply with each hour.

And what had he done? Stirred up something that was better left alone. He didn't know if Lily was ever going to look him in the eyes again.

He'd just switched off the burner when she and Angie rolled in a double stroller. Grace and Sophie looked as if they were content and almost asleep.

Crossing to the refrigerator, Angie pulled out milk and orange juice, snagging the coffeepot and bringing it to the table. "You should go back to bed," Angie told Lily as they pulled out their chairs.

"I have laundry to do, and I want to make up a couple of casseroles and freeze them so we can just pull them out this week if we need them."

Although Mitch sat at the table with them, Lily

glanced down at her plate. She picked up a slice of toast, took a bite and set it down again.

For the next ten minutes, the lump in Mitch's chest grew as he and Angie made conversation.

Finally, his breakfast eaten, he asked Lily, "Can I talk to you for a minute before I go?"

Her attention automatically went to her daughters, but Angie reassured her quickly. "I'll watch them. Go ahead."

There were so many things he wanted to tell Lily as they stood in the foyer. But he couldn't think of one. She was wearing jeans and a pink sweater and looked as if she were going to face the new day with determination and courage, the way she always did.

He knew what she wanted to hear from him, so he said it. "You were right. Last night was a mistake. I was out of line."

"You weren't the one who started it," she admitted honestly. "I don't know what got into me."

"You were grateful for a little help," he said with a smile that didn't come from inside.

"A *lot* of help," she returned, gazing into his eyes like she used to.

"Are you going to be okay when Angie leaves for work?"

"I'll be fine. It's Raina's day off. She's coming over."

He nodded, sure her friends would give her any help she needed, at least for a while. But he also knew Lily wouldn't want to burden them and she'd soon be taking all of it on herself.

They couldn't get involved for so many reasons. What if Lily ever saw his scars, learned his fears? The last relationship he'd tried a few years ago hadn't worked because of all of it. Nothing had changed since then, and on Lily's part, her grief and her connection to Troy was sustaining her in some ways. Missing and longing for him meant loving him. She wasn't ready to let go of that. Still, Mitch didn't know how to walk away from her. He couldn't because he'd promised he wouldn't.

"I'll call you in a couple of days, just to see if Grace and Sophie are settling in. If you need anything, you have my number."

She reached out and touched his arm, probably feeling the same wall he did, a wall they were both standing behind so they wouldn't get hurt.

"Thank you," she said softly.

He left the Victorian again, realizing he didn't want her thanks. What he *did* want was still a mystery to him.

A few weeks later, Mitch was driving home from work when he decided to call Lily. They'd had a *brief* phone conversation last week because neither was comfortable with what had happened and they couldn't seem to get back on that "friend" footing. Now her cell phone rang and rang and rang until finally—a man picked up.

"Who is this?" Mitch asked, surprised by the male voice. A repairman, maybe? But why would he have Lily's cell phone?

"This is Craig Gillette. I'm the manager of Sagebrush Foods."

"Sagebrush Foods? I don't understand. Where's Lily Wescott?"

"Mrs. Wescott had an incident in our store. She's okay now but…"

An incident? What the hell was that? "Put her on," Mitch ordered.

Apparently speaking to the authority in Mitch's voice, the man said, "Sir, I can't right now. We've got two crying infants and she's feeling a little dizzy."

Dizzy? "You tell her not to move. I'll be there in five." Mitch didn't give the manager time to protest or approve. He stepped on the gas.

Minutes later Mitch rushed into the store, scanning the produce area. Rounding a corner, he spotted Lily in the canned goods aisle, holding a paper cup. There were cans of green beans all over the floor around the folding chair where she sat. The twins were ensconced in their stroller. Sophie's little face was screwed up in displeasure, but Grace seemed content for the moment to stare at the bright lights and rows of colorful cans.

Mitch let his training prevail rather than the fear that threatened his composure. In as calm a voice as he could muster, he asked, "What happened?" followed by, "Are you all right?"

Lily looked so pale, and all he wanted to do was lift her into his arms and carry her somewhere safe. But the twins were a concern, too, and he had to get to the bottom of what had happened.

"I just felt a little dizzy, that's all," she said in a soft voice, taking another sip of water. "I haven't gotten much sleep lately and I ran out of diapers…" Grace reached out a little hand to her and Lily reached back.

He got the picture much too well and he didn't like what he saw. His guess? She'd felt faint and she'd run the stroller into the corner of the green beans display.

"Did she pass out?" he asked Gillette.

"No, sir. We wanted to call an ambulance, but she said she just needed to put her head down between her knees for a while—" He stopped when Lily gave him a scolding look as if he were divulging too much information.

Mitch went to Lily and crouched down beside her, looking her over with a practiced doctor's eye. "Be honest with me. Do I need to call an ambulance?"

There were deep blue smudges under both of her eyes. Her hair was a disheveled ponytail and she wore a sweatsuit. This wasn't the Lily he was used to, with her composed attitude, neat hairdos and tailored clothing.

Looking up at him, she forced a smile. She was clearly exhausted.

With his fingertips to her neck, he felt her pulse beating fast.

"Mitch," she protested, turning her head.

His fingers stayed put. "Quiet for a few seconds," he suggested.

Her pulse was definitely racing.

"No ambulance," she said.

"Then tell me what's going on. But drink that water before you do." He guessed she was dehydrated.

"You're acting like a doctor."

"I'm also acting like a friend."

Their gazes met and Mitch could see she was remembering their kiss as vividly as he was, even in these circumstances. Just friends? Not likely.

She didn't argue with him, but rather drank the cup of water.

"Are you still dizzy? Should I call Hillary?" Their colleague was her OB/GYN.

"No. I'm seeing her in a few days for a follow-up. I know what's wrong, Mitch. Not enough sleep, not enough liquids, probably not enough food. I forget to eat when I'm busy. Please don't scold."

He would have, but he could see she realized what he'd known could happen all along—she was overwhelmed.

"Let's see if you can stand on your own."

He held her around the waist and helped her to her feet. She felt slight to him. She'd definitely lost weight. He should have been checking in with her daily, no matter how uncomfortable things were between them. So much for looking after her.

His body was responding in ways it shouldn't as he kept his arm around her waist and they walked a few steps down the aisle.

"Do you think you can walk to your car on your own steam? I'll drive yours then walk back here for mine."

"I drove over here for the diapers because I didn't want to bother anyone," she muttered, then added fiercely, "I'm capable of walking to the car."

At least she wasn't protesting him driving her home. He wanted her to understand the seriousness of what was happening to her. But that discussion would have to wait until she was on the sofa with her feet up and Sophie and Grace were fed and diapered.

In the house a while later, they sat on the sofa, hips practically touching, watching the babies in their cribs on the monitor. Mitch had found laundry in the washer and dryer, bottles in the sink, and had coaxed a little information from Lily. The babies now had a fussy spell that lasted from after Angie left in the evening until well after midnight. And they were nursing at least every three hours. She *was* exhausted and dehydrated and had to do more to take care of herself. But she couldn't do that unless the twins needs were met first.

Mitch began, "You need help, Lily, and you've got to get it before you can't take care of Sophie and Grace. Hire an au pair who will stay at the house for free rent."

He shifted so they weren't quite so close as he expected Lily to protest. She didn't. Rather, she just looked pensive. "I really hadn't thought about doing that. I don't know if Angie would like having a stranger move in."

"She can probably see you need help, too, but doesn't know what to do about it. Talk to her. Talk to Raina and Gina. Maybe they'll know of someone who needs a job and is good with children. But you can't go on like this."

"I know. Believe me, Mitch, I do. What just happened scared me. I just wish—" She swallowed hard. "If Troy were here—"

Mitch watched as she blinked fast and faced the cold splash of reality once more. He didn't know whether to cover her hand with his or move even farther away. Everything had become so complicated between them.

After a few moments of silence, Lily seemed to pull herself together. "Thinking about Troy…" She stopped. "His sister Ellie might be the perfect person to help me."

"Isn't she in Oklahoma?"

"Yes, but Troy's mom and Ellie have wanted to visit. Maybe they could come and help out and maybe…" A smile bloomed on Lily's lips. "Maybe Ellie could stay! She could set up her web business from here. I'm going to call Angie first. If she's agreeable, then I'll phone Ellie."

Lily picked up the handset from the end table.

As she dialed a number, Mitch realized he should be happy she was going to get the help she needed. Yet part of him knew that if Troy's sister came to assist her, Lily could stay entrenched in the past instead of moving on.

That shouldn't matter to him. But it did.

Chapter Five

Lily hung up the receiver and glanced at the glass of juice Mitch had brought her, now empty. She knew better than to let herself become dehydrated. She knew better about a lot of things. She should be grateful Mitch had called right when he had. Troy had always maintained, *There are no coincidences.* She'd always laughed when he'd said it, but maybe he was right.

She found Mitch in the laundry room, pulling baby clothes from the dryer. "You don't have to do that," she said.

He just arched one heavy brow at her and removed the last of the Onesies, settling them in the wash basket.

"I ordered takeout from the Yellow Rose." He glanced at his watch. "It should be here in about fifteen minutes."

"Takeout? But they don't deliver unless—"

"I ordered two dinners for tonight, and three more. You should have enough for a few days so you don't have to worry about cooking."

She knew better than to protest. She should have ordered food herself. She'd intended to cook, but with Angie on the late shift, it had seemed a bother when she had so many other things to do. Still, almost fainting had scared her. She had to eat, drink and get some rest.

"That was a long phone conversation," Mitch commented, carrying the laundry basket into the kitchen and then the living room.

"Just set it on the coffee table," she said. "I have to divide the clothes. I keep some down here, and the rest upstairs."

After he set it down, he asked, "So is the cavalry coming?"

She smiled. "Troy's mother is going to stay for a week. She doesn't want to leave his dad for longer than that. But Ellie will drive her here and stay as long as I need her. She said she could use a change of scene, and Texas seems like a good spot. She's going to bring her sewing machine and make baby clothes and get her website up and running while she's here. If the three of us get along well, she might stay indefinitely."

"I assume since she makes baby clothes, she likes babies."

"She worked at a day-care center for a while, so she's had more practical experience than *I* have."

"I'm glad that's settled. When are they coming?"

"Next week."

"And in the meantime?"

"In the meantime, I'll get by. But I'll take better care of myself."

"That's a promise?"

"It's a promise."

There was about six inches of space between them that seemed to be filled with all kinds of electricity. Lily couldn't understand why, when she was around Mitch now, every nerve in her body tingled a new message.

"Why don't you take out the clothes you want to keep down here, and I'll carry the rest upstairs."

She took a few outfits from the basket and laid them on the coffee table. As Mitch lifted it again, she found her hand going to his forearm.

He pulled away and she realized she'd clasped his scarred and injured arm. "I'm sorry," she said.

He put down the laundry and took a step closer to her. "There's nothing to be sorry about. I'm just not used to having anyone touch me there."

"Does it hurt?"

"No."

"Do you ever let anyone see it?" She didn't know why the personal question had rolled off her tongue so easily, but what had happened at the grocery store had solidified the bond between them.

"Do you?" she prodded. "You wear long sleeves, winter and summer."

"Why does it matter?"

"Because we're friends and I'd like to know."

His expression remained steady, his voice steely. "Most people can't handle seeing scars. They're fascinated by them, but they're afraid of them. They want to ask questions, but they turn away."

"Do you think I'd turn away?"

The two of them were breathing the same air, standing in the same space, but a shield went up in Mitch's eyes that sent him somewhere apart from her. Suddenly she suspected why.

"Have you been in a relationship since you returned from Iraq?"

He started to swivel away from her to go into the kitchen. She wouldn't let him evade her that easily. She didn't touch him this time, but just slipped in front of him so he couldn't take another step without running into her.

"Lily," he said with exasperation. "I don't want to talk about it."

"Have you ever talked about it…talked about *her?*"

"No."

"Just as you haven't talked about Iraq."

"That's right."

Men! Lily thought. Troy had been the same way. He hadn't spoken to her about his earlier deployments, and she hadn't pushed. She had imagined that he'd eventually confide in her. But they hadn't had time. And maybe if he had confided in her, she would have been more prepared—

"So don't talk about Iraq," she conceded.

"But tell you about my love life?" Mitch asked, almost amused.

She realized how ridiculous she was being, when Mitch was a private man who didn't reveal much at all! "I guess I just need something to think about besides my own life right now."

That shield was still in his eyes but his face took on a gentler look.

"Okay. I'll do this once." He jammed his hands into his trouser pockets. "I was back over a year. I'd gotten a fellowship in endocrinology in Dallas and met Charlene, who was a reporter for the local news. She wanted to do a story about my new specialty and why I was changing, but I told her no. After a few tries and a few conversations, we started going out. I wore long sleeves most of the time then, too. One night I took her out to dinner. Afterward, things progressed naturally but when we got to the bedroom and I took off my shirt— She couldn't bear to see my scars, let alone touch them. That's when I realized reality was just a little too difficult for most people to handle."

"Most *women*," Lily murmured, realizing how little emotion Mitch had put into that recital. "That's what you meant to say."

"Maybe I did."

"Not every woman is the same." She could see right away that he didn't believe that. "The scars are more extensive than on your arm and hand," she guessed.

"Yes. They're on my shoulder, back and side, too."

Lily thought about what he'd said but kept her gaze from falling to his shoulder, or to his flat stomach. She was feeling almost dizzy again. Could that be from imagining Mitch without his shirt? Was she different from that reporter? Would extensive scars make her want to turn away?

The doorbell rang.

Mitch took a step back, looking…relieved? Was *she* relieved that the personal conversation was over? Or did she *want* to delve deeper? Somehow she knew Mitch wouldn't let her do that. At least, not tonight.

"So what's for dinner?" she asked brightly, knowing the Yellow Rose delivery had arrived at the door.

Getting to know Mitch any better would mean ties

she might not want…problems she didn't need. Getting to know Mitch better could lead to another kiss.

Neither of them wanted that—right?

Lily's cavalry arrived and Mitch stayed away. He knew it was best for both of them.

Almost a month after the grocery store incident, he received a call as he sat at the desk in his spare bedroom, ready to check email and eat dinner—a slice of pizza and a beer. When he recognized the number on his cell phone, he quickly swallowed his mouthful of pizza and shut down his email program.

"Hey, Lily. How's it going?"

When he'd called to check on her a couple of weeks before, Troy's mother had just left Lily's home and Ellie was settling in. Mitch had known Lily didn't need him there, or even want him there. He knew what had probably gone on while Troy's family was with her—lots of remembering.

It was best that he stay on his side of town and not interfere.

"Darlene and Ellie have been wonderful. They gave me a chance to pull myself back together, get my diet straightened out and find a sleep schedule. And Ellie's definitely going to stay. Angie really likes her, and we all get along great."

After a long pause, she asked, "Why haven't you been over lately?"

"I really didn't think you needed another visitor. Besides, the practice is picking up. I've been working late many nights."

"The beginning of May is a time for growth and

thinking about the future. I can see why the practice picks up this time of year. I miss it."

"I thought you might."

"Don't get me wrong, I love taking care of Grace and Sophie. Doing that, even with Ellie here, is enough to keep me busy all day. But working with you and Hillary and Jon and the staff is part of my life, too."

"So you're coming back?"

"I have to, Mitch. I'm going to see how the summer goes with Ellie, then I'll give you all a definite date."

Lily sounded less frazzled, more peaceful, maybe even a bit happy. He guessed the babies were bringing her joy, not just work, and that was lifting her up, fulfilling her in a new way.

She went on, "They're both cooing. And they're fascinated by their mobiles. You've got to come see them, Mitch, and meet Ellie."

Ellie was Lily's family now, along with her friends. He would bet a week's pay that their first meeting was going to be...uncomfortable. He thought about what type of visit this should be, how much time he should spend with Ellie and Lily, how much time with the twins.

"Have you been out of the house much?"

"Nope. The twins keep me a prisoner," she said with a laugh. "Seriously. I went to the grocery store again last week. This time I made it without knocking anything over. But that's been about it."

"Would tomorrow night be convenient?" he asked. "I could meet Ellie, see how the babies have grown, then take you for a drive. In fact, we could drive to the lake to hear the outdoor concert. How does that sound?"

"That sounds wonderful! But you realize, don't you,

I'm going to have to call back here every fifteen minutes to see what the twins are doing."

"That's a mother's prerogative. Why don't you check with your housemates to see if they mind your leaving, then give me a call back. I think the concert will be a nice break for both of us."

"Your idea sounds perfect. I'll get back to you shortly."

"I'll talk to you soon," Mitch said and hung up.

He didn't know whether to hope for this idea to go through or not. It could become more than a casual outing. Then he grabbed hold of reality again. Not if they *wanted* only casual. After all, it would be easy to stay casual. Lily could tell him all about the memories she and Troy's mother and sister had stirred up during their visit.

Casual would be the theme of the evening.

"How long have you been working with Lily?" Ellie asked on Saturday evening.

He'd arrived a short time before and looked in on the twins, who'd been finishing their supper. They were asleep in their bassinets now and Lily had gone upstairs to change.

Studying Ellie, he noticed she wore her light brown hair in a short, glossy bob that swung against her cheek. The style accentuated her heart-shaped face. At twenty-six, she was ten years younger than the brother she obviously missed.

Mitch tried to answer her question without becoming defensive. After all, who could blame her for watching out for her sister-in-law. "We've worked together for two and a half years."

"Troy mentioned you," she admitted. "Something about playing pool at the Silver Spur Grill."

"We did."

"He said you were in Iraq and had to leave the Guard for medical reasons." She looked him over as if expecting to find his injury and her gaze settled on his hand. She quickly looked away.

"I did," he answered crisply, not intending to go into *that*, even for Troy's sister. The screws the doctor had put in his shoulder and leg, his missing spleen, never mind the damage to his arm and hand, had shut down his ability to serve. Most of the time, no one could tell he'd been injured.

It was time to go on the offensive with Ellie. "Lily tells me you worked in a day-care setting."

"For a while," she responded.

If he got her talking, she might relax. "But you like to sew?"

Looking surprised that he knew a detail like that, she responded, "I started making customized outfits for gifts for friends and relatives. They became so popular, I was getting orders. That's when I decided to open the store. At first I did pretty well, but then when harder times hit, even folks who had the money for those kind of clothes decided to spend it elsewhere."

"I hope your web-based business takes off for you."

"I hope so, too. But in the meantime, I'm going to enjoy taking care of Grace and Sophie. Did you spend much time with them when you brought Lily home from the hospital?"

She clearly wasn't giving up on turning over every leaf of his association with Lily. But he didn't have anything to hide—not really. "Two babies are a handful. That's why I think it's important Lily get away for a bit tonight."

Ellie's green eyes canvassed his face as if searching for motives. Finally, she admitted, "I'm glad the weather turned warm enough."

At that moment, Lily came down the stairs.

Automatically, Mitch turned her way. She was wearing blue jeans and a red blouse with a yellow windbreaker tossed over her arm. She'd fashioned her hair with a clip at the nape and she looked...fantastic. Her blue eyes seemed even bluer tonight as she gave him a tentative smile. He couldn't look away and she seemed to be as immobilized as he was...

...Until Ellie cleared her throat and asked, "How long do you think the concert will last?"

Lily burst into motion, as if in denial that the moment of awareness had ever happened. "Oh, we won't stay for the whole concert, and I'll call in to check with you. That's the nice thing about going to the lake. I don't have to worry about anybody being bothered if I make phone calls during the concert. Since this is the first concert of the season, the audience will be sparse. So call me if the least little thing is wrong, or you think I should come home."

Lily talked very fast when she was nervous, and that's what she was doing now. Her last comment led him to wonder if she was looking for an excuse not to go. Was it because she was still uncomfortable since their kiss? He'd find out shortly.

Lily gave Ellie a list of instructions along with phone numbers, then hiked the strap of her purse over her shoulder, took a last look at the monitor, blew a kiss to the image of her daughters and went out the door.

On the drive to the lake they didn't talk, but rather enjoyed the peaceful scenery—ranches and cotton fields that spread as far as the eye could see, tumbleweeds rolling by.

After he turned off the main road, down a gravel lane, and bumped over a dusty area used as the parking space for the concert, Lily finally said, "I think I'd forgotten how green everything is at this time of year, how spring smells, how the sky turns purple and orange at sunset. In some ways, I feel like I've been locked in a closet since last summer, not really seeing what was around me. Except the twins, of course."

"You've faced a lot of change in the past ten months."

She lowered her window and took a huge breath of outside air as the May breeze tossed her hair. "I don't want to go back into that closet again."

"Then don't. You have help now. While you're on leave, take some time for yourself, too. Figure out who you are again in your new life."

Turning to him, she reached for his arm, and he guessed she didn't even realize she'd done that. "You've been through this, haven't you?" she asked.

Her fingers on his forearm seemed to send fire through his body. Trying to smother it, he responded roughly, "You know I have. I'm not sure major life change is anything anyone welcomes, especially when it's borne from tragedy."

He gently tugged away from her touch. "Come on. Let's go to this concert."

His body still racing with adrenaline from their

contact, Mitch pulled a blanket from the backseat. They headed toward the people gathering in a large pavilion. They didn't see anyone they knew as Mitch dropped the blanket on one of the park benches facing the bandstand. The sides of the pavilion would block the wind and Lily could always wrap herself in the blanket if she got cold.

Their shoulders brushed. Mitch considered moving away, but didn't. Still, he was glad they hadn't recognized anyone. He didn't want Lily having second thoughts about coming. Something told him Ellie would be grilling her when she got back, and she'd have plenty of second thoughts then. He was just glad she'd accepted his invitation tonight, even if it was only to escape her figurative closet for a little while.

The quartet that performed with oboe, bass, clarinet and guitar played instrumental versions of popular songs. The crowd didn't grow much larger as Mitch was sure it would have if this had been a country-and-western or bluegrass band, or even an oldies night. But it suited his purpose to be here tonight with Lily, to listen to calm and easy music so she could relax. Even when she called home, no worry lines fanned her brow as Ellie reassured her that her girls were fine.

When Lily recognized a song, she hummed along. Her face was in profile as she gazed toward the lake, and he could study her without being afraid she'd catch him. Her hair waved in gentle curls under the barrette. Her turned-up nose was so recognizable on Sophie and Grace. Lily's bangs were long, brushed to one side, her brows a shade darker than her hair as they drew together when she concentrated on the music. She'd never worn much makeup, but tonight he noticed a sheen of gloss on her lips.

He could watch her all night and not tire of her expressions, the tilt of her head, the slant of her cheeks. He felt desire grip him again.

At that moment, she turned away from the music toward him…as if she wanted to sneak a peek at *his* expression. They both froze, their gazes locked, their bodies leaning just a little closer until the press of their shoulders was noticeable. Mitch reminded himself that there were so many reasons to keep away from Lily.

The music ended and the quartet announced a break.

Not moving away, Lily asked, "What do you think?"

About her? About the night? About the music? Which was the question to answer?

"My mother would have called them a dance band."

Lily blinked as if she hadn't expected that at all. But then she rallied. "Did she like to dance?"

Letting out a silent sigh of relief, Mitch leaned back so the pressure between their shoulders eased. "She didn't go out dancing, if that's what you mean. She didn't date. She always told me she didn't have time. She'd say, 'Who could work and have time for a man, too?'"

"A modern philosophy if I ever heard one," Lily joked.

Mitch chuckled. "Maybe so. But once in a while, she'd put on the radio and I'd catch her dancing around the kitchen. She always got embarrassed, but I could tell that if she'd had the time and a partner, she'd be good at it."

To his surprise, Mitch felt his phone vibrate against his hip. When he checked the caller ID, he recognized the number of a friend, Tony Russo. "I should take this," he said.

"Go ahead. We can go back to your SUV. I really should be getting home."

Because of that pulsating moment when he'd almost kissed her again? "You're sure?"

"Yes."

The certainty in her answer told him she didn't want to take the chance of staying longer, the chance that darkness and a starry sky might urge them to become more intimate.

A few minutes later, Lily stood beside Mitch at his SUV, wondering why she had agreed to come with him tonight. This seemed so much like a date and it just couldn't be! She'd known right away Ellie didn't approve when she'd told her where she was going.

She had to ask herself...would Troy approve of her being here with Mitch tonight? Troy's approval still mattered to her. She fingered her wedding ring, still feeling married.

Inhaling the scents of spring on the wind, she attempted to stay in the moment. She exhaled confusion and loss, in favor of life and music and the sliver of moon above. She was aware of Mitch's conversation, his deep laugh. He asked about someone named Jimmy and reported he'd gotten an email from Matt last week.

She was learning Mitch had more facets than she'd ever imagined. He had depth she'd never known about. He had a past he didn't want to talk about.

Now, however, when he ended his call, he smiled at

her. That smile both comforted her and made her breath hitch!

"An old friend?" she guessed, taking the safe route.

"Yes, Tony served with me in Iraq."

Surprised he was forthcoming about that, she asked, "Is he coming for a visit?"

"You heard me mention the bed-and-breakfast."

She nodded.

"Every year, the first weekend in December, I get together with servicemen I knew in Iraq. We alternate locations and their families come, too. This year it's my turn to host."

"What a wonderful idea!"

"We usually start planning this time of year to get the best airfares and accommodations. We have a money pool so if someone can't afford to come, the cash is there to draw on."

"How long does your reunion last?"

"Friday to Sunday. My house will be home base on Saturday. Do you have any ideas to occupy kids?"

"Besides enlisting someone to play Santa Claus?" she joked. "I used to do some face painting."

"You're kidding."

"No. I'm *not* just a doctor. I have an artistic bent."

He laughed. "That would be perfect."

A bit of moonlight drifted over them as they stood close. The look in Mitch's eyes was recognizable to her. He'd had that same look before he'd kissed her outside her bedroom.

When he reached out and stroked her cheek, she didn't pull away. She couldn't. There was something about Mitch that drew her to him, that made her want to forget her inhibitions, her idea of propriety, her sadness and loss.

"Lily," he murmured as the stars bore witness, as the moon seemed to tilt, as the ground trembled under her feet. The touch of his fingers on her face was filled with an aching longing.

But then he dropped his hand to his side and opened the passenger door. He didn't have to say anything and neither did she. They knew they couldn't kiss again. If they did, they might not stop there.

Ellie, Sophie and Grace were waiting for her. She didn't want to be any more confused when she walked in that door than she already was now.

Chapter Six

Time rolled by so fast, Lily could hardly count the days. She spent a lot of time thinking about Mitch, of how he'd touched her face at the lake. That night they'd silently but tacitly backed away from each other. Because of Ellie? Because they both feared their feelings were inappropriate?

The last week in May, Lily pushed Sophie and Grace's stroller into the office suite that was still familiar to her. Yet when she looked around at the sea-foam-green furniture, the rose carpeting and the green-and-mauve wallpaper, she didn't feel as if she *did* belong any more. She'd only been away three months, yet it seemed like a lifetime.

"This is where I work," she told Ellie, motioning to the reception area, the glass window behind which their receptionist Maryanne sat, the hall leading to exam rooms, office suites and the lab.

"It's really kind of...cozy," Ellie remarked as if she was surprised. "I think I expected white walls and tile and a sterile atmosphere."

"We try to keep it relaxed," Lily explained. "The couples and women who come to us are stressed enough. The more relaxed we can keep the process, the better."

"How many doctors work here?"

"Four, as well as two nurse-practitioners, two techs and our receptionist."

Lily rolled the stroller up to the receptionist's window.

Maryanne slid the glass open and grinned at her. "We miss you, Dr. Wescott," she said to Lily.

"I miss all of you, too," Lily returned, meaning it. Helping other women have babies was important to her, and even more so now, since she knew the joy of her twins.

She introduced Ellie.

Maryanne came out of her cubicle to coo over the babies. "They're adorable. I'm so glad you brought them in. And at just the right time. Everybody's on their lunch break. Go on back to the lounge."

Ellie took a peek down the hall. "Maybe I shouldn't go with you. I don't want to interrupt anything."

"Don't be silly," Lily said. "The practice is usually closed from twelve to one every day. That's why I was glad when we finished with Tessa right on time. I know Hillary will want to meet you. When I had a checkup with her, I told her about your baby store and your customized outfits. She has a one-year-old. She could be your first paying customer in Sagebrush."

Although Lily had attempted to prepare herself to see Mitch again, she didn't feel ready. Not after their awkward parting the evening of the concert.

As soon as she pushed open the door to the lounge and saw Mitch sitting at the table with Hillary and Jon, she was tossed back to that night, standing close to him by his SUV, the heat of his fingers a scalding impression on her cheek.

Mitch stood as soon as he spotted her and Ellie, the white lab coat he wore giving him the professional appearance that had been so familiar to her before the night of the banquet, before Grace and Sophie had been born.

The twins were the center of attention now as everyone crowded around. Lily was glad for that, relieved to be able to introduce Ellie to her colleagues, grateful that no one could see how being in the same room with Mitch affected her. Lily couldn't believe it herself. Maybe she just didn't want to believe it.

What kind of woman was she? She'd loved her husband, loved him to the moon and back. He'd only been gone for ten months. Many nights she still cried herself to sleep, missing him, needing him, longing for him. Her reaction to Mitch didn't make sense. Not at all. Before the twins were born, she'd never looked at him as anything but a colleague. But now, as everyone babbled to the babies and chatted politely with Ellie, Mitch's gaze passed over Lily's lilac top and slacks then swiftly returned to her face. His appraisal left her a little short of breath.

Hurriedly, she ducked her head and bent to scoop

Sophie from the stroller. "I don't know what I'd do without Ellie," she told everyone. "I seem to need six hands when these two are crying at the same time."

"So when are you coming back?" Hillary asked, her short chestnut hair fringing her face.

"Probably in November," she answered, not knowing what the next months would bring.

"You take your time deciding," Jon said. He was tall and lean with narrow black glasses that made him look scholarly.

Hillary asked, "May I hold Sophie?"

"Sure."

Hillary took the baby and settled her in the crook of her arm, looking down on her with the affection moms feel for kids. "I believe these little girls are going to be petite."

"Maybe. Or they could eventually grow as tall as Troy." Lily felt the need to mention his name, to bring him into the conversation.

Jon leaned a little closer to her. "How are you doing, really?"

"I'm okay. It's just the world's very different without Troy in it. Some days I expect that. Other days I expect him to come walking through the door, pick up Grace and Sophie, to figure out which one will look for his approval and which one won't."

Hillary had obviously overheard. She said, "I'll always remember Troy, Lily. I really cherish the table he made for me. It's absolutely beautiful craftsmanship."

Lily vividly remembered the piece of Troy's unfinished furniture still in storage. In fact, he'd been in the last stages of completing the plant stand she'd asked him to make when he was deployed. So much was unfinished and Lily didn't know how to complete the tapestry of the life that had been hers and Troy's.

Mitch had heard their conversation, too, and turned away, crossing to the refrigerator, closing the top on a juice bottle and setting it inside. His actions were slow and deliberate. She knew she'd brought up Troy to put a boundary around herself again, a boundary that would keep Mitch out. Why had she dropped in today? To catch up with old friends? Or to see *him?*

As Hillary moved away, rocking Sophie and cooing to her, Lily's gaze landed on Ellie, who was glancing toward her and then Mitch. No one else seemed to notice the vibes between Lily and Mitch, but apparently Ellie did.

Lily hung out with her colleagues in the lounge for a while. They all wanted to take turns holding the twins and see if they could distinguish between the two. As Lily had suspected, Hillary asked Ellie to tell her all about the clothes she created.

Stepping away from the group with Grace in her arms, Lily went in search of Mitch. He was her friend, and they would be working together when she returned. She had to keep communication open between them. She had to know what was going on in his mind. Maybe it had nothing to do with her. If it didn't, she'd be relieved. At least that's what she told herself.

She found him in his office, at his computer. She stood there for a few moments, listening to Grace's little soughing sounds, studying Mitch's profile. Her gaze went to his hands as his fingers depressed keys. His left hand was faster than his right and she wondered if the fingers on his right hand hurt to use. What kind of pain did he experience on a daily basis? With what he'd told her, she guessed his injuries had left repercussions. On the other hand, were the memories in his head more painful than anything physical injuries could cause? She wished he could talk to her about all of it. She wished—

Moving into the room, she said, "You should still be on your lunch break."

"A fertility specialist never sleeps," he joked. "I have a couple coming in this afternoon because the time is right."

"They're going the artificial insemination route?"

"For now. In vitro doesn't fit into their budget." His gaze went from Lily to Grace. "She seems content."

Lily checked her watch. "Probably for about fifteen more minutes."

Rolling his chair back, Mitch stood and approached her. His large hand gently passed over Grace's little head, his thumb brushing her strands of cotton-soft blond hair. "So you just decided to stop in or did you and Ellie have errands in the area?"

"Sophie and Grace had appointments with Tessa. Since we were in the building…" She trailed off.

"You wanted to stay in touch."

"I think it will be easier for me to come back to work in the fall if I do."

He nodded.

"Mitch…" She didn't know what she wanted to say, or how to say it. "I need to talk about Troy."

"I know you do. That was another good reason for Ellie coming to stay with you."

"You left the lounge and I thought—"

"I told you I have clients coming."

"I know." She felt so stymied for the right words to

say. She could say, *I want to be around you, but when I am, I feel guilty.* Yet that couldn't come out because she and Mitch were both fighting becoming any closer.

She bowed her head, placing a tiny kiss on Grace's forehead, trying to figure out what she was doing in this room with Mitch and why she had actually stopped in today.

Yet Mitch wouldn't let her stand there, stewing in her own confusion. He slipped one knuckle under her chin and lifted it. "I think we're both feeling things we don't believe we should be feeling. You don't know whether to run in the other direction or pretend we're just friends."

"I don't want to pretend!"

His brows arched as he gave her a crooked smile. "That *is* the crux of it."

"Lily." Ellie was standing in the doorway with Sophie, studying the two of them standing close, Mitch's finger under her chin.

He quickly dropped his hand to his side while Lily turned to face her sister-in-law. "I know. They're both going to start crying for lunch soon."

"If you'd like to use my office, you can," Mitch offered. "I have work to do in the lab."

Crossing to his desk and reaching for a file folder, he picked it up, then stopped in the doorway. "It's good to see you again, Ellie."

"You, too," she said politely.

Mitch stood there for a few moments as if waiting to see if Troy's sister had something else to say. But she didn't. After a last glance at Lily and the twins, he strode down the hall.

Lily waited, not knowing if Ellie might have something to say to *her.* But her sister-in-law just moved toward the door. "I'll get the diaper bag." Then she was gone, too, leaving Lily with Grace in Mitch's office with very chaotic thoughts and feelings.

"They sure like those swings," Angie observed a week later as Lily came into the kitchen and watched her putting together a casserole for lunch.

Lily stirred the white sauce she was cooking and glanced over at her content daughters. "They're settling into a real schedule."

"Where's Ellie?"

"She went shopping to get material she needed."

Angie poured herself a cup of coffee and took a seat at the kitchen counter. "Mitch hasn't been around for a while. Did you two have a fight or something?"

Or something, Lily thought. "I saw him when I visited everyone at the practice."

"That was a week ago. He stopped in to see Sophie and Grace every day when they were in the hospital and he worried about you. It seems odd he hasn't called or dropped by more."

"I think he's giving me space."

Angie studied Lily over her mug. "Do you want space?"

"We're just friends." If she repeated those words often enough, she might believe them.

"I know that. And I know he's watching over you because Troy asked him to."

Lily found herself wanting to protest, to say that wasn't the only reason. Yet she wasn't sure she should. She didn't know what was in Mitch's mind. "I feel I owe him so much for everything."

"So why not call him and ask him to dinner?"

Angie made it sound so simple. On the one hand, Lily would love to do that. But on the other, she wished she and Mitch could have a little time alone, maybe straighten out everything between them.

"I could go to his place to cook dinner," she said aloud, testing the idea.

From the doorway, several bags in her arms, Ellie asked, "You want to cook dinner for Mitch?" There was wariness in her tone and an element of disapproval.

"He did so much for me, including encouraging me to call you. I'd like to thank him."

Ellie came into the kitchen and dropped her bags on the table. Then she went to the twins and crouched down, greeting both of them.

"I'm off for the weekend," Angie offered. "I could watch Sophie and Grace if Ellie has plans."

"No plans tomorrow. Just the concert with you in Amarillo on Saturday," Ellie said to Angie, without looking up. "I can watch them."

"Are you sure?" Lily asked. "Because I could invite Mitch here instead."

"No," Ellie responded, standing. "It's fine. Angie and I and Sophie and Grace will have a girls' night together. It will be a blast, even if the babies can't eat popcorn yet."

"Before we make too many plans, I'd better find out if Mitch wants me to cook for him. I'll leave a message on his cell phone." She picked up the cordless phone in the kitchen before she lost her nerve.

An hour and a half later, when Mitch returned her call, Lily had just finished breast-feeding both babies.

It was much easier now than when she'd first tried to juggle their needs.

"I got your message," Mitch said. "Is everything all right?"

Lily looked down at her sleeping daughters. "Ev-erything's fine. I…" She cleared her throat. "If you're going to be home tomorrow evening, I'd like to cook you dinner."

"Home? As in at my house?"

She laughed. "Yes. Angie and Ellie offered to watch Sophie and Grace, and this would be my way to thank you for everything you've done."

He didn't say, "You don't have to thank me," because they'd gone through that routine before and he probably knew it would fall on deaf ears. "A home-cooked meal would be a nice change," he agreed noncommittally.

"What's your favorite meal?"

"Why don't you surprise me."

"You're not going to give me a hint?"

"Nope. I like everything."

"Okay, I'll stop at the market and then come over."

"I'm taking off tomorrow afternoon to meet with the couple who own the bed-and-breakfast around three. But I should be home by four. I can tape a spare key under the garage spout in case I'm tied up longer."

Lily was surprised Mitch was taking off, but she knew planning the reunion was important to him. "That's perfect. I can get started and then when you arrive, we can really catch up."

"Catching up sounds good," he responded, as if he meant it.

Lily's heart seemed to flutter but she told herself it was just her imagination.

After she ended the call, she wondered if she was doing the right thing. But showing her appreciation was important to her. No matter what Mitch said, she believed it was important to him, too.

She'd find out tomorrow night.

Lily found the key behind the spout on Friday and let herself into Mitch's brick ranch-style house situated on the outskirts of Sagebrush. She liked the looks of the outside with its neat plantings and tall fencing, and the protected entrance where she'd set the grocery bags on a wooden bench that perfectly fit the space. Slipping the key into the lock, she pushed open the door and stepped inside.

To the right of the small foyer, a door led into the garage. Beyond that lay a rambling living room. It was huge, with a fireplace, tall windows and a cathedral ceiling with a fan. The comfortable-looking furniture was upholstered in masculine colors, navy and burgundy. Distressed-pine tables and black wrought-iron lamps sat in practical positions around the furniture. She was surprised to see only a small flat-screen TV in the entertainment center rather than a larger model. But then maybe Mitch didn't spend much time watching TV.

The kitchen was straight ahead and she eagerly picked up the bags, took them in and set them on the counter. Stainless steel appliances looked shiny and new. An archway opened into a sunroom where French doors led outside to a large rustic brick patio. A round table and four chairs nestled in a corner of the dining area of the kitchen under a black wrought-iron chandelier. She liked the clean lines of the house, its spaciousness, its practical floor plan.

She was unpacking the groceries when her cell phone rang. She thought it might be Mitch telling her he was on his way. Instead, she recognized Raina's number and happily answered. "How are you?"

Her friend said, "I'm in labor!"

"You're not due till next week," Lily said practically.

Raina laughed. "Tell that to our son or daughter."

"Where are you?"

"At the hospital. Emily is with me."

Lily knew Raina was comfortable using a midwife, but her husband hadn't been so sure. "How is Shep handling this?"

"Let's just say he drove here under the speed limit but that was a struggle. Now he's pacing while Emily's trying to keep the mood relaxed."

Raina had wanted to have a home birth, but she'd compromised with Shep. Since Emily and Jared had managed to bring about changes at the hospital to include a midwife in the birthing process, there were two suites there now that were supposed to simulate the comforts of home. The birthing suites provided the advantages of delivering a baby in a more natural setting while having a doctor nearby should any complications arise.

"How are *you* handling labor?"

"I can't wait for this baby to be born. Wow," she suddenly exclaimed, "I'm starting another contraction and it's stronger than the last one. Either Shep or I will let you know when the baby's born. Talk to you later."

Lily thought about her own contractions, how they'd come on so suddenly, how Mitch had helped her. In some ways, that night seemed eons ago.

After considering her options, Lily had decided to make Mitch something she had never cooked before. She'd found the recipe for chicken in wine in her favorite cookbook. It wasn't complicated. It just required a little time to prepare. Today she had the time. She'd brought along her favorite pan and started bacon frying in it. Rummaging in Mitch's cupboard, she found other pots and pans she could use. After she sorted her ingredients, she prepared the chicken to fry in the bacon drippings.

A half hour later, the chicken was browning nicely when she heard the garage door open. She took a quick look around the kitchen. She had managed to set the table before she'd started the chicken. She'd brought along two place mats, matching napkins, as well as a vase filled with pretty, hand-carved wooden flowers. Mitch's white ironstone dishes looked perfect on the dark green place mats.

Lily heard the door from the garage into the foyer open then Mitch's deep voice calling into the kitchen. "Something smells great."

And then he was there in the doorway, tall and lean, his almost black eyes taking in everything at a glance. He wore blue jeans, black boots and a navy henley. Skitters of sensation rippled up and down her spine.

They just stood there for a few moments, staring at each other. He assessed her white jeans and pink top with its scoop neckline. "Shouldn't you be wearing an apron?"

"The clothes will wash."

"Spoken like a mom."

Moving forward into the kitchen, he caught sight

of the table and stopped. "You've gone to a lot of trouble."

"Not really. You're just not used to a woman's touch." As soon as the words were out, she knew she should have thought first before speaking. Letting the thoughts in her mind spill free could land her in deep trouble.

Mitch didn't react, simply hung his keys on a hook above the light switch. "I don't know how long it's been since I walked into a kitchen with something good cooking. Do you want me to help with this?" He motioned to the stove and the sink. "Or do you want me to get out of your way?"

"You're welcome to help, but if you have something more important to do—"

"Nothing that can't wait," he said, washing his hands. "I worked in the yard earlier this afternoon."

"I like your house, and the way you've decorated."

His brows drew together as he dried his hands on the dish towel. "Maybe you can tell me the best way to set it up to entertain twenty to twenty-five people for the reunion weekend. I'm afraid space will be tight."

"What about a fire pit on the patio, depending on the weather, of course. It might draw a few people out there to toast marshmallows."

He studied her with one of those intense looks again and she knew it wasn't just the heat from the stove that was making her cheeks flame. "What?"

"You have great ideas."

Smiling to herself, she turned back to the chicken, deciding it was browned just right and that she had to concentrate on the meal so she wouldn't focus too much on Mitch. "My next great idea is that I'd better watch what I'm doing or your kitchen could go up in flames."

He chuckled. "What do you need help with?"

"Can you open the wine? I need a cup. I have everything else ready to simmer." She dumped in onions and celery, stirring to sauté them a bit, added carrots, chicken broth and the crumbled bacon. After Mitch loosened the cork and poured out a cup of wine, she took it from him, their hands grazing each other, hers tingling after they did.

Moving away from him, she poured the wine into the pot, put the lid on and set it to simmer, glad the major part of the meal was finished.

"Now what?" he asked.

"I need three apples peeled and sliced into that pie plate. I'll make the topping while you're doing that. Tell me about your meeting. Will you be able to reserve rooms at the bed-and-breakfast?"

When Mitch didn't answer, she looked up at him and saw him staring down at the apples. At that moment, she realized the request she'd made, as well as the mistake of asking him to do that kind of task.

"I've learned to do a lot of things with my left hand," he said matter-of-factly, "but using a knife to slice apples isn't one of them."

"Mitch, I'm sorry. I wasn't thinking."

"There's nothing to be sorry about. Why don't I look through my collection of DVDs and find something we would both enjoy?"

She wanted to put her arms around Mitch. She wanted to breathe in his scent and kiss him, letting him know the use of his fingers wasn't an issue between them.

"Okay," she said lightly. "I'll be there in a few

minutes." That was all the time she'd need to slice the apples, mix them with cranberries and pour on a topping.

Then she might have to decide just where she stood where Mitch was concerned.

Chapter Seven

Mitch knew he shouldn't have reacted as he had. It had been a very long time since something so simple had pushed his buttons. After Iraq, he'd been grateful he'd survived. He'd been grateful he could retrain in another specialty. He'd been grateful he had a life.

The truth was, he could have peeled an apple with his left hand, but those slices would have been chunky and choppy, maybe still bearing some skin.

At the practice, he spoke with couples, analyzed their needs, helped them decide which process was best. He calculated cycles, administered drug regimens, analyzed test results, sonograms, fluoroscopic X-rays. He could facilitate artificial insemination procedures. But he couldn't peel and slice an apple to his liking.

He could help bring life into the world, but he couldn't perform surgery to save a life.

Why had that fact hit him so hard just now?

He shuffled through the DVDs lying on the coffee table without paying attention to the titles. He was vaguely aware of the scent of cinnamon and apples baking, adding to the aroma of the chicken and wine. But when Lily stood in the doorway for a couple of moments before she took a step into the living room, he was elementally aware of her.

As she sat beside him on the sofa, only a few inches away, he wanted to both push her away and take her into his arms. It was the oddest feeling he'd ever experienced. Desire bit at him and he fought it.

"Dinner will be ready in about twenty minutes," she said, as if that were the main topic for discussion.

He could feel her gaze on him, making him hot, making him more restless. Facing her, he concluded, "Maybe this wasn't such a good idea."

"Eating dinner?" she asked, a little nervously, trying to make light of what was happening.

"Cooking together, eating together, watching a DVD together."

"I want to be here," she assured him, her eyes big and wide, all attempts at teasing gone. It was as if she were inviting him to kiss her.

He balled his hands into fists. "Lily—"

Reaching out to him, she touched the tense line of his jaw. "I don't know what's happening, Mitch, but being here with you is important to me. Maybe that first kiss wasn't as intense as we both thought it was. Maybe it was just an outlet—"

He was tired of analyzing and debating and pushing away desire that needed to be expressed. His hands slid under her hair as he leaned toward her, as he cut off her words with his lips. For over two years, he'd kept his desire for her hidden, locked away. Now, unable to resist, he set it free.

Passion poured out. Lily responded to it and returned it. For that reason, and that reason only, he didn't slam the door shut. He didn't throw the combination away again. She was softness and goodness and light in his hands. When his tongue swept her mouth, she wrapped her arms around his neck and held on. He was caught in the storm that had been building between them since the day he'd first held her. Warning bells clanged in his head, reminding him he should stop kissing her and pull away. But those warning bells seemed distant compared to the hunger that urged him on.

He sensed that same hunger had built in Lily. She wasn't holding back. Nothing about her was restrained.

The sounds of satisfaction Lily was making were driving Mitch crazy. His hand slid from her hair and caressed her shoulder. He could feel the heat of her skin under her knit top. Was she on fire for him as he was for her? Would she consider this kiss another mistake?

His hand slid to her breast. He knew if he didn't breathe soon, the need inside him would consume him.

Lily leaned away just slightly, as if inviting him to touch her more. His control was in shreds. He tore away from the kiss to nuzzle her neck as his hand left her breast and caressed her thigh.

When she turned her face up to his again, her eyes were closed. At that moment, Mitch knew this could be a very big mistake. What if she was imagining Troy loving her? What if she just needed someone to hold her and any man would take the form of her husband?

He leaned back, willed his heart to slow and found his voice. "Lily, open your eyes."

The few seconds it took for Lily to find her way back to the sofa seemed unending. She'd been so lost in pleasure that the sound of Mitch's voice—the request he'd made—seemed impossible at first.

When she did open her eyes, she was gazing into his. They were so dark and simmering, filled with the questions that took her a moment to understand. Until he asked, "Were you here with me?"

Her reflexive response was, "Of course, I was here with you." But as soon as she said it, she had to go back and think and feel. She had to be honest with Mitch and herself. As he didn't move an inch, she whispered, "*Mostly* here with you."

While she was kissing Mitch, had she been longing for Troy to be the one making love to her? Shaken by that question, as well as the aftermath of the passion that had bubbled up inside her like a well waiting to be sprung, she jumped when the cell phone in her pocket chimed.

Mitch seemed just as jarred. The resigned look on his face told her he knew she had to take the call. After all, Sophie or Grace might need her.

She checked the screen and then glanced at him. "It's Raina. She's in the hospital in labor. I have to find out if everything's okay."

Just then, the timer went off in the kitchen. Mitch rose to his feet. "I'll check on dinner," he said gruffly.

Lily closed her eyes and answered Raina's call.

Swallowing emotion that was confusing and

exhilarating, as well as terrifying, Lily cleared her throat. "Raina?"

"It's a girl, Lily! We had a *girl*." Her friend's voice broke.

"That was pretty fast."

"Once we got here, it was like she couldn't wait to get out. You've got to come see her, Lily. I know you… understand."

Lily did understand Raina's history, the loss of her husband and dreams unfulfilled. Now she'd captured those dreams again. "I'm at Mitch's."

Raina didn't miss a beat. Her joy was too big and broad. "Bring him, too. Shep could use a little distraction. He's hovering over both of us. Eva's here with the boys but she's going to leave in a few minutes. They're so excited about their new sister that they're getting a little rowdy."

"I'll call you back after I talk to Mitch."

"If I interrupted something, I'm sorry. You can wait to visit tomorrow."

Yes, she could. Yet she knew the joy Raina was feeling. She knew this was a once-in-a-lifetime experience for her.

After she and Raina ended the call, Lily went into the kitchen, where Mitch had taken the apple dessert from the oven and set it on the counter.

"Raina had a baby girl," she announced brightly.

"I bet she and Shep are ecstatic."

She remembered Mitch had met Shep the night of the awards dinner that now seemed forever ago. "She'd like us to come see the baby."

"Now? She wants company?"

"You know how it is with new moms. They're so

proud, so full of life. And Raina and I, we have a special bond. She says we can wait until tomorrow, but I don't want to let her down. The chicken should be finished. Do you want to have dinner first?"

Mitch glanced at the kitchen clock. "Visiting hours will be over soon. Let's put it in a casserole. We can warm it up when we get back."

"I can go alone."

"Would you rather go alone?"

Their intimacy on the sofa was still fresh in her mind and in her heart. She wanted to stay with him...*be* with him a little longer.

"I'd like you to come along."

He gave her a hint of a smile. "Then let's put this away and get going."

Lily thought she'd jump out of her skin every time Mitch glanced at her in his SUV. Their awareness of each other was so acute, it was almost uncanny. She suspected Mitch was feeling the same way when he flipped on the CD player. Both of them had agreed to go to the hospital because that was the easier thing to do. She'd almost gotten naked with Mitch, almost let him make love to her. Then what would they have had to say to each other?

At the hospital, alone in the elevator as they rode up to the maternity floor, Mitch turned to her. "I don't feel as if I belong here."

"Here?"

"The maternity floor. With your friend."

"My guess is Shep will be glad to see a friendly male face. He's not real comfortable with the softer things in life, if you know what I mean. But I think Raina's changing that."

"Softer things in life, meaning women having babies, pink blankets, nurses cooing?"

"You've got it."

Mitch almost smiled. "That does take some getting used to."

"I guess the transition from trauma surgeon to fertility specialist wasn't always easy for you."

"Fortunately I was able to rely on some of the research skills I'd acquired while I was in med school. I was a teaching assistant for a professor studying T cells, so analyzing data and studies wasn't foreign to me. I think the hardest part was learning to act as a counselor sometimes to couples who were stressed out because they'd been trying for years to have a baby and couldn't. All kinds of things popped up. I suppose that's why we have Dr. Flannagan as an adjunct."

"Vanessa is good. I've sent couples to her who are indecisive or who can't agree on what they want to do. Do you know Vanessa well?" Lily asked.

"No. We had lunch together once to discuss a case. She doesn't like to skate on the surface and I didn't want to be psychoanalyzed, so let's just say we didn't socialize after that—we stuck to business."

Lily was surprised to find herself relieved that Mitch hadn't gotten on well with the pretty psychologist. She admonished herself that she had no business being possessive. She had *no* rights where Mitch was concerned.

After Lily and Mitch signed in at the desk, Lily caught sight of Shep in one of the family waiting rooms. Joey and Roy, Shep and Raina's older boys, stood in the doorway as if ready to leave. Eva, their nanny, had one arm about each of them while Manuel, Shep and

Raina's almost three-year-old, was throwing a tantrum, his arms tightly holding Shep around the neck, his tears as heartbreaking as his sobs.

"Daddy, you come home, *too*," he wailed.

Shep spotted Lily immediately and said above Manuel's wails, "Don't you tell Raina about this."

"She'd understand."

"Hell, yes, she'd understand. She'd want me to bring them all into the room so they could sleep with her."

Lily had to chuckle because she knew Shep was right. "She'd call it a birthday sleepover," Lily joked.

Mitch groaned. "I think you're going to have to do better than that to cheer this little guy up. So your name's Manuel?" Mitch asked, bending down to him, looking into his eyes.

At first Lily thought the little boy would play shy. Instead of hiding in Shep's shoulder, though, he pulled himself up straighter and studied Mitch. "What's your name?"

"My name's Mitch." He pointed to Lily. "You know her, don't you?"

Manuel nodded vigorously. "She and Mom are BFFs."

The adults all looked at each other and broke out into laughter.

"Who'd you hear that from?" Shep asked.

"Joey. He knows."

"Yes, he does know lots of things," Shep agreed with a grin he couldn't suppress.

"Maybe you should go home and make sure everything's ready for tomorrow when your sister comes home," Mitch suggested. "I bet your mom and dad would both be surprised."

Eva stepped in. "We could cut some roses and put them in pretty vases. Your mom would love that. We can make sure everything in the baby's room is just right."

Manuel stared at Eva.

Adding another incentive, she offered, "I can turn on the new baby monitor and you can watch the lights flicker when we make noise in the room."

Swiveling toward his dad again, Manuel screwed up his little face. "Okay."

Shep tapped the pocket of his shirt. "I'll give you a call before bed and you can say good-night to Mom. How's that?"

"That's good," Manuel assured him, climbing off his dad's lap and taking Eva's hand.

After hugs and kisses from all his boys, Shep watched them leave the maternity floor with Eva.

"Man, that's tough," he muttered. "It breaks my heart when they're sad."

Lily patted Shep's arm knowing that before he met Raina, he never would have been able to admit that.

"I'm going to visit the new mom," Lily said.

Shep studied Mitch. "You want to get a cup of coffee with me?"

"Sure," Mitch answered, exchanging a look with Lily that told her she'd been right about Shep needing a break.

"See you in a bit," she said with a wave, and headed for Raina's room.

When she entered her friend's room, she stopped short. This was a woman who had her world together.

The head of the bed had been raised and Raina was holding her infant daughter. She looked absolutely radiant and Lily almost envied her calm sense of satisfaction.

"Hey, there," she called softly from the doorway.

"Hey, yourself. Come on in. Meet Christina Joy McGraw."

"What a beautiful name! Did you and Shep decide on it together?"

"He just said he wanted something pretty and a little old-fashioned. I added Joy because that's what she's going to bring us." After passing her hand over her baby's head, Raina looked beyond Lily. "Where's Mitch?"

"He's keeping Shep company for a cup of coffee."

"This is a rough day for Shep, but if he drinks more than two cups, he's not going to sleep tonight."

Lily laughed. "I don't think he's going to sleep anyway. You *do* know he's going to stay here with you."

"He said something to that effect, but I thought he was kidding."

"Uh-uh. He's not letting you or that baby girl out of his sight for very long."

After they both stared down at the infant, Lily taken with her raven-dark hair and eyes, Raina asked, "Did I interrupt something when I called? I never imagined you'd be with Mitch."

"Oh, I just decided to make him a thank-you dinner. It was easier to do at his house."

"Did you eat?"

"No, we put it in a casserole for later. It will be fine."

"I have lousy timing," Raina murmured.

"No, actually you have very good timing."

The two women exchanged a look.

"Do you want to tell me what's going on?" Raina asked.

"Not here. The men could come back. Besides, I'm not sure anything is going on. Nothing should be going on, right?" If there was one person to ask about this, that person would be Raina.

"I waited nine long years to find love again. You don't have to wait that long."

"But what if it isn't love? What if I just miss Troy so much, long to be held so much, that I mistake something else for real emotion?"

"Is that what you think is happening?"

Lily sighed. "I don't know. When I'm with Mitch, I actually can't think sometimes, let alone figure out the best thing to do."

"Then don't do anything until you're ready to do whatever's right for you."

"You make it sound so easy."

"Yeah, I know," Raina said with a wry smile. "If I'd taken my own advice, I wouldn't have this little girl in my arms right now. Do you want to hold her?"

"You bet I do."

Shep sat across from Mitch at the cafeteria table, staring down into his coffee. "When Raina went into labor—" He shook his head. "I don't think I've ever gone into such a panic."

"I know what you mean," Mitch said, thinking about that night at the banquet, Lily's contractions, knowing the twins would be premature.

Shep didn't say anything for a moment, but then remarked, "So you felt that way when Lily went into labor?"

What kind of trap had Mitch just walked into? He kept silent.

"You being a doc and all," Shep went on, "I would think you'd be more matter-of-fact about it."

He would have been with anyone else, but not with Lily. No way was he going to admit that out loud. Then it didn't seem he had to. Shep was giving him a knowing look that made Mitch feel uncomfortable. One thing Mitch never thought he'd be was transparent. He expected another question, but it didn't follow.

Instead, Shep took another sip of his coffee and set it down again. "Raina and Lily have become really good friends. They have a lot in common."

"Raina's been a great support for Lily since Troy died." He might as well just get the subject out there so they weren't trampling around it.

"I heard you've been, too."

"You heard?" Mitch tried to keep the defensiveness from his voice, but he was worried that gossip was spreading about him and Lily.

"That night at the banquet when you carried Lily off. Raina told me Troy had left a letter asking you to look after her. That's why you're with her again tonight, right?" Shep inquired blandly.

Lily had told Mitch about Shep's background and why he'd wanted to adopt. She'd always spoken admiringly of him and Mitch knew her to be a good judge of character.

So when Shep stopped beating around the proverbial bush and added, "When I met Raina, nine years had passed since her husband died. Even so, we had a few bumps in our road because of it."

"Lily and I aren't—"

"Aren't serious? Aren't involved? Only friends? I get that. No one's judging you…or Lily."

"Maybe *you're* not, but Troy's sister is and I can't blame her for that. Even *I* know Lily's still vulnerable and I should watch my step. But how do you keep a promise to protect someone and step back at the same time?"

"That's a tough one," Shep admitted. "But if you care about her, you'll figure out the right thing to do, without interference from anyone else." Shep drank the last of his coffee. "Thanks for coming down here with me. I want to be with my wife and baby, but I needed a little break just to settle down a bit."

"I understand."

Shep nodded. "So are you ready to meet my daughter?"

When Lily and Mitch returned from the hospital, they warmed up dinner and ate at the table Lily had set. She called Ellie to see how the twins were doing and to give a report on Raina.

After she closed her phone, Mitch asked, "Ready for dessert?" and brought the apple crumble to the table.

"I have to get back home. Sophie and Grace are okay but I don't want Ellie and Angie to feel as if I've abandoned them."

"You haven't. A couple of hours away will do all of you good."

"I know, but—"

"You don't have to run off because you think I might kiss you again. I won't, if you don't want me to."

Lily felt her heart start hammering. "That's the problem, Mitch. I think I want you to."

Although another man might have acted on that subtle invitation, Mitch didn't. He set the dish on the table and started scooping dessert out for both of them.

"You don't have anything to say to that?" she asked quietly.

"Shep thinks we're involved."

Lily felt rattled that the subject had come up between the two men.

"I didn't start that conversation, if you're wondering," Mitch assured her.

"No, I wasn't. I guess I was just surprised."

"Everyone who cares about you is worried about you. It's natural that they're going to watch what you're doing."

"I hate to think I'm being watched," Lily murmured.

"In a good way."

After Mitch took his seat again beside her, she confessed, "Raina thinks we're involved, too."

"And what do *you* think?" he asked, his dark gaze penetrating, assessing, questioning.

"I think I'm scared. I think a kiss means more than I want it to mean with you."

"We did more than kiss," he reminded her.

She couldn't look away, didn't look away, wouldn't look away. She had to be as honest as she could with him. "I'm not sure where we're headed, Mitch. A lot of hormones are still driving me. What if we go up in flames? How much damage will that do to either of us? I've never had affairs, even before Troy. I was always in committed relationships. So what's happening between you and me—"

"Isn't a committed relationship."

"We're really on sandy footing," she said with a shake of her head.

He didn't disagree.

"But I like being with you," she continued. "I feel so alone sometimes, but not when I'm with you."

"We're back to the friends-versus-more question," he said.

Suddenly Lily was tired of the seriousness of it all. She was a widow with two babies to raise and sometimes she just wanted to scream. "Why do we even have to decide? Why are we worried about affairs and committed relationships? I mean, why can't we just enjoy being together?"

A light smile crept across his lips. "You couldn't be saying we're analyzing too much."

"I'm saying I need to take some deep breaths and not worry so much, and maybe *you* do, too. Yes, I think about Troy all the time, and how much I miss him, and how much the babies would love to have him as a father. But he's not here, and I can't pretend he will be again."

"You still love him a lot."

"Yes, Mitch, I do. But that love can't fill up my life twenty-four hours a day anymore. I have to start making room for a different life."

"And?" Mitch prompted.

"And," Lily repeated, then hesitated a moment.... "And Ellie and Angie are going to a concert in Amarillo tomorrow. They're going to stay overnight. So why don't you come over around four and we'll take the babies for a walk. Then maybe we can toss around some ideas for your Christmas weekend. That will be looking ahead and it should be fun. I can plan a menu. You can decide who will be Santa Claus. We'll just hang out."

His gaze was still on her, seeing into her and through her. They had to both figure out what they wanted and maybe the only way to do that would be to spend some time together.

"You just want some help with Sophie and Grace," he teased.

After considering what he'd said, she shook her head. "No, I want to hang out with you."

If she thought Mitch had ignored her invitation earlier, she could see in his eyes now that he hadn't.

Leaning toward her, he reached out and moved a stray wave from her cheek. Then he rubbed his thumb over her lips, leaning even closer. "Does hanging out involve kissing?"

"Maybe," she said with a little uncertainty.

His lips came down on hers and the rest of the world fell away.

Chapter Eight

Mitch pushed the double stroller down the street, noticing the darkened gray sky and the storm clouds that had gathered. He felt a similar storm inside of himself, agitating to be set free.

We're just going to hang out together, he repeated in his mind like a mantra.

Strolling beside him, Lily bent to make sure Sophie and Grace were happy under their canopies. Lily wore a yellow sundress with strawberries appliquéd around the hem. He wondered if she'd dressed up for him or if he was reading too much into her choice of a simple dress on a warm June day. She'd tucked her hair behind her ears and held it in place with two pretty mother-of-pearl combs. She was a vision that plagued his dreams and unsettled his days.

When she straightened, she flashed him a quick smile. "You're staring."

"Caught in the act," he joked. "You look pretty today. But more than that. Freer somehow."

"It was nice being in the house alone with the babies the few hours before you came. Don't get me wrong. I'm so grateful for how Angie and Ellie help. I love being housemates with them. But I also like the feeling that I'm Sophie and Grace's mother and no one means as much to them as I do. Isn't that silly?"

"Not at all. But you don't have to worry. Their eyes are starting to follow you. They know you're their mother, no matter who takes care of them. You have an innate bond with them, just as they do with each other. Nothing will change that."

"Not even me going back to work?"

"Not even."

The breeze suddenly picked up, tossing Lily's hair across her shoulders. "Uh-oh," she said, looking up. "We might not make it back before it rains."

"The rain could hold off," he assured her, yet he knew it probably wouldn't. Once the weather cycle was set in motion, nothing could stop it.

"I'm not wearing running shoes. *You* are."

"I promise I won't race ahead of you. Sophie and Grace are protected by the state-of-the-art stroller your friends gave them. So I don't think we have to rush on their part."

Still, he rolled the stroller around in a half circle and headed back the way they'd come.

Lily stepped up her pace beside him. "I don't like sudden storms."

"You'd rather have planned storms?" he asked, amused.

She cast him a sideways glance. "I know you think that's funny, but just imagine. What if you knew ahead of time about the crises in your life? You could prevent them."

"Maybe. Or maybe fate would just find another way to get you to the same spot so you'd have to make the same kind of decisions."

"Oh my gosh! You're a philosopher and I never knew it."

Mitch had to laugh. "That's one title I've never been given."

"It's a compliment," she assured him, with a teasing tone in her voice that made him want to tug her into his arms and kiss her right there and then on the street. But in Sagebrush, that would almost be a spectacle.

She must have guessed what he was thinking because she slowed for a moment. He didn't stop, and she took a couple of running steps to catch up.

The wind buffeted them with a little more force now and large, fat drops of rain began to pelt them. Lightning slashed the sky not so far away and thunder grumbled overhead. The flashes and booms reminded Mitch of faraway places. He fought to keep memories at bay. Even though he was practically jogging with the stroller, he took deep, even breaths, reminding himself where he was and what he was doing.

A half block from the Victorian, the rain became steadier, rat-a-tatting on the pavement, pelting the leaves of the Texas ash trees blurred in Mitch's peripheral vision. The thunder became a louder drumroll.

Mitch blocked the sound as best he could.

Almost at the front yard of the big, blue house with its yellow gingerbread trim, Lily's sandal caught on the uneven pavement. Mitch sensed rather than saw what was happening and training took over. He reached low for Lily, catching her around the waist before she fell. Her body was warm, her shoulders slick with the rain dripping down. One of her arms had surrounded his waist as she'd steadied herself to keep from falling. His face was so close to hers he could almost feel the quiver of her chin as emotion and desire ran through them both.

Yet they seemed to recognize where they were and what they were doing at the same time because in unison, they murmured, "The twins."

Mitch tilted his forehead against hers for just a moment then released her and pushed the stroller up the walkway to the porch.

Lily unlocked the door while he easily lifted the stroller, carrying it up the steps and into the foyer.

Moments later she switched on the Tiffany light to dispel the shadows while he rolled the twins into the living room and stooped down at Sophie's side of the stroller to see if any pelts of rain had made their way to her.

Lily did the same on Grace's side. "They're dry," she said with amazement.

"At least their clothes are," he returned with a wink.

When Lily laughed, he felt as if he'd done something terrific. He also felt as if the lightning strike had sent supercharged awareness through *him*. When his eyes met Lily's, he knew she felt the same way.

Ducking her head, she lifted Grace. Her pink-and-yellow playsuit with the dog appliquéd on her belly was a little big. It wouldn't be long until she grew into it, Mitch knew.

Grace cooed at Lily and Lily cooed back. "You're a happy girl today. How would you like to sit in your swing?"

Grace's little mouth rounded in an O and her very blue eyes studied her mom's face.

Mitch held Sophie in the crook of his arm. "Do you want to join your sister?"

Sophie's outfit was pink-and-green with a cat appliquéd on the bib of her overalls. When she waved her arms and oohed and aahed in her baby language, Mitch chuckled.

He and Lily set the girls in their swings and wound the mechanism that would start the motion. Then of one accord, she and Mitch seemed to come together, standing close behind the twins.

He brushed his hand down her arm. "I think you need a towel." She was wet from the rain and he was, too. The result of that seemed to be steam rising from both of them.

"I need to change," she murmured but didn't move away.

He fingered one of her combs. "I like these in your hair."

"They were my mother's," she replied softly. "I haven't worn them very much. I was afraid something would happen to them. Suddenly today I realized she wouldn't want me to just leave them in my jewelry box."

Lily's skin was lightly tanned as if she'd taken the babies for walks many days in the sun. He clasped her shoulders and ran his thumbs up and down the straps of her dress. "I've been wanting to kiss you since I got here."

"I've wanted you to kiss me since you got here."

She tilted her head up and he lowered his. He told himself to go easy, not to scare her with too much need. He didn't want to need her at all. But the moment his lips settled on hers, he couldn't keep the hunger at bay. The feel of her in his arms was exquisite, the soft pressure of her lips was a temptation that urged him to claim her. When his tongue thrust into her mouth, her gasp was only a preliminary response. She followed it with a tightening of her arms around him. A return taste of him became a chase and retreat that had them pressing their bodies together.

Outside, a bright flash of light against a darkening sky was soon followed by thunder that seemed to crawl up one side of the roof and down the other. The crackle and boom sounded very close.

All at once the light in the foyer went out and the hum of the refrigerator ceased.

Mitch held Lily tighter, ended the kiss and rubbed his jaw against her cheek. "The electricity." Huskiness hazed his words. "The lightning must have hit a transformer."

After a few moments, she leaned away from him. "I'd better find the oil lamp in case we don't have power for a while. I had a stir-fry planned for supper."

"We'll have to make do with lunchmeat and cheese."

"I made a coconut cake. We don't need power to eat that."

"You have flashlights and candles?"

"I think they're under the kitchen sink. The oil lamp's upstairs. I'll get it when I change."

"Go ahead. I'll watch Grace and Sophie until you come back down. Then you can stay with them while I rummage."

After a last longing look at him, sending the message their kiss had ended much too soon, she ran upstairs.

Mitch took a hefty breath.

Sandwiches eaten, candles and oil lamp lit, Lily forgot about time and just lived in the moment. She and Mitch had talked as they'd sat on the sofa and exchanged fussy babies. They'd played patty-cake and peekaboo with Sophie and Grace in between talking about books they had read, movies they'd seen, first experiences swimming, diving, surfing, hiking. There seemed to be so much to talk about. Yet underneath it all, whenever their gazes met or their fingers brushed, memories of their kisses danced in her mind.

After a few hours, Lily breast-fed Grace while Mitch bottle-fed Sophie. Sophie finished first, and he laid her in her crib, starting her mobile.

They'd brought the oil lamp to the babies' room while they fed them. A flameless candle Mitch had found in a cupboard glowed in place of a night-light. Shadows were heavy in the room and Lily could see Mitch caring for her daughter, gently making sure she was settled, watching her for a few moments, then touching his fingers to her forehead.

He would make a wonderful father.

Turning from the crib, he stooped to pick up the bottle he'd set on the floor. "I'll wash this out."

Grace had stopped suckling and her eyes were closed.

Lily raised her to her shoulder until she heard a little burp, and then she carried her to her crib, settling her in for the night, then she took the oil lamp to the bathroom where she set it on the vanity. A small candle burned next to the sink where Mitch was rinsing the bottle. He'd rolled up his shirtsleeves and for the first time, Lily saw the scars on his right forearm. She didn't look somewhere else, but studied the lines that still looked raw…the gashes that had healed but would never fade away.

Slowly she raised her eyes to his.

He turned off the spigot and blew out the candle.

He was about to roll down his sleeve when she stopped him, her hand clasping his. "You don't have to hide them from me."

"They're ugly."

"No, they're a badge of honor." Without thinking, only feeling, she bent and kissed one of the welts.

"Lily." He said her name in a way he never had before. His words were thick with need, with desire that needed to be expressed.

Her lips lingered on his skin for a few seconds, maybe because she wanted to anticipate what might happen next, maybe because she was afraid of what might happen next.

When she straightened, he took her face in both of his hands. "Do you know what you're doing?" he asked, his voice raspy.

"I'm feeling," she said without apology.

"Damn," he growled, wrapping his arms around her, possessing her lips with his.

His kiss was long and hungry, wet and wild. Lily felt like someone else, like a woman who could throw caution to the side and be free from the chains of what she should and shouldn't do. She kissed Mitch with a fervor that shocked her, yet gave her hope.

Lily's breasts pressed into Mitch's chest. Instead of trying to touch her with his hands, he let their bodies communicate. His breathing was as hot and heavy as hers. They fit together with perfect temptation, perfect anticipation, perfect exhilaration. He seemed to wait for some sign from her that she wanted more and she gave it, pressing even closer. She felt his hardness, the desire he'd been controlling up until now. There would be no turning back from this.

She didn't want to turn back. She wanted tonight with Mitch. Did he want her as badly? Would he let his scars be an issue?

She lowered her hand from his shoulder and insinuated it between their bodies, cupping him, leaving him with no doubt as to what she was ready to do.

Still holding her securely, Mitch backed her out of the bathroom...across the hall...into her bedroom. The area was pitch-black, the glow from the oil lamp in the bathroom the only light, reaching just inside the door. But that didn't stop them. The dark seemed to hold some comfort for them both. Once they were enveloped by it, their mouths sought each other, their arms embraced, their fingers touched. The dark held more excitement than anything else.

Mindlessly, Lily reached for Mitch's shirt buttons.

He searched for the edges of her top and somehow managed to pull it up and over her head.

After he'd tossed it, she asked, "Do you have a condom?"

His hands went still on her waist. "Yes, I do." He

reached into his pocket, pulled out the foil packet and dropped it on the nightstand.

They'd both known this night was coming, hadn't they?

"I'd hoped," Mitch said honestly. "That's why I brought it."

His hands slid to her bra and unhooked it. She shrugged off the straps quickly and leaned forward, kissing his chest. She couldn't see but she could feel hot skin against her lips. Her hands became her eyes as she ran them down his flat abdomen and stopped at the waistband of his jeans. His belt was pliant but fought her hands as she tried to unfasten it. He helped her with it. A few moments later, he'd shed his sneakers, jeans and briefs. She'd flicked off her sandals. Now he slid his hands into the waistband of her shorts, sliding them down her hips along with her panties.

She knew he couldn't see much more than shadows, either, and she asked, "Should I light a candle?"

"No time," he muttered as he pushed her hair aside and kissed her neck, trailing his lips along her collarbone. His foray to her breast made her restless, flushed and needy.

"Mitch," she moaned, but he didn't stop. He just kept kissing lower, down her belly to the mound between her thighs. She couldn't let him be that intimate. She just couldn't. The reason why eluded her.

She grasped his shoulders and said again, "Mitch."

This time she felt him shift, felt his head tilt up. He straightened, flung back the covers, and climbed into bed, holding his hand out to her.

Thunder grumbled again outside and she thought fleetingly of Grace and Sophie and whether or not they'd awaken. She listened as the sky rolled but heard nothing from the babies' bedroom.

As if he read her mind, Mitch asked, "Do you want to check on them?"

She knew she'd hear them if they awakened, even without the monitor. "They'll let us know if they wake up," she replied, crawling in beside him, moving closer to him.

He wrapped his arm around her and stroked her back. "You'll have to tell me what you like."

She suddenly couldn't speak and didn't know why. So she tilted her head against his and finally managed, "I want *you*, Mitch. Kiss me and everything else will be okay."

His lips were searingly hot, his tongue an instrument of pleasure that urged her to caress his back, his sides, his manhood.

"Lily," he gasped. "Are you ready?"

"Yes, Mitch. I am."

Reaching to the nightstand, he grabbed the packet and ripped open the foil. After he slid the condom on, he stretched out on top of her, letting her feel his weight. He spread her legs and lay between them. As he braced himself on his elbows, she tensed a little. He must have felt it because he kissed her again until all she wanted was him filling her, giving her pleasure, helping her to forget.

Forget what? a little voice inside her head whispered, but she ignored it, not bothering to find the answer.

When Mitch entered her, she *was* ready. Each of his thrusts made her call his name, asking for more. Mitch's body was as slick as hers with their passion. His chest slid against her breasts as they rocked, tempting each other, provoking each other to the next level of pleasure. Lily held on tightly as a strong orgasm overtook her, shaking her world until it was upside down. Mitch's shuddering release came moments later.

She felt as if the storm had somehow come inside. Stunned by the pleasure still tingling through her, she also felt overwhelmed by the intimacy she'd experienced with Mitch. She wobbled on the verge of feelings that terrified her and she didn't know whether to run or to hold on to Mitch for dear life.

After Mitch collapsed on top of her, he whispered in her ear, "Are you okay?"

She didn't know how to answer him, but gave him the response that would be easiest. "Yes, I'm good."

He kissed her cheek then rolled onto his side, taking her with him, their bodies still joined. "Do you want me to check on Sophie and Grace?"

"In a minute." She was still catching her breath, still trying to absorb what they had done, what she had done.

"Talk to me, Lily."

"Just hold me, Mitch. Just hold me."

"I shouldn't fall asleep with you. I could have a nightmare."

"It doesn't matter, I don't want you to leave."

So Mitch stayed and she held on, unsure what morning would bring.

Lily snuck glances at Mitch as they made breakfast the next morning. The night before, the first time the twins had awakened, Mitch had climbed out of bed quickly. Lily wondered if he'd slept at all because he'd seemed so wide awake as they fed Sophie and Grace and settled them once more. Afterward, Mitch had kissed her and she thought they might make love again. Instead he'd said, "Get some sleep. I'm going to bunk on the couch. When the electricity clicks back on, I'll make sure everything's working okay."

"Mitch, you could sleep with me."

But he'd shaken his head and she'd known better than to argue.

The twins had slept later than usual this morning, so it was almost ten o'clock as she scrambled eggs and Mitch fried bacon. Sophie and Grace faced each other and babbled in their swings.

She hadn't talked to Mitch about last night. They'd been too busy changing, dressing, diapering and now making breakfast. What she wanted to ask most was, *What did last night mean to you?*

However, as she was about to begin the discussion, the front door swung open and Angie and Ellie charged in, overnight cases in hand. They gave some attention to the babies and then stopped short when they saw Mitch.

Cheerfully, Angie tried to set the tone. "Good morning."

"I didn't expect you back so soon," Lily remarked. "How was the concert?"

"It was wonderful," Angie replied. "I felt like a teenager again. Brad Paisley is one hot dude."

Lily forced a laugh because Ellie was being so quiet.

Angie slipped a CD from her purse. "I got his new one."

"Did you have a good time?" she asked Ellie. Mitch silently listened, forking the slices of bacon.

"Yeah, it was great. But we heard you had storms last night and a lot of the electricity was out. We were worried. That's why we got up early and drove back. I tried to call but the phone must not be working. It just kept ringing and you didn't answer your cell, either."

"Oh, I'm sorry you worried," Lily apologized. "My cell was out of power when the electricity went down and I unplugged the charger so it wouldn't get damaged if there was a surge." She felt as if she were overexplaining and Ellie was eyeing her and then Mitch. Lily felt uncomfortable.

"Did you have any trouble getting back?" Mitch asked. "Trees down? That kind of thing?"

"Just a tree down on Alamo," Angie answered when Ellie didn't. "Branches here and there. We heard a tornado went through Odessa. That's why we were worried. How did Sophie and Grace do with the storm?"

"They didn't seem to mind," Mitch said with a smile.

"How long have you been here?" Ellie inquired.

Mitch looked to Lily, obviously deciding to let her answer. She felt suddenly unsettled, as if what had happened with Mitch last night was definitely all wrong. She was the mother of three-month-old twins. What was she doing having an affair? What was she doing making love with a man when Troy hadn't been gone a year? What was she doing trying to find a life when her old one still seemed so real?

Suddenly plagued by doubts, she answered, "Mitch came over last evening to visit. While he was here, the electricity went off. He stayed to make sure we were all safe. He slept on the couch and when the power came back on, he made sure everything was working right again."

She sensed Mitch's body tense. With a sideways glance at him, she saw his jaw set and his mouth tighten. She didn't dare look into his eyes.

"I see," Ellie responded.

Silence shrouded the kitchen until Angie broke it. "We bought donuts at the convenience store. I left them in the car with the souvenirs. I'll go get them."

"I can throw more eggs into the pan," Lily offered. "We have plenty of bacon and toast."

Mitch switched off the burner, fished the bacon from the pan and let it drain on a paper towel on a dish. But then he said, "I think I'll be going. Everything's back to normal here and the three of you can catch up."

Lily reached out a hand to him. "Mitch, you don't have to go."

His gaze locked to hers. "Yes, I think I do."

Lily felt her heart drop to her stomach. The look on Mitch's face told her that her explanation to Ellie hadn't been what he'd expected her to say. She slid the eggs from the pan onto a serving dish and set it on the table.

"I'll be right back," she told Ellie. "I'm going to walk Mitch out."

Mitch stopped by Sophie and Grace, jiggled their feet, gave them a last long look, then went to the living room. Making sure the timer on the swings would keep the babies content for a little while longer, Lily bent down and kissed them both. She passed Angie in the living room and saw that Mitch had already gone out the door.

"What's up?" Angie whispered to her.

"We'll talk later," she told her friend, not knowing what to expect when she went outside.

Lily had never seen Mitch angry. A sense of calm always seemed to surround him. But now, even though he was still, he wasn't calm. His brown eyes simmered with an emotion she didn't understand. She thought he was accusing her of something and she went on the defensive.

"You could stay for breakfast."

"If I stayed and Ellie asked what happened last night, what should I tell her?"

Maybe the emotion she was witnessing in Mitch's eyes wasn't anger. It was something worse. It was betrayal.

Her hands suddenly felt clammy. "I couldn't tell her what happened."

"I understand you want to keep your life private. I understand you're afraid you'll hurt her feelings. I understand that you feel she'd be upset if she thinks you're moving on. What I don't understand, especially after last night, is that you gave her the impression I was like a security guard seeing to your safety. Why are you afraid to admit to yourself what happened last night. We were *intimate,* Lily, as intimate as two people can be. Do you want to erase that from your memory?"

The breeze tossed her hair across her cheek as she self-consciously looked around to make sure no one was walking anywhere nearby. Glancing over her shoulder, she needed to be certain neither Angie nor Ellie were in the foyer, listening.

"I don't know what to think about last night," she admitted. "I'm not like that, Mitch. I don't seek pleasure to wipe out—"

"Loss and grief and memories?"

"Why are you so angry?"

He ran his hand over his face and considered her words carefully. "I don't think I'm as angry with you as I am with myself. I should have known better. I should have known you weren't ready."

She remembered him asking her last night, "Are you ready?" He'd meant so much more than the physical. Deep down, she'd known that.

"The dark made it easy," he decided. "The dark let you think, subconsciously at least, that you were with your husband again."

She wanted to protest. She wanted to scream that he was wrong. Yet how could she? She didn't know if he was wrong or right. She didn't know if last night had been about her and Mitch, or if it had been about her needing a man to hold her. She felt awful. She felt as if she *had* betrayed him.

"I'm going to leave before I say something else I shouldn't," he muttered. "It's probably better if we don't see each other for a while."

For a while? How long was that? She'd be going back to work in November. He didn't mean that long, did he? But she had her pride and he had his. She'd hurt him badly and now she had to suffer the consequences.

He took his car keys from his pocket. "Take care of yourself, Lily."

Moments later, he was driving down the street away from her.

Taking a deep, shaky breath, she tried not to think or feel and went inside to Grace and Sophie.

Chapter Nine

Late November

Lily sat across from Mitch in his office, hardly able to bear the awkwardness that had developed between them.

She'd been back at work for two weeks and had only caught glimpses of Mitch. He had definitely made himself scarce. The only reason they were in the same room together now was because they had to discuss a patient. "Joan Higgins has high levels of FSH, which definitely lowers the quality of her eggs. I think further testing is indicated."

Mitch nodded, keeping his gaze on the notes on his desk.

After he'd left the Victorian that morning in June, he'd emailed Lily every few weeks to inquire about her health and her daughters'. *Emailed*. He was doing his duty and keeping his promise to Troy without truly getting involved.

Could she blame him?

Lily desperately wanted to blurt out to Mitch, "I miss you," yet she knew she couldn't. She'd hurt him greatly by making love with him while she grieved for her husband. But he'd hurt *her* by walking away as he had. If he could leave her life so easily, what had that night meant to him? What if they'd continued the affair? Would he eventually have opened up to her? Would he have been ready to care for her and the twins out of more than duty?

"I'll order further tests," he agreed, ending their discussion of the patient.

They sat in awkward silence.

Finally Mitch laid down his pen. "How does it feel to be back at work?" His expression was neutral and he could have been making polite conversation with any of their colleagues.

"It feels good to be back. But I miss Sophie and Grace," she added honestly, as if he were still the old Mitch. "I miss not being able to hold them whenever I want. I mostly miss not hearing every new baby word first."

"You could come in part time," he suggested, as an employer might.

"I might be able to do that for a month or so, but I need my salary. I can't just think about the moment, I have to think about the future."

When their gazes collided, they were both thinking about taking pleasure in the moment, and the night neither of them would forget. At least, Lily hoped Mitch wouldn't forget it. She knew *she* never would.

Mitch pushed the papers on his desk into a stack, clipped them together and tossed them into his in-box. "It's getting late. I won't keep you any longer. I know you want to get home."

"Sophie and Grace are really growing and changing."

He looked surprised she'd started up the conversation again.

Reaching into her lab coat pocket, she drew out a small picture portfolio. "These are the latest pictures… if you'd like to see them. I can't believe they're already nine months old."

Maybe she was making it difficult for him to refuse to look, but right now she needed to see emotion from him, something more than a polite facade meant just for her. She'd ached for him all these months, but she hadn't been able to do more than answer his emails in the same tone he'd sent them—politely and with pertinent information. Yet seeing him and working with him again, she realized how much she'd lost when he'd walked away.

As she slid the little booklet across the desk to him, she confessed, "I need to keep their faces close by."

He stared at the small album for a couple of seconds and then picked it up. After he leafed through it, he stood and handed it back to her. "They're beautiful kids, Lily. I imagine in a few weeks, you'll have their picture taken with Santa Claus."

Yes, the holidays were coming and she found she didn't want to celebrate them without Mitch. Did he feel anything when he looked at Sophie and Grace's photos?

Did he wonder if the monitor was still working? If the sun rose and set now without her feeling grief twenty-four hours a day? What could she say to him to bring warmth back into his eyes?

She returned the photos to her pocket and rose to her feet. Obviously, he wanted her to leave. She could feel the figurative miles he was trying to shove between them. She'd let him do that for the past five months because she hadn't known what else to do, what was fair, what was necessary. But she couldn't merely leave things like this, emotions all tangled up, words gone unsaid, desires left unfulfilled.

"Mitch, what can I do to fix this?"

He didn't pretend to not know what she was talking about. "I don't think there's anything to fix."

It had taken courage on her part to bring it up, but he had shot her down without a glimmer of understanding...without a glimmer of hope that they could reestablish the connection they once had. She felt foolish and embarrassed. She should just go home to the people who loved her and wipe from her memories everything that had happened with Mitch.

She'd almost reached the door when she felt his hand on her shoulder. That simple touch brought back everything—the long, wet kisses, his hands on her body, the orgasm that had swept her to another realm. She hoped the naked feelings weren't showing in her eyes.

"I don't know how to fix it," he admitted. "We crossed the line and we can't go back."

The five months that had passed had seemed like a lifetime. If she told him she was ready now, would it be the truth? Would he believe her?

"We could start over," she suggested.

"As what? Colleagues who once had sex and now are trying to renew a friendship?"

His words hit her solar plexus squarely, just where he'd intended. Yet she couldn't give up. "Maybe," she answered truthfully. "We can't deny what happened, but I hate this…wall between us. You were there when Grace and Sophie were born, and now you've just dropped out of their lives."

"I thought the emails—"

"Mitch, you sent them from a sense of duty, because you made a promise to Troy. I didn't know if you really cared. I didn't know whether to email you pictures or describe how I rolled their strollers through the sprinkler and they loved it, or how their hair was finally long enough to put little bows in."

He dropped his hand from her shoulder as if he could see the pictures, too, the pictures of *them* as they'd been, not just the twins. "I walked away because it was the right thing to do."

"For *me* or for *you?*"

"For both of us."

He didn't look or sound as if he had any regrets. That hurt—a lot. She shook her head and accepted what seemed to be inevitable. "If you want to just be colleagues, that's fine. We'll figure out eventually how to relate on that level."

She would have gone again, but this time the huskiness in his voice stopped her. "Lily."

When she swung around suddenly, she saw a flicker of something on his face…and she waited, hoping.

"What did you have in mind?" he asked.

If that wasn't a loaded question! But she did have

something in mind. She just didn't know if he'd go
for it.

"How are you celebrating Thanksgiving?" Lily asked.
It was only three days away. If he had plans, so be it.
She'd figure out something else.

"I plan to pick up a turkey dinner at the Yellow
Rose."

She noticed the lines around Mitch's mouth seemed
deeper. "And take it home and eat it alone?"

"I guess that's not how most people celebrate Thanksgiving, but afterward I was going to make some phone
calls, to make sure everyone was still coming next
weekend."

His reunion weekend. The one she'd thought she'd be
involved in. "Would you like to come along with Ellie
and me to Raina and Shep's?"

Considering that for a few heartbeats, Mitch finally
answered, "Are you sure they wouldn't mind having an
unexpected guest?"

Her heart seemed to jump against her chest. "Shep
said Eva bought a turkey big enough to fill the entire
oven. I'm sure they won't mind."

"You already checked this out with Raina, didn't
you?" he asked suspiciously.

"Actually, it was her idea. I mentioned things were
strained between us here."

"Women," he said with a bit of exasperation. "Do
you have to tell each other *everything?*"

"Not everything," Lily assured him quickly.

There was a darkening of Mitch's eyes and she knew
he'd caught her underlying meaning.

"Ellie might not like the idea," he pointed out.

"No, she might not. And for her sake, it might be better if we meet at Shep and Raina's ranch."

"Doesn't this take us back where we started?" he asked with such soberness she realized much more was going on under the surface than he was revealing.

"No, it doesn't. Because I'll tell her I invited you. I'll make that clear."

It was easy for her to see that Mitch was debating with himself.

Although she didn't want to say acceptable words just because he wanted to hear them, she did. "If you don't want to come, that's okay. I understand. I just thought maybe we could ease back into…friendship."

"With a crowd around?" he asked, the corner of his lip quirking up.

"Sometimes conversation comes more easily that way."

"And kids are always great buffers."

"Yes," she agreed, now holding her breath, waiting for his answer.

He gave it in the form of another question. "What time does Thanksgiving dinner start?"

When Raina pulled Mitch into a bedlam of bubbling voices, running kids and chattering adults, he knew he must be crazy. He could be sitting home alone, in front of a takeout turkey dinner—

His gaze found Lily right off. At the stove, she was testing the boiling potatoes. Her hair was arranged in a wispy version of a bun that made his fingers tingle to pull it down. She was wearing a calf-length suede skirt with tan boots, and a long multicolored blouse with a concho belt slung low on her slim waist. When she turned to wave at him, he could read her apron that proclaimed in block lettering, I'd Rather Cook Than Clean.

As Shep came toward him, Mitch offered him a bottle of wine. To Raina, he handed a bouquet of colorful mums.

"You didn't have to do that," she said.

"I wanted to." He really had. It was nice of them to include him.

How much did Lily want him here? Maybe she just wanted them to work together without snubbing each other. That would be a far cry from becoming friends again. Friends like before Troy had died? Or friends like after the twins were born?

Lily's babies were sitting in play saucers in the kitchen so she could keep her eye on them. Eva was conversing with Ellie as they made a salad together. Ellie had given Mitch a glance and lifted a hand in his direction, but that was about all.

This could be one interesting Thanksgiving dinner.

Although he knew it wasn't in his best interest, he did want to see how Sophie and Grace had grown.

It had been more than difficult to stay away from Lily and her daughters all these months. But he'd felt it was the right move to make. She'd needed time to recover from Troy's passing. And even now he doubted enough time had passed. But today was about getting a real look at her life again. If he had to try to watch over her without getting involved, then somehow he'd manage that.

He hunkered down at Grace's play saucer, helping her ring a bell, spin a wheel and study her face in the mirror. She giggled at him and reached out to touch his jaw. That tiny hand on his chin made his heart squeeze uncomfortably, so he gave it a gentle pat and moved on to Sophie, who seemed a little more sedate. After all, she was the older sister, even if it was only by two to three minutes. She was slower to let Mitch join in her private game, but eventually she welcomed the intricacies of his set of keys and would have kept them if not for her mom intervening.

"She'll put them in her mouth," Lily said. "I try to keep her toys as sterile as possible, but you know how that is."

"Actually, I don't, but I can imagine with their crawling all over the floor." He looked around at the saucers and stroller and the high chairs. "You must have brought a truck."

Lily laughed.

"The high chairs and stroller fold. Ellie stowed them in the back of her car." She glanced back at the potatoes. "I'd better finish those if we want them ready with the turkey."

"Do you need help with the pot?" It was huge and, he imagined, quite heavy.

"Sure. That would be great."

As he stepped around her, his hip brushed hers. That minor connection of their bodies threw him more than he wanted to admit. He stood in front of the stove and reached for the pot. As always with Lily, physical contact sent his system into a rush forward toward something out of his reach. He thought that might have diminished in their time apart.

It hadn't.

Coming here today had been stupid. He avoided her gaze as he drained the potatoes into a colander in the sink, steam billowing up all around them. *This isn't the first time,* he thought ironically.

"Into the mixing bowl?" he asked, looking at the bowl on the counter.

She nodded, avoiding his gaze, too.

They were a pair. No, *not* a pair, he corrected himself. Just two individuals with wants and needs that couldn't be fulfilled.

He saw Lily go over to her daughters and consult with Raina, who was playing with them, her own five-month-old cuddled close on her lap. Then Lily returned to the mixer.

"Raina said I could put in whatever I want, so here goes."

"Whatever you want?" he asked. "I thought they just got butter and milk."

"That's the plain version," Lily explained with a smile, starting the mixer. "I like to add a little pizzazz."

She added pizzazz all right. With fascination, he watched her add sour cream, milk, chives and a blob of butter for good measure.

"No cholesterol there," he muttered.

She jabbed him in the ribs. "It's Thanksgiving."

He liked the feel of her friendliness again. He'd missed her a lot over the past five months. In his email inquiries, he'd wanted to ask question after question—about the babies and about her. Yet he'd known he had to, in large part, leave her alone. He should have done that to begin with. Today, however, with her close by his side, within kissing distance, inhaling the familiar scent of her perfume, he saw keeping a wall up between them was either very smart...or very stupid. What would an affair do to them? Was she even open to one? Were either of them really ready to move on?

After whipping the potatoes into a delicious white frenzy, Lily stuck in a spoon, took a fingerful and poked it into her mouth. She rolled her eyes. "Just right. Try some?"

He'd watched that finger go into her mouth. He'd watched her lips pucker up. He'd watched her lick it. If there weren't so many people in the big kitchen, he'd kiss her. But there were and he didn't. Instead he put his finger on the spoon, curled potatoes onto it and popped it into his mouth.

"Just right," he agreed, his eyes locking to hers, his gut telling him they weren't finished and might never be.

Mitch barely heard the sound of scraping chairs and laughter and the clatter of silverware.

He *did* hear the doorbell ring. Soon after, the door opened and he heard a woman's voice call, "We're here."

Shep picked up the turkey on its platter and carried it to the table, explaining to Mitch, "It's Raina's mom and brother. Ryder just got off his shift."

Mitch knew Raina's brother was a cop.

Ryder and Sonya Greystone came into the kitchen and were introduced to Mitch. Sonya said to him, "I hope you're a big eater, like Shep. I made pumpkin, apple and cherry pies, and I don't want to take any home."

Shep gave her a bear hug. "You don't have to worry about that."

Mitch had never experienced anything like this Thanksgiving celebration—so many people who seemed like family and really cared about each other. Then he realized that conclusion wasn't true. When he and his buddies and families got together, it was a similar feeling. Family meant something different to everyone, and he was suddenly glad he hadn't stayed home today and eaten dinner in front of a football game.

In the next few minutes, he helped Lily transfer the potatoes from the mixing bowl to a beautiful serving dish embellished with roses and gold trim. He stared at it for a second and Lily asked, "Mitch?"

In the midst of the holiday chaos, he said in a low voice, "This dish reminds me of one my mom used when she tried to make the holidays a celebration for the two of us."

"Holidays are supposed to be about memories and traditions and loved ones, even when they're not still with us."

He'd walked into that one. When his gaze met Lily's, he expected to see sadness on her face. Instead, he saw an emotion more poignant.

She said, "If you'll put those on the table, I'll set the twins in their high chairs."

In the next few minutes, everyone was seated around the huge, rectangular table. Even Joey and Roy seemed awed by the amount of food in front of them.

In the moment of quiet, Shep said, "Let's all give thanks for being together today."

Mitch didn't know where the chain started—maybe with Shep's children—but everyone held hands and bowed their heads, remembering Thanksgivings past, grateful for the opportunity to be together like this with more than enough food for everyone to eat.

Lily had taken Mitch's hand. He intertwined his fingers with hers and she looked over at him, her eyes questioning. He didn't have the answers to those questions. They'd have to just see where today took them.

After dinner, Mitch and Shep played a board game with Roy and Joey while Eva recorded everything she could on a video camera. Every once in a while Mitch glanced over at Eva, who was sitting on the floor beside Manuel as he rode a high-tech rocking horse. The letters of the alphabet appeared on a little screen in front of him the longer he rocked back and forth. Grace and Sophie crawled around Lily and Ellie's feet, while Raina played with her daughter in one of the play saucers.

Roy shouted, "I won," and everyone cheered as he moved his marker into the winning block.

Mitch moved to the sofa while the boys ran to the playroom for another game. Aware of Grace crawling over to him, he smiled when she sat before him and raised her arms. He knew what that meant. It had been a while since he'd held one of the twins, a while since he'd felt as if he should.

A baby's needs always trumped overthinking, so he bent and lifted her up to his lap. At nine months she was a heartbreaker. He could only imagine how beautiful she'd be as a teenager, when someone would have to protect her from overeager guys who would date her.

Grace grinned up at him and snuggled into his chest as if she were just waiting for a place to enjoy a comfortable nap.

Ellie, who'd been talking to Raina's mother and Eva across the room, came to sit beside him. She patted Grace's leg. "Tired, little one?"

"The day's celebration has wiped her out," Mitch said amiably. He didn't know what Ellie thought about his being here today.

"She only had a short nap this afternoon before we came."

Mitch touched Grace's name embroidered on the front of her pale green overalls. "Did you make this?"

"Yes, I did. I finally got the website up and running last month, and I have orders."

"So you're thinking about staying in Sagebrush?"

"That depends on Lily. Mom asked her to come back to Oklahoma and raise the twins there. That way she and my dad could see them more often and give her all the help she needs."

Mitch remained silent. Finally he said, "Lily seemed happy to get back to work. She'd have to find a practice in Oklahoma City or start her own."

"That's true. But Oklahoma City is a medical center. I don't think she'd have a problem starting over there."

Grace's tiny fingers rubbed up and down against Mitch's sweater as if it were a security blanket.

"What if Lily decides to stay in Sagebrush? Will you support that decision?" Mitch asked.

"Do you think you can convince her to do that?" Ellie asked in return.

"This isn't about convincing. It's about what Lily wants and where she wants to raise her daughters."

"You sound so removed from it. Don't you care?"

Oh, he cared. More than he wanted to admit—more than he dared to admit. "I won't persuade Lily one way or the other. She has to make up her own mind. If she doesn't, she'll have regrets."

"She asked you here today." Ellie's voice was almost accusing.

"I'm not sure why she did. As you know, we haven't seen each other for a while." Ellie was the type of woman who wanted the cards on the table, so he might as well put them there.

"You two have a connection," Ellie said softly. "One anyone can see."

"Anyone can?"

"You can't hide it, even though you both try."

Mitch smoothed his hand over Grace's hair, tweaking the little green bow with his finger. "And how do you feel about that?" he asked Ellie.

"I don't think it matters how I feel."

"Yes, it does." Mitch could tell Ellie that she was the reason he and Lily hadn't been in real contact since June. On the other hand, she wasn't actually the root of the problem.

"Lily asked you here today without my input," Ellie confided.

Mitch gave Ellie a regarding look. "What would your input have been?"

Ellie kept silent.

So he said something he probably shouldn't have. "I think Lily feels she needs your permission to move on."

That widened Ellie's eyes. "You're not serious."

"Yes, I am. We probably shouldn't even be having this conversation, but I thought it would be better if we cleared the air. I don't know what's going to happen next, but I do know Lily deserves to be happy."

He'd said too much. He'd tried to take himself out of the equation as much as possible, but that was difficult when he thought he had a stake in it. It was difficult when he felt as if Lily and the twins owned a piece of his heart.

Seeing them talking, Lily crossed to the sofa with

Sophie in her arms. Sophie was rubbing her eyes and her face against Lily's blouse. "I think we'd better get these two home. In a few minutes they're either both going to be asleep or fussing because they're tired."

Mitch carefully picked up Grace and stood with her. "I'll help you pack the car. I should be going, too."

"I can take Grace," Ellie said, reaching for the little girl.

Mitch aided in the transfer, wondering just how seriously Lily might be thinking about moving to Oklahoma City.

While Ellie watched the twins, Lily and Mitch took baby paraphernalia outside to Ellie's car. The weather had turned colder. The late-November wind blew across the parking area and through the corral across the lane. Lily opened the car door while Mitch slid the high chairs inside, along with a diaper bag. At the trunk, he adjusted the stroller to lay flat.

After he shut the lid, he regarded Lily in the glow of the floodlight shining from the back of the house. "Ellie tells me Troy's mother wants you to move to Oklahoma City." He'd never intended to start like that, but the question had formed before he could think of anything else to say.

Although she wore a suede jacket, Lily wrapped her arms around herself as if to ward off a chill. "I'm surprised she told you that."

"Were *you* going to tell me?"

"I don't know. After the past few months…" She trailed off. "If I went to Oklahoma City, you wouldn't have to worry about your promise to Troy."

"Is *that* why you'd move?"

She turned away, as if making eye contact was too difficult, as if she couldn't be as honest if she did.

But he clasped her arm and pulled her a little closer. "What do you want, Lily? A different life in Oklahoma?"

"I'm thinking about it. I have good friends here, but Troy's parents are Sophie and Grace's grandparents. I'm not sure what the right thing to do is."

"Whatever makes you happy."

She gave a short laugh. "And how do we ever really know what that will be?"

He'd meant it when he'd told Ellie he wouldn't try to persuade Lily one way or the other. They'd have to set aside the question of her moving...for now. "I'm glad you asked me to come today," he said after a long pause.

"Are you?" Lily's voice was filled with the same longing Mitch felt. They'd been apart and he'd hated that. He just didn't know if they should be together.

"I never experienced a holiday quite like it," he explained. "I haven't had a place to go for holidays in a long time."

"I think Sophie and Grace remember you. They're so comfortable with you."

"And how comfortable are you with everyone watching?" He swore under his breath. "That didn't come out right."

"Yes, it did. I know what you mean. But we weren't really together today, were we?"

He had to make a decision now, which way was he going to go with Lily. He could just cut her out of his life. But wasn't that in itself making a decision for her?

"How would you like to go to the tree-lighting

ceremony on Sunday at the library? We can show the twins all the lights and let them listen to their first Christmas carols."

She only hesitated a few moments. "I'd like to do that."

He didn't ask her if she'd ever been to the tree-lighting ceremony with Troy. He didn't want to know. Although he longed to take her in his arms and kiss her, he didn't. This time, they were going to take small steps toward each other to find out if that's where they wanted to be.

Maybe Sunday would be a beginning. Maybe Sunday would be an end.

At least he'd know one way or the other.

Chapter Ten

"It pays to have connections," Mitch said with a grin as he stood inside the library, peering out the long window with Sophie in his arms. Raina's mother was the head librarian and had told them they could settle inside for as long as they wanted.

Lily was holding Grace, peering outside beside Mitch. Her arm was brushing his. Every time it did, he remembered everything about their night together—everything about her hands on his body and the shake-up of his soul. Not for the first time he wondered if he wanted Lily simply because he shouldn't have her.

Mitch suddenly felt a hand on his shoulder and tensed. As he turned, he relaxed. "Hello, Mr. Fieldcrest. Are you and your wife going to enjoy the tree-lighting ceremony?" Tucker Fieldcrest and his wife owned the

B&B where his friends would be staying this coming weekend.

"We surely are. I was going to call you this week, but now I don't have to. I just wanted to tell you, we're all ready for your guests."

Mitch introduced Tucker to Lily. They all chatted for a few minutes and then Tucker motioned to the crowd gathering outside. "They're almost ready to light the tree. You'd better get your place. I'll see you Friday night." With a wave, he left through the library's huge wooden double doors.

"He seems very nice," Lily said, after the older man had gone outside.

"He and his wife Belinda are good people. They're cutting us a break, only charging half the normal room rates. They insisted they'd be empty this time of year anyway, and our veterans deserve more than reasonable room charges."

"Absolutely," Lily said emphatically, and Mitch knew what she was thinking about. Yet she surprised him when she asked, "So, do you still need activities for the kids? Would you like me to come over and paint faces?"

"I roped Matt into playing Santa Claus and I was hoping that would take up the whole afternoon. But if you're still willing, I'm sure everyone would appreciate it."

"I'm still willing."

To do more than face paint? he wanted to ask. All the words that passed between them seemed to have an underlying message. When he'd asked her to come along tonight, he'd thought of it as a sort of date. But did she think about it that way, too? Did having the twins along make it merely an outing they could enjoy together?

He'd drive himself crazy with the questions, especially when Lily looked at him with those big, blue eyes and a smile that again brought back their night together in vivid detail. It was ironic, really. They'd had sex in the dark but every moment of it was emblazoned in his mind in living color. Sometimes he thought he could see those same pictures running through Lily's thoughts, but that could be wishful thinking.

"Let's get Sophie and Grace bundled up so we don't miss their expressions when the tree lights glow. Do you have your camera?"

Lily patted the pocket of her yellow down jacket. "Right here. But I don't know how we're going to hold them both and take their picture at the same time."

"We'll figure out something," he assured her. Sophie suddenly took hold of his nose and squeezed it a little, babbling new consonant sounds as she did. He laughed. "Getting impatient, are you? Come on, let's cover that pretty blond hair with your hat and hood so you stay warm."

Once the girls were dressed, Mitch and Lily pushed the stroller down the side ramp to the sidewalk. A fir tree stood on the land in front of the eighty-year-old, two-story brick library. The storefronts farther up the street were all lit up with multicolor lights, more than ready for Christmas shoppers. Grady Fitzgerald owned a saddle shop in the next block and Mitch thought he caught a glimpse of him and Francesca with their little boy on the other side of the tree. Lily waved to Tessa and Vince Rossi, who'd brought their children, Sean and Natalie, to watch the ceremony.

"Gina and Logan are here somewhere," Lily said to Mitch, leaning close to him so he could hear her amidst the buzz of people talking.

She pulled the camera from her pocket. "You hold the stroller and I'll take your picture."

"Lily, I don't think—" But before he could protest, before he could say he hated to have his picture taken, she'd already done it. Turnabout was fair play, so he motioned her to the back of the stroller, snagged the camera from her hand and took more than one of her with her girls. Sophie and Grace seemed to be mesmerized by the people passing by, the stand with the microphone where the mayor stood, the wind carrying the smells of French fries, corn dogs and hamburgers from the food cart parked not far away.

As the mayor, Greta Landon, came to the mike and started her remarks, Mitch handed the camera back to Lily. He swooped Sophie out of the stroller and said, "If you hand me Grace, I can hold them both up, and you can take their picture when the lights go on."

After Lily lifted Grace from the stroller, she transferred her to Mitch. As she stood close, she tilted her chin up and was almost near enough to kiss. She said, "This was a great idea. Maybe we'll start a tradition."

If you don't leave Sagebrush for Oklahoma City, he thought. He believed he was so good at not giving anything away, but he must have been wrong about that. Because Lily backed away as if she couldn't reassure him she would be staying in Texas. Her impulsive exclamation had been just that—impulsive.

Just like their night together.

At that moment, the mayor announced, "Let this

year's Christmas tree glow brightly for all the residents of Sagebrush."

The tree came alive with blue, red, green and purple balls. Strand after strand of tiny white lights twinkled around those. Mitch witnessed the expression on Sophie and Grace's faces, and their wide-eyed awe was priceless.

Instead of looking at the tree when the Christmas carols began playing, Lily's face was Madonna-like as she gazed at her girls. Then her eyes locked to his. Something elemental twisted in his chest.

The twins already seemed to be developing their own language. They babbled to each other and the gibberish was almost in a cadence that Mitch thought of as language.

Lily leaned in and kissed both of their cheeks, then snapped a picture of Mitch holding them. "What do you think of all those lights?"

They waved their hands at each other and at her.

All of a sudden, Hillary was at Lily's side, carrying her own daughter. "Look who's here," Hillary said, taking in Mitch, Lily and the twins. "Since when are you two seeing each other outside of the office?"

"Since tonight," Mitch answered, matter-of-factly. "We're sharing some Christmas cheer. How does Megan like all this?" If there was one thing Mitch knew, it was that talking about someone's children always took their mind off anything else.

Still, Hillary gave him a knowing look. "She loved it, but now I think she's ready for bed. Besides, I don't want her out in the cold too long. How about you? Are you going to go back into the library for some complimentary hot chocolate?"

He and Lily hadn't discussed that, but he imagined what her answer would be. "We're headed home, too."

Hillary shifted Megan to her other arm. "Well, it was good to run into you without your lab coats on. I'll see you tomorrow." Then as quickly as she'd appeared, she was gone.

If Lily was going to take issue with what he'd told Hillary, this wasn't the time or place. He said, "Let's get them into the stroller and roll them to the car, unless you really would like some hot chocolate first."

As Lily took Sophie from him, she replied, "We can make hot chocolate back at the house."

Hmm. They just might be in for that discussion after all.

Lily had been surprised tonight at what Mitch had said to Hillary. For all those months he'd seemed as far away as the North Pole. But when he'd asked her to come along with him tonight, he seemed to have established a now-or-never attitude. However, everything was unsaid. Everything was up in the air. Everything was up to them.

How should she feel about his proprietary statement? Were they going to be a couple? Could Mitch make a lifelong commitment if that's where they were headed? What if she decided she shouldn't stay in Sagebrush? All the questions were terrifying, along with the life changes they could provoke.

But for tonight?

The warm and fuzzy feelings from the tree-lighting ceremony lingered as they drove home.

After they pulled into the drive, gathered the girls and the stroller and rolled them up the front walk, Mitch asked, "How will your housemates feel about us coming back here?"

"I guess we'll find out."

Her flippant reply almost seemed like a challenge.

Once in the living room, he found Angie and Ellie watching a forensic drama on TV while they strung popcorn to use as garlands.

"You're getting ready for Christmas?" he asked as a hello.

Ellie looked up, shot him a forced smile, then went back to stringing.

Angie responded to his question. "We all like to do home-crafted decorations, so it can take a while."

Without thinking twice, he took Sophie from her stroller, unzipped her coat, took off her mittens and hat and picked her up.

"Ma-ma-ma-ma," she said practically, as her sister chimed in with the same syllable.

He laughed and asked Lily, "Two bottles upstairs?" She nodded.

"If you need some help…" Ellie called.

"You look like you're busy," Mitch said. "We'll be okay." Taking the lead was second nature to him. Would Lily mind? She didn't give any indication that she did.

"I put bottles together," Angie said. "They're in the refrigerator in their bedroom."

Mitch glanced over his shoulder as he carried Sophie upstairs, right behind Lily with Grace. He wasn't surprised to see Ellie's gaze on them.

In the twins' bedroom, Mitch and Lily stole glances at each other while they fed the girls and readied them for bed. They'd been super-aware of each other all night, but hadn't been able to act on that awareness. Now they still couldn't, with Sophie and Grace to care for and Ellie and Angie downstairs. The whole situation was frustrating, titillating and exciting. Mitch knew he'd thrown down a figurative gauntlet tonight, and Lily had to make the decision whether or not she wanted to pick it up. She could deny their bond as she had once before. Maybe he was just waiting for her to do it again. Maybe he wanted the safer route. Maybe living alone was preferable to caring about a family. Maybe he didn't think he deserved a family. Because he had come home but others hadn't?

It was a lonely route, yet he was used to it.

Once the twins were comfortably settled in their cribs, once Lily had kissed them both and he'd simply laid a protective hand on each of their foreheads, Lily and Mitch left them to sleep by the glow of the night-light and stepped into the hall. This was about the most privacy they were going to have.

At least that's what he thought until Lily said, "I need to turn on their monitor in my bedroom."

Lily's bedroom. Visions raced through his mind.

Lily went ahead to her nightstand and switched on the monitor. He stepped over the threshold and shut the door.

She didn't move and neither did he for a moment. Then he saw that flicker in her eyes, the memory of what it was like when they were together. He covered the two steps to her, lifted her chin and looked deep into her eyes. "I told Hillary we were dating."

"I know."

"Do you have an opinion about that?"

"I didn't protest."

"No, mainly so you wouldn't embarrass us both."

"That wasn't the reason."

"What was?" he demanded, tired of waiting, yet knowing that with Lily all he could do was wait until she was truly free of yesterday.

"Because I want to spend time with you, Mitch—*with* the twins…*without* the twins. I can't tell you everything's going to go smoothly. I still miss Troy." She looked down at her hand, and he did, too. Her wedding ring glistened there, as real now as the day Troy had slipped it on her finger.

"And *I'm* used to being alone," he admitted.

"Do you like that?" she asked with the spirit that was all Lily.

He almost laughed. Almost. But the question had been a serious one. "I used to think being alone was the only way I could deal with my life on my terms."

"And now?"

"I'm open to finding out differently. That's all I can give you right now."

The expression on her pretty face said she didn't know if that was enough. He didn't, either. But as he bent his head, kissing her seemed a lot more important than the future.

He brushed his lips against hers, maybe to test her, to see how much she wanted. But the test became his to pass or fail. She responded by twining her arms around his neck and slipping her fingers into his hair. He'd wanted to take everything slowly with Lily. This time they'd take it easy. This time he'd make sure she knew what she was doing. This time, she wouldn't want to deny what was going on between them.

But the moment her fingers tugged at his hair as if

she wanted more, undeniable desire rushed through his body.

Making himself slow down, he kissed her neck, and asked, "How much time do you think we have?" He leaned back to check her expression, to see if she felt guilty about being in her room with him, to see if what her housemates thought mattered.

"A few minutes," she responded. "Ellie and Angie will wonder if everything's all right."

A few minutes wasn't enough time. So he didn't waste a moment more of it. His mouth came down on hers possessively, coaxing, teasing, plundering. Still the moan that came from Lily's throat gave the kiss more power as they both gave in to the primal quality of it. He thrust his tongue into her mouth, felt her soft, full breasts against him, and knew he was more aroused than he'd ever been. His hands slid down her back and he pressed her into him. She shivered and the trembling of her body made him wonder what he was doing. Their kisses awakened him to the raw need inside him. What if that need could never be satisfied? What if Lily, too, turned away from his scars? After all, the last time, they'd made love in the dark. What if he had a nightmare while he was lying beside her? How would she react?

The questions flooding his brain doused the far-reaching, fiery tendrils of his desire. A good thing, too, because he might have pulled her onto that bed, undressed her and joined their bodies no matter who was downstairs.

Tearing himself from her and the kiss, he stood away so he wouldn't reach for her again.

Looking a bit dazed, she said, "Wow! Those few minutes sure went fast."

He rubbed his hand over his face. "You get to me."

Smiling, she replied, "*You* get to *me*."

What bothered Mitch was that, despite the rush of passion that had enfolded them, the smile on Lily's face and in her voice didn't touch her eyes. Neither of them seemed happy about it.

"I'm looking forward to this weekend, Lily, but if you don't want to take the time away from Sophie and Grace, I'll understand. I'll be busy playing host, so I don't know how much time I'll have for…us."

Her hands fluttered as if she didn't know what to do with them, so she stuffed them into her front jeans pockets. "Why don't we just play it by ear? I'll see what kind of day the girls are having and then decide."

"Fair enough," he responded. Yet what he'd suggested didn't seem fair at all. He'd just given her an out, and she might take it…just as she might still move to Oklahoma City and leave her life in Sagebrush behind.

Midweek, Lily softly descended the steps into the living room, not wanting to awaken anyone. Sophie and Grace were snuggled in for the night. Angie, on day shift now, had turned in around the same time as Ellie after the evening news.

But Lily couldn't sleep. The decision whether or not to go to Mitch's on Saturday was gnawing at her. Every time she ran into him during the course of the day, she knew he was wondering if she'd be there or not. She felt that if she decided to go, she would be making a commitment.

A commitment to Mitch when she still wore her wedding ring?

She'd had lunch with Raina today, who had given her

a DVD copy of the video Eva had recorded on Thanksgiving. Lying in bed, feeling more alone than she'd ever remembered feeling, Lily decided she needed to watch that DVD.

After she inserted the disk in the machine, she sat on the sofa, perched on the edge of the cushion, pressing the buttons on the remote. The video sprang to life and she watched Thanksgiving Day come alive for her all over again. The living room at Shep and Raina's had been full of lively chatter. Mitch sat on the floor with Joey and Roy, his long legs stretched out in front of him, crossed at the ankles. The boys said something and Mitch laughed. He had such a deep, rich laugh and she rarely heard it. But he'd laughed often on Thanksgiving Day. Because he'd been relaxed? Because kids surrounded him? Because the two of them were together with friends in a way they hadn't been before?

The moment Grace raised her arms to Mitch and he'd lifted her onto his lap brought tears to Lily's eyes. He was so caring and gentle with the girls. Yet Lily sensed he still withheld part of himself. He didn't want to get too attached. Because in being attached to them, he'd be attached to her?

"You should be asleep," a soft voice scolded.

Startled, Lily dropped the remote.

"Sorry," Ellie said, coming to sit beside her. "I didn't mean to scare you."

Bending to the floor, Lily found the remote and hit the stop button.

"This is Thanksgiving," Ellie noticed, staring at the freeze frame on the TV, the still image of Mitch holding Grace.

"Raina gave me a copy today. She thought I'd like to

have it for posterity," Lily said with a small, short laugh that she had to force out.

"You don't have to stop it on my account. I was there, remember?"

"I know, but I thought—"

"Stop tiptoeing around me, Lily. You don't have to. I know how I reacted at the beginning of the summer when Mitch was around. I'm sorry for that."

"You had every right to feel whatever you were feeling."

"I had no right to dictate who you should or shouldn't see."

"You didn't."

"Then why didn't I see Mitch around for almost six months?"

"That was *my* fault, not yours. I wasn't ready to open my heart to another man."

Ellie pointed to the screen. "It looks as if you're trying to figure out if you're ready now."

"If I have to figure it out, that means I'm not?" Lily asked, in turmoil about it. Yet that's what she was feeling.

"I don't know, Lily. Troy is still real to me. He's still my brother. I talk to him, and I listen for his advice. Is that crazy or what?"

"I don't think that's crazy at all. I still do that, too."

"Then maybe you should ask him about this," Ellie advised her.

The two women sat there for a few moments in the dark, with the silence, staring at the frozen picture on the TV in all its color and high definition.

Now that she and Ellie were having an open talk about this, Lily went to her purse on the foyer table and removed her camera. It had been in there since Sunday night.

"I want to show you something," she said to Ellie, sitting beside her sister-in-law again.

She switched on the camera, pressed the review button and brought up a picture. She was standing in front of the town's Christmas tree with the twins in their stroller. Then there were a few shots of Sophie and Grace by themselves, their faces filled with awe, the excitement of their first Christmas shining from their eyes. The miracle of Christmas was starting to unfold for them. She wanted the holiday to be filled with kindness and love and sharing so they'd never forget the importance of giving all year.

The final picture was Mitch holding Sophie and Grace, gazing into the camera with the intensity that was all his. Even though he was smiling, she knew he had questions about what the future held for all of them. Their attraction to each other couldn't be denied. But it muddied the already stirred-up waters. As Lily studied his face, her heart tripped. Her gaze fell to his smile and her stomach somersaulted. Staring at him holding her twins, she felt as if she could melt.

Lily flipped again to the photo of herself with Sophie and Grace, then the other one with Mitch. She said in almost a whisper, "I'm falling in love with him, and it terrifies me."

"Why?"

"Because I've lost everyone who loves me. Because Mitch has an area of his life he won't open to me. Because I'm still attached to Troy and afraid to let go."

"So what are you trying to decide?"

"Mitch's reunion with his buddies from Iraq is this

weekend. Saturday they'll be at his place most of the day and he asked me to come over. I'll be setting foot in an area of his life he kept closed off to me. He said we won't have much time alone, but after everyone leaves, we might."

"Are you asking my permission?" Ellie asked with a hint of a smile.

"No. I guess what I'm asking for is your blessing."

Ellie's gaze dropped to the end table by the sofa where a picture of Lily and Troy stood. Then she lifted it to the TV screen. "Go, Lily. You have to. It's the only way you'll know for sure if you're ready to move on. That's the best I can do."

Lily switched off the DVD player and set the camera on the coffee table. "Let's have a cup of hot cider. I want your opinion on what I'm thinking of giving to Angie and Raina for Christmas."

"You want to be distracted from what's really going on in your mind."

Ellie knew her too well because she was right.

Chapter Eleven

Mitch opened his door to Lily, trying to adjust his thinking about today to include her in it. His gut always twisted a little when he saw her…when her blue eyes looked at him with so many questions he wasn't sure he'd ever be able to answer. "I wasn't sure you'd come."

She had a cake holder in one hand, a paint case in the other. "I told you yesterday that I'd come to help."

Yes, she had. They'd been passing in the hall and she'd stopped him with a touch of her hand on his elbow. He'd felt the heat from it the rest of the day, though he'd told himself that was impossible. Had his caresses branded her the same way?

Stepping aside so she could enter, not sure what her presence meant, he pointed to the far end of the kitchen.

"I put the desserts on the table. The deli trays are in the fridge and the barbecued beef is in the slow cooker."

"It sounds as if you have all of the bases covered."

Except the base with her on it. He nodded to her carrying case. "Paints?" The mundane conversation had to get them through, although the question he wanted to ask was—would she stay the night? Too much to expect?

"Yep. And I have some board games and puzzles in the car. Along with Santa Claus, you should have the kids covered."

"I have a table set up for you in the sunroom."

After she unzipped her parka, he moved behind her, taking it from her shoulders. He hadn't been *this* close to Lily all week, though each time he'd passed her in the hall he'd wanted to haul her over his shoulder, carry her to a closet for privacy and kiss her. She'd left her hair loose today and he caught the scent of it as his hands closed over her jacket and red scarf. She was wearing a Christmas-red sweater with black jeans, dangling gold earrings and black shoe-boots with tall heels. She looked incredible.

When she glanced over her shoulder, their gazes collided and he bent his head to kiss her.

But that kiss wasn't to be. His doorbell rang and he swore under his breath. Not that he didn't want to see his visitors. But every private moment with Lily was precious.

"I'm nervous," she admitted with a shaky smile, as he hung her jacket and scarf over his arm.

"Why?"

"Because these are your friends and I'm not sure I belong here."

"I felt that way at Thanksgiving until Raina and Shep made me feel comfortable. Relax, Lily. These are just families who share a common bond. *You* share it, too."

His words didn't seem to reassure her. He wanted to wipe the anxious look off her face with a touch…with a few kisses. But he couldn't. His guests were arriving and he had to play host.

The next half hour passed in a whirlwind of guests entering and introductions being made. Lily had no trouble making conversation, as Mitch had known she wouldn't. She was easily drawn to the moms with kids, and to one of Mitch's best friends, Matt Gates, who was an ER doctor in Houston. After everyone else had arrived, Jimmy Newcomb's wife, Robin, drove their van into a space the guests had left for them in Mitch's driveway. All of the guys went outside in case Robin needed help. But the Newcomb's van was equipped with a wheelchair lift and, fortunately, Mitch's house had only one step to navigate to push the wheelchair inside.

"I don't want to make tracks in your carpet," Jimmy said to Mitch as he wheeled into the kitchen.

"You can go anywhere you want to in my house," Mitch assured him.

Robin and Maya, Tony Russo's wife, set up the kids in the sunroom with games and puzzles, drawing paper, pencils and crayons, while Lily arranged her face paints on a small table. The children began asking questions right away and she explained what she could do. Soon they were lined up, pleading with her to paint a Christmas tree or an angel, a reindeer or a butterfly on their faces. Once when Mitch looked in on her she was telling them about Christmas traditions around the world.

Another time, the children were explaining how they celebrated Christmas. He realized how much he wanted Lily to stay tonight. It had to be *her* decision. As she took a few breaks, he suspected she was calling Ellie to check on Sophie and Grace.

In the course of the afternoon, he attempted to spend time with everyone. He lit a fire in the fireplace, pulled bottles of beer from a cooler, made pots of coffee. When darkness fell, he set out the food. He'd ordered more than enough, and he was glad to see all his guests looked pleased to be there, sitting near the predecorated Christmas tree he'd bought at the last minute. Reunions could bomb. But this group had too much in common. Feelings ran deep and so did loyalties.

Matt had brought his Santa paraphernalia and stowed it in a spare bedroom where Mitch had stacked presents for the kids.

As most of the guests enjoyed dessert and Lily sat on the couch deep in conversation with Robin, Matt beckoned Mitch to follow him into the hall.

"Ready to sweat in that Santa suit?" Mitch asked with a grin.

Matt grimaced. "You're going to owe me for this one."

"Not if I can help it. You're going to love doing this so much you'll want to do it every year. If the gifts are too heavy in that flannel sack—"

"Do you think practicing in the ER is making me soft?" Matt inquired with a raised brow.

"Not for a minute," Mitch assured him.

"Before I forget, I want to give you something," Matt said, taking out his wallet and slipping out a business card.

"What's this?" Mitch glanced at it and saw the name, address and telephone number of a doctor—the head of the Hand and Trauma Surgery division at the hospital where Matt practiced.

"Eric Dolman is good, Mitch. The best I've ever seen. He's performed nerve grafting and conduits, as well as nerve transfers, with success. If you want to return to surgery, you might want to fly to Houston to see him. I could probably get you in on short notice."

Mitch's gut tightened. "I have a new career now. I was told surgery could cause more damage than I already have." He flexed his fingers just thinking about it.

"Look, Mitch. I know about survivor guilt. Most of us carry it. Maybe it's time to lose it and reach out for something you deserve to have. If you don't want to go back to trauma surgery, that's your decision. But Eric might be able to restore full use of your hand."

Mitch heard a noise and swung around. Lily was standing there and had obviously cleared her throat to make her presence known. She was holding her cell phone and probably looking for a quiet place to make her call.

"I didn't mean to interrupt," she told both of them. "I was just trying to find—"

"A little quiet?" Matt filled in with a smile. "That's hard to do around this crowd." His grin faded, then he became serious. "Tony's wife told me you lost your husband to Afghanistan. I'm sorry."

"Thank you," Lily replied, looking down at her phone where a picture of her twins stared up at her.

Matt tapped the card Mitch was still holding. "Don't lose that. Call him anytime. Just mention my name." Then he strode down the hall to the bedroom.

Lily's blue eyes found Mitch's. "I really didn't mean to interrupt. I overheard a little. This doctor could repair the damage to your hand?"

If Mitch was going to even think about doing this, he had to run it through his own mind first. "The risk could be greater than the rewards."

"But if you could return to surgery—"

"Lily, I don't think this is the time or place to have this discussion. Can we just table it for now?"

"Does that mean you'll want to talk about it later?" she challenged.

Not only was Mitch hesitating to start a serious relationship with Lily because of her memories...but also because of his. She might want too much from him, a closeness he didn't know how to give. She was pushing him now, and that made him restless and uncomfortable. So he was honest with her. "I don't know. I need some time to think about what Matt said. I might want to research this doctor. I might not want to discuss surgery at all."

He saw the hurt on Lily's face, and he knew he was closing her out. But this was sacred territory to him. She didn't understand the ramifications of everything surgery could stir up. Not only memories of his time in the hospital and rehab, working to change his specialty to endocrinology, but also the cause of it all. He didn't talk about *that* to anyone.

More gently, he told her, "I'm going to set up the kindling in the fire pit. After Santa leaves, we can toast marshmallows with the kids."

"I'm sure they'll like that," Lily said, much too politely.

He left her in the hall, believing that after the marsh-mallows were toasted, she would leave.

Lily opened one side of the French doors and stepped outside onto the red-and-gray brick patio. It was huge, running along most of the back of Mitch's house. But three high stone walls framed the outside of the patio, giving it a protective feel. Mitch, Jimmy and Matt sat by the fire, talking, mugs of hot coffee in their hands.

She walked over to them, zipping her parka. "The kids want to come out and sing Christmas carols before they all go back to the bed-and-breakfast."

"Tell them to come on," Mitch said, rising to his feet.

Lawn chairs were scattered across the bricks, where after Santa's arrival and departure some of the older children had toasted marshmallows for the younger ones under their parents' watchful eyes. Now the fire had died down and short flames licked at the remaining logs under the mesh fire screen.

Lily didn't have to convey Mitch's invitation to the guests inside. As soon as she turned toward the door again, all the children and adults who had gone for their coats poured out. Light from inside shone on the closest section of the patio. The rest was lit by a half moon and so many stars she couldn't count them all if she tried. For Mitch's guests who lived in cities, this had to be a treat. Those who lived in more rural areas knew how to appreciate the beauty of the winter night.

Jimmy's little boy, who was eight and had Rudolph painted on one cheek, grabbed Lily's hand and pulled her toward his mom and dad. "Stand over here," he told her.

She did and found herself beside Mitch.

The night was turning colder and a light wind blew over the stone walls, but she felt protected in the cocoon of the patio, although her breath puffed white vapor in front of her.

Beside her husband, Robin suggested, "Let's take hands."

A hush fell over the group and even the little ones reached for a hand on either side of them. Lily found one of her hands in Mitch's, the other holding Jimmy's. She was emotionally moved in a way she couldn't even begin to express, especially when Maya's sweet voice began "Silent Night." Lily's throat closed as she tried to sing along with the words.

All is calm. All is bright.

How these men deserved calmness and bright.

Instead of holding her hand now, Mitch swung his arm around her shoulders.

What was he feeling at this moment? What had this night meant to him? Would he talk to her about it? Would he talk to her about the possible surgery?

Sleep in heavenly peace. Sleep in heavenly peace.

She suspected all the men were thinking about fallen comrades and maybe how lucky and grateful they were to be alive…to be here together. She thought about the Purple Heart medal tucked away in her jewelry box and how well Troy would have fit in here tonight.

After the last verse of the Christmas carol, moms and dads herded up children and one by one thanked Mitch for his hospitality. She heard him say, "It'll be your turn sometime. Then I'll be thanking you."

He'd gone to a lot of trouble to put this weekend together and it showed.

Inside the house again once more, Mitch saw his guests to the door. Lily stowed food away while he made sure Jimmy accessed his van without difficulty.

"You don't have to do that," Mitch told Lily when he returned to the kitchen.

Actually she'd been grateful for something to do. She knew what *she* wanted to happen next, but she wasn't sure how Mitch felt. "There's not much left. A few pieces of chocolate cake, a half dozen cookies. Some guacamole and a bag of corn chips."

She covered the remainder of the cake with plastic wrap and set it on the counter. "Matt was a great Santa."

"He's always the life of the party," Mitch replied.

The echo of "Silent Night" and the picture of the group gathered outside would be lasting. "Jimmy's a remarkable man. Robin explained a little of what their life is like since he became paralyzed. They're both courageous people."

"She stuck by him when he wasn't sure she would."

"She loves him."

"Sometimes love isn't enough."

Mitch's decisive words seemed to echo in the kitchen. Lily didn't know if he was going to ask her to stay the night, but if he wasn't, she wanted to discuss the surgery on his hand.

He was standing by the counter perfectly still as she moved closer to him. "Nothing can change what happened to Jimmy in Iraq." She took Mitch's hand and ran her thumb over the top of it. "But maybe you can change some of what happened to you."

Mitch pulled away from her, his expression closed. "I told you—surgery could have repercussions."

"I understand that. But a consultation would do no harm."

"I'd have to take time off."

"The practice slows down over the holidays," she reminded him.

His jaw became more set. "I don't want to be a guinea pig. I don't want to be given false hope or become a statistic."

"You haven't even *met* this doctor. You don't have the information you need to make an informed decision."

He blew out a frustrated breath. "Lily, I don't want to argue about this."

"Fine," she said agreeably. "We don't have to argue. I'm merely making a few observations." Then stepping even closer to him, laying her hand gently on his tight jaw, she whispered, "I care about you."

The tension in his body was obvious in his granite-like expression, the squareness of his shoulders, his legs defensively widened. Did it come from more than this interchange between them? After all, although he'd never admit it, this had to have been an emotional day for him.

Looking deeply into her eyes, he seemed to try to see to her very essence. She stood silent, holding her breath.

Then he covered her hand with his. They stood that way for what seemed like hours. The ice maker in the freezer rumbled as it made new ice. The heating system pinged as it battled against the cold night. Lily could feel the pulse in Mitch's jaw jumping under her palm.

Finally he dropped his hand and wrapped his arms around her. When he kissed her, his raw hunger excited her need, ratcheted up the desire that had been building between them, told them both that coming together again would be an explosion of passion.

After Mitch broke the kiss, he leaned away slightly and asked, "Will you stay tonight?"

"I thought you'd never ask," she replied a bit shakily.

Moments later, sitting on the corner of the bed in Mitch's room, her earrings in her palm, Lily ended her call with Ellie. She'd switched on one of the dresser lamps when she'd entered. Now as she glanced around, she saw Mitch's minimalist taste reflected here, too. The bed's headboard was dark pecan, as were the dresser, chest and nightstands. The lamps were a combination of wood and black iron, with the dresser top uncluttered. Yet the multicolored rug beside the bed looked handwoven. The afghan on top of the brown suede-like spread seemed to be hand-knitted.

Rising to her feet, she walked to the dresser and laid her phone and earrings there. She hadn't packed an overnight bag. Because she hadn't wanted to think tonight was a sure thing?

When Mitch entered the room, her body knew it. She didn't turn around but rather raised her gaze in the mirror.

He came up behind her, his eyes on hers. "Everything's okay at home?"

She nodded.

Sliding his arms around her, he pulled her tight against him. "We both smell like wood smoke," he growled against her ear.

Feeling him strong and hard against her body, excitement coursed through her. Her breaths became more shallow, and already she was tingling in the places she imagined he might touch.

"Wood smoke can be sexy," she teased lightly.

"*You're* sexy," he returned, his hands covering her breasts.

Lily trembled from head to toe. At that moment her need for Mitch was go great, she felt she could melt in his hands. Even though she'd stopped breast-feeding, her breasts had remained larger than they once were. Now as they lay cupped in Mitch's palms, she was grateful for every sensation, every nuance of feeling. Yet she understood that feeling would be so much greater with her clothes *off*.

"Undress me," she requested with an urgency that Mitch could obviously hear.

His low chuckle vibrated against her back. "Sometimes making out can be more scintillating with your clothes on." His hands moved down her stomach to the waistband of her jeans.

"Aren't we going to do more than make out?" she asked.

His answer was rough against her ear. "Eventually."

Mitch's foreplay was driving her crazy. All she wanted to do was crawl into bed with him, their bodies naked and exposed to each other's hands and mouths.

Before she realized what Mitch was going to do, her jeans were around her hips, held up by his thighs. His hands slid inside her panties and cupped her. She'd never felt like this—on the verge of an orgasm without even a kiss.

"Do you know how often our first time together

plays in my mind?" he asked with an erotic rasp to his words.

She had those same pictures in her mind. The continuous loop the visions made came to her at odd times and could make her blush.

His finger slipped inside of her and she moaned, needing to turn and face him.

But he wouldn't let her. "Watch in the mirror," he commanded.

There was something so sensual about what they were doing, and the way they were doing it. She'd never watched herself enjoy pleasure. When she lifted her gaze to his and stared at their reflection, his fingers started moving again. Her breath caught. She stared into his eyes as her body tensed and then released in swirls of muscle-melting sensations.

After the orgasmic release, she lay her head back against his shoulder. He held her tightly.

After a few moments of letting her catch her breath, he said, "Let's take off those boots. They make your legs look like a million bucks, but I think they could be dangerous in bed."

They undressed each other beside the bed, and this time—unlike the first—they did it by the glow of the lamp. If Mitch had given her pleasure to blunt the experience of what she was about to see, it hadn't worked. All of her senses seemed even more sensitive to everything that was revealed. His body was hard and muscled and strong, attesting to his workouts. Silky black chest hair formed a Y, arrowing down his flat stomach, around his navel. But red scars from surgery streaked his side. The heel of her hand slid over them as she sifted her fingers through his chest hair.

"Lily," he breathed, "we can just get in bed—"

"No."

She wanted to see. She wanted to know. She needed to feel.

His shoulder and arm were mottled with zigzagging scars, bumps and ridges, and she could only imagine the pain of his injury. She kissed the arm that he kept covered the whole way down to his wrist. Then she took his hand in hers and brought it to her lips.

He again murmured, "Lily—"

He'd undressed her first, but now she finished undressing him. When he kicked his jeans and briefs aside, she rested her hands on his hips and gazed up into his eyes.

Then he was kissing her and his tongue was in her mouth and hers was in his. She couldn't seem to reach far enough to explore or hold him tight enough against her to hear the beat of his heart. She wasn't even sure how they managed moving, but they fell or rolled onto the bed, so hungry for each other they didn't have enough words or touches to express it. Mitch's fingertips stroked her face. Her hand passed down his thigh and cupped his arousal. They were frantic to kiss each other all over, to explore erogenous zones, to stoke their desire to the limit. Mitch's scent had become familiar to her and now it was like an aphrodisiac she couldn't get enough of. The intensity of their foreplay made her body glisten, her heart race, her limbs quiver in anticipation of release. She didn't want to admit how, at that moment, Mitch blotted out everything else in her world. She didn't want to admit to having this mindless passion she'd never felt before. Yet she had to face what was happening, how deeply she was falling, how inexorable their attraction was.

"I need you," she confessed with sudden tears closing her throat.

Mitch reached for a condom, prepared himself, then rose above her. He took her hands, one on either side of her head, and interlocked his fingers with hers. When she raised her knees, he entered her with a thrust of possession that made her gasp. Her climax began building from the first stroke. She wrapped her legs around him, swimming in pleasure that was bigger than the ocean, wider than the universe, higher than heaven.

"Open your eyes and look at me," Mitch commanded, and she knew why. He wanted her to make sure she knew who he was.

"Mitch," she cried, assuring him she did.

His rhythm became faster. She took him deeper. The explosion that rocked them both should have blown the roof off the house.

But it didn't. It simply left them both breathless and gasping and exhausted from a union that had been months in the making.

Lily lowered her legs, loving the feel of Mitch's body on hers. She wanted to postpone the "where do we go from here" moment for as long as she could.

At first, Lily didn't know what had awakened her. A shout. Groans.

Mitch wasn't in bed with her.

Another shout and she finally was alert enough to know what was happening.

She grabbed Mitch's flannel shirt from a chair and slipped it on as she ran from his bedroom to the guest bedroom next door. Mitch was thrashing in the bed, calling a name—Larry. He was drenched in sweat, breathing hard, eyes open but unseeing.

Lily had learned about post-traumatic stress disorder but didn't know whether to awaken him, or whether to get too close. She'd read about the cut with reality that occurred when flashbacks became more real than life itself. What had triggered this? Being with fellow servicemen who knew what war was about? Sitting around the fire? Talking about surface life yet never going too deep?

Grabbing the metal waste can, she banged it against a tall, wrought-iron floor lamp. The noise was loud and seemed to penetrate Mitch's nightmare. He sat up, eyes open with awareness now, and stared at her still holding the waste can.

When he passed his hands down his face, rubbed his eyes and forehead as if to try to erase everything he'd just seen, she slid into the bed beside him and attempted to fold her arms around him.

He prevented her from doing that and pushed away.

"Everything's fine now, Mitch. I'm here."

"Your being here doesn't change what happened over there." His voice was gravelly with regret, sadness and too many memories.

"Maybe it's time you tell me about it."

"You don't want to hear this, Lily."

When she clasped his shoulder, he flinched, but she didn't remove her hand. "I might not want to hear it, but you need to say it out loud. You need to talk to somebody about it, and right now I think I'm the best person. Just stop fighting your subconscious, Mitch, and let it out."

"Do you think talking about it is going to take away the nightmares? Get *real,* Lily."

"I don't know if talking about your experience will take away anything. I suppose it could make memories worse for a while. But suffering in silence isn't the answer, either."

In that silence Lily could hear Mitch's breathing, still not quite as regular as usual. She could feel his doubt, as if revealing *anything* could make his nightmares worse. But she sat there steadfastly, her hand on his shoulder.

His voice was detached when he said, "I got used to the scud alerts, the bunkers, the MREs. It's amazing what can become normal. I not only cared for our soldiers, but for Iraqis too, many of them children with shrapnel injuries. The sound of artillery shots and mortars coming back at us became a backdrop."

Stopping, he seemed to prepare himself for remembering. Sending her a look that said he didn't want to do this and he was going to get it over with quickly, he continued, "We had spent a couple of days cross-training with ambulance teams, going over procedures. We slept when we could catch minutes, sometimes an hour."

After a quiet so prolonged she didn't know if he'd continue, he did. The nerve in his jaw worked and she could hear the strain in his voice when he said, "I was traveling in a convoy when RPGs came at us. The next thing I knew we'd hit an IED."

Lily was familiar with the military speaking in acronyms. RPG stood for rocket propelled grenade…IED, improvised explosive device.

Mitch's face took on a gray pallor as he forced himself to go on. "Blood was *everywhere.*" His voice lowered. "The man beside me was…gone. At that point I didn't realize the extent of my injuries, because adrenaline raced so fast I didn't think about anything except helping anybody who was hurt. My ears rang, though. And rounds were still bouncing off the Humvee even though it was burning. I helped two men from the vehicle, but I saw others who'd been tossed out by the explosion. There was fire all around. I spotted Larry and somehow reached him. He had a hole in his thigh—the femoral vein—" Mitch closed his eyes. "Tony covered me with an M16. All I could think of was that I had to stop the bleeding. I *had* to stop it. What seemed like wild shots zinged over my head. Everything was on fire," he said again. "So I threw my body over his. I heard a muffled yell. I finally saw part of the Humvee had been blown away from the fire. I dragged Larry behind it. Someone handed me a piece of a shirt. I tried to staunch the blood. Then I…must have blacked out."

Mitch took a deep breath…stared away from her… into the past. "I had recollections of the medevac, but other than that, the next thing I knew I was waking up in a hospital in Germany, my spleen gone, internal injuries repaired, a pin in my shoulder and another in my leg."

By the time Mitch finished, tears ran down Lily's cheeks. She hurt *for* him and *with* him and couldn't even fathom living with his memories. She wrapped her arms around him, and he was rigid with resistance. Yet she kept holding on and wouldn't let go.

"Larry died," he said, his voice rough. "Larry died."

Leaning her head against his, she didn't even breathe. After what seemed like an eon, she murmured, "Don't send me away. Let me sleep here with you."

Whether Mitch was too exhausted to protest, too

awash in the past to care, he slid down under the covers, letting her hold on.

She didn't fall asleep again until she heard the deep, even rhythm of his breathing. Then she let herself slumber with him, knowing morning would come sooner than they both wanted.

Chapter Twelve

In the morning everything always looked different.

That's what Lily thought as she awakened, reached across the guest room bed and found that Mitch was gone.

He'd slept in the bed with her most of the night. She'd awakened a couple of times and cuddled close to him with her head on his shoulder. He'd been asleep then... she could tell. But something had made him leave now and she had to admit to herself that that was her biggest fear—that he would leave. If not physically, then emotionally.

Their physical reunion last night had been spectacular. What he'd shared with her about Iraq had been wrenching. Did he have regrets about that now? Was that why he'd left the bed?

She glanced at the clock and saw that it was 7:00 a.m.

She knew he was meeting his friends at the bed-and-breakfast for brunch, but that wasn't until ten o'clock. She caught up the flannel shirt she'd discarded last night and slipped it on. She'd shower and dress after she found out where Mitch had gone.

After she buttoned his shirt from neckline to hem, she realized how silly that was. She certainly hadn't been so modest last night. She'd never felt so wanton or so free...so hungry or so sexual.

Sunlight poured in the hall skylight, a new, bright December day with Christmas right around the corner. What gift could she get Mitch?

She hated feeling uncertain like this. She hated not knowing how deep his feelings ran. Were they just having an affair?

That possibility made her heartsick.

She smelled the aroma of coffee and heard Mitch's voice before she saw him. He was pacing the kitchen, talking on his cell phone. He went to the French doors and looked out as he listened.

Spotting his jacket around the kitchen chair, a mug of coffee half gone, she wondered if he'd sat outside this morning in the cold before he'd come in to make his phone call. Who was he talking to? Jimmy? Matt?

Then she heard him say, "Dr. Dolman, I appreciate what you're saying. I searched your articles online this morning." There was a pause. "Yes, that too. I trust Matt. But I wanted to check out your credentials for myself."

Dr. Dolman. The surgeon who could possibly repair Mitch's hand. If Mitch was going to talk to him, why hadn't he discussed it with her? Why had he disappeared from the bed without a "good morning" or a kiss? Last night had meant the world to her. Decisions they each made would affect the other's life. Unless they weren't really "together." Unless last night hadn't meant what she thought it did.

She felt hurt and knew she shouldn't. This was *his* life. This was *his* decision. But she did feel let down. She'd thought last night they'd gotten closer than any two people could get.

Mitch sensed her presence and turned, finding her in the doorway. For a moment their gazes met, but then his mind was on the conversation again and he looked away, shutting her out.

At least that's the way it felt. She wouldn't eavesdrop if he didn't want her there.

She returned to the master bedroom and bath, catching the scent of Mitch's soap still lingering in the shower. She'd thought maybe they could shower together this morning. She'd thought—

Stop it, she chastised herself. Disappointment pressed against her heart as she showered quickly, found a blow dryer under Mitch's sink and blew most of the wetness from her hair. She'd dressed and was picking up her own phone to call the Victorian when she heard Mitch coming down the hall.

She closed her phone and waited.

He saw her standing there with it in her hand. "How are the twins?"

"I don't know. I haven't called yet."

The intimacy they'd shared last night seemed to have been lost. The electric buzz between them was still there, but there was nothing comfortable about it. She kept quiet to let him choose the first topic for discussion.

He asked, "You overheard some of my conversation?"

"Not much. Just the name of the doctor Matt told you about last night."

"Dr. Dolman."

She nodded.

"I was up early, went outside and did a ton of thinking."

She wanted to ask, *About us?* But that obviously wasn't what was on his mind.

"I thought about everything Matt said. He thinks I have survivor guilt."

"Do you?" she asked.

"Hell, I don't know. But I did think about why I wouldn't want to get my hand fixed. Yes, there could be more damage. But it also has to do with the life change I made."

"In other words, why rock the boat?" she inquired.

"Exactly. Yet I've never been a half-measure person. Why in this?"

There were only about three feet between them but it seemed like so much more.

He went on. "Dr. Dolman's success rate is outstanding. I made an appointment with him for Tuesday afternoon."

Tuesday was Mitch's day off. He could reserve an early flight and be in Houston before noon.

"I see," she said.

Tilting his head, he studied her. "I thought you'd be happy about it."

She *was* terrifically pleased he'd made the decision. "I am. But why didn't you wake me up to talk about it? Why did you leave and cut off the closeness we'd shared? Why didn't you think I'd want to be part of whatever you decided?"

His back became straighter, his stance a little wider, as if he had a position to defend. "Why do you think?"

"I'm not at all sure."

"You're insightful, Lily. Take a guess."

"Mitch…"

"No woman has ever touched my scars. *You* did. No woman has ever seen me in the throes of one of my nightmares. *You* did. I never told a civilian back here what happened over there. But I told *you*. If I had stayed in that bed this morning and you'd opened your eyes and I'd seen pity or worse yet, dismay, that even after all these years I still haven't gotten a handle on my own subconscious—" He stopped abruptly. "I just didn't want to have to deal with that."

She didn't know what to say. There were so many levels to his statement. She didn't know how to separate it into all the aspects they needed to examine.

So she stated what was obvious to her. "Why would I feel pity? Mitch, you're a decorated hero. You were awarded a Silver Star, a Purple—"

"I'm *not* a hero. I didn't save Larry's life."

"No, but you tried. You risked *your* life."

"Results matter…in surgery, in helping couples conceive, in life."

Shaking her head, she sank down onto the corner of the bed, hoping he'd do the same. "You expect too much of yourself. And maybe you don't expect enough of me."

"Maybe that's because I think in your mind you're still married."

His words struck her hard and stole her breath. "Did I act like I was still married last night?"

"Did you feel guilt afterwards?"

"No, I didn't," she said almost angrily.

Then he looked down at her hand in her lap. "Then why are you still wearing your wedding ring?"

"This is about my *ring?* You're jealous because I can't forget my husband?"

"I'm *not* jealous," Mitch protested with a vehemence she almost believed. "It's not about that," he concluded. "It's about your ability to let go of Troy so you have something with me."

The thought of letting go of Troy absolutely panicked her! If she let go, didn't that mean their love hadn't been very strong? If she let go, didn't that mean Sophie and Grace would never know their real dad? If she let go, and Mitch left, what would she have then?

He must have seen the color drain from her face. He must have seen how shaken she was, because he covered the few feet between them and clasped her shoulder.

But his touch, which still sent scalding heat through her body, activated her. She stood and pulled away from him. "I have to go home to Sophie and Grace."

"I know you do." His voice had lost its edge and was gentler than she expected. "But this is something we've needed to discuss and haven't."

"I thought we were discussing your surgery." Her feelings for Mitch had been simpler when the focus was on *him*.

"If I have surgery, I'm doing it to move on. You say you want to move on, but I don't know if that's really true."

She was stymied for a response and didn't know what he wanted from her.

"Why don't you go home, get the twins and meet me at the bed-and-breakfast for brunch?"

"I don't think that's a good idea." The words reflexively spilled from her.

"Why not?"

"Because…because I don't know what kind of night they had. I don't know if they're fussy or content. I should have called first thing and I didn't."

"Why didn't you?" he probed.

Because you were on my mind, she thought. "Because you left and I didn't know why."

"I only went as far as the kitchen."

Maybe that was true, but it hadn't felt that way at the time.

"I need to go," she whispered. More than anything, she needed to hold Sophie and Grace. To kiss them. To feel the bond she had with them.

Seeming to understand that, Mitch nodded. "Okay. I'll help you carry your things to the car."

Lily felt shell-shocked…as if her whole world had just crashed in. Mitch had turned the tables so effectively she didn't know who was more conflicted…or which one of them could figure out where they could go from here.

On Tuesday evening Lily sat at the kitchen table with evergreen boughs, ribbon and gold bells spread across newspaper. She was making a wreath for the front door while Angie and Ellie added more Christmas touches to the rest of the house. The last time she'd looked they were arranging a nativity set on the table by the sofa.

When the phone rang, she called into them, "I'll get it," went to the counter and picked up the cordless. The caller ID simply read Out of Area without a number.

"Hello," she answered, afraid to hope the caller was Mitch. Yesterday he'd been busy at the office tying up loose ends, cramming appointments together, going over histories of his patients with Jon and Hillary in case he got tied up in Houston. When she'd asked him about the brunch, he'd said everyone hated to leave the bed-and-breakfast, but they all had to get back to their lives. He'd given her one of those "Mitch" looks that was intense and full of meaning.

But then Jon had buzzed him and he'd rushed off. He didn't seem to be shutting her out, yet he didn't seem to be waiting for anything from her, either.

Before she'd left for the day, she'd placed a note on his desk, wishing him luck.

"Lily, it's Mitch. Are you tied up?"

She wanted to say, *Yes, my stomach's tied in knots and I'm worried about you.* Instead, she replied, "Sophie and Grace are sleeping. Ellie, Angie and I are decorating."

"I wanted to let you know Dr. Dolman believes I'm a good candidate for surgery. He has a slot open on Friday afternoon, so I'm going to stay, have some tests and then let him operate."

"That soon?" she murmured.

"I had to make a decision, Lily. This surgery will either work or it won't. One way or another, I'll know, and I'll adjust my life accordingly."

That's what Mitch did. He adjusted his life to fit whatever happened to him. His history had shown her that. He was a decisive, confident man who didn't stall or procrastinate or wait…unless waiting fit into the big picture. How long would he wait for her? Maybe his patience had already come to an end.

"Anyway, I'm staying at the Longhorn Inn. Matt said I could crash at his place, but he's starting a three-day rotation and will be tied up. I wanted to give you the number where I'll be in case my cell is out of reach. Got a pen and paper?"

She grabbed a pen and tablet from the counter. "Go ahead." She jotted down the number he gave her. "How long will you be in Houston after your surgery?"

"I'll be discharged the next day, but Matt wants me to give it forty-eight hours until I fly. If all goes well, I'll be back Monday. I can do physical therapy in Lubbock."

If all goes well.

"What about after you're discharged? Doesn't someone have to be with you?"

"I'll be fine, Lily. Matt said he'll have one of his doc friends check on me."

She hated the fact Mitch was going through this practically alone. Like most men, he probably didn't want anyone to see him when he wasn't at his best. But she didn't like the idea he'd be alone after surgery. She didn't like the idea that he was in Houston alone now.

After a long silence, Mitch asked, "So, did you put up a Christmas tree?"

"Yes, we did. Complete with a lighted star on top. Sophie and Grace haven't seen it yet, though. When they wake up they won't know what to think."

"You're lucky they're not walking yet. You can still keep most things out of their reach."

"Except for the tree. Angie hung ornaments that wouldn't break on the bottom. I have a feeling they'll have a few tantrums until they realize they can't touch it."

"They have to learn boundaries."

There was a commotion on Mitch's end. "Someone's at my door, Lily. It's probably room service."

"You're just having dinner?"

"After the consultation, I talked to Matt and then drove around for a while. I needed to…think. I wasn't hungry then. But after I got back and showered, the idea of food sounded good."

"I won't keep you then."

"I'm sorry you're going to have a heavier load this week because of my being away."

"Don't be concerned about that, Mitch. Hillary and Jon and I will be fine."

"Okay, then. If you need anything, or have any questions about my patients, just call."

"I will. And Mitch, I'll be praying for you…that everything goes well."

"Thanks, Lily."

When his phone clicked off, she set down hers, the hollow feeling inside her seeming to echo with Mitch's voice.

Angie came into the kitchen and saw Lily standing there, staring at the phone. "What's going on?"

Lily told her about Mitch's consultation and surgery. "He shouldn't be there alone," Lily murmured when she was finished.

"Who should be with him?" Angie asked.

Lily knew what Angie was suggesting. "I have Grace and Sophie to think about. And the practice."

"Take them with you."

Suddenly Lily heard a cry from the baby monitor.

"That's Grace," she said. "I'll find out what's wrong." On her way out of the kitchen, she glanced back at Angie. "I feel pulled in so many directions. I can't think about going to Houston. At least not tonight."

"Tomorrow will come soon enough," her housemate suggested.

Lily knew she was right.

On the way home from the office on Wednesday, Lily took a detour. After arriving at the outskirts of Sagebrush, she turned down a road where she hadn't driven for over a year...almost sixteen months. Mid-December darkness had already fallen and she glimpsed farms along the road with Christmas decorations and lights twinkling from eaves, gables and shrubs in front yards.

Eventually Lily reached an illuminated lane where a security guard was housed in a cupola before a high fence. She presented ID to him and a key. After a few taps into his computer, he okayed her, opened the gate and let her drive inside.

She passed row upon row of storage compartments, some looking more like closets, some the size of a garage. The area was well lit and there were no other cars around. It didn't take her long to find the row, and then the storage compartment that she was looking for. She didn't think as she parked in front of it. She tried not to feel. If she let herself feel now, what would happen after she went inside?

She did check her watch and knew she couldn't spend a whole lot of time here. Not today anyway. Sophie and Grace were waiting for her.

After she unlocked the combination, she inserted the

key into the padlock. Two levels of security. Now both were just barriers, locking her out of memories that she'd stored because they were too painful to see, listen to or handle.

The roll-up door stuck and she wondered if she'd have to call the security guard to help her heave it up. But then it gave way and rolled open, revealing the remnants of her marriage. At least the physical ones.

Stepping into the past, she looked around and her eyes burned. It was the cold, the staleness of the compartment, the boxes upon boxes that almost sixteen months ago she couldn't bear to donate or toss away. Moving to the Victorian had accomplished more than giving her an economical place to live, friends to support her, room for her twins to grow. Moving there so quickly after Troy had died had removed her from a good dose of the pain of losing him. She'd been nearly numb when she'd packed up her belongings and his. She'd sent a lot of Troy's things home to his mother, knowing she'd treasure them. But the rest was here in front of her, making her eyes go misty with the remembrance of what was inside the boxes.

She could sit here and go through them one by one. They were labeled and she knew what she'd find. But she hadn't come here to open a box with souvenirs from her Caribbean honeymoon with Troy or CDs they'd once listened to together. She'd come here to find something that would tell her whether she could meld the past with the present…if she *could* really move on. Besides cartons, she had to step over and around Troy's saws and metal boxes that held sets of chisels or a Dremel tool. Finally, after she'd moved a circular saw housed on its own table, she found what she was looking for in the corner.

She had asked Troy to make this for her. It was a multi-tiered plant stand fashioned in oak. Almost finished, it simply needed a last smoothing with fine sandpaper, polishing and then a coat of acrylic.

At least three feet high, the plant stand was bulky as she pushed it from its protected place to the front of the storage compartment and ran her hands over it, imagining Troy doing the same. Now tears really pressed against her eyelids. Giving in, she let them come and didn't even try to brush them away.

When she heard a sound, she realized an airplane was buzzing overhead. At the edge of the compartment, she lifted her gaze to the sky. The moon was bright, almost full, and brought back the memory of standing at the fire pit on Mitch's patio singing "Silent Night." Her nose was numb. Her fingers were stiff. Her feet were cold in her high-heeled pumps. But the cold didn't matter now as she stood still, just letting every feeling in her life wash over her.

Her gaze lifted to the moon and she suddenly saw something to the east of it—a shooting star. It glowed, streaked, then vanished.

Like Troy?

Turning away from the sky, she ran her hands over the solid wood again. She heard the question in her head as if someone were standing in the compartment speaking to her. *Do you love Mitch?*

Searching for the answer here, in the midst of her past life, she knew she did.

Why? that little voice asked again. *Because I asked him to look out for you?*

Reverently she slid her hands over the oak grain, straight and crooked, with imperfections and beauty despite that. She and Troy and Mitch had imperfections and beauty, too. No, she didn't love Mitch because Troy had asked him to watch over her. She loved Mitch because of who he was, and who she was when she was with him. She loved him because he was passionate and intense, and tender and caring. She loved him differently than she'd loved Troy. Whether or not that was because of Sophie and Grace, she didn't know. All of a sudden she just knew her love for Mitch was right.

Yes, it had come along at a time when she was still grieving. And maybe she'd miss Troy for the rest of her life. Loss wouldn't go away merely because she wanted it to. But Troy had so often told her, *There are no coincidences.* On and off, over the past nine months, she'd tested what she'd felt for Mitch. And every time, the desire, the aching to be with him, the dreams that appeared when she let herself think about the future couldn't be denied.

With one hand on the plant stand, she looked down at her other hand, where her wedding ring gleamed in the white moonlight. She slipped it off her finger and set it on the top shelf of the stand.

It was then that she felt warmth seeping into her body, as if someone had given her a giant hug. The sensation only lasted a matter of moments. Then once again she felt her cold nose, her stiff fingers, her numbing feet. She picked up the ring and slipped it into a zippered pocket in her purse. Then she pushed the plant stand out of the storage compartment, determined to fit it into her car.

She had to get home to Sophie and Grace and make an airline reservation to Houston.

Chapter Thirteen

The nurse ran the IV and Mitch watched the drip. This surgery was really going to happen.

Although Matt had stopped in a little while before, the one person Mitch wanted to talk to was Lily. But she was back in Sagebrush.

When the nurse left Mitch's cubicle, he flexed both hands, staring at his right one. Someday in the future, if not able to perform surgery, he might have fuller use of his fingers. Would he feel whole if he did?

He doubted it. Because he realized now he didn't need the use of his fingers to feel whole. He needed Lily. That need had been supremely evident the night of the reunion when they'd made love. Somehow, on that night, attraction and chemistry had transformed into something else entirely.

It had transformed into love.

He hadn't had the courage to admit it or the courage to feel it until he'd awakened the following morning holding her. Yet at that same moment he'd had doubts about Lily's ability to love again…doubts about her ability to freely make any kind of commitment to him. If he pushed her, he'd lose her.

He'd almost lost her when his ego had slid between them in June and his pride had convinced him to put time and distance between them. He'd almost lost her again when he'd prodded her about her wedding ring on Sunday morning.

Would she cut and run? Would she decide loving Troy for the rest of her life was enough? Were her feelings not deep enough to allow a future to develop between them?

He wanted her here to talk about all of it—his past mistakes, his future possibilities, her independence, their passionate hunger that went deeper than pheromones. He hadn't asked her to come, because she had Sophie and Grace to consider first. He hadn't asked her to come, because he knew if he pushed too hard she'd slip away entirely.

Turning away from the IV stand, he closed his eyes and tried to blank his mind.

Lily rushed down the hospital corridor hoping she wasn't too late. She had to see Mitch before he went into surgery. She *had* to.

The past three days had felt like a global marathon.

When she'd returned from the storage unit, Ellie had helped her carry in the plant stand. She'd also noticed the absent wedding ring. When Lily had explained what she wanted to do, Ellie had offered to take care of Sophie and Grace while she went to Houston. Angie had been at home, too, and when Lily couldn't find available seating on a flight, she'd called her brother-in-law, billionaire Logan Barnes. He'd booked Lily first-class seats. Both Angie and Ellie convinced her the twins would be well taken care of. Lily didn't have to worry about anything... except what Mitch was going to say and do.

Now as Lily headed for the information desk in the surgical wing, she was afraid. She loved Mitch Cortega with all her heart. But what if he'd lost patience with her? What if she was too late? What if he rejected her and she'd made a fool of herself?

She kept going anyway, almost at a jog. If she made a fool of herself, so be it.

When she reached the desk and inquired about Mitch's whereabouts, the woman asked, "Are you family?"

Lily said blithely, "I'm his fiancée."

Narrowing her eyes, the clerk asked if Lily knew his date of birth.

"I do. It's January twenty-first."

A tad less warily, the gatekeeper of this surgical unit next asked for his home address and telephone number.

Resigned to this delay, Lily rattled them off.

Finally the clerk pointed her in the direction she should go, advising, "Follow the yellow floor line."

Doing so, Lily almost ran toward the surgical waiting area, found cubicle number six and peeked around the curtain.

There Mitch was, lying on a gurney, an IV line attached to the hand that wouldn't be undergoing surgery.

She wondered if he'd already been given medication to relax, if he'd even be aware that she was here.

Crossing to the bed, she stood beside it and asked softly, "Mitch?"

His eyes opened. They were clear, alert and totally flabbergasted. "Lily? What are you doing here? My surgery was delayed an hour and they haven't given me anything yet. So I know you can't be a hallucination." He sat up and looked ready to climb out of the bed.

She laid a hand on his shoulder, stood as close as she could without jumping into bed with him, then plunged in. "I had to see you in person. I had to tell you before you went into surgery."

"What? Did something happen to Sophie or Grace?" The lines on his forehead cutting deep, his expression showed his extreme worry.

"They're fine. Ellie and Angie are taking good care of them."

Now he just looked totally perplexed.

She took his hand, stroked the scars on his arm and gazed deeply into his eyes. "I love you, Mitch. I couldn't let you go into surgery not knowing that. You've been so patient and I don't know if that patience has run out or not. But I do love you. I want to be with you. I want a future with you."

He didn't look as ecstatic as she thought he might, as she'd *hoped* he might. Instead, he looked troubled. "What happened, Lily?"

He didn't believe her! In fact, he seemed to consider her appearance as impulsive, that she might change her mind tomorrow. She stayed close to him, her hand still on his arm. Somehow she'd make him understand. "I went to the storage compartment where I kept everything

I didn't move into the Victorian. Troy's tools are there, and the plant stand he made for me before he was deployed."

Mitch began to say something but she didn't give him the chance. She rushed on. "The stand isn't finished and I'd like to finish it. And then I want to put it in your sunroom where it can hold plants or flowers and remind me of the love Troy gave me. It's part of my past, Mitch. Troy is part of my past. And I'll always hold his memory dear in my heart. I don't think it was a coincidence he chose you to look after me. He used to say, 'There are no coincidences,' and I believe he was right. When I was standing there looking at the moon and spotting a shooting star—I'd never seen one before in my life—I remembered standing by the fire pit with you and singing 'Silent Night.' My whole being just understood I should finally admit what I've been feeling. I *do* love you, Mitch Cortega. I'm ready to commit to you for the rest of my life. If you aren't ready, that's okay. We'll figure things out as we go. *Together.*"

She could see that what she was saying and feeling and meaning took a few moments for Mitch to absorb. But then he opened his arms to her. "Come here."

She didn't hesitate. If someone came in to take him to surgery, they could just take her along, too!

On his lap, with his arms around her the best he could manage it, he kissed her with such soul-stirring passion she thought she'd melt right into him.

But then he broke the kiss and lifted his head. "When we made love Saturday night, I was forced to admit to myself I was doing a hell of a lot more than watching over you. I hadn't tried the word *love* on what I felt. But on Sunday, I did. I guess I was embarrassed after the bad dream. I woke up thinking I had to do *something*. If you weren't ready, then I had to prepare myself for whatever life dealt. The best way to do that was to see if I could have my hand repaired."

"I was hurt you didn't talk about it with me," she admitted, knowing she had to be honest with him about everything.

"I'm sorry. I guess I thought I'd given you too many pieces of myself and this was one I had to take control of."

Stroking his face, she said, "I want all of you, Mitch. Not just the strong parts or the perfect parts. I'll support you no matter what happens, whether we return to our practice or whether you want to go back to trauma surgery. And I have no intention of moving to Oklahoma. I'm staying in Sagebrush with *you*."

Taking Lily's hand, Mitch smiled. "This isn't the place I'd imagined we'd be talking about this. I want to give you romance and flowers and music to remember the day by, not the clanging of hospital trays. But it seems like I've waited for you for so long, and I don't want to wait a second longer. Will you marry me?"

"When?" She'd be ready today if that's what he wanted.

"Soon. As soon as we can fly back to Sagebrush and arrange it. I don't want to wait a minute more than I have to to be your husband. And," he hesitated, then continued, "a stepfather to Sophie and Grace."

"You're not going to be a *step*father. You're going to be their dad. Troy would want that. I know he would."

Mitch kissed her again, just as the nurse swung back the curtain.

They were oblivious, lost in passion and promises they yearned to share.

Epilogue

"This is as unconventional as it gets," Mitch murmured to Lily, folding his arm around her in her cream wool cape. As long as she was in his arms, the world was good and he slept peacefully during the deep night hours. Marriage would gift them with the future they both wanted and needed.

Twinkle lights were strung around the border of Mitch's patio. The fire pit was lit, giving off warmth. The minister from Lily's church had agreed to perform the service. He'd told her early evening was fine. Afterward, he could return to his congregation for Christmas Eve midnight service.

Fortunately, the weather had cooperated and even Mitch had to admit his patio looked wedding-ready. The stars were crystal clear and the slice of moon glowed with silver-white light. An arbor, also decorated in evergreens and twinkle lights, housed the minister as Lily and Mitch stood before him, ready to say their vows.

Lily cast a glance at Ellie, who was holding Grace, and at Angie, who was carrying Sophie. The twins were bundled up in their pink snowsuits and mittens, their noses barely peeking out from their hoods. Gina had dressed Daniel similarly in blue, and Logan held his son so he could see what was going on, too, as Eva stood with Hannah ready to help with the kids. Shep and Raina had brought along Joey, Roy and Manuel. Tessa and her husband, Vince, held their children's hands, while Francesca and Grady as well as Emily and Jared stood by with their children. Within driving distance, Tony and Jimmy had brought their wives, children and Christmas along with them. Beside them, Lily and Mitch's colleagues watched from along one stone wall where the twinkle lights flickered high above them.

Lily had wanted them all here to witness this joyous celebration. She loved Mitch so much she wanted everyone who could to share their joy. They'd only be outside for about ten minutes and then they'd go inside for their reception, which would be homey and all theirs.

In a low voice beside Mitch, Matt said, "You two couldn't wait until spring, could you?"

Mitch shook his head. "Not a chance. You and I both know each day is a precious gift, and I want to spend them all with Lily."

Lily cuddled closer to Mitch, not at all cold, just wanting to feel him near. He was wearing a black, Western-cut leather jacket. His hand and wrist were still bandaged. After Christmas they would fly back to Houston for an exam by the doctor and decide whether

Mitch was ready for physical therapy. The surgery had gone well, but it might take time for him to have use of those fingers again.

Reverend Allbright made some opening remarks and then said, "I understand the two of you have vows to make to each other."

"We do," they said in unison.

"Whoever wants to go first," the kindly older man invited.

Lily took Mitch's hands, one bandaged and one not, in both of hers. "I know how important vows and promises are to you. I promise to love you from morning till night and every minute in between. I vow to be your partner, lover and friend and I will always respect your opinion in raising our girls. Each and every day, I will try to bring happiness into your life and will be proud to call you my husband."

Mitch cleared his throat and held on to her as tightly as she was holding on to him. "I was broken when I met you, in ways I didn't even understand. Your acceptance, passion and caring have changed that. Having you and Sophie and Grace in my life has healed past wounds. I want nothing more than to be your husband and their dad. You are everything I've ever wanted, the woman I didn't even know I hoped to find. I love you, Lily, and I will cherish you, protect you, honor and respect you every day of our lives."

The minister opened his hand to Lily. Raina handed her a wide gold band and Lily placed it in the minister's hand. Matt handed Mitch a circle of diamonds and Mitch placed that in the minister's palm, also.

Reverend Allbright said, "These rings embody the circle of love that you have promised each other. I give them to you now to slide onto each other's fingers in memory of this night, the vows you have made and the love you will share."

Lily took the ring again and slid it onto Mitch's finger. "I thee wed," she said solemnly.

Mitch took the ring from the minister's hand and slid it onto Lily's finger. "I thee wed," he echoed, just as solemnly.

They held hands and faced forward again.

Reverend Allbright smiled. "I now pronounce you husband and wife."

Mitch took Lily into his arms and she lifted her face to his. Their kiss was an embodiment of everything their ceremony had entailed.

When Mitch raised his head, he said loud and clear, "I love you."

She kissed him again and buried her nose by his ear. "I love you, too."

Everyone around them was applauding and they realized they weren't alone in the universe. With her husband beside her, Lily went to Grace and lifted her into her arms. Mitch did the same with Sophie and they came together for a group hug.

"Can we cut the cake now?" Joey asked.

"We can cut the cake," Mitch announced happily, tickling Sophie.

After more hugs all around, they headed into Mitch's house, ready to begin their lives and the future they would build together.

* * * * *

JOIN US ON SOCIAL MEDIA!

Stay up to date with our latest releases, author
news and gossip, special offers and discounts, and
all the behind-the-scenes action
from Mills & Boon...

 millsandboon

 millsandboonuk

 millsandboon

It might just be true love...

MILLS & BOON
MEDICAL
Pulse-Racing Passion

Set your pulse racing with dedicated, delectable doctors in the high-pressure world of medicine, where emotions run high and passion, comfort and love are the best medicine.